TRUTH TO TELL

By Aline Templeton

KELSO STRANG SERIES

Human Face
Carrion Comfort
Devil's Garden
Old Sins
Blind Eye
Deadfall
Truth to Tell

MARJORY FLEMING SERIES

Evil for Evil
Bad Blood
The Third Sin

TRUTH TO TELL

ALINE TEMPLETON

Allison & Busby Limited
11 Wardour Mews
London W1F 8AN
allisonandbusby.com

First published in Great Britain by Allison & Busby in 2026.

A CIP catalogue record for this book is available from the British Library.

First Edition

ISBN 978-0-7490-3343-9

By choosing this product, you help take care of the world's forests. Learn more: www.fsc.org.

FSC
www.fsc.org
MIX
Paper | Supporting responsible forestry
FSC® C018072

Printed and bound in Great Britain by Clays Ltd. Elcograf S.p.A

EU GPSR Authorised Representative
LOGOS EUROPE, 9 rue Nicolas Poussin, 17000, LA ROCHELLE, France
E-mail: Contact@logoseurope.eu

For Philip and Emma Templeton,
my legal consultants, with much love

PROLOGUE

November 2024

At this dead hour of the morning, the lorry park was deserted. It was a bitterly cold night, with rain falling that had an edge of snow, and under the sickly yellow lighting the great lorries and tarpaulined trailers were dark and bulky as huddled beasts.

It had gone well so far for the predators. With practised skill they had disabled the alarm, opened one rear door and stealthily accessed the refrigerated interior; boxes of lobsters, langoustines and scallops that would never now reach their French destination were piling up already in the white van.

In the driver's seat the young man, his thin, sensitive face contorted in anxiety, was drumming on the steering wheel, muttering, 'Hurry, hurry, hurry,' under his breath. He didn't do this from choice; it had started as a favour to an old friend who'd suffer if manpower for an operation wasn't delivered.

Callan couldn't deny the money was welcome. As a

sous chef in a smart Glasgow restaurant he was paid a pittance for an unfeasible number of working hours; the owner liked to describe the job as an apprenticeship that would lead to Michelin stars and a glittering celebrity career, making temporary poverty worthwhile.

Admittedly, his predecessors in the job hadn't been notably successful but he had a romantic soul and he'd fallen in love with the craft, seduced at first by a simple physical pleasure in the smell of sizzling onions or grated lemons; as he began to appreciate the more subtle scents and tastes – fresh herbs, grated truffle, brown butter – and relish the mental challenge of enhancing them, it became a passion.

The work was punishing, the failures painful, but he was picking up the necessary skills – assessing the cooking of a steak by touch alone, knowing precisely when to add a squeeze of lemon to bring out flavour, or to finish a sauce with cold butter for gloss.

But not long after he'd got the job, six months ago, they'd come calling, as he'd been afraid they would, knowing he'd never be brave enough to refuse. Anyway, there'd always been a lot of 'don't ask, don't tell' in catering and prime seafood delivered at surprisingly low prices was seldom questioned provided Chef could claim he had no idea what happened at the back door.

As a result, a thriving industry had developed, intercepting the goods in transit. His friend had put the old Robin Hood gloss on it – 'You're only taking from the rich bastards' – but Callan still squirmed; how often had his mum said, 'You're better than that'? And he certainly wasn't going to tell his girlfriend about it because she was definitely better than that, much better. She was a few years older than he was, clever, classy, with her own little catering business; she'd covered for Chef's holiday once and somehow they'd become an item. She was the most wonderful thing that had ever happened to him; he'd have infinitely preferred not to lie to her but if he'd told the truth it would be over.

They'd held the threat of telling her over him too when he'd tried to refuse – not his friend, but the bosses. He'd been scared and had given in, so here he was chewing his lip and twitching as Gav and Paddy carried out more refrigerated cartons, desperate for the moment when the van was full and they could leave. He had the engine running ready, his foot poised over the accelerator.

Perhaps it was the icy cold that made Gav, inside the lorry, fumble the pile he was passing down to Paddy. He made a clumsy movement to save it.

And the lorry started rocking. With a startled cry, Paddy ran for the van as Gav dropped the boxes and scrambled to the ground but a man with a great black beard had jumped down from the driver's cab – a bear of a man, an angry man, roaring his rage. He was sprinting to cut off Gav's escape.

Before Callan's horrified eyes, a gun appeared in Gav's hands. They'd never run into trouble before and though he'd guessed they might carry a weapon, 'just for protection', he hadn't allowed himself to believe people like Gav and Paddy, good lads both, would use it. Now Gav was pointing it directly at the driver, his hand trembling; he was short and slight and would be no match for his furious assailant. Callan could hear him yelling something, presumably warning the man to back off.

He didn't. He launched himself at Gav, there was a loud bang and he fell to the ground.

Just like that. Surely Callan's whole precious, beautiful world couldn't disintegrate about him in only ten seconds? Numb with shock, he took a moment to respond to the screamed 'Hit it!' as Gav flung himself into the van.

Now there was movement everywhere as other drivers, asleep in their cabs, were wakened by the shouting and the shot. The white van screamed out of the lorry park and gained the motorway as the first of the police cars, with blue lights and sirens, sped past on the other side, heading north.

They were intercepted on the outskirts of Glasgow. The false plates on the van had been flagged up from CCTV at the site of another lorry raid; they were doomed.

As Callan, shaky and sick with fear, sat in the cell waiting to be charged, he began to realise that he was guilty of an even worse crime than driving a getaway car – cowardice. And he would pay for it with his life.

February 2025

She was waiting, just waiting. Since the first frantic flurry when she'd been spun like a pinball from one place to another, waiting was all she had done in this nondescript flat, in this nondescript street, in a nondescript Scottish town near Glasgow. And she'd be wise to stay nondescript too, if she wanted to survive.

She hadn't the energy to do more than stare out of the window at the pewter-grey sky. The sullen rain that had been falling all morning onto the grey pavements was soaking dark patches into the grey rendering on the tenement building opposite, and from the greyish-beige of the walls, curtains and chairs in the sitting room of the flat there emanated a sort of miasma of despair.

A bit like grief, really, once you realised that all the frantic sobbing in the world wasn't going to change anything and that all you were left with was a bleak, sunless reality.

In the unutterable horror of the aftermath she had spilt out to the police every scrap of information she had, information that would have to be disclosed to the defence when the trial eventually called. They had played fair, giving her stark warnings about the risks and the consequences but she had gritted her teeth and gone on out of – what? A need to offer mitigation for Callan's crime, by way of expiation for her part in the tragedy? Or just an old-fashioned thirst for revenge on those responsible? Oh, certainly that! She was angry – beyond angry. Anyway, she had stood firm, even when the horror had started.

They knew who she was, of course, and where she lived. After the night when she'd come home to find a black car parked outside her flat and lights on where no lights should be and had fled, the police machine had swept into action with supreme efficiency. She was their star witness and she was precious: they put her in a safe place where they could guard her while they wiped out her past.

She didn't mind the thought of walking away. She was an only child; her parents were dead; she was by nature a bit of a loner who got by with a number of pleasant acquaintances rather than friends.

The months she and Callan had spent together seemed, looking back, to exist in glorious technicolour compared to the restrained black and white of her previous existence. And the life her handler had in mind for her wouldn't even be that – just more grey. The woman from the National Crime Agency who had been working on the back story they would be helping her to set up was coming this afternoon to start sorting out the details.

She hadn't realised how exhaustive the process would be. There were endless forms to fill as she cancelled bank account, gym membership, car insurance, various subscriptions and everything else that could connect her to her past, and then more forms to apply for reinstatement of the essentials, right down to a new National Insurance number. She'd never appreciated how documented her life was.

Then she was subjected to psychiatric assessments, counselling, endless questions – did they really need to know about her political opinions and her sexual orientation? – as slowly, inexorably, Janet MacNeish faded to a pale ghost of herself, like a photograph exposed to strong light.

Today when Christine came they would be talking about her future. Christine knew her most intimate details, but Janet wasn't even permitted to know her surname, which made for an uncomfortable balance of power. Not that she was aggressive; she was merely supremely confident, a bustling woman with neatly cropped grey hair and a professionally friendly manner.

Janet knew what she would suggest. She probably had already selected the town, well away from Glasgow, where what was left of Janet by then could vanish into decent obscurity.

When she offered her coffee, Christine said, as she always did, 'Thank you, dear, milk and one sugar – though I know I shouldn't! Now, I know you've had to be very patient, but we've been working hard and I'm pleased to say we've got just the right thing for you lined up. We thought you'd be safer out of Scotland meantime anyway, and this is a flat much like yours in Glasgow, not far from the centre of Manchester. It's easy to be anonymous there, and with your cookery skills finding work's no problem.'

'Yes,' Janet agreed.

There'd been a bit of a tussle earlier over what to call herself. She'd always hated Janet – a prissy, buttoned-up sort of name – though it was possibly unreasonable to feel that with a more interesting name she might have had a more exciting life. She'd written the odd article for cookery magazines under a *nom de plume* but the connections were slight enough not to pose any threat, and she was determined to retain that tiny part of her old self.

Christine wasn't impressed. 'It's a *memorable* name, Susanna,' she pointed out. 'What you want is a name that doesn't draw attention to itself – like Ann Smith, say.'

'I'm sorry, Christine,' Janet said firmly. 'I have to live with it for the rest of my life, and this is my choice. Susanna Bruce.'

Christine never took rejection well. By way of a rearguard action, she said, 'Anyway, why this particular one? It's not your mother's maiden name, is it? That would be entirely unsuitable – it's quite easy to find that out—'

'No.'

'Or one that anyone could connect with you?'

'No,' she said again.

Christine looked at her narrowly, but then sighed. 'Well, as you said, it's your choice.'

Janet had won that battle but she'd seen that Christine, a very experienced operator, had been suspicious and realised she'd have to do better when it came to the bigger lies she was planning to tell later.

Now Christine said, opening her briefcase, 'I've got pictures here for you. It's in Manchester, very nice, everything very practical and up to date.'

As she handed them over, Janet took a deep breath. 'I'm very grateful for your efforts but this isn't what I want.'

Christine looked shocked. 'But it's perfect for you, dear! You'll be able to do what you do now, find another gym, make new friends, set up in catering . . .'

'The thing is, I don't want a city. I've always meant to move to the country one day, and this is the ideal opportunity.'

'That's a dangerous idea. Make no mistake, they'll be out looking for you and in a small place, a newcomer would be obvious. Yes, Manchester's a city but there's plenty of countryside round about, and parks and things—'

'I know where I want to go – a small place up on the north-west coast. There are internet workers fleeing city life all over the Highlands now so it wouldn't be seen as at all unusual.'

'Somewhere you know? Somewhere you have some connection with?' Christine was positively quivering with anxiety. 'No, certainly not! You'd stick out like a sore thumb and it's far too close to Glasgow anyway – you'd be signing your death warrant! There's no way we can allow that.'

Janet didn't exactly have a death wish but the threat

didn't bother her as once it would have. She said calmly, even as she lied through her teeth, 'There's no connection, beyond having been there on holiday as a child and it's the most beautiful place I ever saw. I don't know anyone who lives there but I know it's easy to get to know people in a wee place. Strangers suddenly appearing would, like you said, stick out like a sore thumb, and I'd be able to see them coming. If they were asking questions about me, someone would tell me, but in Manchester they could be next door and I wouldn't know – and you've warned me yourself that they could come for me anywhere.'

Christine went on shaking her head and giving half a dozen different versions of the word 'no', until Janet said, again with perfect calm, 'If I need to withdraw myself from protection, I shall.'

It worked, of course. She was the main pillar propping up the prosecution case and they needed her alive and able to testify. Now she had set her terms, the accommodation became available.

It was, as she had demanded, in the little township of Ardelour in Wester Ross, normally let to tourists but now hers on a six-month extendable lease. Christine had been scathing about it.

'There's nothing to do up there. You can't live on a view, and you'll get tired of it and we'll have to go through it all again. Still, it's your decision, but I think you're . . . going to regret it.'

The telling pause suggested she had only just stopped herself saying the unprofessional word 'mad'.

* * *

There were occasions in those early winter days when she found herself thinking of that conversation, like the days when the great storms hurled themselves across the Atlantic with screaming winds that wrapped themselves round the little house beside the moor above Ardelour, rocking it to its ancient foundations, and the days when she would wake up to a sea of white mist and a world so profoundly silent that she could believe she had gone deaf, and then there were crying days when there was nothing to distract her from her thoughts of what she had lost.

But she had come for a reason. Callan had said to her once about Ardelour, in that soft Highland voice that made everything sound like poetry, 'Sometimes you just look and look, hardly able to breathe because it's so beautiful.'

'Breathtaking, you might almost say,' she'd replied, teasing him.

He'd smiled. 'Oh, I know people say that. But there – it really is.'

He loved his birthplace, clearly, but he'd vetoed a suggested visit. When she'd asked him why, he'd actually shuddered and said, 'It's not—' then hesitated before offering, 'wholesome.'

A strange word, she'd thought then. Gaelic was his first language and she'd wondered if he was thinking of some Gaelic word that had translated oddly into English.

He'd gone on, 'That's all behind me – right? Let's talk about now, when I've got the woman I love, and the job I love, and about how I'm going to show you that I can make you an omelette that really is, for the very first time, the *perfect* omelette.' It had been his current obsession.

She'd often thought about that reaction. He was such

a gentle soul; was there a history of bullying, abuse, even, that had left him traumatised? Even after months together all she knew was that his parents had left Ardelour and gone to live near his sister in Canada. His past was a book he'd not only firmly closed but padlocked away like a teenaged girl's journal, as if he was afraid opening it might release some demon within.

Even when it reached the desperate stage, he still wouldn't give her the little gold key. He was shattered, not eating, not sleeping; he admitted it was all linked to Ardelour but when she'd tried to tease out what that meant, all he would say was that he'd made 'bad choices'. He was prepared to shop Gav, who'd used the gun, but with stubborn loyalty he wouldn't tell her anything about the 'friend' whose involvement in crime had drawn him in.

The policewoman who had brought the envelope with her name on it, found after Callan took a lethal overdose, had handed it over stiffly, suggesting without enthusiasm that she should stay with Janet while she read it.

She refused the offer with numbed lips then collapsed onto a chair as if she'd been pole-axed. Shock had left her dry-eyed so that she could read that he was so sorry, but he couldn't take any more.

Prison – you know what they do to you if you're not a hard man. And I grassed so I've got real enemies now too. I'm not waiting for them to come for me. I was never good enough for you and I've dragged you down into the dirt. I've lied to you, and I can't face seeing how much you must despise me. Have the life you deserve. My love's yours for ever, though you'll maybe not want it now.

She still suffered the pain from that dagger-thrust. She'd known about his lies already because of their disastrous effect and it had made no difference to her love; her heart had ached for Callan in his lonely agony of fear.

In the bleakness of grief and helplessness, only the red flame of her anger felt real. The one thing that mattered was to find out how it had come about and who the 'friend' with Callan's blood on his hands was. It was then she'd taken the decision that meant she was here in Ardelour, and here she would stay until she had. She still wasn't sure what she would do then. She wasn't sure at all.

The rental's living room had a big modern window looking out over Loch Torridon and she'd begun an evening habit of watching the changing weather, rain, sun or storm – often all three in the course of a few hours – with a glass of wine and a book of poetry, though often it went unread. Mostly she sat thinking – agonising, really.

Guilt shadowed her like an over-faithful dog. Callan had come in that night distraught that a man had died – 'A man with a wife and kids, maybe' – because of what he'd been part of. If she'd known then his assurance that this had been a one-off wasn't true, would she still have taken the principled attitude and urged him to help the police with whatever information he had?

She'd been so sure that, with a blameless record and a good lawyer to do bit of plea-bargaining, it would result in not much more than a slap on the wrist – as well as a conscience that would let him sleep at night, which he hadn't been doing. He'd been in the habit of turning to her for advice and he'd been persuaded. A man had died, after all.

She'd been unpardonably naive. Ignorant of his record for petty crime as a teenager, and the number of times he'd actually driven the getaway car, she'd given him advice that had proved – yes, quite literally fatal. Conventional morality was all very well, but how did it weigh in the scales of justice compared to a young man's life? Her views had changed, and it was a particular irony that her own belief in truth and justice had resulted in her having to live a lie for the rest of her life.

Tonight, after one of the rare glorious days, the sun was sinking into a golden sea as darkness gathered. The loch was millpond-calm, its creamy waves seeming almost too lazy to break on the shore, and in the distance the Torridon mountain peaks were hazy blue, shading towards a purplish-grey: a symphony of colours.

He hadn't lied about that, at least, she thought with a small, bitter smile. It was so beautiful it was almost painful. The village was pretty too, with cottages and houses scattered as if at random up behind the little street that hugged the shore. It seemed idyllic to the tourists who came and fantasised about a life in Arcadia.

Yet this was the place, she was now convinced, that had so damaged her lovely, sensitive Callan. He'd been weak, perhaps, but that wasn't a crime – more a disability.

With the law's delays, it would be some time before the case called in the High Court in Glasgow. However much she might want to stay withdrawn and nurse her pain, she couldn't afford to do that for much longer. The civilised glass of wine had already shown a tendency to be not one, but two – or even, sometimes, many more than that.

Apart from anything else, she had a living to earn; the

money from selling her Glasgow flat wouldn't last for ever. She didn't doubt she could set up something – catering for the Airbnb tourists, maybe, and doing freezer meals that she might persuade the local store to stock during the winter. She'd presumably be cooking lasagne and chilli rather than the veal *scaloppine al limone* that was popular for directors' lunches, but maybe in time she could introduce speciality items for her own satisfaction.

The best thing about it was that it would help her get to know people, first for her own safety and then as a way to find out more about this 'unwholesome' place. And it boosted her morale to know that while they might be looking for her, they didn't know she would be quietly stalking them.

April 2025

The police came to whisk her away at last to give her evidence in court, picking her up in a discreet grey car before dawn and bringing her back at midnight days later. It wasn't likely anyone would be stumbling around the moors behind Ardelour in the darkness, but even so she was grateful they'd taken every precaution as, by police request, Janet MacNeish made positively her last appearance.

She'd known how tough the questioning would be as her evidence was challenged, but she hadn't realised how personal it would be allowed to get. She was still feeling bruised, as if the ruthless attacks on her integrity, her memory, her morals and her motives had been physical punches. She'd managed to stay calm and clear but her head and her back ached from the tension of holding herself together and as she was driven back she was so stiff she wondered how she would manage to get out of the car.

The jury had retired to consider its verdict over the weekend. The inspector who'd supported her throughout promised her he'd call her whenever it came in, warning her that they might well think that evidence of reported speech, however truthful, was unsatisfactory, and not to take it personally if they acquitted Gavin Thomson.

Whatever he said, an acquittal would still feel like a personal slap in the face and when the phone rang at last her hand was shaking as she picked it up.

'Guilty,' the inspector said, 'and largely thanks to you. You're a brave woman – I only hope you feel it's worth it. Goodbye, Janet MacNeish.'

As she set the phone down, she realised this was the last time anyone would call her by the so-familiar name. Stripped of it, she felt oddly disembodied, as if she had become a wraith.

But she'd done what she'd promised; now she must be brave enough to make the new life work. With a sigh and a little shudder, she fetched a glass of wine and sat down in the chair by the window, picking up the book she had left there. It fell open at a poem by the first-century Chinese poet Li Bai.

The birds have vanished from the sky
And as the last cloud fades away,
We sit together, the mountain and I
Until only the mountain remains.

CHAPTER ONE

April 2025

Catriona Fleming was standing in the atrium of the Glasgow High Court with her leader in the trial that had just finished – David Mackintosh, a senior advocate rumoured to be on the point of taking silk.

She'd been gratified to be brought in as his junior; her appearances so far had been mainly in the Edinburgh courts so it was good to widen her experience. Best of all, they'd won their case.

'A pleasing outcome,' he said with satisfaction. 'Good job, Cat. You unearthed that deposition for me just in time. His Honour was getting a bit tetchy.'

'Bit of a stress moment, I have to admit,' she said, laughing. 'Just glad it worked out.'

'I owe you a drink for that before we get the train back to Edinburgh,' he said but she shook her head.

'Thanks, David, but I'm getting a lift back from Kelso. He'd a meeting here today and then heard the jury was about to come back in a case he'd an interest in. He's sticking around for the verdict.'

'Back to work, then? Keeping all right?'

'He's only just been passed fit but he's fine, thanks. This is something that happened a while ago – murder linked to a raid on a food lorry. It was all a bit of a tragedy with a sidekick killing himself after being charged as well.'

'I remember that case – made the headlines at the time. Was Kelso involved?'

'Not directly – just giving evidence about the Serious Rural Crime Squad's take on the general freight theft problem at that time, I think.'

'Come up with new angles for robbing the honest citizens all the time, don't they? Still, I suppose if they didn't, we'd go out of business,' David said. 'I'll leave you to it, then, Cat. And like I said – a good job. I'll be back in touch. Best to Kelso.'

Cat smiled her thanks then sat down on a bench to wait, glowing at the pat on the back. She'd enjoyed working with him, and that was definitely a nod that he'd put more work her way. It might even be noticed by other senior advocates who might be looking for a junior – all useful stuff.

Unconsciously, she twiddled the emerald-cut aquamarine on her left hand, starting to think about the wedding plans that were never far from her mind at the moment. Betsy, Kelso's six-year-old niece, was obsessively drawing brides' and bridesmaids' dresses that leant heavily on white meringue for their inspiration, but Cat was very much aware that this would not be Kelso's first wedding and was determined to keep it simple.

They both had friends and family who'd want to come to wish them well, though. They would all have to be wined and dined, however informally, which meant she'd have to set up a packed programme for the next visit to Kirkluce to include seeing the caterers, the minister, the photographer and the florist. Kelso had insisted that he'd be perfectly happy with whatever arrangements she made and that there was no need for his opinion, but there wasn't a chance he was getting out of it.

Her brother, Cameron, and sister-in-law, Annelise, had offered to host it at Mains of Craigie, and Cat herself had tried to offload responsibility for the arrangements onto her mother but Marjory Fleming, notorious for her lack of domesticity, was having none of it.

'I'm happy to do the grunt work like dealing with the people getting the big barn into shape for the reception, but when it comes to choices and style, you and Kelso are on your own. I'm not sure we have the same tastes at all – I've never forgotten that all-black bedroom you insisted on having.'

'And you've never let me forget it either! For crying out loud, Mum, I was only ten at the time,' she protested. 'We like the same sort of things now.'

But she hadn't got anywhere with that, so they both – '*both*' she had said firmly to her reluctant fiancé – would be heading down there for a weekend for the jigsaw of appointments she'd designed.

The light caught her ring as she moved her hand and she looked down on it with a fond smile. Kelso had worked hard enough at his physio to be able to present it to her in traditional style on the Praia do Sancho beach in Brazil, the local stone echoing the colours of a summer sea. It had been wonderful, but when friends had said it must have been hard for her to come back to real life, she couldn't agree. Ordinary life with Kelso back to his old self after the high drama of his serious injury and the long, gruelling recovery was all she could want.

There he was now, walking briskly down the corridor from the courtrooms and beckoning to her. As she got up and hurried after him she could see there was a trickle of chattering people emerging from the court behind him.

'I just wanted to get away before his supporters appeared,' he said on the way to the car park.

'So how did it go?' she asked as they set off at pace.

'Fine, for what it was. He'll be going down for a good stretch, but the trouble is he's a nothing, just a stupid greedy little ned. We didn't get anywhere near the organisation behind the raid and even if he'd been one of the bosses, if you take one out half a dozen others move in to occupy the space you've created.

'This one was unusual in that the driver was killed. Normally they're pretty careful to avoid that sort of thing. It's become much the same as shoplifting when it comes to prosecutions – as long as there's no violence they'll only get a fine they write off as a business expense.'

'We've been talking about it around the courts,' Cat said. 'We're always instructed to say they're doing it because of the cost-of-living crisis, though if I'm honest the cases I've dealt with have been more about greed than need.'

'The freight theft gangs are highly professional now and they know all the rules about the length of drivers' shifts and research the places they like to stop. There's been a particular Scottish problem over the last bit with the high-value luxury goods like whisky and seafood that have to be transported from the producers down via Inverness. The companies have been trying to vary the schedules but it's getting increasingly difficult – there are paid spies all over the area who provide tip-offs and a gang is called in.

'They actually seem to be developing hubs in rural areas where there's almost no policing now. You can understand how it happens – there's a lot of poverty, not many jobs going, and if you're on benefits any little side-hustle is welcome.'

'They probably see themselves as edgy modern-day highwaymen,' Cat said thoughtfully. 'Life on benefits is dreary and defying the law probably adds a bit of excitement.'

'And how did David Mackintosh's law-defying client get on today?'

Cat beamed. 'Oh, we won. But what *do* you mean, law-defying? I can't imagine how you could possibly think that. Not at all – it was just an accusation of fraud that apparently had merely been a misunderstanding, which David managed to explain to the court's satisfaction. His client was very pleased and David was pleased with me too. I got a definite hint that he might use me again.'

'It probably only means more work for us to do later – no, don't hit me! I'm pleased you did so well. I think we should celebrate – there's a jazz night at the pub tonight.'

'Sounds good to me.' As they turned onto the motorway, Cat said, 'Did they say much about the poor guy who killed himself?'

'Only as it related to the evidence of his girlfriend. That was what nailed the killer, but I'm a bit haunted by her. She was allowed to give evidence from behind a screen, but she didn't sound the usual ned's girlfriend type. She was certainly taking her life in her hands by agreeing to stand up in court. They'll have taken a contract out on her already so I guess she's been in police protection ever since it happened.'

'What will that mean – a new identity?'

'Yes, being cut off from everything and everyone relating to your past life – and knowing there are people who'll be looking for you who could find you without warning at any time.'

Cat shuddered. 'What a dreadful punishment for doing the right thing! We've a big problem getting witnesses to testify even at a level when it's only going to mean a bit of aggro. I can't imagine what it must be like to be cut off from your family and friends for ever – bleak beyond belief.'

'She's certainly a very brave woman.'

'Or else,' Cat said, 'just have been very, very angry about what happened and looking for revenge.'

Despite having the shadow of the court case looming over her, Anna Bruce had been busy in the intervening months – Anna now, not Susanna. She'd sort of believed that her dull name was responsible for her unadventurous spirit, but disappointingly, the new name didn't seem to have made any difference and she was still the same: practical, sensible, down-to-earth. Bruce was all right – a good Scots name – but though Susanna had been fine as a pen name, in real life it made her feel much as she had when her mother had forced her small unwilling self into a frilly party dress.

Her first practical steps had been to get the hygiene certificate for her kitchen and buy a chest freezer and chiller to install in the shed in the garden. She'd established her supply chain: a mixture of online orders from Tesco along with farms and local businesses that she'd sussed out for wonderful produce, especially smoked fish and venison and fresh seafood.

Advertising on the community noticeboards was free and orders started coming in remarkably quickly. There were a few small villages around the Torridon area that each had its own little shop selling basic provisions and frozen goods and there was a popular café too that needed constant supplies of home baking. Somewhat to her surprise, she'd even had a steady trickle of orders for catered meals; with six Munros in the area, groups often rented an Airbnb for a climbing weekend and there were second homes with regular family gatherings too, from time to time. If there was someone at the big house on the Ardelour estate she often got an order for an evening meal; indeed, there were bookings in her diary already for parties in August for the shooting.

The trickle threatened to turn into a flood after Easter and once she knew the trial date she'd had to be ruthless about keeping her diary clear, telling disappointed clients she was off on holiday. She'd been nervous that the trial would overrun, but having been delivered back the previous afternoon she found herself now with the luxury of a full day to prepare for the lunch order she was to deliver the following morning.

Anna finished her coffee then started to set out her *mise en place*, ticking off the items in her notebook. It was always a soothing activity, needing concentration that stopped her mind from whirring in its usual pointless circles and it had been her coping mechanism over these difficult months.

Tomorrow's order was for a family party. They wanted a seafood platter to start with; that would mean a trip to the smokehouse she favoured, and a visit first thing next morning to the fishery on the shores of Loch Shieldaig, up along the Applecross road. She'd found it surprising that it was so difficult to buy langoustines and lobsters in the area where they were brought out of the water, but the bulk of their catch went off live to Spain, and she was lucky to have a contact locally who'd let her buy on the doorstep.

She decided to make a start with the lemon cheesecake that had been requested as one of the desserts. She went to the chiller for the three lemons that had come with the order delivered the previous day, then stopped in dismay. Unnoticed mould had started on one of them and then spread to the second. And you couldn't get the serious citrus hit the cheesecake required with one measly lemon.

Fresh produce was always a bit of a hit-and-miss affair when it came to the local shop. Some lemons would be ordered, certainly, but whether there would be any left depended entirely on demand. A vivid picture sprang to mind of the teeming shelves of the Waitrose just round the corner from her Glasgow flat and she bit her lip.

She didn't want to squander her precious extra prep day on a trawl for lemons and she certainly didn't want to have to drive to the Co-op in Kyle of Lochalsh, but the client, though loyal, was fussy and she'd take it badly if she didn't have her favourite dessert. Still, she might strike it lucky and anyway, the sooner it was done the better. She could drive on to the smokehouse afterwards.

Anna checked through the rest of the menu to make sure that everything else was in order and that the grapes for the chicken and grape salad hadn't suffered the same fate as the lemons, then went out to her second-hand Volvo hatchback, sturdy enough for Highland weather and, with the back seat down, roomy enough to take trays and boxes for deliveries.

There was a brisk breeze coming off the sea but at least it wasn't raining. The village was deserted apart from a man and a woman wandering around aimlessly. When she parked on Shore Street, the man, wearing walking boots and a cagoule, crossed the road towards her.

The opening up of the tourist season had made her nervous and an unknown man approaching her was enough to make her tense up; this one looked harmless enough, but how could you tell?

As she got out of the car, he called, 'Excuse me, do you know when the café opens?'

She answered politely but without encouraging warmth, 'It should be open by now.'

'Well, it isn't,' he said. 'Will it be open later?'

'I don't know.' She crossed the road and walked along to the shop.

'It's closed too,' he called after her with what almost sounded like triumph in his voice.

Ignoring him, Anna tried the door for herself, but he was certainly right; the shop was closed, and the café had a blunt notice, *CLOSED*, on the door. Frowning, she walked further along to the pub. It wouldn't be open yet, of course, but usually there would be someone working there that she could ask. Today there were no lights on inside, and when she cupped her hand and peered in the window, there was no sign of activity. This was definitely odd.

As she got back into her car, she heard the man saying to the woman, 'That's the trouble with the teuchters. Too lazy to get themselves out of bed in the morning.'

At least she could go to the smokehouse, then work out what to do – phoning the other small shops she dealt with to find out which of them had lemons in stock would probably be best. But as she drove off she was puzzled. Why would everything be shut on a normal working day?

Shona Macintyre would be able to tell her. She had a house beyond the Ardelour peninsula, up the Applecross road, with a smokehouse alongside. She'd inherited the business from her father, having come back as a single mum with one son, now in his twenties. The hot and cold smoked salmon and sea trout were common fare in the smokehouses around, but Shona stocked smoked duck and venison too, and even smoked cheeses, and ordered in the venison sausages for one of Anna's most popular dishes. As a result of that, Shona had become the closest thing to a friend that she dared to allow herself.

But the smokehouse was shut. She could smell the wonderful peaty smell, but there was no one around tending the racks. She rang the house doorbell, but there was no answer and she went unhappily back to the car. What could have happened while she was away? Oh, there were other smokehouses and of course she could drive around and pull together the ingredients she needed, but this was a bleak illustration of her biggest problem: there was no one she could ask.

As she had said to Christine all that time ago, in a wee place it was easy to get to know everyone and now she pretty much did, at least by sight. The weather always gave you something to talk about for a minute as you passed in the street and from a security point of view she could be confident that, as she'd said, if anyone came asking questions about her, she'd hear about it, and in the down season strangers did indeed stick out like a sore thumb. But what she, a city girl, hadn't appreciated was how hard it would be to get included in the life of this close-knit community.

She regularly had pleasant chats with her clients, but the grapevine of local gossip, more efficient even than the internet, didn't reach her because she was just an incomer – and from observation, still would be in fifty years' time. She sometimes felt she was living behind a pane of plate-glass, unable either to reach out or bring anyone in.

How could she? Friendships arise from shared experiences, but there are rules for growing them successfully, as in any other human activity. 'Where did you come from?' is an obvious opening gambit that slides easily into, 'Oh yes, I went there once – do you know the so-and-sos?' and the carefully constructed lies that formed her back story wouldn't lend themselves to detailed examination. Though she'd been prepared to lose her past, she hadn't quite appreciated the extent to which she'd compromised her future.

The dispiriting thing was that she was no nearer to

finding the key to unlock Callan's past. She could look with a darkly suspicious eye at young men around his age like Brodie Campbell and Jago Innes but she couldn't ask direct questions without putting herself in deadly danger; she knew no more now than she had when she came in January, and she was beginning to dread that she never would. And what other purpose did she have in life? Anna had told herself she'd feel better once the case was over but now she was feeling lower than ever as she drove away.

Fortunately the little store in Torridon had a recent delivery of lemons and the smokehouse nearby could provide what she needed. She drove back along the coast, turning off onto the single-track road that ran between great rocks looming on either side and along the narrow neck leading to the Ardelour peninsula, then through the village and up to the cottage beside the track to a farmer's field just below the moorland.

As she got out and slammed the car door, a grouse whirred up, startled, giving its alarm cry, 'Go back, go back!'

For a moment she stood, watching its flight. Then her lip twisted and with an audible sigh she walked into the house.

John Wilson was in the shed his wife liked to call the studio and he referred to privately as The Doghouse. Tchaikovsky's *1812 Overture* was blaring out at full volume and he was working on a canvas propped on an easel, his palette loaded with shades of orange, red and black. With a broad brush, he was slashing at it with strong, warring strokes that felt good, as if giving way to artistic rage might purge his need to give way to ill-judged fury.

At the sound of footsteps on the path outside, he froze, then moving quickly he grabbed a sheet, threw it over the painting and swung his stool so that he was facing the trestle table on the back wall where watercolour paints were laid out, as well as a small half-finished painting of the view from Ardelour over Loch Torridon to Beinn Alligin and Liathach. It was very pretty and he looked at it with loathing as he took up his brush.

He didn't turn his head as the door opened but he could feel someone standing behind him. Then to his astonishment, his eyes were covered by a woman's hands and he caught the musky scent of her perfume.

She was laughing as he turned around. 'Zoe! What the hell are you doing here?'

'I just got bored on my own and I couldn't think what else to do.'

'I thought you were Mairead – she could be back any minute.'

'Oh, turn that row off – I can't hear myself think. She won't,' she said firmly. 'Not for a good while. I saw her driving through, heading along for the wake. Jago's gone too.'

'So you didn't go to the crem?'

She shook her head. 'Depresses me, that kind of thing. Right, come on. Where is it, then?'

John watched her move about the shed: slender, olive-skinned, with thickly lashed brown eyes outlined with winged flicks. She had curly brown hair rioting round her elfin face, and tattoos and piercings as well – disfiguring, he would once have said, but she was still the sexiest woman he had ever seen.

He was twenty years older than she was, he reckoned, though she was evasive about her age, and he sometimes thought she'd seduced him as some sort of in-joke that he didn't quite get, but he was happy to go along with it for as long as it lasted. He worried about Jago sometimes, but perhaps he didn't mind. Mairead, on the other hand . . .

'What do you mean, where is it?' he blustered.

'Oh, for God's sake, Jo-Jo, don't waste your booze-laden breath – ah, here it is! Famous Grouse – that's a cut above your usual rot-gut. Mairead have a fit of generosity?'

'Doesn't know the meaning of the word,' he said with some bitterness. 'No, got a cheque from a gallery in Glasgow who actually sold one of my oils – the stuff I ought to be doing.'

'That's not what she would say.' As she spoke she was hunting through the untidy shelves, cluttered with prepared canvases and tubs of brushes and paint-spattered palettes as well as odd bits and pieces that didn't have anywhere else to go apart from on the floor like a lot of other stuff, before emerging triumphant with a smeary small tumbler. 'Why the hell don't you have any decent glasses?'

'Because Mairead would wonder why I needed them,' he said, taking out his own similar one from under the table while Zoe washed hers at the sink, then poured for them both.

She sat down on the daybed John used when he came home drunk and wanted to avoid his wife, and he eyed her with some nervousness. 'I don't know when she might be back—' he began, and she laughed again, that irresistible throaty laugh.

'Don't worry, I have no designs on your body today. No way do I want to lose my nice wee job in the café – Mairead and I are getting on great.'

Zoe got up restlessly and went over to lift the cloth covering the easel and assessed the painting, head on one side. 'Feeling as bad as that, huh?'

'She drives me mad. This is going well – got a bit of energy to it, but oh no, I'm not to be allowed the time for serious art by she-who-holds-the-purse-strings. I'm not saying I'm Picasso, but I could produce good stuff for the galleries if I didn't have her screaming at me to drop it and get on with chocolate-box painting by numbers.'

'They sell well, though – fifty quid a time and we sold three at the weekend. There's only two left in stock so you'd better fire up the production line. And if you think just covering the easel with a cloth and sitting at the table will fool Mairead, it won't. The place stinks of oil paint and you've got it all over your fingers too.'

She finished her drink, then her slim hand with its blue acrylic nails and the start of the climbing vine tattoo that spiralled up her arm, leading the eye across to a heart in the hollow at the base of her throat, turned his head towards her to give him a lingering kiss. 'Just something on account,' she said. 'I'd better leave you to it.'

She left John feeling dizzy, as she so often did. At least she'd be off the premises before Mairead came back, but why had she come? She never had before. 'Just got bored,' she'd said, and it sort of rang true. It possibly explained their relationship, if he was just *faute de mieux*.

He should be feeling elated about the oil that he'd sold, but it had only spelt out to him how his artistic potential had been crushed out of him by living here, where there was none of the energy of a buzzing artistic scene that would have raised him to being the great artist he knew, just knew, he could have been; the sense of failure and bitterness ran deep. It was all about money – or rather the lack of it.

Of course, he'd known that as a young, struggling artist you had to expect to be poor, but he did like the finer things in life and when on a painting trip up here he'd met Mairead, he'd told himself he could paint anywhere and allowed himself to be seduced away from artistic poverty. Not that she was ever exactly a siren, but she was good in bed and a great cook; best of all, she had utterly believed in his talent and was happy to support him on her income from the café so he would have all the time he needed to produce the paintings that would change everything. That belief was long gone, and with the pandemic and the cost-of-living crisis, things had been hard for a long time. Oh, he did have his finger in one or two little ventures, but his only official contribution to living expenses came from the watercolours and the series of art courses he ran in the village hall – for one of which Zoe, to his amazement, had signed up.

She had a natural talent, but it was obvious that she was only playing at it – and with him, probably. It hadn't been long before she was staying behind to help him clear up and one thing had led to another.

He looked at his watch. Mairead wouldn't be long now so he'd better sit down like a naughty schoolboy and finish that watercolour. If he was able to take it through to his wife before she came to chase it up, she wouldn't smell the oils and start another of their debilitating rows.

John took a step back to look at the painting before he covered it up again, and winced. He was kidding himself – that was an indulgence, not a painting. He needed space to breathe and to think, and there wasn't a lot of that when you were a prisoner in a dismal shed from which you could only escape by walking along the passage beside the café and shop that was the ground floor of their house, under the eye of a woman who had missed her vocation as a prison guard.

He took up a palette knife and in a spasm of pure rage turned it on its edge to slash again and again through the canvas.

CHAPTER TWO

Everything always stops from respect when there is a funeral in these small communities. If the end of a life well-lived is being celebrated, it brings everyone together and it won't be long before the wake becomes a sort of party and sooner or later someone will say what a pity it is that the deceased couldn't be there to enjoy it too.

This one wasn't like that. The service at the crematorium in Inverness had been well-attended but a lot of people had drifted off afterwards and hadn't come back to the house. What could you say that hadn't been said before – and no doubt would have to be said again?

Mairead Wilson stayed to speak to the boy's mother, who was looking as if she didn't know where she was, but as Mairead reached her she tried to smile.

'You were always so good to Donnie. And he wasn't the only one – look at that lot over there.' She gestured to group of young men. 'Nice lads, really, you know.'

Mairead nodded, moving on to allow someone else

to take her place, ready to leave as soon as she decently could. Too many memories, too much guilt . . . far too much guilt. Her throat tightened.

'Something in the water that makes them do that, is it?' another woman had murmured bleakly and Mairead had nodded, with a strained smile.

And that was Brodie Campbell now, just putting in an appearance, his manner somehow suggesting that he was bestowing his presence. Mairead eyed him narrowly as he went over to a couple of young men, engaging them in a conversation that had them shifting a little uneasily. He liked to see himself as the Big Man, the embodiment of the law, being gamekeeper for the big estate – the law as he defined it, more commonly known as physical assault.

She'd known him as a child. She'd known all the bairns who hung around the café on the way home from school and she'd usually been good for a biscuit or maybe even a wee slice of cake, but she drew the line at Brodie, a bully and a two-faced cheat even then. She knew some of the stuff he was into later and he'd done well for himself – people who had no scruples usually did.

He didn't stay long. On his way out he had given her a cold, unsmiling nod and she couldn't suppress a shudder, feeling angry that he was able to affect her that way.

It was mainly the family that was left now, along with the two men Brodie had spoken to – two of 'her laddies' who'd come to show respect to a mate, but who lacked the social skills to extract themselves. She made her way over to them and they greeted her with sheepish smiles.

They were in their twenties now. Fergus Matheson had admittedly had a bit of a false start but he was back on the right track now and was still the bright-faced fellow he'd always been; Craig Lothian, though . . . Her heart sank as she saw his pallor and dull eyes. Lacking kids of her own, she'd mothered them and it was like a stab in the heart. What a terrible world it was now for the young – but what had she done to improve it?

'Hello, lads. I'm away home now. You coming?' she said, and they followed in her wake like obedient ducklings.

Which left Jago Innes, who had no conscience and would linger until they stopped serving the drink. Her lips tightened as she glanced at him, with his chain necklaces and pierced eyebrow and his arms tattooed so that he looked part human, part lizard. He claimed to be a Traveller, but it had been obvious from the start when he parked his mobile home on a patch of waste ground just above the shore that he was no such thing – one of those New Agers, more like, who always made claims of spirituality but still seemed to get involved in dirty stuff – very dirty, in some cases. He certainly hadn't travelled far; his family had lived up around Torridon and there'd been no shortage of money, at least before his hippie parents had started running through it.

He'd made the site an eyesore, with motorbikes coming for repair and failed engine parts left scattered round about in the overgrown grass. The mobile home itself, decorated with fairy-lights and dangling crystals, looked out of place in its surroundings and even walking past you were assailed by a smell that his partner might claim was joss sticks, but Mairead's head didn't button up the back.

She couldn't quite place his girlfriend. With her colouring, Zoe Cooper might well be of Irish Traveller stock but she'd never volunteered any personal information and nowadays you didn't like to ask. It was only recently that Mairead had taken her on to replace the woman who'd been waitressing for her for years but had been tempted away to take a job in one of the hotels. She wouldn't have trusted Jago within a mile of her till and she'd been very doubtful, but with the wages being offered there was only one applicant.

Zoe, though, had surprised her; she very effectively managed the tables and the shop and the seventeen-year-old schoolgirl who helped out, leaving Mairead free to cook her popular light lunches and teas and even give her time for business stuff. She was a bit inclined to take off at short notice but she was otherwise reliable and could be left to deal with the takings and close up the café so that if Mairead had to be away, she needn't shut the place and lose money.

That mattered. Times had been so hard and the debts had mounted during the bad years of lockdowns and the cost-of-living crisis so that the business had teetered on the verge of going under. Shore House, her family home, was part of herself; if she lost it, she'd feel crippled and vulnerable, like a snail that had lost its shell. She'd set up the café to be able to keep it when her parents died and she'd been proud of the way that it had prospered until Covid hit like a bludgeon to the back of the head. She wouldn't submit; bloody but unbowed, she had flogged her guts out, not caring what she did, grabbing as if she was crazy at anything that would bring in the cash to keep it afloat. And they'd pulled through – no thanks to the useless slob she'd saddled herself with.

Mairead sometimes asked herself, plaintively, how she could have been so blind to his faults. Compared to the locals, fishermen and farmworkers mainly, he'd seemed kind of glamorous then, floating in from the city as a visiting artist with a vision, destined for great things and, poor fool, she'd been young enough to be dazzled. She couldn't deny that he'd been good-looking then too – still was, she supposed, in a raddled sort of way, though the ponytail that had looked a bit raffish when he was younger now was grey and, in her opinion, frankly sad.

He'd moved in with her and for the first years of their marriage, with him doing nothing except producing paintings that rarely sold, money had been too tight to think of having bairns, and by the time they might have, she'd realised how fundamentally idle he was, and how delusional. The only paintings that had ever been commercially successful had been the little landscapes that sold to tourists, and persuading him to do the artwork he so blatantly thought beneath him took up time she could ill spare. She'd acquired a man-child instead of the kids she could have had. The boys who drifted off once the begging-for-cakes years stopped were a very limited substitute – though they came back soon enough when they were in trouble. She'd have divorced John long ago if she hadn't known he'd ruthlessly take her to the cleaners and all that she'd worked for so tirelessly would crash in ruins about her.

As she drove back to Ardelour, her mind was on the demands of the day. It had been a sacrifice to close for the morning since it was just after the Easter break when there were more tourists around and she could hope to make enough to see her through the long tough winter months, so she'd have to open up this afternoon. With a variety of homemade cakes always displayed on the counter on stands with glass domes, it had become a destination café for people all around the area and it was important not to disappoint them.

Keeping up supplies had always been a challenge, but it was easier now that she'd been able to rely on Anna Bruce, a caterer who for some odd reason had moved here recently. She'd been away on holiday, though, and now Mairead had to hope she'd got back and would deliver as promised tomorrow. The last frozen coffee and walnut cake had been taken out of the freezer yesterday and though there was still a fruitcake, she'd probably be as well to whip up a Victoria sponge ready for the afternoon opening. Anyway, it would take her mind off what had just been happening. The coincidence had left her feeling sick and she really couldn't afford to think about it any more.

Just as she slowed down for the narrow entrance to the Ardelour road, she heard the snarling roar of a motorbike's engine, and Jago Innes, unhelmeted, shot past and cut in so that she had to brake sharply to let him make the turn in front of her. He grinned and waved.

It did occur to her that if she'd accelerated instead of braking at that point, it would have made the world a healthier place.

The air in Anna Bruce's kitchen was heavy with the delectable smell of baking, of spice and of citrus, and she sniffed appreciatively as she took the last of the cakes out of the oven and left it to cool with the others so that she could ice them in the morning, ready to take down to the Shore House Café before it opened.

She'd been glad to get the commission, not least because she'd hoped it might at last give her a route to acceptance into the community. Good cooks tend to enjoy talking food and she'd tasted enough of Mairead's light lunches to know that she was, indeed, a good cook, but that had never happened. Anna's cakes were accepted with polite praise and conventional remarks would be made about the weather or the occasional delivery problem before Mairead retreated into the kitchen at the back, with never an offer of a chat over a cup of coffee. Anna had given up trying now, but it so clearly said that she didn't belong and left her feeling bruised.

Someone had explained that the café and shop was the ground floor of Mairead's family home, a three-storey Victorian house on the shore that had been built by a prosperous skipper in the days before the 'silver darlings' – the herring – so disastrously deserted their fishing-grounds.

Mairead Wilson was interesting. She'd probably been quite good-looking as a girl, though with her height and strong features she'd always have been more likely to be described as handsome rather than pretty, and in middle age her face had hardened into lines that suggested life had been a disappointment. Anna suspected that it might have had something to do with the husband, a sort of aging-hippy type, who didn't seem to do anything much and was most frequently to be seen in the pub with a group of cronies.

The pub – oh dear. Anna was tired as she finished clearing up in the kitchen; it had been a hard day's work and what she wanted to do more than anything was to get out the Sauvignon and sit at the window. The view was particularly seductive this evening, the sea midnight dark and flecked with white caps, the streaks of cloud underlit with red and gold by the sinking sun.

But she had decided earlier that however reluctant she might be, she must go down to The Ship tonight to see whether there was any obvious reaction to the trial verdict. She'd been listening to Radio Scotland while she worked and it had certainly featured on the news, with a further discussion about the problem of freight thefts, but it hadn't even mentioned Callan. If Gavin Thomson hadn't any local connection it might easily have gone unnoticed.

There was one person, though, who would definitely have been taking an interest – the 'friend' who was to blame for his death, the 'friend' who would undoubtedly know about the part she – or rather, Janet MacNeish – had played in getting the guilty verdict, who might have shared that knowledge with his own little circle, who might even now be sitting round a table in The Ship talking about it.

She'd be as invisible to him as a fly on the wall. From early on Anna had made a practice of dropping in at the pub, even once she'd realised that the tight-knit circle of regulars wasn't going to draw her into useful conversation. She knew John Wilson from the café by sight, and the nice man from the shellfish fishery always gave her a wave, but apart from that she was ignored – often that conversation was in Gaelic too, which, while not deliberately intended to be excluding, had that effect.

There was a small table in a corner where she could sit with her glass of wine, not drawing attention to herself, while she studied her mobile phone. They were used to her now, and it was a good observation point. To start with she'd been on edge, constantly watching for any threat but now she recognised pretty much everyone, she'd relaxed. A stranger was always easy to spot and even with tourists starting to appear, she'd become adept at categorising them: the climbers, the sightseers, the boaties coming in from the small yachts that sometimes moored out in the bay, the Airbnb groups of families and sometimes friends, none of whom showed the smallest interest in her. She was confident now that she'd made a good choice of a place where no one would think to look for her.

Of course, the pub might not even be open tonight. She hadn't been down to Shore Street since the morning and it was possible that everything had stayed shut. She was guessing there must have been a funeral and she remembered one a few months ago when quite clearly the wake had gone on well into the night; she could still hear the sounds drifting up in the wee small hours.

The Ship was open and not only that, it was quite busy tonight. In addition to the regulars, there was a noisy group at one table, hill walkers from the look of them, and a couple of girls standing at the bar – teenagers escaping from their holidaying families to look for some action, Anna guessed. That wasn't unusual.

They were finding it in the shape of Brodie Campbell, russet as a fox with his red hair, sharp face and light brown eyes, his huge shaggy lurcher lying at his feet as he stood at the bar. They were giggling as he chatted them up, the alpha male staking out his territory, enjoying the dagger looks from a couple of young locals.

He was certainly charismatic, but Anna didn't like him.

He was always throwing his weight around, and someone had said he knew everything that was going on and had a finger in a lot of pies; she'd noticed the way he would go around chatting first with this one then another. He was gamekeeper to the big estate that owned the grouse moor up behind Ardelour and there was allegedly a wife and child in the tied cottage near the big house but Anna had never seen her.

He was known to be trigger-happy when it came to what he called vermin, which included foxes, crows and any other predators that saw grouse chicks as a tasty snack, and there had been a fuss when he'd been accused of poisoning a hen harrier. It was never proved but there had been several protests in the village after that – mostly shouting and the occasional stone thrown, but with no nearby police presence it had been alarming for the residents at the time.

He'd swaggered his way through it and local sentiment was robust anyway. The shoots brought much-needed employment and money to the area and country folk in general feel less guilty about their effect on nature and the planet than those who enjoy the luxuries of a city lifestyle.

As Anna passed him on the way to the bar, he didn't so much as glance in her direction. He never did – never had, in fact, right from the start. She wasn't his type and now she was of no more interest than the rest of the bar furniture.

'Of course, when you have to deal with guns all the time, you can't take any chances,' he was saying, and when one of the girls giggled and said, 'You make it sound like the Wild West out here!', Anna heard his reply, 'And don't think it isn't!'

The Ship was the only bar in Ardelour, a fairly basic drinkers' pub, one of a small group owned by someone in Fort William. With few local youngsters available for bar jobs, the staff changed a lot, seemingly supplied by an agency; many were from Eastern Europe and when Anna asked the pleasant young woman who served her why the pub had been shut, she wasn't very hopeful of getting an informative answer and she didn't get one, only, 'Sorry, don't know. Just, we were told we weren't needed till the evening.'

When she looked round, she saw that Jago Innes was there, sitting with a group of four other men, their heads together in a low-voiced discussion over the big round table in the window. She didn't recognise any of them, but safe in her cloak of invisibility she wasn't troubled by that.

The small corner table she favoured was nearby, but someone was sitting at it already. Normally she'd have looked round for somewhere else, but this was an opportunity she couldn't afford to miss.

'Do you mind if I sit here?' she said to the occupant, indicating the empty chair.

He was an older man in a navy Guernsey sweater and there was a pair of binoculars on the table beside him – a twitcher, she reckoned. His plate held pastry crumbs from one of the microwaved snacks that were all The Ship offered by way of food and now he was enjoying the rest of his pint while he did a crossword. He looked up, flustered, saying, 'Er – no, of course not,' and moved slightly to let her go round to the other seat. As she thanked him and sat down, he eyed her nervously – as if, thought Anna with an inward smile, he reckoned she was on the pull.

She took out her mobile as reassuringly as she could and he went back to his crossword, though she thought guiltily that he was probably hurrying his drink to escape the embarrassment and that she'd spoilt his enjoyment of it.

There was definitely some sort of consultation going on at Jago's table but, tucked right into the corner, she wasn't close enough to hear what it was about. When the persecuted man opposite her rose and left with a polite nod, she moved very quietly round to his place.

Even from there, she couldn't hear much. They seemed to be taking particular care to keep their voices low; the odd word she picked up related to timing, and some people coming up from the south. There was the odd bark of laughter when the voices rose again, but it wasn't long before she realised that whatever they might be talking about, it wasn't anything to do with the trial.

Discouraged, she finished her wine and was on the point of leaving when Brodie Campbell abandoned his fan club and came across.

'I've just noticed who your friends are, Jago,' he said. He was almost bristling with aggression. 'Nice company you keep. What are you doing up here, Connelly? If you're sniffing around now we're getting the birds ready for the season, you can forget it. There's security patrols with dogs going around the moor.'

The man, small and dark with deep-set eyes, looked up with a smile that exposed uneven teeth. 'Patrols?' he sneered. 'You and whose army? Big place, the moor, Brodie boy. Could lead you a fine dance, always supposing that was what we had in mind. But I can't think why you're getting fashed, with us just coming up for a wee visit and a bevvy with our pal here. Want to watch your mental health, pal, looking for trouble at every turn like that.'

Campbell's face flushed red. 'I'm fashed because you're a set of Glasgow bams and I'll be on the phone tonight tipping off the polis that you're hanging around.'

That provoked a laugh. 'Ooh, I'm scared! Well, lads, we could wait around until they turn up, if it wasn't I've got a business meeting tomorrow afternoon.'

At the raised voices, heads were turning. The atmosphere was electric as Brodie stood glaring down at him. At a loss, Anna thought, and sure enough, he turned away. But then he yelled, 'Listen up, everyone. As long as this lot is hanging about, I'd advise you to be sure you lock your doors carefully.' Then he stalked out, the dog instantly rising to follow him.

There was an awkward silence for a moment, before the chatter started up again. Brodie, Anna thought, must have been furious at losing face like that in front of the teenagers, who were now looking very uncomfortable, but there was no doubt Jago was annoyed as well.

He rose abruptly. 'Let's go back to mine,' he said, and the others followed him out.

Anna waited for a minute or two, then did the same. She wasn't particularly surprised that there was bad blood between the two men; she'd always reckoned Jago was into drugs and very possibly more than that, while law enforcement, at least as he interpreted it, was Brodie's job. Jago and Brodie were both regulars and the same sort of age, but never drank together, moving round each other like a couple of wary dogs. She'd never seen active hostility before, though.

But it was clear this had nothing at all to do with Gavin Thomson's trial. It felt as if the waters had simply closed over her and she had to face it, she was getting nowhere. In which case, was there really any point in her staying here, instead of taking up the offer of a neat flat in Manchester with a gym and Waitrose nearby? But the quest for understanding about what had happened – and yes, perhaps even for revenge – had been her only purpose in life, and if she abandoned it, what would be left? Nothing but a gaping black hole, sucking her down into oblivion. She felt despair as she trudged back up the hill to bed. And it would be another busy day tomorrow.

Iona Campbell could tell from the way he drove in that Brodie was in a bad mood. The gravel spurted up under the car wheels as he arrived, far too fast, and then slammed on the brakes. When he jumped out he banged the car door shut and she sighed heavily. He hadn't been gone long enough to be drunk; something, or more likely someone, must have upset him.

She went through to the kitchen to put the Scotch pies in the oven and warm up the baked beans. At least the baby was asleep; if Rosalie was awake and fretting when Brodie wanted his tea, it was enough to put him a bad mood so when he was clearly in one anyway, it was a mercy she'd settled tonight.

The big question was always whether to acknowledge a mood or ignore it. Sometimes if he could be brought to think about something else he'd forget about it. As he came in, she called, 'That's good! Your tea'll be ready before the match starts. I know you were looking forward to it.'

It wasn't going to work tonight. 'Oh, sure! I was, wasn't I, but instead I'm going to be out all night patrolling. Jago Innes has brought up some effing scum from Glasgow and they'll have come for a raid on the grouse. I'm going to phone the polis to tip them off but I know what they'll say – "Contact us when something's happened." Fat lot of effing use that is! How would I explain to the consortium that a whole truckload of grouse has gone – birds I spent the whole year nannying – and we'll be short when it comes to the Twelfth?'

Iona's heart sank. The Glorious Twelfth of August, when the grouse-shooting season opened and all the fat cats appeared with their fancy guns and fancy women, who always took a shine to Brodie, was her least favourite time of the year. The consortium was run by a group of them who took turns to come and stay in the big house and make all sorts of demands that meant she had to rush round doing cleaning and shopping for them.

Brodie took great pride in his gamekeeping skills. When it was a disappointing year for grouse, as it sometimes was – having sea eagles out there breeding on an island in the loch didn't help – everyone got tetchy, but this had been a good year up to now, so it really would be too bad if that creep Jago Innes wrecked it all.

The lurcher came through as she prepared the meal, delicately hinting at his hopes of supper. It was the only time Luath paid her any real attention; he was a one-man dog, though being a Highland gentleman he was always courteous, watching Rosalie as she crawled about with a sort of puzzled benevolence.

'Good lad,' she said as she put his bowl down and

he acknowledged her with a small wag of his tail, then consumed his meal with dignity rather than haste.

Brodie ate, then went out, the dog at his heels. She could only hope he wouldn't find them; neds from Glasgow were dangerous, not like the locals who by and large were only interested in nabbing a few pheasants and who were well aware of his reputation for delivering what he liked to call 'summary justice' when necessary. The list of his enemies was a long one.

It was, she was thinking as she cleared the table, as if he took this as an insult, as if any theft would be an attack on him personally. She'd known him all her life, from the time when, with his father a hopeless drunk and his mother so feckless she couldn't even send him to school in clean clothes, he'd had to fight down the contempt of the kids from luckier families. She understood the insecurities that made his status as the guardian of the Ardelour estate so important to him and made him react violently to any humiliation – well, he had a temper. He'd red hair, after all – what did they expect?

It was a great pity their first child hadn't been a red-haired boy. Iona had seen the disappointment on Brodie's face when he saw Rosalie, who from the first had favoured her mother with her curly fair hair and blue eyes. He could be charmed by her when she was behaving well – who wouldn't be? – but it worried her that he seemed to only love her when she was good.

Oh, her marriage wasn't perfect, but then, whose was? She'd been brought up to count her blessings: he made the sort of money not many did around here and he wasn't mean with it. He might shout, but she always gave in and did what he wanted, so he'd never actually hit her. She had girlfriends who seemed to have an unfortunate tendency to run into doors whereas he'd given her a nice home and a precious baby.

Had she been in love with him at the start? Probably – though it always puzzled her that people talked about that so easily. That thing Prince Charles had said before the disastrous first marriage, 'Whatever "in love" means,' was a good question, but if you were smart you didn't waste too much time looking for an answer.

She'd thought Brodie was going to be patrolling the moor and hadn't noticed him taking the car, but she heard him driving in now, calling, 'I'm back,' as he went through to the sitting room, sat down and turned on the TV.

That was a good sign. Iona joined him, saying, 'You weren't long. I thought you'd maybe be out half the night.'

With Luath lying at his feet, he was already absorbed in the game. 'What? Oh, I just decided to work smart and check on the scum instead of the moor. They've parked this wee clapped-out campervan next to Innes's, and they'd never be able to get that up as far as this. Even if they do come hanging around, Luath'll let me know. There's something going on, though; I've noticed one or two other things lately and I got through to one of the lads I know in the Inverness force and he said they'll be on the lookout. It'll not be tonight. Can you get me a beer?'

As she went to fetch it for him, she could hear him screaming at the screen, 'What do you call that? Moron!'

She poured the beer and picked up a packet of crisps to take through with it. Just a typical match evening in the Campbell household.

CHAPTER THREE

'Ooh, very fancy!' Zoe Cooper said, taking cakes from Anna Bruce before the café opened. 'Carrot with cream cheese frosting – that's my favourite, though your ginger and lime comes close. So clever – I can't boil an egg.'

Anna smiled politely. There was always something about the way that Zoe said things that made her suspect she was making fun of her.

'Not as easy as all that to boil an egg, if you're at all fussy about it being soft or hard,' she said. 'Will these do you until Monday?'

Zoe looked along the counter. 'I think so, but I'd better just check with the boss.' She disappeared into the kitchen and Anna could hear them discussing it.

She'd been planning to ask her about the café having been shut, but instead of coming back to the counter, Zoe stuck her head round the kitchen door and said, 'Yeah, Mairead says Monday will be fine. Thanks a lot,' and then retreated.

Anna shrugged. It seemed she was fated never to know who had died – not that it mattered; she would likely not have known them well anyway. Now she had to drive on to pick up langoustines at the fishery.

The wind was whipping the loch into ruffling waves today and the sky was leaden grey. It almost seemed as if the weather was in tune with her mood; pathetic fallacy, they called that, and the scenery made it worse – those bare, eroded volcanic slopes, barren of growth except for the scrub on the lower levels. Those Torridon hills were two hundred and fifty million years old, she'd been told, formed by the shifting of tectonic plates along a fault, two hundred million years before ever the Himalayas rose from the Indian plain. They were an uncompromising ancient statement, beyond any comprehension.

She was glad to see the flotilla of floating tanks that meant the next turn would be into the yard of Logan Fisheries. It was quiet at this time of the morning; if it was one of the days when the van took live crustaceans on the first leg of their journey to France and Spain, it would have left earlier and Angus Macdonald would be in his office muttering Gaelic imprecations over the tranche of paperwork he would have to complete ready for the next consignment to be sent off to Europe.

The first time she'd come into the office to ask if there was any way she could buy langoustines direct before they were sent away, she'd overheard him and though she hadn't known what the words actually meant, their tone was a clue, as was the way he'd turned red and spluttered when he saw her. She'd burst out laughing and by way of apology he'd let her buy the langoustines he kept under the counter for a few favoured locals with whom he had a very personal arrangement – cash only, since it was all contracted to Wester Ross Seafood, the export company.

She'd been heartened to be included in that select group and her bleak mood lifted a little as he greeted her with a beaming smile on his round, cheerful face. He always liked to know how she was planning to cook them, being particularly struck with the idea of a whisky sauce she'd described to him.

'So what are you going to be doing with them today, then, my lass?'

'Just garlic butter and lemon, I'm afraid, nothing exotic.' She gave him her order.

'You'll not go wrong with that anyway,' he said, getting up to fetch the shellfish from the chiller.

It was at that moment it struck her that here was the opportunity she'd been waiting for all these months – to bring up the subject of the thefts from the lorries. She could almost hear Christine's prissy voice warning that showing interest in it could fatally expose her and she accepted it was dangerous, but the depression she was struggling with had made her fatalistic.

When he came back, she had her questions ready. As he put the package down in front of her, saying, 'Now what I'm wanting to know is, how can I get an invite for when you're serving one of they posh recipes?', she laughed, then said, 'Actually I was thinking about you yesterday. I was listening to the radio and there was an item about someone going to prison for a theft of langoustines from a lorry. Killed the driver, apparently. Has that been a worry for you?'

Angus's face darkened. 'It's shocking, that – the poor man. But us – och, we'd be hardly worth their while – just a small company and not a likely target either, with them being transported live in their own wee tubes in the vivier tanks. You mind I told you before, they're kinda sensitive and die just to spite you, so if you went hauling them out the tanks all you'd end up with would be a consignment of stinking fish. And we don't go onto the motorway either, just meet up with one of the big exporters where the packs can be transferred direct to their tanks for the journey down to the ports, so it's only the local roads to Inverness. But even so, aye, it's a dirty world out there.'

'Do you have to vary the times you send them out?' He looked at her quizzically and she went on, 'Well, they said something about firms having to do that.'

He frowned. 'Well, six in the morning suits us fine and we'd be needing to liaise with the buyers if we wanted to change it, so I just think we'll be leaving it at that. For now anyway.'

Anna sensed his withdrawal and kicked herself – that had been meant to open up the conversation and it had done the opposite. 'I was just wondering if I'd have to change my timing here,' she said hastily. She'd hoped to be able to mention, ever so casually, that she'd heard of a local lad being involved but she couldn't, now.

She picked up the package and counted out the cash for what was, to put it delicately, an unofficial arrangement. She was just turning to go when she thought of asking about the closures the previous day.

'Oh, perhaps you would know. Everything was shut yesterday morning. Was it a funeral?'

Angus nodded. 'Aye, that's right, a funeral. Very sad – just a young man. Killed himself.'

It felt like a punch in the throat and for a moment she couldn't speak. When she said, 'Oh, how awful!', she hoped he wouldn't notice how strangled her voice sounded.

'It is that. His poor mum.'

'Who – who is she?'

'You'll maybe know her – Shona Macintyre, has the smokehouse down the road there?'

'Shona? Oh no! Yes, I know her, and I used to see the son in the smokehouse occasionally. Donnie, was it?'

'That's right. Hadn't his troubles to seek, mind you.' He looked at his watch. 'Was there anything else? The boss is coming in this morning.'

Anna took the hint that being found with a customer where no customer should be would be awkward for him, tucked her parcel in her bag and left. She was trembling as she drove out and when she came to a lay-by she pulled in and collapsed with her head on the steering wheel as the anguish of grief swept over her like a wave. It never took much to set her off and this was the worst yet.

When she got control of herself at last and sat back, mopping her eyes, she tried to focus on what she should do. Shona was the nearest thing to a friend that she had, but in a situation like this, going to see her might be intrusive. Better perhaps to wait a day or two – or was she just looking for an excuse because she didn't trust herself to manage the conversation?

If Shona didn't want to talk, she could just give her the brush-off – or even tell the friends and family who'd be no doubt supporting her to do that. And she did want her to know why she hadn't been at the funeral – she would hate Shona to think she hadn't cared enough to bother.

Anna dug in her bag for her make-up and did her best to cover up the ravages of tears, then set off for the smokehouse.

Jago Innes was in the middle of a phone call when the string of crystals by the door jangled and Zoe Cooper came in. He stopped mid-sentence and eyed her warily.

'What are you doing here? Thought you were at work today.'

'Coffee break,' she said, dropping onto the bench under the long front window of the motorhome. 'Don't mind me.'

He wasn't tempted to accept the invitation. He ended the call with a brief, 'Get back to you,' shut down the laptop that was open on the desk in the area that he liked to consider his office, and said, 'Not usually honoured with your presence during the day. I thought you and Mairead spent any down time closeted in the kitchen shredding reputations along with the lettuce.'

It was making him uneasy. She'd been out the previous night, working at a bar along in Torridon as a second job, and the lads had been tucked up in the campervan before she got home and he'd been asleep. He'd been asleep too when she'd left for the café this morning and they should have been away well before that, so there was no reason for her to take an interest in what they'd told her was just a drop-in when they'd been having a wee break, going round the North Coast 500.

'So what's going on?' she said, giving him a gimlet look from under the heavy eyelashes that were, improbably, real.

'Don't muck me about with their daft "wee break" story.'

He'd suffer for it if he said, 'None of your business,' but he risked, 'Oh, just business,' instead. 'They've a scam running in Glasgow they thought I'd maybe come in on, but I've too much else to do. I've a big online project starting.'

Zoe was still looking at him and he had to stop himself running his finger round under his collar at the back, conscious that the story didn't quite add up and Zoe was no fool. But after a long, uncomfortable moment she got up.

'I don't care what the hell they do, as long as Joe Connelly doesn't go causing trouble here. The council has been looking for an excuse to get us kicked off the plot and I'm not wanting to move again.'

'No reason why they should,' he lied. 'If they do something it'll be absolutely nothing to do with me.'

After the door had shut behind her, he gave a long sigh and sat back in his office chair, frowning. It wasn't like her to accept a story that was as full of holes as a dragnet, so she'd been lying too. What did that mean? That she'd a scam going herself that couldn't stand the light of day? How was it possible to share a space that wasn't much more than sixty by twenty feet with her and yet know so little about what went on in her head?

Theirs was kind of an odd relationship. They'd been together for a good while now but if one morning he woke up and found she'd left him without explanation, he wouldn't even be surprised. It was more surprising, really, that she hadn't.

And it was surprising, too, that he'd never felt inclined to do that himself. He got bored easily and he'd never been a stayer when it came to women. But then with Zoe, every day was a surprise – or a shock, even, and their fights could be epic, but boredom didn't come into it. You couldn't predict what she was thinking or what she'd be doing next minute, never mind next day.

She'd said, right at the start, 'I am the cat who walks by itself and all places are alike to me. Don't try to put me in a cage.' He hadn't known what the first bit meant, but he'd taken the warning to heart, and in fact it suited them both. No questions: not when she took off somewhere or came home late from work in Torridon, and not when he went to Glasgow for 'business reasons'. She never even wanted to know when he'd be back.

That freedom was probably what had kept them together – that and the sex, of course. And one day it wouldn't be enough for her and yes, she would just go. When he was in one of his dark moods he often felt there was more to it than that – there had to be, something she knew and he didn't.

But she fed his restless mind and he wasn't going to risk losing her by asking the forbidden questions, any more than an addict would risk pissing off his dealer and losing his supply.

Such an odd thing, time. After they'd come and broken the news, it had raced past so crazily that she'd had to work late into the night to get all the formalities completed – not that it mattered, since she couldn't sleep when she went to bed, apart from in brief snatches of oblivion, which were so much worse than lying awake since afterwards she must go through the agony of remembering all over again.

Today, Shona had checked three times already to see if her watch had stopped. It hadn't: it was still only half past nine, with a whole empty day ahead of her. She was tired, bone-tired, but she couldn't find sleep, even though the pills the doctor had given her still hung about her, leaving her mind feeling fuzzy round the edges. When she tried to focus it on anything it felt like peering through smeary glasses.

She was alone. There had been well-meaning offers to sit with her but she'd turned them down, unable to bear futile chat meant to take her mind off what had happened. Anyway, she couldn't forget what they thought of Donnie, what they'd thought of him since the day she'd come back home from London as a single mother with a baby, a beautiful little boy who, with his huge brown eyes and tight black curls, favoured the father who hadn't stuck around long enough even to meet him. She'd called him Donald after her own father, an elder in the kirk, whose unexpected and unquestioning support had given her confidence to refuse to accept the shame she was expected to show, and from then on had held herself aloof.

If only Donnie had! But Donnie had been everybody's friend at the little primary school, always cheerful and smiley; among children, the cruel, old-fashioned prejudices that had so distressed his mother didn't seem to exist. He was a bit naughty, too, and naughty children were always popular, at least with their peers. Perhaps she had spoilt him, her little golden boy. But then . . .

The knock on the door sounded tentative. She wasn't expecting anyone to call; her near neighbours had all punctiliously done their neighbourly duty already so that she had enough fish pies in the freezer to last until Christmas. Did she really want to open the door to yet another 'I'm sorry for your loss', since she still hadn't worked out the correct response? For a moment she stared at the door, almost as if she could see through it to whoever was on the doorstep.

A distraction might help fill up her achingly empty day. She got up slowly, half-thinking the caller might already have given up, but no; Anna Bruce was standing there, looking as uncertain as her knocking had sounded, and saying, 'Tell me to go away, if you'd rather I did.'

Shona stepped aside, waving her in wordlessly.

Anna stepped forward, but hesitated on the threshold. 'I've only just heard what happened. I've been away for a couple of weeks and I wanted to explain that was why I didn't come yesterday,' she said.

Shona hadn't actually noticed; she had gone through the funeral and the wake like a zombie. But she said, 'Oh, don't worry. That's all right.'

'I don't want to intrude on your grief, because I don't begin to know what to say to you. It's just so inexpressibly sad.'

'Sorry for your loss' was easier to deal with than this. In another moment Shona was going to break down, and she hadn't done that in front of anyone else. She managed, 'Yes, it was.'

'I only came to say that if there's anything at all I can do – food, for instance, if you're not up to cooking – let me know.'

Framing a refusal, Shona began, 'You're very kind,' but Anna was shaking her head.

'No, I'm selfish. When life is so cruel, there's nothing I can do that can make a difference, but being allowed to give the tiniest practical support would make me feel less helpless, whatever it might do for you.'

Shona stared at her. 'That's an interesting way of looking at it. It would explain all the fish pies.'

Anna smiled. 'The standard thing, isn't it? I . . .' There was an appreciable pause before she went on, 'I had a bereavement myself, not long ago, and it struck me then.'

Shona noticed now, as she hadn't before, that Anna's eyes were swollen, as if she'd recently been crying. 'Come in and have a cup of coffee,' she said.

Anna made no attempt at small talk, simply saying, 'Tell me about Donnie,' before she even sat down at the kitchen table.

That was thoughtful. She'd liked her from the start, even though Anna was so reserved that she never seemed to get to know her any better. Had she, Shona wondered now, realised from her own experience that it was easier to talk when you had something else to do? As she filled the kettle, fetched the mugs, the coffee and the milk, it all started to pour out: the sunny, happy child, who had grown up to be the prisoner of so many demons.

'There's nothing for them here so they move away,' Shona said as she brought the coffee over and sat down. 'But Donnie had a good job working with me and his grandad – they were great pals from the start. I thought it would be better than letting him go off to the big city.

'But it's a bad place, this. So safe here, you'd think, so beautiful, but it's like a big rosy apple that's full of maggots when you bite into it. The ones who escape are the lucky ones. Donnie's not the first, you know.'

Anna stiffened. 'Not the first?'

'There's been another two in the last few years. Making bad choices, they call it, and there's plenty of vices here to choose from. Drugs, gambling, a bit of theft to finance it all . . .'

'But I've never seen anything like that!'

Shona gave a small, bitter laugh. 'Oh, you wouldn't. But if you looked a likely client, they'd find you. Drugs? Half the kids round here get drawn into the county lines racket – a phone call, and they'll do a personal delivery. Jago Innes is always running a book on something and if there's anything special you want, I've no doubt he could arrange stealing to order.'

She could see she'd shocked her guest. 'It started with Donnie when he went to secondary school. It's a long way – couple of hours a day travel – and for a while someone ran a hostel where they could stay during the week. Of course he wanted to go there with his mates. Dad and I didn't like it, but he got his own way.

'Later it emerged that it was operating almost as a sort of secretive cult, with rules and initiation ceremonies and patterns of behaviour. There was always trouble – shoplifting, vandalism, even break-ins so the police were involved. Later the place was shut down – too late for us, though. That was how we lost him.'

She was struggling now with tears. After a long pause, Anna said huskily, 'Do you – do you know what made him do it?'

'His life had become a living hell and there was nothing I could do to stop that. Years of struggle, treatments, vows to get clean that never lasted. It was ketamine, at the last, and his body was breaking down – constant pain, nausea.' Now she was openly crying. 'The note said, "It hurts too much." He couldn't see another way out. At least now he's up there on the hill in the burial ground looking out to the sea and he isn't hurting any more.'

She hardly heard Anna saying, in a choked voice, 'In Glasgow I knew a young chef who came from here and he killed himself too.'

'Hello, Mum,' Cat Fleming said. 'I got your messages. Sorry to be elusive – I was stuck in court waiting to see whether my case would go off.'

'And did it?' Marjory Fleming asked.

'Oh yes. Our client hasn't deigned to turn up so far and now the sheriff has lost patience. What were you phoning about?'

'It was just I was talking to the mannie about transforming the barn into a palatial reception venue and he needs more specific details now.'

'Actually, I was going to phone you myself. I've been calling round and there are a few more things—'

She heard her mother groan. 'No doubt. There would be, wouldn't there? Look, I'm standing in the Tesco car park and it's raining. I'm away home now so why don't you get your ducks in a row and call me back?'

'I've got a conference with a solicitor later this afternoon and I'm going to grab a sandwich but I can find a nice quiet café and scribble down a list.'

'Good idea. I've always believed that writing a list clears your mind. And if you write at the top, "Respond to the messages from Mum", you can score that off and it'll make you feel better.'

'I know, I know, and if I write "Start making a list" I can score off that one too. Speak soon.'

Her mother had said it was raining but then the weather was always worse over in the west and here the city was basking in April sunshine. Cat walked on down one of the streets that led off the Royal Mile to a small café that did better sandwiches than Pret but was unglamorous enough to put off the tourists who were already starting to infest the city. She always preferred Edinburgh in the winter when it reverted to being the auld grey toon, stark and elegant, and you didn't have to dodge your way around street performers and milling crowds when you were moving from court to court.

She'd contacted Kirkluce friends with wedding experience and then lined up a caterer, a photographer and a florist with glowing references. They were to be married at St Columba's in Kirkluce, the Flemings' family church, whose minister had been tolerant about their shamingly irregular attendance, but he would certainly want to talk to bride and groom before he agreed to take the service, so that had to be scheduled as well.

They really needed to go down to Mains of Craigie for the weekend and finalise the details – they didn't have much time now. It would be good to see everyone too; Lewis was growing at a ridiculous rate and tiny Ross was at the stage when they change by the day.

Before she committed to it, she'd needed to check with Kelso when he could get away – in the force you couldn't rely on weekends that were technically 'off'. But when cornered he agreed that the coming Saturday should be all right, though when she explained about the wall-to-wall meetings he showed signs of alarm, pointing out that you could never be sure what might come up.

Darkly suspecting that this might have something to do with his reluctance to get involved in the practical details, she said firmly, 'Oh, I'm sure it will be fine. I'll just touch base with Mum and then start on a round of phone calls.'

It would be a relief to get all the jigsaw pieces slotted into place.

That had been completely insane. Anna Bruce got back home and collapsed into a chair, having called herself a dozen different kinds of idiot on the way back from Shona Macintyre's.

It had all been so emotional. They had both been crying, and somehow she had blurted out her confession about Callan. And Shona had known him; he was one of the two suicides she'd mentioned. He and Donnie had been almost the same age, and she at once started asking about him – where had she met him, what had he been doing?

The questions had brought her to her senses; she had retreated as best she could, said she'd only met him when she was helping out in a Glasgow restaurant and had remembered him when the whole sad business was in the news.

'I thought he was, you know, one of the lucky ones,' Shona had said. 'He got a wee job helping Mairead in the kitchen and that was what gave him the chance to get out. But it was too late for him anyway, wasn't it? They wouldn't let him escape.'

Starting to feel sick already about what she'd blundered into, she still couldn't stop herself asking, 'They? Who are they?'

Shona sighed, then shrugged. 'Couldn't give you a name. It's spread through everything, like knotweed, getting more powerful out there all the time. Jago Innes could probably tell you – and Brodie Campbell too, the way he gets into everything. He's a bad man – probably worse, in his way, than Jago. But at least now I don't have to lose sleep worrying about what might happen next.'

She was looking exhausted. Anna would need to leave, but before she did she'd had to decide quickly what it was best to do for her own safety. If she swore Shona to secrecy, Anna was sure she would respect that. On the other hand, considering she'd tried to make her interest in Callan sound very casual, it would suggest that this was important for some reason and make matters worse.

She was very angry with herself. But the upside was that she had at long last learnt more of what lay in the locked diary that was Callan's past and she started trying to piece together what she had found out. She had suspected he had suffered abuse of some kind, and Shona's talk of a cult with initiation ceremonies would fit with that, and help to account for his flat refusal to return to Ardelour, a place he'd clearly loved but would never return to. Not even in death.

The tears had come again when Shona had talked about the grave on the hill, looking out over to sea; Callan had been cremated at the request of his next of kin, the parents in Canada who hadn't even come to the stark little funeral.

Still, she knew how he had come into cooking and that

earlier another young man he would have known had killed himself; suicide can almost be called contagious. There probably wasn't a great deal more to know, apart from the one big thing: who was the 'friend' to whom Callan had owed his silence – and why?

Anna tried to convince herself that the shared confidence wouldn't matter, that Shona wouldn't think it was information interesting enough to pass on, and there was nothing to connect Susanna Bruce with anything at all.

She had to pull herself together and get on with the lunch party catering and at least it gave her other things to think about. But when she went to bed at night and lay in the darkness looking out at the stars as she always liked to do, the doubts came creeping.

Were people already wondering what had brought her to this out-of-the-way place? If anyone raised the subject, Shona would have no reason not to repeat what Anna had said – and indeed, might well ask her later whether Callan was the reason for her coming here when next she saw her.

She'd actually come to believe that she was safe here, detached from reality. There was no reason why anyone should be interested in her, just another refugee from city life, and she'd felt herself invisible as she sat there in her little corner of the pub – sublimely unaware that there was bound to be gossip about the stranger in their midst.

There was no way round it; she'd been a fool. She lay awake for a long time and when sleep did come it was accompanied by vivid but unconnected dreams.

It was the lights that disturbed her first – the headlights of cars sweeping across her window as they came up the track that ran past her house to the field just below the moor. Then she heard car doors slamming, rough male voices, high, excited barking from dogs.

She leapt up in total panic, her heart racing so that she could hardly breathe. Had they found her? Had Shona been the 'friend' Anna had been looking for and had she walked into a trap of her own making? Shona could have summoned them with a phone call.

Her darkest fears had been of the stranger with the knife creeping up behind her, or the dark car slowing beside her and opening a door to drag her inside. She had not for a moment imagined anything on this scale and she stood paralysed with shock as she waited for the hammering on the door.

CHAPTER FOUR

Mairead Wilson hadn't been sleeping – far too much on her mind – and the unaccustomed sound of night traffic driving along the upper road in Ardelour drew her to the window of the big back bedroom on the first floor of Shore House.

It faced up towards the moors on the hill above the town and she sat up, blinking at the red figures on the digital radio by the bedside: 02:45. She dragged herself out of bed and drew aside the curtains. It was dark and clouds were whipping across the sky but by the fitful light of a half-moon she could see there were vehicles gathering on the edge of the big field that ran the length of the township, just below the moor. There must be five or six cars and SUVs; a silver Discovery raced up to join them as she watched.

Mairead could see lights going on in one or two nearby houses; there was a lot of noise now, with dogs released from the cars racing around barking ecstatically and men shouting at them. As she watched, they moved forward into the field with torches, then suddenly a huge spotlight was turned on and by its light she could see the dogs surging forward. It looked as if they'd spotted their prey.

Behind her, John stirred. 'What the hell's going on?' he muttered.

'It's them and their bloody hare-coursing. They've just switched on a light to confuse the poor creatures. It's late in the year for that – high time they left them alone.'

'Not when there's money to be made. What do you bet Jago Innes is running a book?'

'Can't think where I'd find anyone to take it.' She picked up a box of earplugs from the bedside table. 'Anyway, I'm going to try to get some sleep.'

'All right for you. I haven't got any earplugs.'

'That's because I don't snore,' she said smugly. She went to close the curtains, then stopped. 'Uh-oh.'

A blue flashing light had just come into view along the main road, closing fast, and then they heard the sound of police sirens.

John got up. 'Looks as if there'll be something worth watching now.'

When the knocking on the door that she had so fearfully expected eventually came, Anna Bruce was still feeling shaken by the fright she'd had. In her panicking state, it had taken her some time to accept that it had nothing to do with her, and even longer to work out what on earth was going on, but after the police arrived she had a ringside seat at the melee that took place below her window, illuminated by the searchlight on top of a police van.

Men started yelling and whistling to recall their dogs. Some managed to bundle them into the cars and take off before police vehicles blocked the end of the track but there was no escape for the three that had been first to arrive and had been boxed in. Escaping across the moor would be pointless; the cars were there to speak to their identity.

As Anna watched, police officers came up the track and spoke to them individually – arresting them, perhaps? There were dogs with them too, a rough-coated, rangy dog of doubtful parentage and a couple of greyhounds and a whippet looking distressed as it wandered round, apparently looking for a missing owner. A woman in a white coat got out of an official-looking van and came up with leads in her hand, clearly meaning to take them away.

That was the point at which things got rough. One of the men launched himself at her and punched the policeman who grabbed him; another was screaming and kicking out. The dogs were milling around barking, and Anna wondered if they too would turn aggressive, but once the man had been subdued and handcuffed, they trotted off meekly enough with the handler.

It had all taken time, and the sky was getting light. Anna had long given up all hope of going back to bed and she was wearing jeans and a sweater when she opened the door.

The officer on the doorstep, a slim young Asian woman who showed her warrant card, introduced herself as PC Sharma and asked if she could have a word.

Just like they always did. Anna felt herself tensing

up – too many memories, too many secrets. She agreed, of course, and the constable came in apologising for disturbing her so early.

She laughed. 'After all this, I could hardly be asleep, could I?'

'No, I guess not, ma'am. You realise what this is about?'

'Hare-coursing, is it? That's a really foul thing to do – they're such beautiful creatures.'

'That's right. Anyway, we've managed to arrest three of them – far too often they get away with it. Can I ask you what you saw tonight?'

'Nothing, I'm afraid, until they were all getting out of their cars. I was asleep and it was only the noise and the lights that woke me. There were about six cars, I think. Seven, maybe.'

'Did you notice any number plates?' As Anna shook her head, Sharma went on, 'Or recognise any of the drivers?'

'No. It was pretty dark and they all went straight up to the field. You arrived not long after that and the ones I saw under the light I didn't know. Sorry to be so little help.'

They were standing in the hall and now Anna took a couple of steps towards the door by way of hinting that the interview was over but saw with dismay that the other woman had taken out a notebook.

'Your name?'

She sighed inwardly. 'Susanna Bruce.' It gave her a qualm to be giving the police a false name and it was with considerable reluctance that she said, 'Perhaps you'd better come and sit down.'

The sitting room felt cold in the chilly early morning air and she switched on the electric fire and put on the light but drew the line at offering coffee; the sooner PC Sharma left, the happier Anna would be.

In the abstract, the questions seemed unnecessary and intrusive, but as a result of long and painful experience, she was familiar with police questioning; it was never restricted to what was directly relevant, on the basis that information had a value in itself.

Anna was tired after her disturbed night and it was a challenge to make sure that all her answers squared with her agreed back story and once or twice when she'd taken a moment, she thought Sharma had noticed that.

At last the notebook was put away and the ordeal was over. Sharma got up and went to look out of the window. The sky had cleared and the tops of the peaks were becoming visible above the morning mist, the rising sun just tipping them with gold.

'That's a great view,' she said. 'Nice place, this. I've never been down this way before.'

Anna came over to stand beside her. 'Yes,' she said, 'I often sit here just looking, especially at sunset, but you do bear the full brunt of the weather coming in off the sea too.'

'I can imagine that,' Sharma said. 'Well, thanks for your time, ma'am.'

She went towards the door, but Anna stopped, staring down to the road where, standing talking to one of the officers, was Brodie Campbell with the big lurcher at his heel. They seemed on very good terms; Campbell said something and then they both burst out laughing.

As she closed the door behind Sharma, she suddenly thought of the scene she'd witnessed in the pub with Jago

Innes and his pals. Brodie had threatened them then with the police and perhaps he'd tipped them off to watch out for trouble. Shona had certainly implied that he knew about what went on in the dark undercurrents of local life.

Perhaps she should tell PC Sharma about it, but that would mean calling her back in and Anna had no taste for being subjected to more questioning. And anyway, it looked as if Brodie would have told them about it himself.

She yawned hugely. She couldn't have had more than three hours' sleep but she had another busy day planned; there were a couple of orders for meals at the weekend and she wanted to get ahead with meals to go in the shops' freezers as well. It was all starting to get busier and busier.

At least it wouldn't give her time to fret over her problems. She switched on the coffee machine. An espresso, or possibly two, should see her through.

Iona Campbell wasn't sure what time Brodie had gone out, but she'd gone in to feed the baby at around midnight, then fallen into a sound sleep until Rosie woke a little before six and then she'd found he wasn't there.

Her heart sank. That presumably meant that there had been trouble up on the hill and he'd be in a surly mood after chasing after poachers all night long. He'd certainly been tetchy yesterday morning after the run-in with Jago and hadn't been much around the house all day, but he'd been in a good mood in the evening, actually playing with Rosie and looking almost doting when she gave him one of her gurgling laughs.

There was no note to indicate where he was or when he'd be back, but what was certain was that he'd be hungry.

With Rosie dressed and on her playmat surrounded by toys, Iona got bacon and eggs and a slice of square sausage laid out by the stove and had put on the kettle to make tea when she heard the car turning into the driveway.

Brodie wasn't in a temper, at least. He'd driven in quite slowly and parked neatly; when he came in with Luath he was grinning broadly, to her great relief.

'Well, that's sorted them!' he said.

Iona put the frying pan on the stove. 'So you got the poachers, did you?'

'Not poachers, no. It turned out Innes's scummy little pals were planning hare-coursing.'

Iona gave an involuntary exclamation of dismay and Brodie frowned. 'Well, I'd not hold that against them. Vermin, hares are, with them carrying the louping ill that kills off the grouse. But it's big business with the betting and the polis have been keen to get at it so after what I told my pal Dave Kirk, they were on the lookout. Didn't manage to get them all, but there's three cooling their heels in the nick right now.

'And the best of it is they'll be leaning on Innes. They knew already about the gambling on the side but they've never been able to make it stick – maybe they'll get him this time. I've given them a pointer or two about that, and another couple of things as well that've been going on – since Callan McIver's mate got the jail, there's been a lot of talk.'

Iona handed him a mug of tea and he went to sit down at the table, even taking a moment to speak to his daughter, who again obliged with a smile. The bacon and sausage were sizzling in the pan and Luath, though too proud to beg, was taking such deep breaths of the tantalising smell that Iona laughed and promised him his share.

It was such a relief that Brodie wasn't in a mood that she felt quite light-hearted; he'd even started pulling faces now to make Rosie laugh. This morning as she put the breakfast on the table she almost felt as if they actually were the sort of family she had always wanted to have.

Jago Innes had had a busy night and he was sound asleep when the door to the bedroom area burst open and Zoe Cooper stormed in.

'Would you like to tell me what in hell's been going on?' she shouted.

It was unfeasibly early. Trying to collect his wits, Jago sat up. 'I don't know what you mean,' he said thickly.

'Oh, sure you do. This is what your mates were here for – to set this up. You said they weren't doing anything that would bring the bastards down on us? Well, they're swarming all over the place now.' As he sat up and made to speak, she snapped, 'And don't lie to me. You're running the book, aren't you? I woke up in the night and heard you on the computer.'

He was out of bed now in his pyjama bottoms, his temper rising to match her aggression. 'Not sure why I would bother to lie. It's none of your business. Anyway, why aren't you at work?'

'Mairead let me have five minutes to come across to talk to you. She got wakened up with all the noise and saw the whole thing – all the cars, the dogs, the lights . . .'

That was bad news, and Jago froze. Trying to sound unconcerned, he said, 'So? What did she see, then?'

'She saw three guys being taken off. Some had got away before the polis arrived but she recognised one that didn't – Richard Armstrong. Pal of yours, isn't he?'

Jago gulped. Could this actually be a nightmare and he was still asleep? Armstrong was a well-heeled estate agent who would sing like a canary if he thought it would help his case.

'So?' he said again. He knew it sounded lame but he couldn't think of anything else to say.

'So I guess they'll be on the doorstep any minute now,' Zoe said. 'And you might like to know that your chum Brodie Campbell was out there helping them. Anyway, I can't stay. Leave me a note if you get arrested.'

Then the crystals jangled and the door was slammed, and she was gone. He hadn't even had the presence of mind to demand that she tell him why it mattered to her so much. He sat down on the edge of the bed, put his head in his hands and groaned.

This just wasn't meant to happen. Hare-coursing brought in big money from the online betting and a surprising number of outwardly respectable folk were happy to get involved because the risk-to-reward ratio was so favourable. It was sort of like summoning up a flash mob; you publicised the venue at the last minute, people turned up, took part and vanished, never giving the police time to home in, and even if you got unlucky you were talking about a fine or at worst a suspended sentence. But they came down harder on illicit betting – a lot harder.

The operation here had been his bright idea – not serious business, just a wee sideline to some of the bigger stuff. It had looked like a no-brainer – an isolated field, well-populated with hares avoiding the grouse moor above, where they were persecuted, remote terrain in a barely policed community. He'd suggested it to his Glasgow contacts; they'd come up for a swift recce and given him not just the nod but a pat on the back as well.

Brodie Campbell, Zoe had said, and he felt a rising tide of rage. He'd hated the man since their schooldays – a bully and a clype they'd all despised. They hadn't taken him seriously that night. 'Strutting like a turkey-cock,' one of them had said after the dust-up in the pub, 'but we're only wanting to borrow his dunghill for one evening,' and then they had all laughed.

They wouldn't be laughing now; the possible ramifications were terrifying. How had he known to tip off the police? A nasty thought occurred to him; had he somehow managed to infiltrate the group that had publicised the event? If he had, what else had he learnt on there – and what use would he make of it? Oh, there'd be a score to settle, but that had to wait.

But what was he doing, sitting here? He needed to get to his computer, close down the group and see what he could do to cover his tracks The police wouldn't be able to look at it without a warrant but once they'd had a chance to grill the guys they'd taken in last night, they might have enough evidence to get one – and who knew what else would unravel then? He still didn't know who the other two they'd picked up were; the situation could well be even worse than it looked to be already.

He was sitting in his office area, still in his pyjama bottoms, frantically deleting files, when he saw the police car drive up outside.

That was, in its way, good news, though he closed down his laptop instantly anyway. Once they'd serious information to go on, it wouldn't be the uniforms who came; it would be the guys in civvies in an unmarked car. He could be pretty sure who he had to thank for their visit and his suspicions were confirmed when he recognised the sergeant who got out, accompanied by a woman PC. He didn't know his name but he'd seen him talking to Brodie once or twice when there had been local problems.

It was a chilly morning and Jago shivered as he opened the door, The sergeant, Dave Kirk, was a big lad who looked even bigger beside the slight figure of the constable and with the identification process complete, his first question went straight to the point.

'It is our understanding that you know something about the crime we're investigating – hare-coursing up by the moors last night.'

Jago gave him a blank look. 'I'm afraid you have the advantage of me, Sergeant Kirk,' he said, his drawl deliberately offensive. 'I haven't a scooby what you're talking about.'

'Perhaps we could come in and tell you about it,' Kirk said, taking a step forward.

'Oh, no, I don't think so. I've really nothing I could tell you about anything that happened last night. I wouldn't be any use as a witness since I was cosily tucked up in bed when all this excitement was apparently happening.'

A wicked little breeze had got up and it really was very cold, standing here with his top bare. Jago gave another involuntary shiver.

'There were just two or three questions we need to ask

you. I'm sure you'd be more comfortable inside,' Kirk said, and the constable added helpfully, 'You're getting goose-flesh.'

He was, too. Outmanoeuvred, he let them in with a grudging wave towards the built-in sofa and, picking up a fleece from a hook by the door, went back to his desk.

'Get on with it, then,' he said. 'But if you're acting on information received from your pal Brodie, you should know that he would tell any lie in the book to get me in trouble.'

Kirk was obviously taken aback that he knew. 'Well . . .'

'I'll tell you what he told you, to save you the trouble, shall I? He said I was in the pub the other night with what he probably termed "convicted criminals". So? I've known them for years, and they've served their time, paid their debt to society, all that stuff – turned over a new leaf, I shouldn't wonder.

'But no doubt Campbell also told you they were behind this crime you say you're investigating. Maybe they were. I wouldn't know. When they dropped by, they told me they'd been doing a trip round the North Coast 500 and I'd no reason to think they weren't. There's nothing more I can tell you, but perhaps you can tell me if you've any evidence to back up Campbell's dirty little smears?'

He'd got Kirk there. The sergeant did his best and prised out the names of the men in question, but his questions got more and more irrelevant until at last he got up and said, more or less snarling, 'Thank you for your cooperation, sir,' and Jago was able to shut the door behind them.

He'd won the first skirmish, which had bought him time

to circulate a warning and start putting damage limitation in place. But winning the first skirmish had never been a reliable pointer to winning a war.

The mobile on the bedside table had to ring several times before Sandy Wallace had wakened up that morning. Indeed, it wasn't so much the ringing phone that woke him as his wife digging him in the ribs and grumbling, 'For God's sake! It's only half past four!'

Still dazed with sleep, Sandy had rolled over to pick it up, blinking blearily at the name. The normal five-thirty was bad enough, but four-thirty was fair ridiculous.

'What kind of time do you call this?' he said angrily.

At the other end of the phone, Angus Macdonald hadn't sounded any more cheerful than he felt. 'It's a message from the bosses. The tanker wants us to do the handover early – something to do with they bastards that keep raiding the vans. They've seemingly had an alert or something and they're changing our time so they can get the next shipment with all the frozen stuff off early. I'm just away in now to get the papers ready for you but you'll need to be here by five.'

'Language, Sandy, do you mind?' his wife had said as he climbed stiffly out of bed with his bad leg giving him gyp and blundered around the room swearing, and she turned over to go back to sleep.

It had been pitch dark, and very cold, when he set out. He was well happed up in three layers with a fleece and a scarf and gloves ready to put on top when he got out of his own car and into the van. The vivier tank in the back had to be kept at 5°C for the boxes of live langoustines in their individual cells; their comfort was clearly more important than that of the poor bloody driver.

In the office at Logan Fisheries, Angus, haphazardly dressed and moving like a sleepwalker, had all the paperwork ready for him, only it wasn't when he checked and he'd had to go and dig around in the files, so it was well after five before Sandy got away. It was still fairly dark, but the sunrise was showing as a line in the horizon.

As he drove along the side of the sea-loch, he could see the little waves slapping viciously onto the shore and after his years as a fisherman he knew what that meant. The wind would be building as the morning went on and he'd likely be driving back in stormy weather. The storms seemed to have got an awful lot worse since they started giving them those daft names.

Sandy sighed. Maybe he was getting too old for this run, certainly if they were going to muck about with the timing like this. He wasn't happy anyway with all this talk about the raids; even though they weren't a target themselves, you never knew what might happen if there was trouble.

Still, there was nothing to do but get on with it now. He switched on the radio and half-listened as he thought about the rest of the day. Around an hour to the rendezvous point on the A9, say ten minutes to get his cargo transferred and to hand over the paperwork, twenty minutes for a coffee and a bacon roll in the café in Achnasheen, and he'd be home in time for another breakfast.

He gave a huge yawn. Maybe he'd manage to doze in his chair after that – it'd be a late night tonight when they were going out with friends for their supper.

At this hour the roads were very quiet, of course, and

on the single-track stretch he'd only passed two or three cars, all locals who understood the system so he barely had to check. But as he turned the corner just before Loch Clair, he came up with an idiot who'd managed to get the passing place wrong and his car, an elderly Ford, had stopped half across the road.

Maybe it had broken down. A man got out of the passenger side and as he came towards him Sandy lowered his window, expecting an apology and a request for help. But as he approached the man pulled a black balaclava down over his face.

Too shocked to do anything, Sandy sat gaping as the man reached the van and the driver of the car, another faceless man, ran up in support.

The door was wrenched open. 'Out!' the first man said, seizing his arm.

All Sandy managed was, 'But you can't . . .' before he was ruthlessly dragged out of the van and forced across the road, then pushed backwards into a deep stony ditch with a little burn running along the bottom of it.

Both men laughed, sounding high on their own success. The driver went back to the Ford, leaving his passenger to jump into the van and take off.

It was all so quick. Still too shocked to take it in, Sandy lay for a moment trying to pull himself together. But the icy water was already seeping into his clothes; he'd have to move because it wouldn't take long for hypothermia to set in.

The trouble was, they'd left him in a sort of jack-knife position. He could squirm, but he couldn't raise his arms high enough to use the edge of the ditch as leverage. All he could do was try to roll sideways, get onto all fours and stand up that way. He spotted a rock on the hill beside the ditch with a ledge that he could grab on to, if he could reach it.

The wind was gusting strongly now and, swathed in his wet clothes, he was losing body heat by the minute. His teeth were starting to chatter, but with grim determination he managed the first part of the manoeuvre. On his knees and leaning on one arm, he stretched and got his hand onto the ledge. Now at least he could stand up.

His bad leg gave way, pitching him headfirst into the hard rock face, knocking him out, and he folded back into the ditch again.

CHAPTER FIVE

John Wilson sauntered down the stairs and into the Shore House Café at just before ten, the most-favoured time slot for coffees, then stopped. Fridays had started to get busy again with weekend folk arriving early, admittedly, but today there was an unusual number of locals in too.

That puzzled him for a moment. There were a few regulars, of course, but for most the coffee and cake here were pricey enough to be more like an occasional treat. Then he realised – there'd been that fuss the night before and until the pub opened this would be gossip central.

All the tables were occupied, and there was even a small queue of people staring pointedly at the occupants to embarrass them into drinking up and leaving while Zoe, trying to be in three places at once, was looking harassed. As he weaved his way through the tables towards her, he heard snatches of conversation: 'took the dogs away'; 'and the noise!'; 'cruel, if you ask me.'

As he reached her, John smiled. 'A bit frantic, eh?'

The cutting look she turned on him left him in no doubt about her annoyance at his late appearance and she didn't even say hello, just, 'Get on the till, will you? The girl says she can't get in until later.'

He never knew where he was with her and now he was feeling aggrieved. 'Can't Mairead give you a hand?'

'You'd prefer to make the lunch, would you?' Zoe snapped, hurrying into the kitchen to fetch coffee for a group that was looking fidgety. She was clearly in a temper and he resented her taking it out on him just because it was busy.

Certainly, he expected to step in when necessary but nothing had been said to him about today. After his disturbed night he'd been sound asleep when Mairead got up, so how could he be expected to know he was needed? It didn't look likely that he'd get his coffee now – and he'd always needed a decent jolt of caffeine to start the day. With a muttered curse, he went to take his place behind the counter.

There was a steady trickle of people coming up to pay, which kept him busy and fuming quietly. When a woman who was actually buying one of his watercolours said, a little skittishly, 'I hear you're the artist! These are wonderful – they capture the very soul of this place! How do you do it?', it took him all his time to make a suitably polite response and not to snarl, 'Just buy a bloody postcard and copy it.'

Towards twelve, the coffee drinkers thinned out and Mairead, having done the prep for the lunches, emerged from the kitchen, looking hatchet-faced.

'Good of you to condescend to join us,' she said over

her shoulder as she swept past to help Zoe with clearing and setting-up.

Clearly the bad mood was catching. 'With being up during the night, I slept in, but you could have wakened me when Ellie didn't appear,' he said defensively.

'We both had a broken night but it didn't stop me waking up in time to come to work. You could try getting out of bed at a reasonable time and at least pretend you have a living to earn,' she snapped. 'And how was I to know it was going to be so effing busy? I'd have had to take time to go up and kick you out of bed while customers were waiting. Anyway, it's quietening down, thank God, now the locals have caught up with the most exciting thing that's happened since the Brodie Campbell protests.'

Realising it would be unwise to respond in kind, John, tight-lipped, said only, 'That's good. Then just possibly I might be allowed to get the coffee I still haven't had?'

Sometimes he hated her – really hated her. Most of the time, if he was honest. She ought to be pleased because it was busy – God knew she was always on about having to worry about turnover. He wasn't going to just stand there and be a punchbag for two bitching women.

John was cautiously edging out from behind the counter when he heard Zoe's phone ring. She glanced at the number then went through ahead of him into the kitchen to take the call.

Three women came in at that moment looking for lunch and Mairead went to deal with them. Seizing his chance to escape without discussion, he followed Zoe and heard her say, 'If I must, I must. With you shortly,' and his heart sank.

'I hope that doesn't mean what I think it does,' he said.

Zoe gave him a cold look. 'Oh, you're there, are you? Well, yes, I suppose it does. I've got something I need to do.' She walked past him and said to Mairead, 'I'm sorry about this, but I've had an urgent message from someone I can't afford to ignore and I need to go. Ellie said she'd be in later and you've got John now.'

Mairead gave a disparaging glance at her husband. 'For what that's worth! For goodness' sake, Zoe – you can see what it's like today – this is all I need, frankly.'

Zoe said nothing, only giving a small shrug and Mairead said, with obvious reluctance, 'Oh, I suppose so. How long are you likely to be?'

'Not sure. Doubt if I'll be back before closing time. I'll just get my coat.' She went through the door, shutting it firmly behind her.

'Well, really!' John exploded. 'That's a bit high-handed! Why didn't you just tell her no, that she can't take off like that when you need her here?'

Mairead was looking after Zoe, deep in thought. It took her a moment to turn to him and say tartly, 'Because she's the best waitress I've ever had and I can't afford to lose her. And keep your voice down – people are staring.' She gave a heavy sigh. 'I *really* don't need this. Oh, you'd better go and empty the dishwasher so we're ready to put out the lunches. Do you suppose you could possibly manage that?' she asked with heavy sarcasm, going to greet a couple who had just come in and ushering them to a table.

The words *If I'm so utterly useless, I might as well leave* sprang to mind but he didn't have the guts to say it when she was in a mood like this – time of the month, probably. His eye fell on a long, sharp knife used for slicing the cakes and he had to fight down the temptation to seize it and use it for a very different purpose. With a bad grace he went through to start stacking the clean plates and mugs.

He'd obviously have to be on waitressing duty, which he hated. Not only was it a menial task that in his heart John felt was beneath him, it called for endless cheerfulness and patience with the punters' demands, however idiotic they might be. And he hadn't even got his coffee yet.

He was just taking an order from a couple with a baby in a pushchair when he heard Mairead talking to someone in the kitchen. That must be Ellie, so he might be let off the hook sooner than he'd hoped. He was feeling more cheerful as he took through the slip.

But there was no sign of Ellie. Mairead was just shutting the back door and when he asked who it had been, she said flatly, 'Oh, just a message.'

John wasn't in the habit of studying his wife's face, but he couldn't help noticing that her brows were knitted together. She'd been out of temper before, and it looked as if whatever the message had been had made it even worse.

Well, it was nothing to do with him. He passed on the order with a shrug and went back to his duties.

It had been towards nine o'clock when Angus Macdonald first frowned at his watch. Sandy Wallace always took his time coming back from the link-up; with the early starts, it wasn't surprising he liked to get a bite of breakfast on the way home. Admittedly, with him being much earlier today, he'd maybe had to wait for the café to open, but even so . . .

He got out his phone and dialled Sandy's number. There was no answer; the phone reception was patchy all round here, so he left a message telling him to call back.

He waited, but there was still no response and he was getting – well, puzzled, certainly, and a bit anxious as well. When the phone rang, he snatched it up, muttering, 'About time too!'

But when he looked at it, it wasn't Sandy. It was a very irritated manager from Wester Ross Seafood demanding to know what had happened to the link-up that hadn't taken place.

'I know it wasn't ideal that we had to change the time, but we'd got a tip-off that there could be a raid and we had to swap around the schedule for the frozen and chilled stuff so we could get it away earlier than planned. Did the message never get through to you? The driver waited for your mannie to turn up – even called him, but got no reply. What's happened?'

With a sinking feeling in his insides, Angus said, 'I'm afraid I can't tell you. It's not like Sandy – rock-solid reliable, been doing the run for years. Something must have happened – the van's broken down somewhere that hasn't any coverage, most likely. I'm sorry about that, believe you me. I'll send a laddie to find out what's gone wrong and get back to you later.'

'Right. I'm afraid it'll just have to be put down as a miss for today, though. I'll call you about further timings later.'

The manager rang off and Angus put the phone down slowly. The langoustines in the tank would survive all right, but that was a payment that wasn't going to come in and the boss wouldn't be pleased. It would probably turn out to be some sort of maintenance problem with the rather elderly van and he'd no doubt be blamed.

With a shiver he stepped out and hurried down to the processing shed by the water's edge to tell one of the workers to go out and start searching. The wind was blowing hard now, driving spray in through the open doors.

The lad he asked shed his oilskins with alacrity and jumped into his nice cosy car with instructions to report the minute he located Sandy and/or the van. Meanwhile Angus tried to carry on with his usual routine but he was constantly looking at the phone, willing it to ring. Surely Sandy could leave the van if it had broken down and walk to somewhere he could pick up a signal? It wasn't likely he'd actually crashed it or anything; by now someone would have seen a wreck and reported it and there was a little nagging worry at the back of his mind. Sandy wasn't a young man . . .

He was dreading phoning to tell the boss, anyway. Logan Ogilvie owned three small fisheries like this one and ran a tight ship, so he was prepared for a difficult interview. But when Angus explained he was surprisingly sympathetic.

'Just hope poor old Sandy didn't fall asleep at the wheel after the early start and drive off the road,' he said. 'It's a bit much that we get jerked around like this by the big guys just because they're not managing to protect their loads. They should have someone riding shotgun in the cabs, to support the driver.'

'It's not them I blame,' Angus said darkly. 'It's they dirty bastards and their raids.'

'Right enough,' Ogilvie said. 'Well, let me know whenever you find out what's happened.'

It was an hour later that the lad phoned in to say he'd gone along the road as far as the A9 and there was no sign of the van, or Sandy, and asked for instructions.

Angus gulped. 'Well – just come back, I suppose.' But what the hell did he do now?

'They've thought up a new wrinkle to keep us entertained,' DC Alex Ritchie said. 'You'll like this new one that's just come in, boss. It's enterprising, to say the very least.'

'Oh? Break it to me gently – what have they done now?' DCI Strang asked, with some trepidation. The Serious Rural Crime Squad had been for some time involved with the task force dedicated to tackling the burgeoning problem with raids on the consignments of lorries and trucks, with the Scottish companies that were often transporting luxury items offering tempting targets. They'd achieved the odd result, like the recent conviction of Gavin Thomson, but the successes were few. Ritchie was working at the Glasgow end of the operation and Strang had a lot of time for him – young, enthusiastic and notably competent.

'Looks like they've taken the van and the driver this time, instead of just the freight,' Ritchie said.

'What? But – that's crazy! It's absolutely guaranteed to spark a full-scale hunt – APBs, helicopters even! Why not snatch the stuff and run, like the playbook says?'

'Ah well, this load's a bit different,' Ritchie said. 'Small fishery, north-west coast, supplies lobsters and langoustines to Wester Ross Seafood, one of the big companies that, as well as selling them chilled and frozen, ships them live to France and Spain, where they're crazy for them, in specialised vehicles – you're talking serious money here. Even so, raids haven't been a problem because apparently nephrons – that's langoustines to the likes of you and me – threaten to die immediately unless they're given everything they want. I know folk like that!'

Strang grinned. 'Go on. And what do they want?'

'What they really, really want, as I understand it, is a tank kept at 5°C. If you grabbed them out of it, all you'd get is boxes of dying fish. Not something you could sell off the back of a lorry in the pub or at the back door of a fancy restaurant, which is where most of the chilled and frozen stuff ends up.'

'So you reckon some enterprising neds have now acquired a fully equipped van that will open up a whole new set of possibilities? Of course, you'd need to have a contact somewhere to get them to the continental markets – English south coast, say, or even Ireland,' Strang said, thinking on his feet. 'I see it's possible if you got a system going there'd be good money in it, when you think what an ordinary lobster costs in a fishmonger's here. So you take the van, slap on false plates and drive off. But a kidnapped driver? What's that about?'

'Pure incompetence, if you ask me, boss,' Ritchie said. 'That's usually the answer when you're dealing with the neds.'

'Certainly it won't be the masterminds that'll be out there doing the risky stuff. Something goes wrong, the hired hands panic and for some reason find themselves with an inconvenient driver on their hands. No sightings as yet, I take it?'

'None. It's just a large white van – we're getting full details, but it's a needle-in-a-haystack job – 1.9 million of them on the roads at the last count.'

'Right. So let's say you're a low-grade crook. What do you do now?'

'Gee, thanks. I'd rather be a criminal mastermind.'

Strang laughed. He liked Ritchie. 'Certainly not, Alex. You're on a simple van-jack and then suddenly this is what happens. What do you do now?'

'If you'd allowed me to be a criminal mastermind, I'd have coshed him, looked around to see where all that seafood had come from, driven him to the nearest accessible bit and dropped him in with a rock tied to his ankle. If I wasn't, I'd still hit him on the head, hard enough to incapacitate him, and leave him somewhere while I drove off, as quickly as I could.'

'That's probably quite a good analysis. So what's happening now?'

'Ah well, that's where you come in. I'm actually on my way up there now. Our DCS talked to your DCS and she seemed pretty keen for you to be involved.'

Strang's heart sank. Detective Chief Superintendent Jane Borthwick – JB – having fought off an attack that might have shut down the SRCS last year, had been determined to consolidate her triumph by getting involved in anything and everything. As DS Livvy Murray had said to Strang, 'If she asks you to go and open the nearest church jumble sale, you will tell her no, won't you?' and he hadn't been sure she was joking.

Ritchie went on, 'The thing is we've got the use of a helicopter that's involved in the searches, doing thermal imagery and stuff. Suppose you just come up to take a brief look – they could pick you up in Edinburgh. You could assess the situation and see what you think, then flip back to Edinburgh when they do another of their sweeps.'

Strang hesitated. He was tempted; it never did any harm to show willing and have JB pleased with you, and anyway he was somewhat intrigued by the thought of someone who seemed to have been thinking outside the box. Those were the dangerous ones, and you were wise to seize any opportunity to get ahead of them if it offered. It sounded as if they'd found themselves in a situation that was far from ideal and they might well be vulnerable.

On the other hand, tomorrow he'd said he'd be free to take Cat down to Galloway and he knew how much trouble she'd taken to set up appointments. Not only that, he was well aware that she knew he wasn't exactly looking forward to the process and if for any reason he wasn't able to do so, she would most definitely suspect he'd done it deliberately.

'You can positively guarantee that I'll be back here, ready to have my scheduled day off tomorrow?' he said. 'My fiancée has big plans and will never speak to me again if I'm not available.'

'Absolutely without fail. That's a promise – the promise of a humble copper who has absolutely no control over anything,' Ritchie said.

Strang gave a slightly uneasy laugh. 'Where is it, anyway?'

'Torridon.'

A place that had his heart. The most extraordinary,

beautiful landscape that returned you to a world when nothing had been fixed, when mountains had moved and created great clefts and valleys long before so much of the rest of the world had begun to take recognisable shape, where the peaks had names that sang in your head – Liathach, Beinn Eighe, Beinn Alligin: Munros that as a climber you were expected to 'conquer' – but he'd never been foolish enough to use the word.

Seeing it from the air would be spectacular too – weather permitting. He couldn't resist. 'Fine, I'll take your word for it.' Cat would understand if things happened to go wrong. Of course she would.

Anna Bruce was performing the delicate operation of separating egg yolks from whites to make a pavlova when her mobile rang. She gave a small start, with the inevitable result that the shell pierced a yolk, making the three whites already in the bowl unusable for meringue, and she swore. Knowing she'd been cutting corners by not breaking it into a separate bowl didn't make it any better and she was aware of sounding abrupt as she answered the phone.

A man's voice said, 'Sorry – bad moment, is it? Would you like me to call back later?'

'No, no, it's all right,' she said, with some resignation. She didn't know the voice, but she knew who he would be; she'd been thinking the other day that she was pretty much due for another liaison call from someone from the National Crime Agency. Every so often some well-meaning person, male or female, would take up her time with questions about her welfare; she would say she was all right, they would probe a little; she would still say she was all right and eventually they would ring off, no doubt putting a tick on a to-do list. They'd even visited once or twice, but mercifully they seemed to have come to accept that perhaps her choice of location hadn't been as crazy as they had at first thought, and that she meant what she said.

Did she, though? Increasingly she was coming to feel her vision of – what? Closure? – had blurred and her life was slipping away as pointlessly as the grains of sand in an hourglass. God knew she still missed him every day of her life and the anger was still there, but it was hard to keep the flame burning high after all these months. She didn't think she was ever likely to find out who Callan's 'friend' was except by chance and if she did, she had no plan for using that knowledge. Had she actually believed she might consider carrying out some sort of revenge? Really?

What she did know was that these official chats weren't any help at all. The man had started to set out his credentials, as they always did, but she'd cut him short with a burst of friendliness, thanking him for his call. The sooner she jumped through the hoops, the sooner she could get back to sorting out her culinary problem.

The man, Martin Williamson, seemed very pleasant. He even knew the area a little and he was clearly keen to tell her all about his experiences – the views, the switchback roads, the birdwatching . . . She was finding it hard to share his excitement about actually having seen a sea eagle fishing, and perhaps her lack of enthusiasm showed and at last he got round to asking if there were any problems she needed help with. Had there, for instance, been any suspicious visitors or incidents that she'd noticed? They always asked that. She assured him that there hadn't been, he reminded her of the dangers, told her to be vigilant – they always did that too – and then at long last rang off, leaving her free to go back to frowning at the eggs.

Best just to tip the yolks she'd painstakingly separated out already back in with the whites to use those for a cake – it would do for the café later anyway. The pavlova was a higher priority so, crossly, she set aside the bowl and started again. Using separate bowls, this time.

DS Livvy Murray came off her shift feeling tired and dispirited. She'd been working on an armed robbery and trying to follow up a lead from a Covert Human Intelligence Source, but every line she'd taken had petered out. As she went towards the cloakroom, she bumped into Angie Andrews, the Force Civilian Assistant assigned to the SRCS, who raised her eyebrows.

'Well, who stole your scone?'

Murray groaned. 'Just a typical day at the office. A lead from a CHIS that went nowhere – he'd been covert, right enough, but the information element was totally missing and he seemed to find it unreasonable that he wasn't going to be paid. Bored out of my skull, frankly. I don't know. After that disaster up in the Black Isle I swore I was never going to go out on another murder investigation, but this is doing my head in. I need a change. I was even wondering if I should apply for a transfer back to Glasgow and hope for a more interesting level of crime.'

Angie laughed. 'Edinburgh's too polite, you think? Oh, we have our seamy sides, as well you know. But I can't say the SRCS has been very exciting lately either, though the boss has just gone off up north by helicopter – there's been another of those raids on a lorry and this time they've kidnapped the driver.'

'Haven't even seen him around recently,' Murray said. 'He still looks odd to me without the scar.'

'Must have been his Cat, getting him into shape for the wedding photos. He was talking about it earlier – it's in a few weeks.'

'Well, I hope it stays fine for them, like they say. See you later!'

Murray fetched her coat and went out into the street. It was a dreich day, much in keeping with her mood, overcast and raining steadily. Once she'd have come away from that conversation hurting inside; now thinking about Kelso married only provoked a tiny, nostalgic ache.

It was definitely time for her to stop drifting and take a grip on her own future. She'd stepped out a few times with the brother of one of her friends, a nice guy who'd a job she didn't understand in some sort of technology, but she wasn't sure it was going anywhere. Geek talk wasn't as entertaining as the gossip in the CID room.

She pulled up the hood of her jacket and decided she'd head for St James Quarter. A spot of retail therapy might be just what was needed.

There was a gusting wind now, bringing in sheets of lashing rain – truly miserable weather. The family heading up to an Airbnb in Shieldaig for the weekend was miserable too as they drove up the A896 with the wipers working overtime and the windows steaming up.

'You know what they say round here – if you don't like the weather, wait a minute,' Ron Davidson said with determined brightness. Torridon had been his choice, and he was regretting it now. 'It's a shame you're not getting a glimpse of the peaks yet. I promise you they're quite something.'

'There are peaks? I would never have guessed,' his wife said icily, which wasn't helpful.

It had been a long and stressful drive after a horribly early start and for someone only used to city driving the passing places were presenting a considerable challenge. Now he had to duck into one to avoid hitting an oncoming car, shooting an irritated glance at Tessa as he did so.

With the manoeuvre successfully completed, he was driving on when four-year-old Noah in the back seat, who had hummed tunelessly for several hours, only breaking off to ask, 'Are we there yet?' with monotonous regularity, said, 'What was that man doing lying in the ditch?'

'What man?' his father asked tetchily. 'I didn't see a man.'

'Well, I did,' Noah insisted. 'Lying in the ditch.'

'Oh, probably working on it, digging it out or something. If there even was a man,' he added under his breath.

The boy was getting shriller now. 'There was, there was,' he insisted.

Tessa sighed. 'You'd better go back or we'll get no peace – you know what he's like. It'll only take a minute.'

Groaning, Ron pulled into the next passing place to set off back to look. Muttering, 'Piece of nonsense,' he zipped up his parka and pulled the hood up then stepped out into the blast.

Watching in the rear-view mirror, Tessa saw him trudge

back along the verge, checking the ditch that ran alongside the road. After a few hundred metres he reached the marked passing place, stopped suddenly, bent over and peered in. When he straightened up he stood rigid for a couple of minutes, then fumbled in his pocket for his mobile and made a call before he walked back, looking shaken.

Noah had been watching too. 'That's where the man was!' he exclaimed. 'What's Daddy doing?'

Tessa, with a sinking feeling in her inside, said, 'Daddy's just finding out if he's all right.'

As Ron opened the door and leant in, Noah said, 'Well? Why was he lying in the ditch?'

His father swallowed hard. 'He just didn't feel well and lay down for a little rest. Mummy's going to take you on to find a café and I'm waiting till his friends come to take him home.'

His wife looked at him with raised eyebrows and he pulled a face. She got into the driver's seat and before she shut the door, Ron heard the child saying, 'I said there was a man lying in the ditch and Daddy wouldn't believe me, but he was.'

'Yes, you were right,' his mother said soberly.

CHAPTER SIX

It was raining when they took off from Edinburgh, raining heavily with a blustering wind sweeping in from the west as they crossed Perthshire. 'Bit of a sporty day,' the pilot called cheerfully as the helicopter lurched and bumped.

'OK, not a problem,' Kelso Strang called back, though without much enthusiasm. He'd never been bothered by travel sickness, but even so the weather was making him feel increasingly uncomfortable. He'd let himself be seduced by the idea of not just checking out an interesting new angle on an ongoing problem but by the thought of an aerial panorama of the Torridon scenery, and after all, they were scheduled to be back in Edinburgh late afternoon.

But from the looks of it now, all he would get would be a bird's eye view of banks of thick cloud, and he was regretting his weakness now. If the conditions got much worse, he might even find himself stranded and he hadn't been brave enough to tell Cat what he was planning to do.

Amazingly, as they went further north the weather, always unpredictable on this Atlantic coast, had one of its mercurial changes of mood. The wind was now sweeping scudding clouds away from the west and as the sun, metallic silver at first, began to strengthen, the peaks started to pierce the mist, one at a time, as if they were being conjured up by a magician. As they swung round to land at the Torridon helipad, Strang could see laid out below him the great bare tops and randomly distributed lochans of the Applecross peninsula, the huge boulders tossed down like wooden building blocks after a toddler's tantrum, the valleys where green vegetation barely clings to the thin soil – a strange, bleak, magnificent landscape.

He'd got his reward, and now it was looking as if there shouldn't be any problem about the return flight. DC Ritchie was pledged to meet the helicopter and bring him back to be returned to Edinburgh and he could see him waiting now. Strang was in good spirits as the chopper put down; he thanked the team and ran towards the waiting car.

He greeted DC Ritchie brightly with a 'Well done, Alex! You made it,' and climbed in before he turned to smile at the other man. It only took one look at his face to wipe away that smile. 'Found him, have they?'

Ritchie nodded. 'I'm afraid so. Dead in a ditch.'

Shamefully, his inward response wasn't an immediately professional one. It was, 'How am I going to tell Cat?'

DC Alex Ritchie was having a bad day. He had set off from Glasgow when the news of the hijack came in, by way of Perth and the notorious A9, which had lived up to its reputation with several delays, and when he reached Logan Fisheries it was to discover that his straightforward fact-finding expedition had become more complicated.

It was unfortunate that he'd arrived ahead of the local force. Emergency calls to the Inverness police were routed through Glasgow and with neither enough staff nor enough vehicles adequate to covering a patch the size of Belgium, as they always said, calls had to be dealt with on the basis of priorities. A body already dead didn't merit urgent blues-and-twos attendance and though it later emerged that a patrol car was on its way to the scene, it could be quite some time before it arrived, given the distances involved.

As he drew into the car park, he thought only that there were quite a few people standing outside talking – discussing the loss of the van, no doubt. He hailed an older man wearing oilskins and asked where the office was.

He got a hard stare. 'Polis, are you? About time too! Over there.'

Feeling faintly aggrieved, Ritchie walked across to the door he indicated. They should have been told that he would be coming to take the details of the theft of the van but only for information; investigating the crime itself would be a matter for Inverness and it seemed they'd failed to appear.

In the little office, he found a middle-aged man, thin-faced and sharp-eyed, wearing what Ritchie recognised as one of the more expensive Barbour jackets. He was perched on the edge of a desk and behind it was sitting slumped a plump older man, with the broken-veined cheeks that spoke to an outdoor life. In contrast to the red of his cheeks, his skin was ashen pale. On the desk there was an open bottle of whisky and there was an empty glass in front of each of them.

There was something he was missing. 'DC Alex Ritchie,' he said, producing his warrant card.

'At last!' the younger man said, getting up and holding out his hand. 'Logan Ogilvie – I'm the owner of the fishery, and this is Angus Macdonald, my manager. I appreciate the problems you have with distance but I have to say it's been hard having to deal with this unsupported. What is the procedure now?'

Ritchie looked from one to the other in some confusion. 'I think there's some sort of misunderstanding. I've come up from Glasgow – you should have been informed that I would be coming to take details about what happened to report back to the task force coordinating the investigations into these raids. Just fact-finding, you understand?'

Macdonald said, 'Aye, they said that.' His voice was shaky and it broke as he said, 'But afterwards they said they'd be sending someone about – well, about Sandy.'

Ogilvie said flatly, 'You don't know, do you? Did they tell you someone was missing?'

'Yes – yes they did.' There was a hollow feeling now in his stomach. 'Do you mean he's been found?'

'Just chucked him in a ditch and left him to die, that's what they did,' Macdonald said, colour coming back to his face as he gave way to anger. 'He was an old man, Sandy – a decent man, worked his whole life. Not so fit now – talked about retiring but he wasn't like they young ones that think the world owes them a living.'

'Yes, Angus. I know. It's very hard.' Ogilvie turned to Ritchie. 'You'll understand he's upset – it was him had to phone and tell Sandy's wife – fifty-six years married.'

Ritchie grimaced. 'I'm sorry. That's a dreadful thing.'

'It is indeed. So – what do we do now?'

'To tell you the truth, I don't know what to say. I'd be glad to help in any way I can but I have no locus in this – it's entirely a matter for the Inverness police force. They won't even know I'm here. Of course I'll let them know at once and liaise with them, help if necessary—'

'But basically there's nothing you can do? Oh, this is ridiculous!'

Sweating a little now, he said, 'I'm quite sure they will have a car on its way to see you. I'll contact them immediately, and there's a DCI coming up from Edinburgh too – in fact I should be going to fetch him from Torridon now.'

That was simple cowardice speaking – he'd left himself plenty of time to assess the position at the fishery so he could brief Strang when he picked him up – and Ogilvie's acid reply, 'They certainly need all the help they can get,' made him flinch. Muttering, 'Yes, yes of course,' he made an ignominious exit.

Alex Ritchie was pleasant, cheerful by nature, and robust enough to have done well so far in police service. He'd come in fairly recently on the graduate programme after a few years in business but was always as ready as any other copper to roll his sleeves up and get stuck in with the physical stuff if necessary. He'd even managed to live down the stigma of having played rugby instead of football and was working now for his sergeant's badge. He hadn't often been exposed to that sort of humiliation and he wasn't pleased with the way he'd handled it; he'd rather prided himself on his ability to deal with a curveball but he'd failed.

He'd been working for some time with DCI Strang on the current investigations and also on the ongoing problems of farm thefts; as a result, he'd taken an interest in the reports of murder investigations Strang had headed and saw him as something of a role model. It had been a big bonus that they got on so well; Strang didn't pull rank and they shared the same sense of humour.

Now, having persuaded Strang to get directly involved, there was more humiliation up ahead. He'd managed to pitchfork him into a homicide inquiry and DCS Borthwick was known to be on a mission to promote the Serious Rural Crime Squad; since she knew already that he was being kept in the picture, there was no way Strang would now be allowed to turn his back on what had happened and walk away if she found out that he was actually in place.

And then there was the guilt of having dropped him right in it with his fiancée too. *Not starring, really, Ritchie*, he said to himself, as Strang got into the car. He broke the news, then set off for Logan Fisheries.

'That's the position, boss,' Ritchie said. 'I'm ashamed of myself for chickening out and for probably landing you in it with your fiancée too.'

DCI Strang smiled. 'Oh, I think this is the point at which I say "*te absolvo*", isn't it? I can't see there was much that you could usefully have done – and Cat understands what the job's like,' he added, sounding more confident than he felt.

It had been a well-constructed briefing. Ritchie was

undoubtedly good at his job and he'd clearly been marked out for bigger challenges, having already been assigned to two of the current national investigations. Probably joining the force when you were older after the discipline of an academic degree made it easier; Strang had watched how Livvy Murray had struggled over the years to get to grips with clarity and brevity.

'That's it there,' Ritchie said, pointing ahead to where the tanks floated on the sea loch.

'Oh, quite small. I thought it would have been bigger. But I suppose there's a good number like that taking their catch from wee local boats as well as the big fleets in places like Ullapool.' Strang frowned thoughtfully. 'Mmm. A raid on a van coming from here isn't going to bring you in a big haul, is it?'

Ritchie said, 'Look! There's a patrol car. The Inverness guys have arrived so that should take the heat off us.'

There was no one in the yard now and work in the processing shed seemed to be going on again. How, Strang wondered, would they cope without the stolen van?

In the office, Angus Macdonald was slumped at his desk looking bleary-eyed. Logan Ogilvie was now sitting on one of the rather battered-looking wooden chairs while a woman PC was standing taking notes in a corner and a tall police sergeant, also standing, broke off what he was saying to look at them questioningly.

Ritchie stepped forward. 'DC Ritchie and DCI Strang. I spoke to the Inverness desk earlier—'

'Oh yes, I got a message.' Looking at Strang, he said, 'Sergeant Kirk, sir, and PC Sharma. I don't know if you want to take over?'

'No, no,' Strang said hastily. 'It's your case. We'll listen in, if we may.'

'I've all but finished here anyway. I've got the details of what happened as far as they know, and we'll be putting out a request for information from anyone who might have seen anything.'

'You'll not get far with that,' Macdonald said, plainly unimpressed. 'That hour in the morning, there wouldn't be a soul about.'

The atmosphere seemed fairly hostile. It looked as if the police hadn't even been offered the shabby chairs to let them sit down.

'You're maybe right, but we have to try.' Kirk sounded defensive.

'Anyway, you've not said what happened to him,' Macdonald persisted.

Kirk hesitated, looking awkward. 'I'm not at liberty to say.'

Ogilive said tartly, 'Well, you know he was found dead. Surely you know if he was beaten up, stabbed—'

'We won't know until we get the police doctor's report.'

'What? You mean you can't just look at the poor man and see? It's quite farcical!'

Kirk, red in the face now, stammered, 'It's just procedure, sir. They won't say until that's been done and I haven't been to the scene myself.'

Feeling huge sympathy for the man, Strang put in, 'There is a reason – it's not always possible to make a judgement at first sight so rather than give out information that might later prove to have been inaccurate, they make it a rule to wait until they can be sure.'

'Mmm. I see,' Ogilvie said, though he was plainly unhappy. 'So, what happens now?'

Kirk said, 'Well, I go back and report the details. Then someone will come to give you a statement to sign.' He turned to the constable who had been standing in a corner, keeping her head down. 'Just check over with them what you have there please, so they can confirm it's right – and maybe add anything else they remember?'

'Told you everything already,' Macdonald muttered, but they listened patiently enough as PC Sharma went through her notes.

There was very little there. The pattern of delivery was long-established; all that was worthy of note was the change of time.

'All right?' Kirk looked anxiously from one to the other, edging towards the door as he spoke.

'And that's all?' Ogilvie seemed ready to erupt. 'There's a man been murdered and this is what you call a police investigation? And what are you two for?' he demanded, turning on Strang and Ritchie.

'Let me explain,' Strang said. 'I can assure you that detectives from the Inverness force will be dealing with the case in depth, but DC Ritchie and I are involved at the national level trying to stop these things happening at all. Since this raid is different from all the previous ones, if you would allow us to talk through the background with you it would hopefully allow us to prevent anything like this happening again.'

He noticed that Oglivie was suddenly looking thoughtful. 'You mean other fisheries could be vulnerable now? I have another three, up and down the coast.'

Sergeant Kirk cleared his throat. 'I'll leave you to it, if that's all right, sir. They're setting up an incident room in the Gairloch police station – I was to tell you that. And if Mr Ogilvie and Mr Macdonald have anything further they want to add, it'll be open in office hours.'

'Well, that will be a novelty!' Ogilvie said savagely. 'Actually speaking to someone in person, instead of calling someone in Glasgow who's never heard of this place?'

Wisely, Kirk didn't respond, only made good his escape, PC Sharma at his heels.

Strang and Ritchie exchanged glances, then sat down. Strang gave him the nod to open the questioning. It would give him the chance to observe, and anyway he was interested to know what line Ritchie would take.

'You said you had other fisheries like this, Mr Ogilvie?' Ritchie said.

'Yes, that's right. So am I to assume that there might be copycat raids? It's an alarming thought – we've considered ourselves immune up to this point.'

Ogilvie was engaged now, leaning forward in his chair, though Macdonald, hunched in his own and giving an enormous yawn, seemed merely confused as Ritchie went on.

'Presumably you will have a problem with transporting the catch from here now the van has been stolen?'

'It will certainly be a nuisance, but we can work with our client to juggle pick-up times, and a driver from one of the other fisheries can do an extra run.'

'So – who would have known that this run would have gone off unusually early?'

Suddenly, Macdonald came to life. 'Not a soul! Didn't

know myself till I got that damned phone call at half past four this morning. Sandy didn't know till I phoned him. But they knew the day before what they were planning to do – said they were sorry about the short notice but it was a question of security.'

'So the only people who could have known earlier than that would have been at the other end? So we would be looking for a mole?'

That was a good point. As Macdonald nodded, Strang put in, 'I get the impression that your normal schedule was common knowledge among your workers, but can you think of anyone recently who was taking what you might think was an unhealthy interest in your timings?'

Macdonald looked vague. 'Can't think anyone would. It's never been a secret, so . . .'

Ritchie was just about to put his next question when he went on, 'Oh, just a wee minute. There's a lady moved here recently – makes a lot of posh stuff for the visitors round about. She's come here—'

He stopped abruptly and Ritchie, puzzled, prompted him, 'Yes? Go on.'

Strang noticed that Macdonald was blushing and he'd given a nervous gulp. 'Well, she just came to ask where she could get fresh langoustines locally—'

Ogilvie said impatiently, 'Oh, for God's sake, go on, Angus! Do you really think I don't know about your little sideline? Just get on with it.'

Macdonald gaped at his boss, then stammered, 'Well, er, she didn't know anyone here and I just did her a favour once or twice. Anyway, last time she was in she started asking about what time our van went off in the morning.

I thought it was kinda funny – nosy, really. None of her business. So I just changed the subject. Don't know why she should be interested, anyway.'

'Can you remember exactly what she said?' Strang asked.

Macdonald looked blank. 'I mind she said something about did we vary the times. Oh, I think it was maybe there'd been something on the radio about a van driver that got killed and we were just chatting about it, as I remember.'

Strang asked with sudden interest, 'The trial that finished recently, with Gavin Thomson found guilty of murder?'

'Aye, that was it,' Macdonald agreed and Ogilvie chipped in, 'Oh, we all knew about that one. There was a local lad involved that ended up killing himself.'

That was even more interesting. 'Local lad?'

Ogilvie said, 'That's right, Callan McIver – grew up here. He was in with a bad crowd but getting the job in Glasgow should have been his chance to change his ways. Clearly it didn't work out like that.'

Strang was aware that Ritchie had glanced at him to see if he wanted to take over, but he said nothing and Ritchie went on, 'Do you have the lady's name and address?'

Macdonald looked pleased to be asked a simple question. 'Her name's Anna Bruce. Nice lady, well-spoken, ken? She's living in the cottage on that track off the top road just as you come into Ardelour – backs on to the moor.'

'I'm sure we can find it,' Strang said smoothly. 'And there's just one more thing I wanted to ask. How much would they be likely to get for the consignment they took today?'

Ogilvie and Macdonald exchanged glances. 'Black

market prices – hard to say,' Ogilvie said. 'When they reach France or Spain, they'll pay £110, £120 a kilo going through legitimate channels with all the paperwork – more, even, but without that, what? Maybe just £10, £20? And we ship them in four-kilo boxes, so if you were trying to sell them from the back of the van you'd have to find a restaurant that wanted as much as that all at once. To be honest, I'm still surprised it was worth their while.'

'Right. I see,' Strang said. 'Thank you, that's been most helpful. Unless – Alex?'

Ritchie shook his head. He was obviously surprised at the lack of follow up, but Strang wasn't about to explain.

God, her head hurt! It felt as if it might split open at any moment; sadness and rage were a lethal combination. Mairead Wilson had never been one to pamper herself; she swallowed a couple of her migraine pills, gritted her teeth and went on setting up what would be needed for the next morning as quickly as she could manage; it could be another very busy day. Zoe hadn't reappeared and there was no guarantee she'd be in on time tomorrow.

She finished her task. Now there was the chance to do what she needed to do, however much she dreaded it; there was still no sign of Zoe, but the café was quiet now and she'd just have to leave John and Ellie to cope meantime. He was bumbling about, looking surly, while Ellie, willing but clumsy, was briskly clearing the tables, every clatter of crockery sending another shaft of pain through her head.

When Mairead walked through the café to the house door and said, 'I'm off out. Not sure how long I'll be,' John looked outraged.

'Are you really wanting me to stay till closing time?' he demanded. 'I haven't got to my studio at all today, and you're always complaining that you need more paintings.'

'Oh, for God's sake, just do it,' she said and walked out, ignoring the waves of hatred emanating from him.

The rain had come on again with a vengeance and the detectives were dashing to the car when Strang's mobile buzzed. He made a face as he pulled it out of his pocket. 'That may be my boss if she's found out where I am.' However, when he looked at it, Cat's name came up – a voicemail message.

'Oh, that's lucky,' Strang said. 'She's going to be late tonight – a case conference or something. And having listened to all that just now, I was thinking that if we can be sure Inverness has the investigation in hand, I might even be able to get away today after all. It doesn't look as if there's much doubt about what's happened and the perpetrators won't be sticking around here waiting to be investigated. And the other thing that struck me is that this sounds like amateur night to me.'

'Absolutely. It could only have been an inside job since Wester Ross Seafood dictated the change in timing, but from the sound of it they weren't going to make a fortune out of that one raid. They maybe believed that having the tank would let them raid other vans with the expensive fresh stuff, but they wouldn't have an inside track like they must have had this time.'

'If they were naive, they might really have reckoned they would get something near the sort of prices you see in restaurants, so it would be worth the risks involved,'

Strang said. 'Anyway, we'd better go and check in at Gairloch, but before we do that, I'd like to have a word with the lady.'

'I know where Ardelour is – it's signposted over a bridge and down a very narrow road. It's not far. In fact, there it is now.'

'Looks as if it's on a peninsula,' Strang said. 'And a narrow road indeed. Must have been blasted through the rocks at some early stage.'

The road widened further on as the land flattened out to make room for a few rough fields with moorland rising up behind, before the place name sign and the first houses appeared. Driving slowly, Ritchie spotted a rough track that ran between two houses on the right-hand side of the road.

'What about that one? It looks as if it leads up to the moor.' As he turned into it, he said tentatively, 'I wondered if you knew something more about that case Macdonald mentioned, boss?'

'I'm certainly interested to meet this lady who was asking questions and has only recently arrived here.'

To Ritchie's disappointment, he didn't give any further explanation, but he was able to park behind a Volvo hatchback – at least the posh caterer must be in.

If she could only take her head off and park it somewhere, Mairead might be able to cope better. For all the effect the pills were having, she might as well have eaten Smarties, and though she'd held herself together so far, it felt as if her thoughts were revolving on a spiked wheel.

Determinedly, she focused on practicalities. If this was going to be one of her worst migraines, what would happen the next day, if Zoe didn't turn up? And what was it that had demanded her immediate attention? An awful lot went on below the surface with her.

She ought to be able to rely on John to stand in when necessary, of course, but she couldn't trust him. When he was caught with his hand in the till, he'd be blatantly unrepentant, saying she'd skin a flea for its hide and a man had to live. She suspected he had other sources of income she knew nothing about, but when questioned he would give her the practised stare of the habitual liar and say he had no idea what she was talking about.

She drove back through teeming rain. Soaked to the skin, she hurried from the car to the café, which hadn't yet closed, and found to her surprise that Zoe was there.

'Oh, thank goodness!' Mairead said. 'I hadn't dared to hope you'd be back today.'

'Didn't take as long as I thought it might. John's scarpered now I'm back. How did you manage?'

'"Somehow", I think would be best way to put it.'

Zoe stared at her. 'You're looking awful. What's the matter?'

It was getting harder to form her words. 'One of my headaches.'

'Well, I can close up. You know what you're like – you should have gone to bed long ago.'

'There's was something I needed to do first—'

'Nothing matters that much. You can barely see.'

'I had to . . .' She faltered.

Zoe's penetrating brown eyes seemed to be boring into her. 'What was it that was so important? For heaven's sake, you could have crashed the car.'

'No, I was all right,' she managed, unwisely shaking her head, and staggered. Only Zoe's swift movement stopped her falling over.

'I'll take you through to lie down before you fall down,' she said, calling, 'Ellie – look after things for a moment.'

With Zoe's arm supporting her, and clinging to the banister, Mairead made it up the stairs to the house. The door of the bedroom was standing open and with Zoe steering her she collapsed at last onto the bed.

'You've a lovely bedroom, Mairead,' Zoe said. 'Now, I'll just draw the curtains, shall I? Oh, nice outlook, too, up over the moors there. Anything more I can do for you?'

'No thanks,' she murmured, closing her eyes and submitting to the pain. She was aware of the bedroom door closing but she didn't hear Zoe going off down the stairs, or the door at the bottom closing. There was just peace, blessed peace.

Iona Campbell looked at her watch again. She wanted to get on with giving Rosalie her supper and her bath, but Brodie hadn't come back for his tea yet.

The police had come round in the morning to talk to him about the arrests the night before, and he'd certainly been pleased about that, but then he'd seemed restless and had gone off to work at the estate office. When he came back for his soup at lunchtime, he'd been a bit on edge, snapping at Rosalie when she started banging on the tray of her high chair so that she started wailing in fright, which didn't make his temper any better. He'd got up then and gone out with Luath, saying he was going to see someone; he hadn't said who and she didn't ask him – he'd tell her if he wanted her to know – but she'd expected him back at five for his tea as usual.

The table was set but she'd had to take the Pukka pies out of the oven before they dried up, because it was half past five now and there was still no sign of Brodie. It wasn't like him and she was beginning to wonder if something was wrong. She couldn't even phone him; his phone was sitting right there on the coffee table.

Once when he'd been out on the moor he'd put his foot down a hole he hadn't noticed and sprained his ankle, but then he'd ordered Luath to go home and fetch her – he was a clever lad, Luath.

But Luath hadn't come back. Anyway, he'd taken the car, so it was maybe just it had broken down or something and she was being silly. No doubt he'd come back in an even worse mood if that was what had happened.

CHAPTER SEVEN

The pavlova was cooling in the switched-off top oven to prevent it cracking, while Anna made a double batch of chocolate brownies to use the eggs she'd messed up. The main oven was pre-heated and ready waiting for them and she spooned the batter into tins.

Sometimes it frustrated her that people's tastes were so predictable; there were more interesting dishes on the menus she sent out but much more often than not it was pavlova and some kind of chocolate cake that people chose. Still, it made tomorrow quite easy; it was a simple supper for a family at an Airbnb in the village and she'd prepared their chilli already. Once the cakes came out of the oven she'd be well set up.

Perhaps tomorrow she could take some time off. She was tempted to put on her walking boots and go for a hike; she hadn't done that as often as she'd thought she would and with no accessible gym she was getting sadly unfit. But she might go to see Shona first.

With Christine's warnings ringing in her ears like a tocsin, she'd been agonising about her foolish indiscretion. Now she was coming round to thinking that warning Shona not to mention to anyone that she'd known Callan was the best thing to do. She could dress it up as being a reluctance to be associated with him in case she might be tainted by his criminal activities, though she would feel a traitor.

Her eyes filled with tears, but she wiped them away with her finger. He wasn't there to be hurt. *You're overthinking this*, she told herself sternly. *See Shona tomorrow and then stop obsessing. However hard it is, you have to move on. And you've work to do now – get on with it*!

She had just put the tins into the oven and set the timer when there was a knock on the door. Anna stiffened. She had no neighbours who were in the habit of coming to her door and if anyone from the National Crime Agency came, they would phone to warn her first. An unexpected caller always set alarm bells ringing.

Of course! she told herself as she went to open it. It would be police coming again about the fuss last night. When she opened it and saw the two men on the doorstep, she had no hesitation in assuming that indeed they were, though they weren't in uniform and she hadn't seen either of them before.

The taller, older man, dark-haired and with hazel eyes, was studying her with what she felt was an uncomfortably piercing gaze, and didn't speak, but the younger man beside him, with light brown curly hair and blue eyes, told her who they were and presented a warrant card. 'Ms Bruce? Could we come in for a minute? We were hoping to have a word with you,' he said.

He had a nice smile – quite buff, actually, she thought. 'Of course. Come through to the sitting room.' She led the way, beginning to feel on edge. There was something about them, something that didn't quite square with her previous assumption.

'Beautiful outlook,' DCI Strang said.

'Wonderful smell,' DC Ritchie said.

Anna smiled. 'I'm afraid they're still in the oven. Do sit down. How can I help you?' She was feeling tired already; she knew how they always went on, all the formal questions, with her having to remember what she was supposed to say.

But DCI Strang didn't go into the procedural questions. He said without preamble, 'The driver of a Logan Fisheries van was killed in a raid that took place early this morning and we are making enquiries. Have you any information about this?'

She gasped. 'Raid – I – I don't know anything about it at all.' Feeling as if she'd been punched in the stomach, she sat down heavily on the nearest chair, afraid her legs would give way.

'Did you know what time the van would be leaving the fishery this morning?'

'Know what time . . . Why would I?'

'I gather you were questioning Mr Macdonald about the van's schedule.'

Trying to collect her wits, she said, 'Mr Macdonald – is that Angus? I didn't know his surname. Oh – it's not him that was killed, is it?'

'No,' Strang said. 'He told us you wanted to know if

they varied the times they went off, and I wondered why you should be interested.'

She remembered now – her failed attempt to draw him into conversation, hoping to find some clue to the identity of Callan's false friend. What to say?

She took a deep breath. 'Oh, that's right – I did. I was just making conversation, really. I'd heard on the radio about a raid on a seafood lorry that had happened a while ago – there was a trial and someone had been found guilty of murdering the driver, and it had just got me thinking what a dreadful thing it was, so when I was there I asked Angus if they had to take precautions – that was all. But – are you saying it's happened again?'

She was aware of DCI Strang listening to her so intently that it was scary. He didn't reply; it was the constable who said, after a moment, 'Could I take your details, ma'am?' He took out a notebook.

'Yes, of course,' she said, trying to stop her voice from shaking. 'Susanna Bruce, though I'm usually called Anna.'

She'd rehearsed the identity questions so many times that it was at least getting easier and the question about her whereabouts today was straightforward enough – 'I was here all day' – but of course there was no verification apart from a pavlova, a pot of chilli and some brownies.

They didn't stay much longer after that. She sat down again after they had left, trying to slow her racing pulse. She'd blundered again in pursuing her self-imposed mission and as a result the police were taking an interest in her now.

And there was something about the way the chief inspector had looked at her. She couldn't account for it, unless he was really thinking that she had somehow been involved in the raid. If it became obvious that she was under suspicion, it wouldn't be long before people started talking about her and by her own stupidity she'd left herself exposed. Somehow she'd been lulled into thinking that here she had a cloak of invisibility – even that by now no one would be bothering about hunting her down.

She hadn't heard the kitchen timer buzzing. It was the smell of burning that brought her to her feet. The brownies were beyond rescue; she tipped them in the bin, then gritting her teeth she fetched more eggs and began again.

At Gairloch Police Station, the Inverness officer now in charge of the incident room, DI Mackenzie, was arrogant and bristling, clearly feeling there was no need to bring in outside help; it was a perfectly straightforward situation. The luckless driver had been pushed into the ditch and it was only in his efforts to get out again that he appeared to have fallen on a rock and split open his head. He pointed out, in a somewhat patronising way, that in all likelihood the gang wouldn't be found up here, so that side of the investigation would be conducted elsewhere anyway and they would only need to establish where the necessary knowledge about the time the van would be setting out had come from.

DCI Strang and DC Ritchie were more than happy to leave it to him. They headed for a café in Torridon where they could grab a late lunch before the chopper was due back and Strang was able to text Cat without even having to mention the risk he'd taken.

Ritchie was bursting with curiosity. There had been a

subtext to the interview with Anna Bruce that he hadn't understood, but all his leading questions had failed to draw Strang out on the subject. He'd been ready to agree that she was a very unlikely accomplice for the raiders, but he clearly wasn't dismissing her from his mind the way you normally would when an interview hadn't been productive.

'They'll probably turn out to have been from Glasgow and it'll be landing on our plate after all,' Ritchie suggested. 'The big boys in the south wouldn't even know about an operation like Logan Fisheries.'

Strang agreed. 'The more I think about it, the more I think they've been very naive. I'd put good money on them messing up and being lifted whenever they try to sell it on.'

'And if they are, the big problem will come when the van is brought in with all those kilos of langoustines – how do you stop them stinking the place out?' Ritchie said. 'Anyway, we'd better be heading for the heliport.'

The chopper came in, well on time. As Strang got in, the pilot said to him, 'You're lucky we didn't have to abandon you. They've picked up the van so we're being stood down.'

'Really? Well, that is good news,' Strang said. And he might even get back to Newhaven before Cat got home.

Iona Campbell had got Rosalie bathed and settled down to sleep, but there was still no sign of her husband. She was hungry now, and it seemed a pity not to eat her Pukka pie, but she didn't really enjoy it. It was so unlike Brodie to be late like this; he'd been in a bad mood earlier and this certainly wouldn't improve it. Telling herself that fussing wouldn't do any good, she turned on the TV to see if *Love Island* could take her mind off it but she kept jumping up to look out every time she thought she heard a sound that might be him returning.

By nine o'clock, she was really worried that something was wrong and she didn't know what to do. She couldn't go out looking for him; she wouldn't know where to start and she couldn't leave Rosalie on her own. There were friends she could call, but if it turned out it had just been some small mishap he'd go radge at her for letting other folk poke their nebs into his business.

He was a grown man; if she phoned the police to report that he hadn't come home for his tea, they'd laugh at her. But somehow she was getting a bad feeling about this; no one would say it to her face but she knew fine that people didn't like him. She couldn't think of anyone she would describe as his friend – the list of his enemies, though . . .

Yes, she did have a really bad feeling. The trouble was she didn't know where to turn. Only . . .

She hesitated, then picked up Brodie's phone from the coffee table. She'd never used it before and she could picture his fury at this violation of his privacy, but she was desperate enough to be brave.

She went to 'Contacts'.

Cat Fleming arrived back at the house in Newhaven and had come in pantomiming exhaustion as she flung herself onto the sofa beside her fiancé, who was set up already with a beer.

'God, I really thought that blasted man would never stop! And I couldn't just say, "Right, I've got the message –

this little toe-rag is a scion of one of your most profitable families of clients so he's to be got off somehow despite my serious doubts about the truth of the line he is spinning us, so now can we both go home?" because with him being a solicitor I need him more than he needs me.'

Grinning, Kelso dropped a kiss on top of her head and got up to fetch her a glass of wine. 'Poor love! You do have to make uncomfortable compromises with your personal integrity in a case like that, don't you?'

'Not at all,' she said firmly. 'When it comes to addressing the court, I shall merely say, "I am instructed by my client that this happened . . ." which is entirely true. The sheriff will of course know that form of words implies that I'm handling the evidence with tongs and won't write me off as either stupid or sleekit.'

'Very ingenious. Did you land the brief?'

'Yes, fortunately. I'm in a lean spell. I did warn you I'd have to be a kept woman, didn't I? Anyway, how was your day?'

'Ah,' he said. 'I've actually had quite an interesting afternoon. There was a kind of weird raid on a seafood van and I got the chance to go to see the set-up in Torridon – they took me there and back in a chopper.'

'Torridon? Good gracious! The weather was pretty iffy too – what if you'd got stranded up there, when we've got everything planned out for tomorrow?'

'Wasn't a problem,' he said, as nonchalantly as he could. 'It was much better there than here. The views were sensational – I'll need to take you up there sometime. Now, I'll put the Charlie Bigham in the oven, shall I?'

He could feel her eyes on his back, but he seemed

to have got off without a direct accusation of reckless endangerment.

'So what was this raid?' she asked as he came back to sit down.

'Oh, a sad business, in fact. They took a van transporting valuable fresh seafood, instead of just raiding a lorry for the frozen kind, and the elderly driver was pushed into a ditch where he had a fatal fall.'

'That's horrible. But what if they'd expected you to stay to investigate?'

'No, no,' he said soothingly. 'Straightforward case, they're handling it up there. And in fact, they picked them up on the M6 and the neds are cooling their heels in a police cell tonight.'

'That's good. No problem about tomorrow, then. I'll give Mum a ring to confirm after we've had supper.'

Cat went into the finer details of the programme while Kelso listened with what he hoped she would see as suitable interest; more than that would be frankly unconvincing.

It was only when they went to the table with their lasagne that he said, 'There was one rather quirky thing today. I went to interview someone who'd been coincidentally involved and I suddenly realised who she was. Remember we talked about the woman who'd been brave enough to testify after the suicide of her partner, at that trial?'

'Yes, of course – the one who'd been forced to go into police protection.'

'That's right. She spoke from behind a screen in court so I never actually saw her, but she had a very distinctive speaking voice and whenever she started talking I was quite sure it was her.'

'How odd! Did you ask her?'

'I couldn't. Even within the force no one is allowed to know, or to try to find out her new identity. They wouldn't give me her details even if I had thought she could be a suspect. And of course I couldn't say anything to the DC who was there, though I know he thought there was something odd about my interest.'

'Another DC working with you? Not Livvy?'

'Oh no, he's with the Glasgow force and he's been assigned to a couple of their big investigations. Marked already for higher things, I guess. I don't know how Livvy is – haven't spoken to her except briefly in passing since I got back to work. But I just can't stop thinking about that woman happening to turn up there.'

Cat looked at him. 'Coincidences very seldom are. That's one of the things you always say.'

'True, and it was where the boyfriend came from, but if it's for any reason other than the sentimental, she's crazy. However, I can't see how she would link into this case. It's obviously been a rather incompetent and very likely local operation – they seem to have managed it only because someone working at the company that does the big runs with fresh seafood to the Continent tipped them off, but that wouldn't happen another time.'

'So what did they think they were going to get out of it?'

'To tell you the truth, I haven't thought about it much. Not my business, I'm happy to say.' He gave a huge yawn. 'Well, I'm for bed. It's been a long day.'

'See you shortly.'

As Kelso went through to the bedroom, he overheard Cat saying to her mother, 'To be honest I have a dark suspicion that he went off hoping for an excuse so he could call off tomorrow,' so she hadn't been fooled. But he'd got away with his risk-taking and tonight he could mentally follow the path he'd taken the last time he'd climbed Beinn Alligin as he dropped off to sleep.

A tired Sergeant Dave Kirk was thankful to be heading back to Inverness, when his phone rang.

'Are you still in Torridon?' his inspector's voice said.

'Just on my way home – not before time.'

'It's only we've had a call about your pal Brodie Cameron.'

That caught his interest. 'Oh aye? Got something more for us, has he? He's working well at the moment.'

'It's not that. His wife's called in on your number to say he's missing – in a bit of a stushie. Expected back at five and now she's worried something's happened to him. Obviously we wouldn't normally take any action yet, but—'

'Yes, but . . .' Kirk said, heavily. He felt a qualm, knowing better than most how many enemies Cameron had – and a CHIS was a precious commodity. 'OK, I'll turn back and go for a wee chat with her.'

'She says the dog's AWOL too, for what that's worth.'

Kirk had met the dog: an impressive beast. Probably had more braincells than its master and certainly better manners. It was smart enough to find its way home at supper time, but it must have stayed with Brodie, wherever he was. He sighed. It had been a difficult day already and it looked set to get worse.

It was a moonless night and as he left the street lights of the village behind to drive up on the tarmac road that ran across the moor, the darkness seemed to gather round him, the only pinpoint of light the Camerons' cottage, about three miles away. He grimaced; there could be no point in going out to start a search before daylight, if Brodie was out there somewhere.

When he reached his destination, though, the SUV he'd seen outside on his morning visit wasn't there, which suggested he wouldn't be – that was something, at least.

Iona Cameron opened the door looking tear-stained and strained. 'Oh, I'm just thankful to see you!' she said tremulously. 'I was going daft with worry and I knew it would be no use phoning the official number, but ever since there was that protest last year I've been feart for him. There's plenty things I don't know about and I just thought maybe you could tell me, was there something going on that would maybe be keeping him? I never thought you'd be coming yourself, though – it's real good of you.'

'No, no, you're fine. He'd been working with us a bit, so we'd like to know where he is as well. All right if I take a seat?'

'Oh dear, where's my manners? Would you like a cuppa?'

'Wouldn't say no. But maybe tell me while you're doing that, what's happened? He was to be coming back for his tea?'

'That's right. Went out after his lunch to see someone, but he always has his tea at five, unless he tells me different.'

'Mmm. He took the car, obviously, but he didn't tell you who it was he was going to see? Or where he was going to see them?'

'No.' Her hands were shaking as she put a teabag in a

mug. 'He doesn't tell me things, not really. But he seemed kind of a wee bit – well, out of sorts.'

'You don't know why?'

'No. Just he was angry with the baby – well, she was making a noise.' She sounded keen to excuse him.

'And the dog was with him and hasn't come back either?'

'He wouldn't be leaving him unless he was told to go.' As she set down the mug beside Kirk, along with a biscuit tin, a child's wail came from upstairs and she looked flustered. 'That's Rosalie – she's been having bad dreams—'

'Away you go. I'll be fine here,' Kirk said. He was thinking hard as he bit into a chocolate digestive.

There'd been so much going on today that it was hard to isolate anything that might be relevant to this present situation. For some time Brodie Cameron had been a valuable source of information for the police, being so well-plugged into the community, and he certainly deserved the credit for tipping them off about the hare-coursing, and a couple of drug busts before. He'd hinted there would soon be more useful stuff he could put their way, but what he hadn't done was pass on any suggestion of a raid being imminent.

Which could simply mean that nothing had popped up on Cameron's network. But Kirk had no illusions about the man he had found useful but hard to like; it could also mean that there had been something in it for him. It wouldn't be the first time he'd suspected him of playing both ends to the middle.

The baby's wails gradually diminished and when Iona came downstairs again, Kirk got up.

'Now, try not to worry too much,' he said kindly. 'He took the car so we know he's not lying injured up on the moor there, and you know if it broke down, he could easily be stranded somewhere and he hasn't even got his phone.'

'That's what I was telling myself,' she said. She sounded grateful for his attempt at reassurance if not entirely convinced, which wasn't surprising since he wasn't convinced himself.

'There's not a lot we can do until daylight,' he said. 'But I'll take a wee drive round the village and see if there's anyone around who might have seen him. Of course his meeting could have been anywhere – we'll widen the search in the morning, if he hasn't turned up swearing about having lost a tyre in a pothole by then. Thanks for the tea – I'm afraid I've done serious damage to that packet of biscuits.'

She managed to smile as she said goodbye, but he had a nasty feeling things weren't going to get better any time soon.

It was late now and the village was deserted when he reached it again, with almost every window dark. The street lights had been switched off; even on a Friday night there wasn't an expectation of what you might call a nightlife in Ardelour with even The Ship shutting its doors at ten-thirty.

Kirk drove down to Shore Street, brightening as he saw that there were still lights on in the back of the pub – doing the clearing-up, no doubt, and it would give him someone to speak to about Cameron. As he got out of the car, he realised from the talking and laughter that there was more going on than washing pint mugs.

A lock-up party, presumably. The last thing they would expect to see around here late on a Friday night was a police officer. He wouldn't be a welcome guest, but it would give them every incentive to be helpful. He went round to the back door and knocked on it loudly, shouting, 'Police!'

A gratifyingly sudden silence ensued, before the door was opened gingerly and a very young woman, pale with fright, asked in a shaking voice, 'What do you want?'

She wasn't a local. Romanian, perhaps, he thought; there were a lot of hospitality staff these days who were immigrants and it might well be that she had reason to be nervous about more than an infringement of opening hours legislation. He had no intention of getting involved in that tonight, though – he'd no authority to start an investigation and that suited him fine.

A man came forward then. 'Oh, sorry, sir,' he said – one of the locals, from the sound of it, with that Gaelic lilt. 'It's just a few of us giving her a wee hand and we were drinking up before we set off home. We're finished now – all right?'

'I'll just come in and have a word with you,' Kirk said. 'How many is "we"?'

There were about half a dozen of them in the pub kitchen, all of them holding glasses. There was another dark-haired, anxious-looking young woman, and the men looked a bit older, early twenties, perhaps. The spokesman said sheepishly, 'Well, I know we shouldn't have stayed on for another drink, but we haven't done any harm—'

'I'm not here about that. Do any of you know Brodie Cameron?'

The women shook their heads, but two of the men

exchanged a look that suggested to Kirk that they did, but retained no particularly fond memories of the encounter.

'He's often in the bar here,' one said. 'He wasn't in tonight, though.'

Then another man said, 'I saw him walking along Shore Street this afternoon – around half past two, I think.'

Bingo! 'Was there anyone with him?' Kirk asked.

'No, apart from the big lurcher that's always at his heels. He was coming from the car park at the end there, I think.'

'Did you see where he went after?'

'No. I was in a friend's house and I'd just happened to look out of the window.'

Kirk took out a notebook. 'Your name?' When he had written down the details, he said, 'Anyone else?' but no one had anything to offer. 'Right – I won't be taking this further. Get out and lock up, and don't do it again.'

He left to a chorus of muttered thanks and hurried along to the car park. And there, sure enough, was Brodie Cameron's SUV – but no Brodie Cameron, and no dog.

He went back to his car and drove to the upper level of the village, driving slowly along the main road, scanning the little gardens of the slumbering households and the fields as he passed as far as the Ardelour sign, but beyond the beam of the car's headlights it was pitch dark. This was pointless.

He suddenly gave a giant yawn. At least there was somewhere to start tomorrow, but this was taking him out of his depth and he'd be as well to go home and get a few hours' sleep before it all kicked off.

* * *

The early sun of a glorious April morning woke the dog. For a moment he was confused; he was cold and wet and very, very hungry, but the familiar scent of his master, lying beside him on the grass, was reassuring and he nudged closer to him.

But his nose told him there was something wrong – there was no comforting warmth or movement and there was a disturbing taint in the air. He didn't like it. He nudged again, then overcome with anxiety sat up, raised his muzzle to the sky and howled.

The man, driving from his house on the shore to his work in Kinlochewe, had just reached the top of the hill where the road turned back on itself to reach the top level of the village. Beyond that, a little path led away along the edge to a small grassy park with a slide and a couple of swings as well as a picnic table with a fine view of the loch and Shieldaig Island. The dog, in obvious distress, was sitting near the gate.

As a regular at The Ship, he recognised it at once, braked and got out.

'Luath!' he called. 'What are you doing here, old lad?'

The dog got up, ran over to him, then ran back to a figure that, now the dog had moved, he could see was lying on the grass, and the man gasped.

There was no mistaking Brodie Cameron's red hair. No mistaking, either, that the great red patch on the grass he was lying on was a pool of blood.

CHAPTER EIGHT

Mairead Wilson opened her eyes with infinite caution. Thanks to the pills, she had slept heavily and the headache, thank God, had eased off, though she was still feeling achy and slightly nauseous. Having gone to sleep so early, she had wakened early too, alone in the double bed; John had presumably slept in the spare room, but she didn't care enough to wonder whether this was out of consideration for her or because he was sulking.

The post-migraine brain fog was making her mind fuzzy, but that was just fine; it made it easier to blot out what had happened the day before – and what was going to happen in the days ahead.

Work, work was the answer; she must get up and get on with all the normal tasks. Saturday was always one of the busiest days and more and more visitors were coming now the weather was better. At least Zoe would be there to help – though of course you could never be quite sure of that, if she got one of those imperious messages.

She had a good three hours now before the café opened, more than time enough to get the lunch prep done, so she'd better face up to going to her office and doing a bit of work on the accounts. Her relationship with her computer was love-hate, with the balance ready to tip to the hate side at any moment. Without it, it would be impossible these days to run a business, but she was also its slave, unable to escape from the tentacles that might reach out for her at any time. She always held her breath as she tapped in her password, but there were no unwelcome messages today and she was able to go straight to the accounts, an activity guaranteed to insulate her mind from intrusive thoughts.

After a useful hour that had left the paperwork up to date for once, Mairead switched off her PC and stood up. She still felt a little dizzy, but that should improve as the day went on and she was thinking ahead to making chowder as the soup of the day when she suddenly noticed that one of the drawers of the filing cabinet wasn't quite shut.

She froze; she hadn't gone into that drawer for weeks, and there was no way she wouldn't have noticed if she'd left it like that. John never came into her office; there was only one person it could have been. And she remembered now – she'd crashed out so comprehensively that she hadn't even heard Zoe leave the room, let alone the house.

Was Zoe actually spying on her? What had she been looking for, and what had she believed she might find? And why should she be interested? She'd been in the office before, putting the takings in the safe when necessary, but Mairead had never seen signs of this before.

There wasn't anything in the files, apart from business papers; Mairead was far too smart to put any of her more shameful secrets on record. Her computer was still secured and she checked every cupboard and drawer without seeing any further sign of intrusion – not that that proved anything. But as she ran through the possible answers to her own questions, the lingering nausea overwhelmed her and she had to run from the room.

'You're not going to need all that soup,' Zoe said as she came into the café, much later. 'Or those either, frankly.'

Mairead, who was just putting a tray of chicken pies into the oven, stopped and stared at her. 'What do you mean?'

'The reason I'm late is that the police have set up a roadblock at the top of Shore Street. I explained I was local traffic and batted my eyelashes at them, so it only took half an hour to persuade the plod on site to contact the plod at the other end, who consulted the oracle at the far end of the phone and eventually agreed that I could be allowed to slip through. But I think you have to take it that there won't be a lot of casual visitors dropping in.'

'I did wonder why we hadn't had a single person looking for coffee so far. What on earth is going on?'

'Can't help you there. They've cordoned off the park at the top of the road and put screens up and there's police swarming everywhere.'

Mairead said, 'That sounds bad. And after yesterday, with those lads arrested . . .'

Zoe, who had been folding napkins, swivelled to look at her. 'Did you know them?'

Mairead's eyes filled with tears. 'Oh yes, I knew them.

Have known them since they were wee boys scrounging cake round the back door. What is it that we do to our young that means they ruin their lives?'

'As if we didn't know,' Zoe said. 'There's drugs put their way when they're innocent babies barely out of primary school.' She took a harder look at her boss. 'How are you, anyway? You're still not looking great. You were in pieces yesterday.'

'Oh, not too bad,' she said. 'You were a real life-saver, scooping me up.'

'You really need to learn to give in when you need to. You said you had gone out yesterday because there was something you had to do, but just tell me, what is there that matters more than your health?'

The door opened and two women, neighbours from along the shore road, came in looking astonished at the deserted café, and headed for the table by the window.

'Goodness me!' one woman said. 'We're a wee bit later than usual, and here was me thinking we'd never get our favourite seat.'

'I saw there was something going on at the top of the road – police cars, even!' the other said. 'Do you know what's happening?'

'Not really,' Zoe said, 'but whatever it is, you're going to be in the front row of the stalls.'

Mairead was already on her way back to the kitchen, saying over her shoulder, 'I'm just going to cook the pies anyway and leave them to cool so I can put them in the freezer.'

Zoe had just asked the ladies for their order when a phone rang.

'Oh, I think that's mine,' one said, groping in her bag. She listened to the voice at the other end, with her eyes getting wider and wider. 'Never!' she said at last. 'No, we're in the café but we've not seen a soul. Right – keep in touch, and I'll let you know anything that happens down here.'

Mairead had turned and was standing in the kitchen doorway. Zoe said, 'Well? What was that? Let us in on it!'

'You'll never guess! They're saying Brodie Campbell's been found dead in that wee park up the road there. Shot, they think, but that's just gossip so far.'

Her companion's face was expressive. It showed shock, certainly, but her mouth was pursed. 'Asked for it, probably,' she said, then after a moment, 'I think I'll just have the Victoria sponge today, Zoe.'

Anna Bruce, having delivered the order to the Airbnb, set off along the Applecross road to pay a visit to Shona Macintyre. She had her walking boots in the back of the car; it was a glorious spring morning and she fancied the walk round the An Aird peninsula that juts out into Loch Torridon. The views would be wonderful today with the sea shimmering steel in the early sunshine and the mountains that hazy shade of purply-blue, and she might even glimpse one of the sea eagles that nested on Shieldaig Island at last; she felt badly in need of the soothing powers of the natural world right at the moment.

The thought of the victim of this recent raid had been haunting her, and she'd been worrying too about the connection the police seemed to have made. Shona might be able to tell her more about it and it might even give her an opportunity to ask for discretion about her confidence. She was concerned for Shona anyway; she remembered all too well the painful process of coming to terms with the hard fact that this was how it would always be, from now on. Sitting brooding was a seriously bad idea; she'd be wiser to open up the smokehouse and keep busy, if she was in a fit state to do it.

But there was a 'Closed' sign on the smokehouse door and when Anna went to the house, Shona greeted her with a wan smile and the marks of distress were clear on her face.

'Are you sure you want a visitor?' Anna said. 'You look—'

'Yes, I know. I look a wreck, but come in – I need someone to talk to. I'm so, so angry, and the worst of it is, it's going to go on happening, isn't it? Even when you manage to cut off the head of one monster it would only mean that you had to start trying to decapitate the next one.'

Struggling to understand, Anna followed her through to the kitchen as Shona set out mugs and switched on the kettle.

'Another two young lives ruined,' she raged. 'I can't bear this place. It's like the island in *Life of Pi* – do you remember that film? It looked like a paradise but it was carnivorous and devoured everything that set foot on it.'

'I don't understand,' Anna said. 'Who are you talking about?'

'The lads that were arrested yesterday – the ones that stole the van.'

'Oh no! Where that poor man died?'

'Yes, that's right. So now they'll be charged with murder

and they're not much more than bairns, the pair of them. It would be an accident – I don't believe for a minute either one of them would have done it on purpose. They're not bad boys, but they'd got Craig Lothian hooked on drugs, just like Donnie, so he was probably off his head at the time. Fergus Matheson . . .' She sighed. 'Well, he'd had his problems a while ago and he's been out of work for months so he probably wouldn't be too fussy about whether taking the van was legal or not. But that way his life is finished.'

It was horribly reminiscent of what had happened with Callan. Anna, who had just taken a sip of coffee, choked. 'Sorry, sorry!' she gasped between paroxysms as Shona quickly brought her a glass of water. 'I just swallowed the wrong way. Thanks, I'm fine. But do you know what the big idea was?'

'The van they took had a special tank for fresh langoustines that are worth a lot of money and I guess the idea was that they could go on to do highwayman-type raids on other fresh seafood suppliers.'

Anna said, 'The police actually came to talk to me, you know. I was chatting to Angus at Logan Fisheries one morning and we mentioned the raid poor Callan got involved in so apparently that made me some sort of suspect.'

Shona stared at her. 'You?'

'Oh, I guess it was merely routine. But do you think you could just not tell anyone about my being friends with Callan? I don't want to make matters worse.'

'Yes of course. Oh, I did actually mention to Mairead this morning that you knew him. She'd phoned to talk about Fergus and Craig – she'd mothered them as kids and she was terribly upset, just like she was when we heard about Callan. He'd helped in the kitchen at the café, you know, and she'd seen that as his escape route so it was a real blow to find that it hadn't worked after all. She was interested to hear you'd met him, but I'm sure she won't go round telling everyone – not really a gossip, Mairead.'

'No, of course not,' Anna said hollowly. You wouldn't have to be a gossip to mention that Anna Bruce had known Callan McIver in Glasgow, and it would only take a stray remark for that knowledge to reach the person she had tried for so long to find – the one who had escaped trial because Callan had protected him. That stray remark, and her own stupidity, had put her in deadly danger. And there was nothing she could do about it.

'It's all just so sad I can hardly bear it,' Shona said, her eyes welling up again.

Anna stood up. 'I was going to go and have a walk – it's such a beautiful day. Why don't you come with me? It always helps, going out into nature.'

'You could be right,' Shona said. 'Just let me get my walking boots.'

He'd sort of been braced for bad news after last night but even so, seeing Brodie Campbell lying there dead was a shock that left Sergeant Kirk feeling physically shaken when he checked in with the guys securing the crime scene and looked behind the screens. Apart from the occasional idiot on a shoot managing to angle his gun the wrong way, firearms incidents were rare and a man being gunned down feet from a public highway was just unreal.

His first thought was gratitude that it wouldn't be his

job to break the news to Iona. Talking to her last night, he'd reckoned she didn't have much of a life with Brodie – a bully if ever there was one – but her new life as a single mother with a small child and no wages coming in would be a punishing one. Not only that, she was living in a tied cottage, which meant that as of today she'd have to rely on the charity of the syndicate who owned the grouse moor to give her enough time to look around for somewhere to stay and get benefits in place. Brodie had undoubtedly been a warm man with all his various activities and Kirk could only hope he'd put enough of it in the bank to cushion the blow for her. He couldn't help thinking about the poor dog too; it had been Brodie's shadow, and faithful dogs grieved like humans.

He'd been tasked with organising door-to-doors, and a pair of constables was just heading off to cover the houses on Shore Street. He knew what he wanted to do, though; he drove along the top road to the mobile home where Jago Innes ran the local end of a crime organisation – at least according to Brodie Campbell.

Everything about it offended Kirk – the site itself, which was unofficial and probably illegal, the weird hippie vibe, the random bits of rusting metal and old tyres in the overgrown grass, the aggressive smell of something that could lead you to go in heavy, only to be told it was nothing but 'joss sticks, bro!' – as if, but they'd never managed to nail him, even with Brodie's keen assistance. It had occurred to him to wonder if Innes would do what he'd done after the hare-coursing and pretend he didn't know anything had happened, to show just how much this could have nothing to do with him, but in fact, he came to the door as Kirk's car pulled up outside.

'They've brought out their big guns, then, I see,' he said, smirking.

Kirk ignored that. 'I see I don't need to tell you what has happened this time.'

'Ah, the jungle drums, the jungle drums! Yes indeed, everyone knows by now. Not much that's very exact, mind you. Sloppy, really – we need more detail.'

'I don't see this as a matter for humour, Mr Innes. I want to have a word with you. Inside?'

'Oh, why not? *Mi casa es su casa* – that's what they say, isn't it?'

He stepped aside, waving him in. Kirk, grinding his teeth, took him at his word and went straight to spin round the chair that sat in front of the computer and sat down on it in a magisterial pose. He was gratified to see that Innes was irritated.

'Did you see Mr Campbell at any time yesterday?'

'No. Why should you think I had?'

'There's no point in beating about the bush,' he said. 'You know as well as I do that you're a major suspect for this.'

'Why?'

The blunt question was clearly intended to throw him, as indeed it had, a little, but he was damned if he was going to show it. 'Let's start with the confrontation you had with Mr Campbell in the pub recently and the hostility towards him that you displayed the last time I spoke to you. You seemed deeply resentful that he had accused you of involvement with the hare-coursing.'

'Reasonable enough, wouldn't you say, since I had none.'

'That remains to be seen. The investigation is still

ongoing, and opening up more every day. Indeed, I'm told that arrests are expected very soon.'

He had the gratification of seeing a flicker of alarm cross Innes's face and went on, 'I'm not going to go there now. Perhaps you can just give me a detailed account of your movements since twelve o'clock yesterday.'

Innes had sat down on the sofa and was now slouching back in it with his crossed legs stretched out.

'Oh, so hard to remember, after all this time!' he said with laboured irony. 'Did I have a sandwich or a wrap for my lunch – or didn't I have anything? I was working online for most of the day and I often just forget to eat. After that, I remember I did make some phone calls and then I had something to eat with my partner when she came back from work – an alibi at last!'

'Your partner – that's Zoe at the café, isn't it?' Kirk had noticed her before – she seemed oddly exotic to be in a place like this.

'The same. Then I went along to the pub about six-fifteen, six-thirty, maybe. Chatted to a few people before I walked home, about half nine, maybe. I'm piling on the alibis now, amn't I? Probably just as well because earlier on I was signally failing. Of course I don't know what time I might be needing one for?'

If he was fishing for an answer to that, he wasn't getting one. Kirk went straight to the interesting point. 'And when you were walking home from the pub, did you notice anything when you passed the park by the top of the hill?'

Again, there was the smirk that made Kirk want to smash it into his face. 'Ooh, you're so sharp you'll cut yourself one day, Sergeant. They should get you into the

CID. Didn't walk past it, did I – there's a path goes right up to the top level and starts just across there, if you look?' He pointed.

Kirk didn't turn his head. There would have been, of course. There probably wasn't any point in asking his next question but he asked it anyway.

'Did you notice that Mr Campbell's SUV was in the car park just opposite the pub?'

'Really? Well, well, well! No, I'm afraid not.'

'You mentioned your partner – could she have seen it?'

'She might well have. Why don't you ask her yourself? You'll find her in the café.'

'Thank you, I will.' He got up. 'I think that's all for the moment, but no doubt there will be further questions later.'

The smirk was back again. 'No doubt. But the answers won't change and you'll have your work cut out to get the ones you want. With the number of people in this place who might have a motive for ending Brodie Campbell, it's going to mean a very useful amount of overtime for you lot. Mrs Kirk can start looking at the brochures for that Caribbean cruise.'

Kirk was proud of himself for concluding the interview without actually decking the man.

Certainly, Innes had been in the vicinity at the time Campbell was shot, but if this was a revenge killing, it was actually more likely that the Glasgow neds with previous, further up the hierarchy, had swooped in to take out the man with evidence to offer as they began feeling the long arm of the law, cold and clammy, about their necks.

Anyway, Kirk's job was to report back, not to decide where this went next, thank God.

* * *

It had felt a very long morning. The minister had been kind, as Cat had said he would be, and Kelso had appreciated his thoughtful counsel about their married life together but he had found it harder to participate fully in the discussions about flowers and table settings. Sampling and pronouncing on canapés was more enjoyable but he was glad when the list had been completed and they could drive to Mains of Craigie for an early lunch.

Bill Fleming was waiting with drinks at the ready when they arrived. Ignoring his daughter, he said to Kelso, 'I reckon you'll be needing this after what she's put you through, son. Where was the police emergency when you were needing one, eh?'

As Kelso took the proffered beer, Cat said, 'Dad! Don't joke about it – that's tempting fate! And it's his wedding as well as mine, all right? Mum in the kitchen?'

She went on through, pausing only to bend down and let Scott lick her ears as the quickest way to calm him down; the dog then transferred his attentions to the disappointingly uncooperative newcomer, eventually giving in and going to lie down by the fire.

In the kitchen, Marjory put a tray into the oven, then turned to embrace her daughter. 'Well, how did it go?'

'He was actually on his best behaviour – I only caught him rolling his eyes twice. And at least it's done!'

'That's good. The steak pie's in the oven, cooked by Cook, not me, you'll be pleased to hear, and it won't be long, so we can go and join the boys.'

They were just walking through when Kelso's phone went. He took it out, glanced at it and winced, then withdrew to the hall as Cat said accusingly to her father,

'If that's what I think it is, it's all your fault!'

'Oh dear,' Bill said, shamefaced.

It was about ten minutes before Kelso came back in, pulling a face.

'Oddly enough, it's a homicide in Torridon, where I was just yesterday, about something else – unrelated, on the face of it, but of course it does raise questions.'

Cat had gone very quiet and Marjory looked at her anxiously. It would be impossible for her daughter not to be haunted by the thoughts of all that had happened the last time Kelso had been summoned away to investigate a murder.

'At least it won't mean the A9 this time,' he said. 'The local force is dealing with it for the moment and then I've pulled rank so I can hitch a lift on the chopper later today when they take up the SOCOs. They'll pick me up around four, if you can drop me off in Glasgow, darling, and then go on to Edinburgh by car, if that's all right?'

'Of course,' Cat said stoically, and her mother silently admired her portrayal of the perfect police wife, while suspecting plates might be smashed next time she had a minute to herself.

'They're actually letting us have accommodation for a couple of people on site,' he went on, 'since someone will need to drive up so we have a car available.'

'Will that be Livvy?' Cat asked.

'Depends whether she's on duty. Anyway, it does mean I don't have to rush off absolutely immediately.'

'That's good,' Marjory said. 'I'd hate to waste the pie. So are you able to tell us the situation?'

'I don't see why not. There's a news conference pending.

It's a gamekeeper who's been shot. There's no background as yet, but touchingly his dog was found beside his body this morning, having been there all night probably.'

'Oh, the poor thing!' Cat said. 'I bet you wouldn't do that, Scotty,' she said reproachfully to the recumbent Scott, who, pleased by the attention, raised his head and thumped his tail.

Bill, defensive on behalf of his pet, said, 'You don't know what he might do in an emergency.'

'I do,' Marjory said. 'Whenever he was hungry he'd go off to the nearest place with a promising smell of food and look pathetic. Now, come through for lunch.'

'No,' DS Livvy Murray said. 'Just no.'

She had come on duty hoping for a quiet Saturday shift; she had a couple of reports to write up and she'd been pleased to find that her favourite seat behind the filing cabinet in the CID room, where she could escape the casual eye-sweep of anyone coming in to find a detective with time on their hands, was available.

In general it worked, but Angie Anderson, the FCA attached to the SRCS, had cottoned on to that particular dodge long ago and now was standing in front of Murray, saying, 'How do you feel about the A9?'

'If I never see the A9 again, it'll be too soon.'

'The good news,' Angie said brightly, 'is that there's lavish provision for accommodation for you this time, so you'd only have to do it at the beginning and the end of the investigation.'

'Lavish?' she said.

'Well, an Airbnb anyway. A Mrs McGregor. At least

you'll get your breakfast. "Old-fashioned comfort", it said.'

Murray was still cynical. 'Old-fashioned's a kind of alarming word. What are the reviews like?'

Angie grinned. 'Mixed, I admit, but it's better than travelling the A9 every day. And there was nothing else available. It's a homicide up in Torridon—'

That was when Murray said, 'No. Just no. After what happened the last time, I've taken a right scunner to those nice wee places that turn out to have a criminal element that makes the Mental Drylaw lot look like a Sunday school class. Can you not find someone else?'

Angie looked at her with surprise. 'You were just saying to me that life was too quiet for you. And Kelso's going to be in charge, of course—' She stopped suddenly, then hastily went on, 'Not that it matters, I know. It'll still be the same A9! I'll check the rota.'

Puzzled by the change of tack, Murray frowned. Then light dawned; the secret she'd never told anyone, that she'd always cherished a slender hope that perhaps one day Kelso might look at her with new eyes, hadn't been as secret as she had thought. That was Angie being kind, assuming that it would be painful for her to go back to the close work relationship now Kelso was spoken for.

Hoping that her face hadn't flared up as much as she felt it had, she said airily, 'Oh. I suppose you're right. I can't complain and try to duck out of it when all that's on my to-do list at the moment is writing up reports. A change of scene might be interesting. But I tell you, the Airbnb better be good.'

CHAPTER NINE

Having slept in the spare room, John Wilson had been able to slip downstairs unnoticed, heading for his studio. Mairead's migraine had been the excuse he'd been looking for to move to a separate bedroom; their sex life now barely existed and having her there at his side, asleep or awake, was a perpetual irritation. He hadn't quite got up the courage to tackle the subject – he wasn't at all sure how she would react – but now if he just went back there each night he had high hopes that it might happen without any discussion at all.

He hadn't meant to sleep late, but here it was almost midday by the time he'd showered and dressed. Instead of getting his Americano in the café, he settled for Nescafé in their own kitchenette so that he wouldn't get trapped into helping out again. He was getting more and more desperate; he hated this place – the isolation, the days that offered nothing more than a bewildering relationship with Zoe blowing hot and cold, and endless rounds of what was in effect the same conversation again and again in the pub. He was becoming conscious, too, that one or two small favours he'd done for the sake of cash in hand, to start up what he was privately calling his running-away fund, were taking him into dangerous territory.

And he'd sold that painting recently. If the gallery could be persuaded to take a few more, he might be brave enough to risk moving to where there was more stimulation and scope for ideas, then sue for divorce. He should do well out of that; after all, he'd given up his own career to support her in the business.

But he needed time to build up his portfolio – time that he was having to waste on paint-by-numbers watercolours and carrying cups of cappuccino and chocolate cake to customers. What he painted had to be disciplined, insightful – inspired, even – not just the slashes of fury that were all that he'd been managing to produce lately. He knew he could do it, given the time and mental space to think, and there was no time like today, John told himself.

As he tiptoed downstairs to the door leading to the garden, he paused to assess how busy it sounded; if it was frantic enough, Mairead would eventually come rampaging through to dig him out and if he had to abandon a developing idea it would be worse than not starting.

There wasn't the familiar noise of rattling cups and saucers and the buzz of talk; he could hear voices, but from the sound of it there were only two or three people. He checked his watch again; this should have been the busiest time for the lunch service.

What on earth could be going on? He hesitated, but he was curious enough to want to find out and given the café was quiet he probably wouldn't be press-ganged on sight.

The only customers were a middle-aged couple sitting at the table by the window, looking a bit ill at ease as Zoe was serving their pot pies. The man was saying, 'We'd heard about the café from friends who visited here last year and they told us about the path down from the top road to get to it, but—'

He broke off as John came in and Zoe turned. 'Well, well – there you are,' she said, then to the customers, 'This is John Wilson, the owner's husband – the artist, you know.' She gestured at the shelf where the little paintings were displayed.

There had definitely been a sarcastic edge to her voice. The customers seemed taken aback, the man looking blank and the woman saying hastily, 'Oh, very nice, I'm sure!'

What had he done to deserve that? Zoe was hardly under pressure today; she must be still in a bad mood about something. Women! He said nothing, only smiled politely and went through to the kitchen looking for Mairead.

She wasn't there. A minute later Zoe came through and without speaking to him went to set out cups and saucers on a tray.

John moved closer to her. 'Like to tell me what I've done? You know, I'm finding it harder and harder to work out our relationship.'

'Don't bother,' she said over her shoulder. 'Too boring to talk about. I've got other things on my mind.'

He gulped. Yes, she was in a mood, and from painful experience with Mairead he'd learnt that instant retreat, if feeble, was also smart.

'Right,' he said. 'Anyway, where's Mairead?'

'Still feeling bad after yesterday. I told her to go back to the house, since there certainly isn't enough for two of us to do.'

He hadn't heard her moving about; perhaps she'd gone to bed. 'But what's going on? Just two in for lunch? Has something happened?'

'You could say. Your friend Brodie Campbell—'

'I wouldn't say a friend, exactly. Not sure he has many of those, actually,' he said. 'What's he done now?'

She gave him a sardonic look. 'You'd better be careful where you say that. He's been shot dead, just at the top of the road here, presumably by one of these people who wasn't a friend. There's cops all over the place.'

He flinched, and saw her looking at him sharply. 'I'm – I'm shocked,' he said. 'Shot? Who on earth would do that?'

'Good question. No doubt they'll be here asking just that any minute now.'

He was edging towards the door already. 'Right. Well, not much point in hanging about. I was just on my way to the studio so if they want me, I'll be there.'

He could feel her eyes on his back as he went out. He just needed a few minutes to steady himself, work out what this might mean – not a lot to him, surely? It would have nothing to do with any silly little errands he might have done – a package here, a message there – but when the police started digging you couldn't tell exactly what they might find.

In the studio, he stood staring at the painting he had slashed and scored, still sitting on the easel there. He'd been going to come in with a renewed purpose and direct himself onto the new life path, but at the moment he couldn't think straight.

There was a Latin tag he'd heard somewhere: *de minimis non curat lex* – the law doesn't concern itself with little things. The trouble was, when you looked around they somehow did, didn't they? There were people in jail right now who'd tweeted the wrong thing.

Oddly enough, it didn't occur to him to wonder who might have fired the shot. Perhaps it was just the feeling that sooner or later, someone would have.

'I've been tasked with giving you such information as we have, sir,' Sergeant Dave Kirk said as he greeted DCI Kelso Strang at the Torridon heliport. 'The transport for the SOCOs is waiting for the equipment to be loaded on and will take them direct to the site, but I'm to take you straight to Gairloch.'

Strang was pleased to see him; the officers on the ground when you were brought in from outside were inevitably a mixed bag and he'd thought Kirk had coped very stoically the day before with the disgruntled Logan Ogilvie.

As they drove, he said, 'I'd certainly be grateful for that. I know the bare facts – where the body was found, and so on – but coming to a situation cold can be very tricky. Give me a broad outline.'

Kirk seemed to be showing the whites of his eyes, Strang thought, at the term 'broad outline', and hastily substituted 'general report'.

'Right, sir. Brodie Campbell was reported missing by his wife last night when he didn't turn up for his tea so I was detailed to go and investigate—'

'Hang on. This was a man who didn't turn up to a meal?'

Kirk turned red. 'Well, he was a CHIS too. He's a local and he's kind of plugged into everything that goes on so he's an important asset. For instance, we made some useful arrests when he tipped us off about a hare-coursing recently—'

Strang's ears pricked up. 'Lucrative businesses, these.'

'That's right, sir. And the one that's bang in the middle of it all is this New Ager who's squatting there right in the village, Jago Innes.'

'So – are we looking at a classic revenge motive here? The big boys that usually turn out to be backing these events?'

Kirk looked uncertain. 'Well . . . he wasn't liked locally, either, to be honest: gamekeeper on the local grouse moor and he's dealt pretty directly with anyone he thinks isn't – well, sort of respectful as you might say, and there was a big protest not long ago when he killed some bird. And . . .' He hesitated.

'Yes? Go on.'

'Maybe I shouldn't say this, but he could have been playing both ends to the middle, sometimes, if you know what I mean.'

'Do you have evidence?' Strang said, then added hastily as he saw Kirk looking alarmed, 'No, of course you don't. Don't let that discourage you.'

It looked as if this was a case that was expanding as he looked at it. He did hope it would turn out that Livvy Murray had been on duty today and would be the officer sent up. Dave Kirk seemed a decent man but lateral thinking clearly wasn't his thing.

'Jago Innes – well, he knew what Campbell had done and according to Campbell it would be him was running the book. Of course he's had time now to wipe his computer but some we've got on a charge are the well-heeled kind that'll sing like canaries if they think it might help.'

Strang smiled. 'I recognise the type. So he's a priority?'

'We've been tasked to do door-to-doors along Shore Street, where the victim's car was found. I went myself to speak to Innes.' He stopped, looking uncomfortable.

'And . . . ?'

'Well, if you'll excuse the expression, sir, he's a right smartarse. Sleekit with it – you'll know that kind too, I've no doubt.'

Oh yes – they all knew. 'Sleekit' – that useful Scots word that suggests 'smooth' and 'sly'. 'Get anywhere with him?'

Kirk reddened. 'Couldn't say I did, sir.'

Strang liked that – an honest man, as he had thought. 'We're just at the beginning. We've time to dig into that. And I gather there are other people who won't be going into mourning either?'

'You could say,' Kirk said with feeling. 'The incident room has had several coming in about this as well as the other business, when we haven't even announced his death officially.'

That sounded good. 'Anything useful?' Strang asked.

'Mostly just folk shopping neighbours who'd had a run-in with the man – there were enough of those! The only direct information has come from a lad I found in the pub drinking after hours after I drove down to the shore in Ardelour late last night and found Campbell's car, and he said he'd actually seen the man walking up the road from the car park in the middle of the afternoon.'

'Possibly the last sighting, do you think?'

'There wouldn't have been many folk around yesterday. The rain was fairly dinging down. That's the station now, sir.'

The Gairloch police station was a smart modern building and there were three badged cars in the car park when Kirk drove in, another with an Edinburgh registration, Strang noted. That was promising, and when Kirk ushered him into the foyer, he was pleased to see DS Livvy Murray waiting for him.

'Well done, Livvy,' he said. 'You must have made good time.'

Murray pulled a face. 'Not exactly, boss – accident on the A9, of course, so I'm only quarter of an hour ahead of you.'

'Oh dear – that makes me feel guilty. Good to see you, anyway. This is Sergeant Kirk, who's our backup at least for as long as Inverness can spare him.'

They nodded to each other, then Murray said, 'DI Mackenzie is waiting to speak to you, boss. I get the impression he's keen to hand over so he can get back to Inverness. He's through this way.'

She led him along the corridor to an office, knocked on the door, opened it, saying, 'DCI Strang, sir,' then added as she retreated, 'I'll just go and check out the accommodation then come back here, boss – all right?'

DI Mackenzie, a man with iron-grey hair and a small moustache, had rather arrogantly assured Strang when last they met that he needed no outside assistance but he was now looking distinctly strained.

'Ah, DCI Strang!' he said. 'Glad to see you. Sit down, sit down! Does that mean the SOCOs have arrived?'

'That's right. They were going directly to the crime scene. Sergeant Kirk has been briefing me on the current situation too.'

'Excellent, excellent. And you have been detailed to take charge of the investigation?'

'I understand that my boss, DCS Borthwick, has suggested that to your DCS Anderson. Are you all right with that?'

'Oh indeed, indeed. With an area the size of Belgium to cover, as you probably know, we're being stretched with the earlier investigation we spoke about yesterday, so it will be a relief not to have to take on the burden of another. It seems it is likely to involve a high number of suspects and in this area checking up on even the licensed firearms will be a major operation. Oh, we will, of course, supply whatever uniform support you need.'

'Thank you. I gather door-to-doors have started already,' Strang said, adding hopefully, 'Sergeant Kirk has been very helpful – may we lay claim to him, at least meantime?'

'Of course, of course. Now, what else is there you're going to need from me?'

He was so obviously anxious to escape that he was sitting on the edge of his seat and it seemed almost cruel to detain him, but Strang hardened his heart. 'The van hijacking case – you said you'd be homing in on the mole who had passed on the essential information. Anything on that?'

'Ah,' Mackenzie said, reluctantly sitting back in his

chair. 'You're not thinking, are you, that the two are connected?' He seemed dismayed at the thought.

'I've no idea,' Strang said. 'But in a place as small as this two such unusual events happening so close together would suggest we should keep an open mind at the very least.'

'Of course, of course. We'll keep you posted with any information coming our way. But so far, I'm afraid we've made no progress – everyone at Wester Ross Seafood has denied involvement.'

'Well, they would, wouldn't they?' Strang said. To his surprise, this was hailed as a witticism.

Mackenzie laughed. 'Ah, very well put, very well put. We'll just have to ask them again, won't we? Now, I'm sure you're going to want to see things for yourself, but naturally this office will be yours when you're ready. If there's nothing else . . .'

He ushered Strang out with the enthusiasm of a sheepdog in a time trial urging the last sheep into the pen, leaving Strang relieved that he wasn't going to have to deal with a man so obviously workshy.

DS Murray drove with a certain trepidation to see what the 'lavish' provision she had been promised consisted of. It proved to be quite a large traditional-style house in the upper part of Ardelour, set in a garden that even to Murray, who had trouble keeping the window box she had inherited with her flat weed-free, looked a bit neglected.

At least there was plenty of room for offroad parking and she put the car in one corner to leave space for other guests and went to the front of the house. There was a doorbell but when she pushed it, she didn't hear it ring. The outer door was standing open and when there was no answer after a minute or two, she stepped into the porch, knocked on the glass of the inner door and stepped back.

The woman who appeared from a dark hall looked to be well into her sixties, matronly, with grey hair in the sort of old-fashioned tight home perm you hardly saw nowadays. When she opened the door she looked as if finding a person standing there on the doorstep was the last thing she would have expected.

'Yes?' she said.

Murray went into the usual routine with her warrant card, but this seemed to confuse the lady even more. She looked at it doubtfully, and then at Murray even more doubtfully.

With a sinking heart, Murray said, 'I understood that there were rooms booked for us here: DCI Strang and DS Murray? Are you Mrs McGregor?'

At last light seemed to dawn. 'Yes. Oh – two rooms. That's right. Somone did say you'd be coming but I wasn't sure what day it was.'

Are you ever sure what day it is? Murray wondered, but she was standing aside to let her in, saying, 'You'd better come in, then,' without much enthusiasm.

Murray's heart sank as she stepped inside. The hall looked like a time capsule, with a hat stand, a sunburst mirror and a brass gong sitting on a brown wood chest, and just off it an open door showed what probably served as an old-fashioned residents' lounge with rather stained wallpaper, pink with medallions. The turkey-red patterned runners on the stairs were very worn, but at least the place seemed clean enough.

'Have you lived here long?' she said, trying to make conversation as she followed her up them.

'Oh yes, for a long, long time. It was my husband's family home, you see. But I'm alone now, and I felt I should share it with people who would otherwise never have a chance to spend time in a historic house like this.'

'I – see,' Murray said. 'How many guests do you have?'

'If I remember rightly yours are the only two bookings tonight, though there are four rooms I'm prepared to let people have. I'm not very busy just now – people seem to expect it to be like these modern places with no soul.' She resumed the climb up the staircase.

Murray gulped. She could read the runes – no en suites. She'd be having the embarrassment of competing with the boss for the shower every morning in their PJs, not to mention any other guests who might be driven by circumstances to book in.

'How many shower rooms do you have?' she said to her hostess's back.

She stopped again. 'Oh, we've never had *showers*. Only Americans want those. There are two bathrooms, of course.'

They reached the top landing. 'That's one,' she said, pointing. 'And this is one of the bedrooms.'

She opened the door onto a huge, high-ceilinged room with a double bed made up with a candlewick bedcover and a purple quilt so puffy that you couldn't tell whether or not the mattress was ancient as well. There was a huge wardrobe and chest whose drawers, Murray was willing to bet, would stick, but it had a pleasant outlook onto the trees at the back.

Mrs McGregor went along the corridor and opened a door on the opposite side. The furnishings were similar but Murray barely noticed them because of the view, looking right across the bay, sparkling in the afternoon sunshine, to the blue hills beyond. She could put up with even a lumpy bed, for a view like this.

And she'd got here first. *First come, first served*, she thought defiantly, even as she knew perfectly well that the hierarchy of rank was so drummed into her that she'd end up in the room at the back.

'That'll be fine,' she said. 'If you can just give me keys and tell me about breakfast . . .'

As they went downstairs, Mrs McGregor said over her shoulder, 'I put breakfast out first thing in the lounge so you can help yourself whenever you like and I clear it at nine. Now, just sign into the book there and I'll find the keys for you.'

It was a sad disappointment. Surely 'old-fashioned comfort' suggested bacon and eggs at the very least, with maybe even a sausage and a tattie scone; what Mrs McGregor had spelt out clearly meant the dreaded variety packs of cereal and she'd no doubt be competing with Kelso for the Crunchy Nut.

'Lavish, huh!' Murray snarled as she drove back to Gairloch.

The SOCOs' bus was parked at the top of the shore road in Ardelour and a white tent had been erected to enclose the scene of the crime, and indeed almost the entire area of the little park.

Strang hadn't previously seen the lower part of the village that ran along the shore of Loch Torridon, an attractive place with what would be a lovely outlook on a less overcast day.

'At least it's not actually raining,' he said in attempt to cheer up Murray, who was downcast after her recce of the accommodation, but the jaundiced look she gave him suggested he hadn't been entirely successful.

A uniform with a clipboard was standing by at the park gate and checked them in. As Strang moved aside the door flap, the familiar tent smell of warm, damp, trampled grass assailed him – but here there was the metallic taint of blood too. Inside, it was a scene of quiet, purposeful activity as the team performed their familiar allocated tasks; as they entered, a camera flash went off with a crack as the team photographer focused on the dead man lying face up in a pool of blood on the ground, an ugly gaping wound in his chest. He had been wearing a heavy jacket, torn open by the force of the blast, and its hood had fallen back to expose his face, his eyes open and his jaw slack, as if still registering the raw shock of the assault.

No matter how often you have seen one, the first sight is always difficult; the savage ugliness of violence to a human body is gut-churning. Strang stiffened for a moment and sensed Murray shift slightly, with a sharp intake of breath, as the team leader, a woman whom Strang had not seen before, came over to provide them with overalls and shoe covers and pulled down the mask covering her mouth.

'It was straightforward enough, as far as we can tell,' she said. 'Shotgun wound: he was shot in the back and fell forward onto his face. We photographed that and then just before you came we turned him over. An extensive exit wound, as you can see – not much visible on the back but considerable spread as the pellets left the body.'

'Indeed,' Strang said, looking at it narrowly. 'I take it you haven't found the gun?'

She grimaced. 'No such luck, and we don't have the cartridge either, though as you'll know even if we had, proving definitively that it was the one used is next to impossible. Weapon of choice for that very reason, often.'

'Indeed. And in this place, with a grouse moor right on the doorstep, shotguns will be two a penny. Anything else?'

'There's evidence of a dog having been here. Seems to have been lying down next to the body – the patch of grass is noticeably drier.'

'Oh, that's so sad!' Murray said. 'What's happened to it, do you know?'

'Taken away by the neighbour who discovered the body, I'm told. Be useful to get hair samples, to tie up the identification.'

'Noted,' Strang said. 'And the gunman – any indications at all?'

She pointed to two officers working on the rustic table and benches. 'They're fingerprinting and checking for DNA as well, of course, but it's a public park and getting anything significant out of so much material is way down the line – there's nothing we've found as yet to give any information about the assailant. There's rubbish over there to be analysed,' she said, indicating a litter bin, 'but of course that could have been left at any time. They're checking for footprints as well but the grass was wet so it's mainly just indentations without any distinguishing features.'

'Do you have any feel for what happened?' Strang asked. It was a question he often put to the team leader; they had considerable hands-on experience, and the answers were often instructive.

'You'll have to get the details from the lab. But . . .' She hesitated.

'Go on,' Strang encouraged her.

'Oh, I shouldn't even speculate, but just looking at the spread, I'd reckon it could be a sawn-off double-barrelled shotgun we're looking for. Possibly even discharged at a distance.'

'Interesting,' Strang said. 'Thanks very much. We'll leave you to it now.'

When they got back onto the road, Sergeant Kirk was waiting for them. Strang said, 'Are there more interviews to be done down here?'

'They're still knocking on the doors, sir, and there's a café I was planning to check out myself – there's a good chance they might have seen Campbell passing the door that afternoon. But you're the boss.'

'Sounds a good plan. Livvy, go with him please, and give me the car keys. I'm going back to the Gairloch office to get organised, and I'll put the DCS in the picture about what's happening.'

Strang was very thoughtful as he drove off. Kirk was clearly convinced that Brodie Campbell had tried one of the many folk with a grudge against him too far – a nightmare scenario for an investigation. Certainly he was the man on the ground, but that could cut two ways: too much local knowledge could stop you looking at the wider picture.

But he too had looked at the extensive damage that had been inflicted and had thought of a sawn-off shotgun, just as the team leader had. It produced a picture as well: a man standing with his back turned to the assailant coming up behind him, a man who more than likely never even knew what had happened. Along with the lack – at least so far – of any incriminating evidence, it had all the marks of a professional hit, and the hare-coursing arrests gave them an obvious place to start – even if Dave Kirk would be disappointed.

He'd clearly got nowhere with this Jago Innes. First thing tomorrow, Strang would take Murray along with him and hold his feet to the fire.

CHAPTER TEN

'So who are we going to see at this café?' Murray asked as she walked down the slope to Shore Street.

'It's usually very busy. Famous for their cakes and the tourists queue up. Can't have had a lot of custom today with all this stuff' – he waved his hand towards the roadblock – 'and by now it'll be closed so maybe just the owner and the husband, who live above the premises, if the waitress has gone home.'

'What are they like?'

'I'm not actually from here, you know, but I've had coffee there a couple of times and I got a lot from the long conversations with Brodie. According to him, they're all dubious characters but then he said that about everyone. He certainly had a pick at Mairead – "a right cow" was what he said – and John Wilson's an artist so that made him a "nancy boy".'

Murray pulled a face. 'A bit of a backwoodsman, then?'

Kirk grinned. 'You could say. He also hinted he might

have something to tell us about him later but that was one of his favourite tactics – talking up the goods for sale.'

Murray filed that one away – fear of being found out was a good solid reason to kill someone. 'And the waitress?'

Kirk paused. 'Well, I've only seen her in passing. She's shacked up with Jago Innes, who Brodie reckoned was in the centre of most of the dirty stuff around here but slippery as an eel, and he claimed she has form too – no details, of course, but again he was on to it and he'd tell us once he'd got everything lined up. But to be honest, looking at her I'd believe anything.'

Murray stared at him. 'Really?'

'Oh, you'll see. Here we are.' There was a 'Closed' sign on the door, but when he knocked on it, a teenage girl came to let them in, still holding a knife and fork she had been wrapping in a napkin ready for the next day's service.

It was a very attractive place with its white walls and cornflower-blue tablecloths, and the typical small shop area featured shelves of tourist magnets, majoring on tartan and pottery Highland cows and seals, as well as small landscapes – the handiwork of the despised husband, presumably. The cakes on the counter, covered by their glass domes, were to die for and Murray, suffering as always from hunger pangs, rapidly averted her eyes. As they stepped inside, a woman came forward.

She was something else. Perhaps she looked extraordinary partly because the setting was so conventional, but Murray saw at once what Kirk had meant. She was mid-height but with her exuberant black curls she looked taller, and her heavily made-up eyes, along with the ring piercing her eyebrow, her golden-brown skin and cyan-blue acrylic nails, made her look distinctly out of place. It was a chilly day and she was wearing a neat black V-necked cashmere sweater that covered her arms but on her hand there was the start of a tattoo of some sort of climbing plant that appeared again above the V, leading suggestively to a heart motif at her throat.

She moved towards them like a cat, Murray thought, fascinated – lithe and self-possessed.

'Ah, we've been wondering why you didn't come in sooner,' she said. 'We saw your lot going into the houses on either side and wondered why they didn't come in. Are we getting special attention?' She seemed, Murray thought, to be silently laughing at them.

'With the big windows here you were in a good position to have seen anyone passing,' Kirk said just as a woman appeared from the kitchen at the back.

She was more the sort of person you'd expect to find in a place like this: middle-aged, weary-looking, with a neat greying bob, carrying a bit of excess weight and getting jowly too. *Those cakes*, thought Murray, sneaking another look.

Kirk made the introductions and Mairead Wilson immediately offered coffee and cake, which he promptly turned down, to Murray's disappointment. Probably just as well – the last thing she needed was jowls.

At this stage their questions were only directed towards finding any sighting of Brodie Campbell the previous afternoon but Mairead and Zoe and Ellie, the schoolgirl helper, had nothing to contribute.

Zoe explained that she hadn't been in the café then, adding, 'Of course you'll be wanting to check with John.

He was on all afternoon. He's in his studio.'

Mairead looked surprised. 'I didn't know that's where he was. I thought he must have gone out.'

'No, he came in around lunchtime, while you'd be in your office. Come this way.'

Zoe led them across the yard behind the café to a shed and opened the door, calling, 'Visitors for you, John,' before she left, giving them a small, neat grin.

Murray hadn't been in an artist's studio before, so the total disorder took her by surprise, as did the painting propped on an easel – a formless mass of reds and black, which had been cut into ribbons. Perhaps that was what they called a Statement, though it didn't state anything intelligible to her. There was only one area that was neat: a table where a paintbox lay open along with smaller brushes and beside it a half-finished painting like the ones for sale in the shop.

There was a smell of turpentine, but it didn't totally mask the smell of whisky. The other thing that was noticeable was that the man was almost twitching with nerves as he got up, saying, 'C-come in. I don't know what you think I can do for you, but of course I'm happy to help.'

'Thank you, sir,' Kirk said. 'We are investigating the murder of Brodie Campbell and we are led to believe that he walked up the street outside from the car park yesterday afternoon, when apparently you were working in the café and might have seen him?'

'Oh, is that all?' Wilson became visibly calmer. 'No, sorry. I was too busy waitressing because Zoe had been called away. Mairead went off somewhere too, so I was flat out keeping the show on the road. Didn't see a thing.'

As Murray and Kirk left and walked up the road to the police car, Murray said, 'I can't believe he actually said, "Oh, is that all?" and then visibly relaxed!'

'It's an invitation to us to start digging, isn't it? What is it he's afraid we were going to ask him?'

'Everyone has secrets, I suppose. We'd probably better let it go till we know more about where we're heading. Let's get back to Gairloch – maybe they've got sandwiches and stuff there. My stomach thinks my throat's cut and the sight of those cakes was pure torture.'

Anna Bruce had been working hard all day. It was for a special birthday dinner and for once the host had chosen some of the more interesting dishes on her menu: asparagus with hollandaise, beef Wellington with all the trimmings and amaretto panna cotta and a chilled lime mousse to follow – just the sort of cooking she enjoyed.

But it hadn't made her feel exhilarated, as it always had before – merely tired.

She glanced at her watch. If she packed it all now and took it to the house, she'd be in good time to brief the hostess about serving up the cold courses and cooking the beef Wellington.

And then – well, back home. It didn't look as if the weather was going to oblige her with the sort of golden sunset that allowed you to blot out everything in the sheer glory of nature. For the last couple of days, even when it wasn't actually raining, the skies had been grey and sullen, her special mountain elusive. She had been trying not to let it feel like rejection.

The greyness of the evening ahead was reaching out to envelop her already, just as it had when she'd been stuck waiting and waiting in that dreary flat near Glasgow. She had started to recognise the symptoms of depression – lack of energy, loss of interest, emptiness – and unless she wanted to sink down into that mire, she had to get herself sorted out. Not only was she no nearer to establishing who Callan had been shielding, she'd all but admitted to herself that she hadn't the first idea what she'd do if she did.

Tonight, she vowed, as she put the last of the boxes into the boot and drove out along the Torridon road to the house, she would stop all this overthinking and make a plan of action, one that almost certainly would involve moving back to somewhere that on an evening like this could offer the distractions of theatres, concerts and the movies. By now, having not seen a single worrying sign that someone was looking for her, she reckoned that after all this time, while she couldn't risk going back to her former life, she wouldn't have to feel too inhibited.

The hostess greeted her arrival with enthusiasm, but Anna became aware that she wasn't really listening to the details of oven temperature and duration that would deliver the beef Wellington to the table in perfect condition.

The moment she stopped speaking, the other woman said eagerly, 'Dreadful thing, that, about the gamekeeper. Are you all right? What are the locals saying?'

Anna stared at her. 'I don't know anything about this.'

Delighted at being first with the news, she said, 'Oh my dear! I was afraid you'd be in shock with that man being shot in Ardelour! A gamekeeper, they said on the news. And his poor dog staying at his side all night – so touching! Can't remember the name—'

'Was it Brodie Campbell?' Anna suggested, feeling hollow inside.

'Yes, that's right!' The hostess brightened. 'Do you know anything about him?'

'No, I'm afraid not.'

Determined to deflect the conversation, she returned doggedly to the oven temperature, and at last managed to escape.

She was feeling very shaken. It was only a few days since she'd seen the man in the pub, twice as large as life as he strutted about, having a stand-up row with Jago Innes – the row she hadn't told the police about after the hare-coursing because, tired already, she'd have been subjected to another bout of personal questions that meant watching out for pitfalls. Living a lie was so hard; how easy it had been when all she'd had to do was tell the truth!

Probably it wouldn't have made any difference if she had, but it would be on her conscience if she didn't go to them now, if it was information that they didn't already have. She gave a deep sigh as she drove home. She'd have to find out first thing tomorrow how to tell the police about it.

And now she was going to switch on the electric fire and get out a bottle of wine, and if this time she drank more than her self-imposed limit, so be it.

Detective Chief Superintendent Jane Borthwick had been in good spirits lately, after her success in promoting the use of the SRCS last year, and she was pleased about this new assignment.

'So you're inclined to think this could be an outside job, rather than part of some local vendetta?' she asked with interest when DCI Strang phoned.

'I'm not jumping at anything, of course – goes without saying,' he said. 'But from what we know so far it looks to have been a neat in-and-out, leaving nothing behind – at least nothing obvious at present. And if the sawn-off shotgun theory is proved right, that's suggestive too, given the profile of hare-coursing. It's tempting to take that line, especially since they've charged participants at the event and we can turn the screw on them to get names.

'Indeed, we have to hope it was. If it does turn out to be a local vendetta, "multiple suspects" wouldn't begin to cover it. They've just handed me a list of statements made already by half a dozen public-spirited citizens drawing our attention to run-ins that had involved Brodie Campbell. I kept thinking of *Murder on the Orient Express* as I read through them,' he said, and Borthwick laughed.

'And the van theft fatality a couple of days ago – does that look as if it's linked in?'

'I've been thinking a lot about that myself,' he said. 'Not on the face of it so far, but I don't like coincidences. Glasgow is dealing with the case and I'm in close touch with one of the officers involved who's part of the raids task force and he'll keep me briefed.'

'That's good. It looks as if you've got an inquiry that's expanding by the minute. I can lean on DCS Anderson to allocate more manpower, if you need it.'

She was obviously enjoying flexing her muscles and

sounded a bit disappointed that he said it wasn't necessary, at least as yet.

'They've sent Livvy Murray up, so I have good support while I try to disentangle the threads.'

She was pleased, as Strang knew she would be. She'd always had a soft spot for Murray, having taken pride in spotting her possibilities right from the start when she'd been a rather unpromising PC.

'That's good. Handy to have someone reliable to cover your back and it sounds as if you'll need all the help you can get at the moment. Good luck, Kelso, and keep me in the picture.'

'Of course, boss,' he said and put the phone down. He sat for a moment, just thinking. It was perfectly possible that it would turn out that the raid on the Logan Fisheries van had nothing to do with this, and that the killing of Brodie Campbell would not only prove to be a hit job, but one that offered leads to follow up that probably wouldn't mean him being kept here for long.

But even in the brief time he'd spent here, he'd become aware of swirling undercurrents in the society that he would be unwise to ignore. And one that was bothering him was the presence of the woman who called herself Anna Bruce.

Jago Innes was working on his computer with frantic speed, as he had been doing for days now. A lot of it had meant cooperating with the Glasgow contacts to make sure they were doing the same; even encryption couldn't stand up to intensive forensic examination, and he was constantly afraid now that they'd seize either his computer or theirs. Or all of them.

When Zoe Cooper came in, he switched off instantly and got up to greet her with a kiss on the cheek.

'Well, hey, stranger! Haven't seen you for a couple of days.'

Her cheek felt cold to his touch, though perhaps the chill he sensed came from the cool indifference of her reaction to him as she went to hang up her coat.

'You weren't up when I left this morning,' she said.

'And you were back so late last night that I'd gone to sleep already,' he countered.

Her only response was a shrug, before she went to the wardrobe and pulled out black jeans and a white shirt.

'Going out again?' he said.

'I have a job, you know.'

'Where is it tonight?' he said.

She was already stripping off the sweater and dark trousers she'd been wearing and apart from giving him a long icy stare, she said nothing.

Even as he felt the cold sweat breaking out on his neck, he couldn't stop his eye following the sinuous vine up her arm and across to the hollow of her throat. 'Zoe, things are getting bad—' he started.

She cut across him. 'Oh, I know that,' she said. 'I just don't know what you think it has to do with me. I warned you long ago about causing trouble and you ignored me. Now look at what you've done!'

When she said that, he actually felt faint and his voice faltered as he said, 'I haven't done anything.'

'Spare me your stupid lies. If that's what you're planning to say to the police, you'd probably better spend a bit of time practising in front of a mirror.'

She had dressed quickly; now she was putting on hoop earrings and a slick of red lipstick and with him following her she walked to the door.

Her voice dripping with contempt, she said, 'I always knew you were a fool, but this is way beyond that. If you're not here when I get back, I'll find out where they've taken you. Or perhaps not – I'll see.'

Jago sat down the nearest couch, his legs giving way. How did she do this to him? Those probing dark eyes had seemed able to read what was in the darker spaces of his mind.

He wasn't worried about police questioning. He'd positively enjoyed playing little games with the plod and seeing him retire hurt, and he felt confident of his ability to deal with whatever they might throw at him.

Zoe was the real danger. She'd go to the police and tell them whatever she knew if it suited her agenda – but he didn't have the least idea what that was.

He mustn't let her get to him like this. He took a bottle of vodka out of the fridge and fetched a glass, then went to his desk again. The first shot steadied him a little but then he put the cap back on the bottle. He had to keep his wits about him as he got on with the job.

There was a limit to what could be done before reports came in. When DS Murray returned to the station with Sergeant Kirk, she found that Strang had been making use of the time to draw up a schedule and listing the 'concerned citizens' statements.

'Can you run your eye over these, Dave? Any you know?'

Kirk shook his head. 'Not personally, but there's a lad

from round here in the incident room and he was saying they were mostly from folk trying to divert suspicion, having got across Campbell themselves. There's one claiming to have heard someone actually threatening him with violence, and I've tasked a PC to follow that one up.'

'Good. Now, I have it in mind to go and speak to Campbell's widow – Iona, isn't it? We need to take a sample of the dog's hairs to tie up that detail for forensic and that might give us a chance to get her talking too. I trust you're up with dog-whispering skills, Livvy?'

Looking horrified, Murray said, 'I don't know anything about dogs, except they have teeth that they use if they think you're taking a liberty.'

Strang laughed. 'In my experience, dogs lavishly present you with suitable material if you so much as get within a hundred yards. The real skill is to avoid getting it on your clothes. I can't think it will be any problem.'

'You're used to them,' she protested. 'Please, boss, do I really have to?'

'Someone does, and I'd better keep well out of it since I've recently been in contact with an overly affectionate Border collie, and that might well cause a certain amount of confusion. Anyway, is there anything we should know about the woman, Dave?'

'Met her for the first time yesterday. Nice lass, small baby – much in awe of Brodie, who was a right bully. Kept her totally in the dark about whatever he was up to, as far as I could tell. Er – would you want me to come to introduce you?'

It was clearly a question hoping for the answer 'no'. Strang said, 'No need. Just tell us how to find her, then off you go. It's a good way back to Ardelour and then a long way back to Inverness for you, but we'll be doing it on our way home.'

'If you could call it that,' Murray muttered darkly, as Kirk departed.

With a low sky and murky clouds, it was already starting to get dark as they set off. Looking about her as they drove back down the side of Loch Maree, she said, 'It's interesting – from having been up further north, I was expecting to have these pine forests piling in on me around here but it's not really like that.'

'Very different terrain,' Strang said. 'The mountains are quite weirdly old and erosion has done a pretty extensive job over the millennia. Wait till you see the Applecross peninsula – it's like a lunar landscape in some places. It was volcanic, of course, and the nearby Great Glen is actually on a fault. I love it myself – not sure it will appeal to you.'

Murray wasn't sure it would either, but she only said that after their last joint commission, she was in favour of anything that didn't involve too many trees. 'To be honest,' she said, 'what's mainly on my mind at the moment is our supper. From what I've seen of Mrs McGregor, she's not the jolly kind of landlady who'll offer to whip up an omelette for a hungry guest.'

'Oh, poor Livvy! You're sounding embittered. There's not a lot in Ardelour admittedly and we'd be very conspicuous there but they've told me about a pub along in Torridon. We won't starve!'

'At least that's *something* to look forward to,' she said gloomily as they reached Ardelour at last and drove up onto the moors in gathering darkness.

'I think that must be the cottage,' Strang said at last, pointing to the only lights that could be seen.

Murray looked, and gave a small shudder. It did look so inexorably bleak out there for a young mum with a baby – of course, a widow now.

As the approaching headlamps caught Iona Campbell's eye, she burst into tears. She had just got Rosalie settled; the baby had been acting up all day, upset by the cars arriving with people who had come to tell Iona things she really, really didn't want to hear and asking questions she didn't know the answer to, and she was at the end of her tether.

She'd only just got rid of her mother, whose questions had all been along the lines of 'What are you going to do now?' and when at last she had completely lost it and shouted, 'I don't bloody know, all right?', her mother had left in a huff, saying, 'No wonder she's difficult, poor wee soul.'

And this, she had little doubt, would be the other sort of questioners, the ones who seemed to think she must know more about what Brodie had done yesterday than she'd ever known about what he did any day of the week. As the car came inexorably across the moor towards the cottage, she got ready to open the door before they could knock and wake Rosalie again. She didn't pause to wipe her eyes; they were welcome to assume that these were a widow's natural distress.

Iona hadn't worked out yet how she felt, except scared. She was still too confused to think straight; she'd actually found herself at one stage thinking, when Rosalie was having a screaming fit, *At least he's not here to hear this, thank goodness*!

There had been a policewoman who was trying to be really nice and sympathetic, but some of the things she'd said, like, 'I know you must be plunged in grief,' simply didn't ring true. The one coherent idea in her head had been, *What on earth will happen to Rosalie and me*?

And here they were now, a man and a woman wearing ordinary clothes but still clearly polis, and she opened the door to them and stood aside limply to let them pass. She saw them exchange glances as they saw her tear-stained face, then came in and repeated the routine with names and cards like they all did.

The boss man was tall and serious-looking; the woman was quite short with a neat dark crop and a sympathetic face. She didn't comment on the tears, only saying, 'I'm sorry, I expect we're all you need, the end of a day like this.'

Iona was too tired to be polite. 'Yes, you are. There's nothing that I can tell you that I haven't told all the others and I'm not answering any more questions.'

She was taken aback when the boss man said, 'We don't want to bother you when you have so much to deal with. You see, it's not you we want to see, it's the dog. It's just a sample of his hairs that the investigators need to have to confirm that he was with his master. Is he here?'

Confused, she said, 'Do you mean Luath?'

'Is that his name? Like Robert Burns's dog?'

She didn't make any attempt to sort that out, only gesturing to the back of the kitchen, where the huge grey lurcher lay, stretched out. Any other time, he'd have been up ready to protect his master's family, but he hadn't even raised his head when the others came in.

'He's not eating. *He's* grieving, if you like,' she said, only realising a moment later the word she'd emphasised.

The woman said, 'Would he be all right if I went over to him?'

She sounded a bit nervous and Iona found herself bridling at the implication that he might not be. 'Of course! He's always polite, Luath. But I don't know what I'll do about him – Brodie's dog, not mine.'

One more hard thing. She could feel tears welling up again and standing there she was starting to feel shaky.

The boss man said, very firmly, 'You're out on your feet. Why don't you sit down and I can make you a cup of tea while DC Murray checks on Luath? I can see the kettle and the tea caddy and I expect I'll find a mug in the cupboard.'

She did as she was told, surprised – but not, she somehow sensed, as surprised as the woman was, from the look she gave the boss man as she went to approach Luath.

CHAPTER ELEVEN

Murray had a lump in her own throat as she came to kneel by the dog. As a city kid, she'd always been wary of dogs, and she'd had more than one painful professional experience with them when performing an arrest. Dirty things, dog bites.

This sad grey gentleman, though, was entirely different; when she tentatively held out her hand towards him, he paid no attention, and you couldn't help but see that he was as deep in mourning as any person might be. As she got up courage to stroke him, she found she was murmuring to him the common platitudes almost as if he could understand, but he didn't seem to hear her. He was taking shallow breaths with his eyes half-open but they were not, as far as she could tell, registering anything. The big idea had been to win his confidence, but she had to conclude that he simply didn't care.

She had picked up a couple of sterile tubes at the station and now she took those and plastic gloves out of her pocket; as she smoothed them down his coat, hairs obligingly detached themselves and it was easy to complete the task. When she straightened up, Strang was sitting with a mug in his hand, talking to Iona Campbell, who had a mug in hers, and there was one waiting for Murray beside the kettle.

'And you must have been very worried yesterday when your husband didn't come home and you didn't know at all where he was,' Strang was saying when Murray came over to join them.

'That was what I kept saying today,' Iona Campbell said wearily. 'They wouldn't believe me when I said that – thought there must be something I wasn't telling them.'

'He seems to have been a very private man,' Strang said. 'I can imagine you wouldn't like to ask him anything about what he was doing or where he was going.'

The tea seemed to have revived Iona. She said, with some force, 'That's right I wouldn't! Couldn't stand anyone interfering with his business and he'd have gone radge if I'd tried, even if I was a bit worried about some of it.'

'Perhaps women do tend to worry more than men, and maybe even recognise the problems a bit better than they do as well,' Strang suggested.

Murray realised suddenly what Strang was doing: Iona had said she wouldn't answer any questions so he wasn't asking any.

And now Iona was nodding her head. 'I worried all the time about the number of folk who really hated him. He didn't care about that as long as he could get what he wanted but I knew it was dangerous. He thought he'd got your lot all wrapped up too – used to joke about them swallowing any daft thing he chose to tell them. Oh, sorry, I didn't mean . . .' She broke off in confusion.

'Not at all. That's just how he saw it, isn't it? But it's easy to see how you would be so worried when he didn't come home yesterday.'

She nodded again. 'There was the protest that time he killed the bird, you see. They were out round the house here, screaming about killing us all, and I know that there were lads poaching he dealt with in his own way – "rough justice", he called it, but sometimes if I was in the village I could see the look one of them would give me, even if he wasn't there.'

There were questions burning on Murray's lips but she had the sense to sip her tea and say nothing as Strang went on, 'That was quite frightening for you. And I suppose there'd be a lot of bad feeling when the arrests were made after the hare-coursing, too.'

'Oh, but he was fair away with himself about that,' she said. 'He thought he'd managed to drop Jago Innes in it – they've been fighting since they were wee boys, you know. That worried me too – Jago's got some bad friends in Glasgow and places. The police came to ask him all about that first thing next morning.'

'So he'd be in a good mood, I expect.'

'Oh, yes,' Iona said, then paused. 'Well, he was until he went out to the estate office later. He wasn't, when he came back for his lunch – quiet and kind of grouchy. That was when he said he'd this meeting but he'd definitely be back for tea. And don't ask me where it was or who it was with, because like I told everyone I don't know!'

Her voice was rising with stress, and Strang stood up,

smiling down at her. 'No, of course I won't. You're very tired and we're going to leave you now to have a much-needed rest.'

Murray saw her moment. 'Mrs Campbell, thank you so much for letting me take the sample from Luath. Such an amazing dog, being there for your husband right to the end, and maybe you can take comfort from remembering that they went out together – and perhaps even remembering what he said to you as they did.'

It was a bit crass, frankly, but it was her best shot. She'd thought it might bring tears, but instead Iona said quite harshly, 'Oh, yes, I do remember. He said, "It's about time I got this sorted out," and I just thought, *Who's he going to offend this time*?'

As they drove back across the moor, Murray said, 'You do wonder after all that what sort of relationship the Campbells had. Did she think he was some sort of romantic hero to start with? Bullying men often come across like that to nice girls at first but they pay for it later. And admittedly she's traumatised, but to go by the way he's suffering, it looks like the dog's the one who loved Brodie, not her.'

As Iona Campbell dragged herself at last to bed, she was turning over the same thought in her weary mind. She'd wondered recently about her marriage, and how you could tell if you were 'in love'; well, it was being spelt out for her now – she hadn't been. She was shocked and scared about everything that lay ahead, but if they'd enough to live on, she and her wee Rosalie would be far better without him.

* * *

Livvy had avoided awkwardness on the landing the night before by lurking in her room until she heard Kelso returning to his and though it wasn't like her to set her alarm for half past six, she was determined to have completed the morning operation that would involve a rather inadequate kimono dressing-gown, bath towel and toilet bag, and reached the bathroom before he was up.

Objective achieved, she stood staring at the bath, which was large with lion's feet like the posh kind in *Ideal Homes*, but this one had ancient stains disfiguring the enamel and taps with greenish corrosion round the base, and when she turned them on, what they disgorged was a disobliging trickle. For a minute she thought there might be no hot water; eventually it came, but it would take half an hour to run a bath at this rate. All she could do was step in once there was enough water to stand in, crouch and swish it around a bit; she always relied on a shower to get her going and this was no way to start the day.

And she hadn't managed to avoid Kelso either. He was just coming out of his bedroom as she left the bathroom, looking quite natty in a navy-blue towelling robe. He didn't seem to be any more inclined to conversation than she was; they exchanged a muttered 'Morning!' as she shot past him.

There was no sign of Mrs McGregor as Livvy came downstairs but she could see that, as promised, there was food laid out on the table in the sitting room – food in the shape of long-life milk, jars of cornflakes and rice crispies, a bowl of sugar, a white sliced loaf beside a bowl holding plastic pots of jam, marmalade and butter, and a small jar of supermarket instant. Oh, and now she looked, two bananas.

Not even a Kellogg's variety pack! Clearly, their hostess's altruism in allowing the peasants to experience her gracious home didn't stretch to offering the traditional country house breakfast. Morosely, Livvy served herself with crispies and sat down in the chair at the end, though at least it meant she hadn't had to decide whether to snaffle the Coco Pops and open herself to ridicule, or be dignified and take the Special K.

She had just put a piece of bread in the toaster when Kelso appeared, stopping on the threshold with a sigh.

'Ah, you did warn me,' he said. 'Well, I suppose it's fuel. Of a sort.'

'You're probably more used to it than I am – no doubt you've had worse in the army,' she said.

'No way the jocks would put up with this. There'd be a mutiny.'

'The kettle's just boiled,' Livvy said. 'At least there's caffeine, also of a sort – I can't face the day without that.'

'Me neither,' Kelso said.

It was weird, having this sort of cosy, domestic conversation. Once she'd have seen it as being a step on the road to the ideal future she had hardly allowed herself to imagine; now she found she was seeing him as if he was already someone else's husband and it felt quite uncomfortable.

Neither was talkative, nor disposed to linger. Kelso was first to get up, saying, 'Straight along to Gairloch after this, all right? It's going to be a busy day.'

'Right, boss, but don't forget your banana or you'll get scurvy.'

* * *

It had been an early start too for Sergeant Dave Kirk, to his wife's irritation, it having been late the previous night by the time he got home; as always in the Inverness force the distances they had to cover took their toll on the family as well. He wasn't going to complain, though, having enjoyed a change from the normal routine stuff and actually working on a murder with the SRCS.

There was a general order out for holders of shotgun licences to be checked today. He thought he probably wouldn't be assigned to that, but when he'd glanced at the list on the board in the incident room, John Wilson's name had caught his eye.

The man's reaction during the interview the previous day had been niggling at him and he was willing to bet it was niggling at DC Murray too: what was it Wilson had been relieved not to be asked about? Maybe it wasn't exactly urgent at this stage in the investigation, but if the boss agreed, he'd be able to say he was just checking Wilson's permit and then he could prod till he'd satisfied his itch to know.

There were cameras and reporters outside the police station when he arrived, some with the furry microphones that meant TV. It wasn't hard to ignore the shouted questions – did anyone ever answer those? – but when he found that Strang and Murray had gone out already and there were no orders for him, he felt disappointed. They had their own way of working, obviously, and this rather spelt out that he was backup rather than an integral part of the team.

Still, it gave him the ideal opportunity to carry out his plan. Running the media gauntlet again, he drove along to Ardelour and parked on the shore opposite the café.

The SOCOs had finished their job and with the roadblock lifted, the café was going like a fair. The hum of conversation dropped right down as Kirk opened the door; it was an effect he was so used to that he barely noticed.

Zoe Cooper was just coming out of the kitchen with a tray. He saw her stand very still for a moment before she swerved towards him with a smile. 'What can we do for you today, Sergeant? If you're looking for a cup of coffee, I'm afraid you'll have to wait for a table.'

'No,' he said flatly, recognising mockery. 'I was wanting a word with Mr Wilson if he's here.'

Turning, he saw that Wilson was presiding at the counter behind the array of cakes, serving a man who was waiting to pay; he caught too the widening of his eyes.

'You'd better take him through to the house, John. I'll cover meantime.' Mairead's voice spoke behind him and he realised she had come out of the kitchen at the sound of her husband's name.

Wilson's face was flushed and he looked flustered. 'Er – yes, of course. I'm sorry, sir – my wife will deal with this,' he said to the customer. 'Come this way, Sergeant.'

Kirk followed him through to the lobby at the foot of the stairs leading up to their flat, where Wilson shut the door, then turned to look at him. 'Well, what is all this about? I told you yesterday I hadn't any useful information.'

'This is just a safety check, sir. I understand that you have a shotgun licence.'

Wilson would never make a poker player, Kirk thought. His tense shoulders had relaxed, just the way they had the day before, and now he was adopting that middle-class snotty tone guaranteed to get up any copper's nose.

'Ah well, one does get an invitation to a shoot from time to time, you know, so of course one has to be prepared.'

'May I ask to see where you keep the gun and the ammunition?'

'Certainly.' He opened a small cupboard set into the staircase and handed a green plastic box to Kirk, which he flipped open.

Cartridges were jumbled together in a random pile and he said, 'This isn't ideal storage, sir. These are a serious fire hazard and having them stored this way right below the stairs risks having the whole house going up and you would find your escape route engulfed.'

Wilson said airily, 'Oh dear. Sorry. Word to the wise – I'll take care of that.'

'And now the gun?'

'Out in the studio.'

He took him through the cloakroom to the door to the yard. Kirk looked around him as he went down the path behind Wilson. 'Not the ideal place for storage,' he said. 'The path down there along the side of the café isn't even gated.'

'You can see the studio's always locked,' Wilson said defensively as he took the key from his pocket and let them in. 'And there's no reason anyone would assume I kept a gun here. I know you're all in a stew about them just now with Brodie being shot, but if someone was looking to nick a gun for whatever reason, it's common knowledge that farmers round about keep loaded shotguns propped behind the kitchen door. That's the safe, in the corner.'

It was a standard gun-safe, looking out of place amid the artistic disorder of the studio. Wilson went to a hook on the wall at the far end and took down a key.

Kirk stared at him. 'Is that the key to the safe? That is absolutely no sort of security.'

'Oh, I suppose not,' he said, making it plain he thought this was a fuss about nothing. 'But I'm useless with keys – I keep losing them and if I can't find one it's a real nuisance. But just for you, Sergeant, I'll keep it in the house somewhere in future.'

The sarcastic tone was wasted on Kirk. He said, 'And the key to your studio? Do you have a spare somewhere for when you can't find that too? On top of the lintel, maybe?'

For once, Wilson looked chastened. 'Well, yes, I suppose so. But anyway, here it is.'

He opened the door. The gun-safe was empty.

DCI Strang checked his computer first thing when he went into the office, having stopped to pick up coffee for them both from a machine in the nearby petrol station – not great, but better than what they'd had.

Confirmation had come in from ballistics that the shotgun used had, indeed, been sawn off. 'So either they reckoned it would make the spread more lethal or they wanted to carry it on them unseen, I suppose,' DS Murray said.

'Or both, of course,' Strang said, a bit absent-mindedly. Also in front of him on the screen was Anna Bruce's name. He'd been intending to go along to Ardelour to interview Jago Innes, but now . . .

On an impulse he stood up and said to Murray, 'I

think we should just knock this one off before we go to grill Innes. I don't think it will take long; I spoke to this woman, Anna Bruce, before and I'd be surprised if she did have anything to do with this, but it's something of an anomaly to find someone like her in a place like this and I'd been wondering why she should be here. She's just phoned the desk claiming to have something to tell us, so that gives us an obvious "in".'

As Strang drove back to Ardelour, he could see that Murray was puzzled – reasonably enough. Anna would have been told to come in to make a statement and any checking out it needed could easily be delegated; on the face of it this certainly wouldn't merit his personal attention.

'What sort of angle are we taking, boss?' she asked.

He didn't quite know what to say. He was concerned about her safety; Janet MacNeish had previously found herself involved in a very murky business and if she had established a connection to that by coming here with her new name, she could be in serious danger. He wasn't legally entitled even to question her about that so there was no way to spell out the risk bluntly. He could only talk around things and see what emerged.

He said, 'She's a caterer. With all the Airbnb stuff around here, she's probably doing quite well out of it but it's an odd thing to do, to come to the back of beyond without a particular reason. She came to our attention because of that raid last week. She'd asked questions about when their van usually set out but she said it was just making conversation because she'd heard a radio report about someone being sentenced for killing a lorry driver in a raid last year – I don't know if you remember?'

'Not the sentence, no, but I do remember the case. A young guy killed himself at the time, right?'

She was impressively on the ball but he wasn't sure that was helpful. 'Yes, that's right. The thing is, when I checked it out, though the young man was working in Glasgow – as she did – he grew up here in Ardelour.'

'I see.'

That was the thing about Murray: she was quick. He never had to spell things out these days – she'd learnt a lot in those last few years. And it looked as if she might have got the point without him breaching the protection order.

'As I said, I think this is peripheral, since I have no reason to suppose that she is likely to have produced a sawn-off shotgun on the basis of what I know about her. In fact, on the contrary, I guess she's on the side of the angels but just possibly she doesn't fear to tread in areas where she shouldn't.'

'I see,' she said again.

He suspected she possibly did. His main task in the interview ahead just might be to stop Murray breaking down – how did they describe it again? The fourth wall, that was it – the barrier between the performer and the audience.

This was a decision distinctly above Kirk's pay grade. He'd been asking for trouble, going out on his own, and now he had to decide whether to do something that would have the media assembled outside the Gairloch police station assuming he was bringing in the murderer.

John Wilson wasn't the man they were looking for, though. Kirk's twenty-five years' service had made sure he wouldn't confuse a simple ned with a real bampot and he was quite clear which one Wilson was. Apart from anything else, a hard man didn't disintegrate at the merest suggestion that someone might think he'd pulled the trigger.

'But – but – I didn't!' Wilson was all but sobbing. 'You have to know, this wasn't anything to do with me! You said yourself – the way I kept the gun was insecure, and I'm sorry, I'm sorry! I'll see to it immediately that this could never happen again – in fact, I'll give up the licence . . .'

Since he now didn't have a gun anyway, it was hardly an issue. The gun, apparently, hadn't even been seen since Christmas when a member of the estate syndicate had invited Wilson to a shoot. But Kirk needed time to think, and there was another question he'd been planning to ask.

'Sit down,' he said.

Wilson subsided onto the artist's stool beside his easel, which gave Kirk, standing, the added authority of superior height.

'Never mind the gun for the moment. Let's talk about the thing you were hoping we wouldn't ask you about when we came yesterday.'

Wilson gaped at him like a landed trout as Kirk went on, 'What is it you've been doing that we might want to know about? And don't even try to act the innocent – what you say will affect how I decide to deal with the present situation.'

It all poured out. Delivery of the sort of packages that Jago Innes didn't want to entrust to his county lines kids, who might blab about where they took them – though of course, as Wilson stressed, he had no idea what was in them. And didn't like to be rude enough to ask, of course, when it really wasn't his business, and it had clearly been a nice little earner.

Kirk found it hard not to look as smug as he felt. He'd got Jago Innes bang to rights, because he'd clearly set up a special service, presumably with a considerable premium for discreet delivery, and though the full majesty of the law was unlikely to be brought to bear on drug-running kids, an exception might well be made for an operation of this sort.

'You could be worth more to us as a witness than as a suspect,' he said, and Wilson's face brightened.

The defence would take him to the cleaners in the witness box, but that wasn't Kirk's problem. All this had given him time to consider what it would be best to do, and now he said, 'I'm inviting you to come to the police station in Gairloch to give an explanation of all this. And I mean now – if you're not there before I am, I'll get you brought in. Right?'

'No problem. And I'll help in any way I can. I can go out the side way – just let me lock up behind you.'

It would have been more dignified, perhaps, not to have said, 'You haven't noticed there aren't any horses left to bolt?' but Kirk said it anyway.

'There's John now, running down the side path, look!' Zoe Cooper said as she came over to Mairead at the counter.

Mairead muttered savagely, 'For God's sake, shush! You don't need to draw everyone's attention,' but as she spoke she realised the customers' heads had been turning already; she could even hear a murmur of 'escaping from the police' and she felt sick.

Even Zoe was looking shaken as they watched John dash across the road, climb into the car and drive off, though she said, in her brittle way, 'Oh really! I know John's not the sharpest knife in the drawer but even he has to see he's not likely to manage a clean break – not unless he took the precaution of nobbling the sergeant first.'

'It's not funny,' Mairead snapped. She was seeing the flashing lights of the aura that might be heralding another migraine and she just wanted everything to stop and the world to go away.

Then the door leading from the house opened and Sergeant Kirk emerged, into an immediate hush. He only nodded to the two women, said, 'Thank you,' and walked to the door to the street.

Zoe protested, 'But you can't just leave without telling us what's happening!'

Reading the room, he had no doubt that she spoke for the rest of them too. Using a form of words that had been useful to him in the past, Kirk said, 'Not at liberty to say,' left, and got into his car to follow Wilson along the road to Gairloch – at least, he trusted that was where he was going. He'd look a right idiot if he wasn't.

He could only hope that the DCI would be there when he got back. He didn't want to be the one who would have to decide what was to happen next.

CHAPTER TWELVE

Anna Bruce was lingering over her breakfast coffee. She knew what she had to do; the person she'd spoken to on the phone had said only that she'd have to go to the Gairloch police station to make a statement. She'd been hoping she could do it over the phone – after all, she hadn't really that much to tell them, just that she'd seen Brodie Campbell squaring up to Jago Innes and his dubious friends in the pub and there'd been plenty of other people around who had probably reported it anyway. But she'd agreed that she would and once she'd finished her coffee she'd have no excuse for not doing it.

If she hadn't been such a wimp and had called the policewoman back that morning after the hare-coursing, it would all have been dealt with already. But she hadn't, and now she might as well get on with it. Just as she gave a heavy sigh and stood up, she heard a car drawing up outside, and she wasn't expecting a delivery. With a sinking heart she guessed who it would be.

And there he was again, the detective with the hazel eyes that had seemed to look right through her. There was a woman with him today, not the bright-faced younger man, and she was holding up her warrant card.

'I'm DS Murray. I think you know DCI Strang?'

'We've met, yes.' She certainly didn't *know* him; she suspected that not many people did and she found that threatening, almost intimidating. He was smiling pleasantly enough, though, as she waved them through to the sitting room.

'I didn't expect such personal attention,' Anna said. 'I was literally just getting up to go along to Gairloch to make a statement.'

'We were coming to Ardelour this morning anyway so I thought if you were in it would save you a journey,' he said easily.

Easily but unconvincingly. She was savvy enough to know that a DCI wouldn't concern himself with the personal convenience of a member of the public; there was more to it than that.

'I hope you will feel it has been worth the effort,' she said lightly. 'I did say on the phone that it was information you may well have been given already. It's just that I was in the pub on Wednesday when there was a stand-off between Brodie Campbell and Jago Innes.'

She gave them the details, about Brodie accusing the men with Jago of being criminals, and the way he was the one who'd ended up looking stupid. 'He took it very badly, shouting out that they were all crooks and he left in a very bad mood. It didn't seem to bother either Jago or the men with him, though they left shortly afterwards. And that's about it. I'm sorry if you were expecting something more helpful.'

'Not at all,' Strang said. 'Do you often go to the pub here?'

Why would he want to know that? She could hardly say she went often enough to become part of the furniture in the hope of gathering any useful scrap of information. 'Oh well, I do go from time to time. It gets a bit lonely working by yourself all day, you see.'

'And have you found it welcoming?'

'Oh – yes, well, I suppose so. I don't have the Gaelic, so I can't really join in with the locals round the bar, but I know a few people just to say hello to and I enjoy that, and of course there are the visitors coming in now too, the groups of climbers and even a few yachties at this time of year. Well, I suppose it's just nice to have the occasional conversation – the sound of a human voice, you know.' She knew she was babbling, and she gave a nervous little laugh.

Neither of her visitors so much as smiled. Strang said, 'But I guess you must have a liking for solitude, living here. Have you been in Ardelour for a long time?'

'No, I moved quite recently. I used to work in Edinburgh but I got sick of city life and I'd always longed to live somewhere like this.' That was an instinctive obfuscation, but then, remembering the claim she'd originally made, she added, 'I visited Ardelour once as a child and I thought it was the most beautiful place I'd ever seen.'

'Indeed,' he said, and as he paused, DS Murray said, 'And have you been able to make friends here, someone to talk to? Sometimes these wee places tend not to be very keen on incomers.'

She said, 'Oh, well, it's understandable – mostly they've known each other for ever and they're just deeply involved with their own community.'

'And as an observer, what impression do you have of that community?' Strang said. 'Two homicides in the last week doesn't suggest a rural paradise, does it?'

Was this why he'd come to see her? Did he think she was holding out on them, hiding something they needed to know? The automatic lie about Edinburgh had been stupid; being completely honest wasn't a problem in this instance. It wasn't the police she needed protection from.

'It's a very troubled place,' she said. 'I do have a friend, Shona Macintyre, who runs a smokehouse out along the Applecross road, and she feels the whole atmosphere is toxic, especially for the young. Drugs are everywhere and far too many of them get involved. Her son was an addict who killed himself, and he wasn't the only one who did that.'

She had felt a catch in her throat as she said that, but she had kept her voice level so it was a shock when Strang said, 'And of course there was Callan McIver, the young chef involved when the driver was killed in that raid last year.'

He was looking directly at her as he spoke, with those penetrating eyes, and, shocked, she realised that he knew. He knew exactly who she was, though she had been assured no one else, even in the police force, would ever be told. Her mouth went dry – if he did, who else might?

But he was going on, still holding her eye. 'I only know about him because I was involved in giving evidence about these raids generally and I stayed on to hear the other witnesses and the conclusion of the trial. A sad business.'

She couldn't mistake the message he was giving her, that he'd recognised the voice that had spoken from behind the screen that had protected her. She moistened her lips. 'Very sad.'

'When there's that sort of flourishing crime within a community, it's likely that it will become attractive to the bigger players and they will home in. It becomes very highly dangerous even for someone only peripherally involved. A generally unhealthy place to be.'

As it might be, someone who drew attention to themselves by asking questions. 'Yes,' she said. 'I can see that.'

He didn't labour the point. 'Is there anything more on that subject that you can think of that might be helpful to us in this present inquiry?' he said, then when she shook her head went on, 'The sergeant here will take a statement from you about your movements on Friday afternoon through to Saturday morning and save you having to do that again when the door-to-door enquiries reach you. She'll give you a contact number in case there's anything later.'

DS Murray got out a notebook, looking, Anna thought, very much as if she'd been in the dark about that little exchange. There wasn't much to tell her: after the police interview, she had made more brownies because the previous lot had got burnt and then sat down with a glass of wine, had her supper and gone to bed.

It didn't take long, and they left. She felt completely wrung out. Strang had definitely been warning her off; she didn't know how much detail he knew, but she'd got the message. She'd more or less made up her mind already to give up what she could now see had been a foolish and risky enterprise – increasingly risky, from what the chief inspector had said. But how best to do it?

She was too stressed to think clearly just at the moment and she got up. It wasn't as if she hadn't enough to do; Mairead was expecting two cakes tomorrow and she always found baking a soothing occupation – carrot cake first, she decided – a general favourite. She had peeled the carrots and was just setting up the processor to grate them when her phone rang.

She looked at the caller number and didn't recognise it – a prospective customer, probably. 'Anna Bruce,' she said.

It was a man's voice at the other end. 'This is Martin from the National Crime Agency. You remember we talked before?'

She did. Very chatty, bird-watcher, yolk ending up with the whites. She'd been distinctly short with him at the time and, feeling guilty, she said warmly, 'Oh yes. Thank you for phoning. How are you?'

'I'm fine, thanks. I hope you are too. This isn't just a routine call; the agency has flagged up the worrying situation in Ardelour at the moment and asked me to make contact. It's been noted that as well as the shooting there has been another lorry raid and if there's any connection to you, your security could be compromised. It's our job to see that you are safe so this is to check that you're all right.'

She was taken aback. 'Oh, I see. Well, it's not a very good place to be just at the moment, to be honest. I've had the police here today taking a statement from me because I saw the victim of the shooting having a row with another man. They didn't phone you, did they?'

He seemed a bit put out at the suggestion. 'Of course not! It's absolutely nothing to do with them, I promise you. It's just that we wouldn't want to see you dragged into this. It could become very complicated. It's not up to us to tell you what to do, but you do seem to be feeling threatened. We can arrange another placement for you right now.'

Could this be the answer to her problem? No more agonising, no more questions – invisible, once again. She heard herself saying, with surprising decision, 'Actually, I'd be grateful if you did.'

'Very wise! The police haven't told you not to leave, or anything?'

'No,' she said firmly. 'I've given them all the help I can. Do I need to tell them I'm leaving?'

'Better not – the fewer people who know anything about it, the safer you'll be. I'll just put it all in hand for you, then.' Martin sounded delighted. 'I'll get back to you very shortly.'

Anna was feeling almost dizzy as she put down the phone. Another step into the unknown – another place – another chance. Possibly even another name, though she'd be sad about that – she'd liked being Susanna Bruce. There would be the same disconnect with her past, admittedly, but she'd be walking away from the mistakes she'd made in what had begun to feel like a pressure cooker.

Abandoning the carrots, she went through to the sitting room and stared out at the mountain – 'her' mountain – that was today festooned with low cloud, the top of the peak just showing against a sky like a livid bruise. She would miss the everchanging beauty but you couldn't live on a view – or the illusion that somehow there was something she could do that would change the hard fact that the love of her life was gone for ever.

'We'll have to move the car, of course, but Innes's mobile home isn't far along this road,' Strang said, driving off. 'Have you seen it? A bit hippie, with what looks like a junk yard round about.'

'Caught a glimpse as Dave drove me down to the café yesterday. The yard doesn't really square with the partner – she's sleek as they come and sharp as a tack.'

'Mmm.'

Murray turned her head to glance at him. He was clearly abstracted. What on earth had been going on back there? He'd hinted earlier that Bruce was in Ardelour because she'd known the young chef in Glasgow – and if that was right, why had she said it was Edinburgh? That probably had some significance. It would have been natural enough to say she'd come here to do her grieving where there were memories of him, but she hadn't. What was she afraid of?

And Strang hadn't mentioned then that he knew Bruce, but she could see that he did. And yet, she didn't know him? He'd been warning her of danger, but seemed to be doing it in some sort of coded way. Very odd indeed.

'Here we are now,' Strang said, drawing up at the side of the road. They had both got out just as his phone rang and Murray stood beside him waiting as he answered it.

He said, 'Oh, for God's sake!' He listened for a few more minutes, then hung up and turned.

'In the car. Back to Gairloch,' he said.

As she obeyed, she noticed that Jago Innes was standing at one of the windows of the mobile home, watching their withdrawal with interest. She also saw that Strang was looking dismayed.

'What was that, boss?' she said.

'Dave Kirk has just brought in John Wilson from the café. You met him, yes?' She nodded, and he went on. 'The idiot had only stored his shotgun so insecurely that he might as well have put it out in the street with a "Help Yourself" notice, and it's gone.'

'For goodness' sake! What does that mean?'

'It probably means,' Strang said through gritted teeth, 'that the idea of a hitman sent in from Glasgow as revenge for the hare-coursing arrests falls apart. And you know yourself, with what you've seen and heard over these two days, the sort of can of worms that would open up.'

'Mmm,' Murray said gloomily. 'We could be stuck for weeks in that sodding Airbnb. But boss, there's nothing to say that even if it is missing, this is the gun we're looking for – it wouldn't have been sawn off, for a start—'

She realised what she'd said even before Strang, with uncharacteristic impatience, snapped, 'Livvy! With your years of service, surely you know that ten minutes with a hacksaw would take care of that.'

Well, that was the last time she'd try to look on the bright side. He could just stew in his misery if that was what made him happy.

Jago Innes watched them leave with interest, and some surprise. He'd been braced for a visit, and nervous too, despite telling himself that he'd have no problem with seeing the next lot off, just as he had the first one. But he wasn't a fool; the local plod wasn't the same as the CID, and it hadn't escaped him that Brodie Campbell's murder had reached first item on the news, even if largely because of the dog. It wasn't even Inverness that the statement had come from; it was delivered by some snotty cow in Edinburgh.

Having worked late, he was more confident about the state of his computer, and Joe Connelly's as well. They'd both been warned that the punters who'd been charged were, as Joe put it, ready to grass to the point where the court would have a green velvet carpet, but they'd be safe enough unless the Crown Prosecution Service could actually come up with corroboration about the gambling – or unless those fat bastards sitting on the bench with their titles could succeed in their plan to abolish the need to have that before the case called in court.

It would also mean, he hoped, that the man and the woman in civvies that he'd seen getting out of the car and then changing their minds could be diverted with that instead of digging deeper into his lifelong hostility to Campbell. They couldn't actually prove a thing about that either, when it came to it; he'd had a barney with him, but who hadn't? He didn't have much of an alibi – but who did?

Yes, he'd be absolutely fine as long as he kept his head – and as long as Zoe wasn't planning something he knew nothing about. He'd heard her come in last night, much later than usual – surely the bars in Torridon didn't go on past midnight? But he'd played dead, and as far as he could tell she'd slipped into bed and gone sound asleep –

the kind of sleep you should only be able to enjoy when your conscience was clear.

But then, she'd never shown any sign of having a conscience at all, had she?

Sergeant Dave Kirk was so visibly nervous that DS Murray had to resist the temptation to reach out, pat his hand and say, 'There, there!'

'I'd no idea that was going to happen,' he bleated to DCI Strang. 'You weren't here when I reported for duty this morning, and since we were supposed to be checking on all the locals with gun licences I thought I could go and check him out. He'd been very twitchy the day before when we only wanted to ask if he'd seen Campbell on the Friday afternoon, and we both noticed that he relaxed when he realised that was all we wanted – that's right, isn't it, Livvy?'

'Absolutely!' Murray said heartily. She'd have liked to say to him that it wasn't his fault that Strang was looking so stern, but she couldn't exactly do that. Instead she said, 'I'd wanted to dig into that too. Did you have any joy?'

Kirk brightened. 'Well, yes. Once we found the gun was gone, he couldn't speak fast enough. He's been a courier for what looks like a bespoke service for posh cokeheads who come down for country house weekends and the shooting around here. Of course he stressed he didn't have any idea what was in the packages, just did what he was paid to do. There are some well-known names, he says, and Jago Innes must have worked out they'd pay a premium not to risk kids doing the deliveries who might run off to the *Scottish Sun* – he was on to a good thing and Wilson benefited.'

'The old "don't ask, don't tell" routine, so he couldn't actually speak to the contents,' Strang said, pulling a face. 'Not perfect from our point of view. Still, well done, Dave. It gives us a line to take with Jago Innes that he might not expect.'

'Wilson's in the holding cell now, sir,' Kirk said. 'PC Sharma is going to take down all the addresses of the houses he delivered to as well as the details of the gun and his movements on Friday, though as far as I could make out he was in the café all day, at least until closing time.'

'The time-of-death estimate isn't a lot more precise than the usual "between the last time he was seen alive and the time he was found dead", though they did decide to live dangerously and suggest that it was more likely to have happened before midnight when the rain stopped – something to do with the position of the body and the ground conditions. What we need is evidence from people who were around in the late afternoon, but no one's come forward so far. The rain was torrential at that time, apparently, and if you were going anywhere you'd take the car, you wouldn't walk, so there may simply have been no one around.'

'He said to his wife that he had a meeting, Dave,' Murray said, to put him in the picture, 'and as he left home with the dog, he said something about it being "time I got this sorted out". So are we assuming that he'd arranged to meet whoever it was in the park where he was killed, boss? Despite the weather?'

'If you remember, he was wearing a heavy hooded jacket,' Strang said. 'What we don't know at all is how long he was there before it happened. For instance, it might be that the park was only meant to be a discreet pick-up point from which he could be taken somewhere else for a discussion.'

'If we're still talking about a hit job, someone may just have stepped out of a car, shot him and left,' Murray said. 'Just because that gun's missing, it doesn't definitely mean it was the gun that was used.' She really liked the idea of a neat solution.

Strang sighed. 'I know. You can get a good price for a decent shotgun and, given the company he was keeping, if Wilson had happened to mention he had one, ears would have pricked up. You said that access to this studio was completely open, Dave?'

Kirk said, 'That's right. There's a path runs down the side of the café and the spare key to the door is balanced on the lintel.'

'So you see,' Murray said, with something like triumph, 'it needn't actually be relevant at all.'

'Oh, you're transparent, Livvy!' Strang said, laughing. 'I know you hate the idea of hanging around here in the Airbnb, but you can't ignore the other evidence – and you needn't hang on to the convenient idea of a pusher having nicked it for unconnected reasons, either.

'Dave, can you tell PC Sharma to find out from Wilson who definitely knew he had the gun, and where he kept it before we let him go? His wife, I would assume, and most likely Zoe Cooper, since she works there – and if she does, very possibly Jago Innes knows as well – another thing to add to our list of things to talk to him about, Livvy.'

'And there's the wee lassie who works there part time,' Kirk put in. 'She's just a schoolgirl but living around here she likely has pals involved in the county lines stuff.'

Strang looked from one to the other. 'Are you two ganging up on me?' he said in faux indignation.

Murray laughed; Kirk looked horrified. 'Oh no, sir! It's just—'

'Don't worry about it, Dave,' Strang said. 'It's just that we all need to struggle against the tendency only to see what fits in with our favoured theory and it looks as if this is starting to get very messy. So let's try to parcel it out. Dave, would you go back to the Shore House Café and talk to everyone individually, try to get a feel for the atmosphere.'

Kirk said, 'Yes, boss,' but even though he'd said 'boss' instead of 'sir' for the first time, Murray thought he looked unhappy at the prospect.

'We'll go and talk to Innes now. All right, Livvy?'

'Yes, boss,' she said, getting up, but she had a nasty feeling that it would be better to allocate her to the Shore House Café interviews along with Kirk if atmosphere came into it. Dave was a man much more into facts than feelings.

'Have you been in touch with Jenny Matheson today?' Shona Macintyre said when Mairead answered her phone.

Mairead suppressed a sigh. 'Oh hello, Shona. Not today, no.' She was drinking a cup of tea as she filled dishes with macaroni cheese for the lunch menu, hoping it might help fend off the migraine that was threatening to return.

'Sorry to interrupt – I know you're busy. It's just that they're saying Fergus has pled guilty to hijacking the van and I know she'll be distraught. I phoned but got no reply and I know how close she is to you. Do you think there might be something I could do to help? I could go to the house and just listen if she wants to talk, but I wouldn't want to be a nuisance. What do you think?'

'I don't think I really can think straight any more. It's all too awful. She knows where you are and she knows where I am, so maybe she doesn't want to talk. He's got a lawyer, hasn't he?'

'Yes, and they're saying it's the lawyer that's said it's what he's to do. He's to blame what happened to Sandy on Craig and say he was drugged up at the time.'

Mairead winced. 'Well, maybe he was. But . . .'

'Aye, I know. But. Well, give Jenny my love if you're speaking to her.'

'I'll do that.'

Mairead put the phone down and went back to the macaroni cheese with her heart heavy as stone and her headache getting worse.

'What was that about?' Zoe Cooper was at the coffee machine as she prepared a tray for an order.

Mairead didn't turn, just saying over her shoulder, 'Oh, just a call from a friend.' She had no wish to talk about the Mathesons' problems with Zoe – or anything else, really, after realising that she'd been snooping in her office.

'That was Shona, wasn't it? I could hear her saying something about a lawyer. Has there been a development in the police investigation?'

The look on her face was very off-putting – almost sort of hungry, Mairead thought. 'No, nothing to do with that. Something else. Do you think that's enough macaroni cheese, or should I make another lot? It's always so popular.'

Zoe filled the cups set out on the tray, but she didn't immediately pick it up. 'There's always "something else" going on in this place. Which one is this?'

Mairead stiffened. The words 'mind your own business' sprang to her lips but she controlled herself; with John away for God only knew how long and a migraine starting, she needed the woman, whatever she thought of her.

She said, 'Look, that couple's chosen the cakes they wanted from Ellie and gone back to the table. We can't stand here catching up on the gossip while their coffee's getting cold.'

For a moment she wondered if Zoe would ignore that and persist, but she lifted the tray and took it out, just as the door opened and Sergeant Kirk came in. There was no doubt she had lost the fight with the migraine. There was another violent burst of zig-zagging lights and now she was feeling sick too.

She heard Zoe say brightly, 'My goodness, Sergeant, we're starting to feel you live here. What do you want this time?'

The whole café would be listening by now. She heard Kirk say soothingly, 'Oh, just more routine enquiries, that's all. Who should I start with?'

Mairead said, 'You'd best come through with me to the house,' and led the way through the house door and up the stairs. If she got him settled in her office, at least if necessary she could make a quick exit to the toilet and not find herself vomiting on the café floor in front of all the customers. She could tell it wouldn't be long now.

CHAPTER THIRTEEN

'I'm reckoning to home in on the courier business,' DCI Strang said as he and DC Livvy Murray drove back to Ardelour from Gairloch, eating sandwiches purchased from the useful petrol station. 'Wilson will have to be allowed to go once he's made his statement and if he gets back to the café and tells them what he's admitted, it'll get back to Innes via the girlfriend. I want to throw him off balance before we get anywhere near the question of the missing gun.'

'Won't Zoe have called to tell him about that?' Murray asked.

'I don't think she knows, as yet. When Dave called me, he said Wilson literally ran to his car without speaking to anyone, and then he had just no-commented as he went back through the café.'

'So that'll be another little surprise. But what's the killer question we want to set up, boss?'

Strang gave a sigh that was almost a groan. 'Wish I knew.

I suppose we see how it plays out and if something stinks we follow our noses. I checked before we left – not a single person has come forward to say they were in the area on Friday afternoon or evening. Kirk had no joy prodding Innes and frankly, I doubt if he'd open up more even if we snarled a bit. By his own admission he was on the spot – so, opportunity. No legal gun, but with his contacts that wouldn't necessarily mean he couldn't find one. He had motive, all right, but that's theoretical and totally useless – unless a gun turns up with his prints on it.'

'Or unless we can find out he was in on something planned by his Glasgow mates,' Murray said doggedly.

'Not sure how we'd do that, are you? Anyway, Inverness will have no problem calling him in for questioning about the drugs and in fact they can probably shut down his dirty little trade for long enough to give Ardelour a bit of respite. Then when it comes to the hare-coursing, it wouldn't be worth forensics' time to call in a computer that he's had plenty of time to scrub clean, especially since we should be able to rely on witness evidence to prove he was running a book – the guys we've arrested will be desperately looking for favours. But when it comes to Campbell – I still can't quite figure out where all that's taking us.'

Murray gave a disparaging look to the slightly limp ham and cheese sandwich she'd taken out of the packet, then took a thoughtful bite. 'OK, he's hated Campbell since school days, according to Iona. He'd be furious with him for dobbing them in to the police over the hare-coursing and probably there's other things too, but actually shooting the man's a bit radical, to say the least. Why would he do it? Revenge?'

'Certainly a classic. But looking at it objectively, what would be in it for Innes? Sure – the satisfaction if seeing his enemy lying dead, but wouldn't it be a rather hollow victory when given the method used it wouldn't even have given him the pleasure of seeing Campbell, the loser, grovelling and humiliated?

'And your much-favoured gangsters, Livvy – would it really be worth it to hire a hitman and take on the risks of discovery and blackmail just to get their own back on Campbell? Admittedly, some of the organisers – and Innes too – may well find themselves out of circulation for a bit but the damage was already done. More often than not, the purpose of a professional killing is to warn others what could happen to them, so that's something to keep in mind.

'Given what we know of Campbell from Dave, I'm inclined to think that this might not have been because of what he'd done, but because of what he might do in the future. He was a valuable CHIS because he'd made a habit of tipping us off when he got wind of an operation being planned – and there he could well have come up against someone with a serious personal interest in stopping him, whether Innes or someone else.'

Murray accepted gloomily that there could be something in that inconvenient theory. 'So?'

'You kick off with the courier stuff, then I'll hit him with the query about the gun and we can take it from there. That's the place now.'

As they went towards the house, Murray's nose wrinkled at a powerful musky scent that she could smell even before the door was opened – something to make it difficult to detect the smell of anything else, perhaps?

It was certainly going to be a tough job to wring anything useful out of him, but she'd always felt she was learning when she worked an interview alongside Kelso, and she loved to learn – and liked to think she was an asset too, now. On the last case, in Moray, there had been no opportunity for long collaborations like this and she was secretly convinced that was why so much had gone badly.

There was a cluster of wind chimes with a sort of bell-pull rigged up to them but she ignored it, giving a firm and business-like knock to the door.

Sergeant Kirk followed Mairead Wilson up the stairs and into a white-painted room that made no attempt to be anything other than an office, with filing cabinets and a desk with a PC and a swivel chair. The wall had several pinboards festooned with what looked like invoices and there was a cheap-looking sofa and two chairs beside a small table.

She said, 'Do sit down.' She didn't sit down herself.

He did as he was told and cleared his throat. 'Mrs Wilson, the first thing I wanted to ask you was—'

Mairead said abruptly, 'Sorry, I'm feeling terribly ill. Excuse me.'

She almost ran out of the room, leaving Kirk staring after her, nonplussed. He hadn't been very keen on the assignment in the first place; being asked to 'get the feel' of a situation took him into a realm he was very uncomfortable with. What sort of 'feel' was this? Was she scared and making an excuse to get out of questioning? Admittedly, he had noticed her stumble on the stairs and now he thought about it, she hadn't been looking well – and now there was the unmistakable sound of someone being sick.

What was he to do? If only Livvy had come with him, being a woman she could have gone to see if everything was all right – in theory, perhaps he could, but he quailed at the thought.

Kirk had a few more minutes of agonising before there was the sound of a flushing toilet and Mairead came back in and sat down, very pale and smelling of toothpaste, but quite collected.

'I'm so sorry to do that to you, Sergeant. I get awful migraines and I'm afraid I was overcome. What was it you wanted to ask me?'

'Oh – right.' He'd better keep it short. 'Did you know your husband had a shotgun?'

'Yes. He gets it out when he's had an invitation from someone to go shooting. I don't think I've ever seen it at any other time.'

'Do you know where it was kept?' The minute he said that, he could have kicked himself and she picked him up on it.

'I knew where it *was*. It was in the gun-safe in his studio. Does that mean it isn't there now?'

Mairead seemed neither surprised nor alarmed – what did that tell him? Did it mean she knew already that the gun wasn't there? Instead of answering, he said, 'Did you know where the key to the safe was kept?'

'No, but knowing my husband he probably had it in some easily accessible place. He was always losing keys.'

'Could he have lost one recently?' He didn't think there

would be any very useful answer but he couldn't think of anything else.

There wasn't. She said, 'Not that I know of,' and somehow there wasn't a lot more to say, except to ask her not to repeat what he had asked to Zoe Cooper when she went down to summon her.

He'd have expected her to ask where her husband was but she had shown no interest. What did that say? Before he'd had time to consider that, he heard hurrying footsteps and Zoe burst into the room.

'Can you make it snappy, Sergeant? We've a full café and Mairead's struggling.'

Her self-assurance made Kirk feel at a disadvantage. 'Sit down, please, madam. Were you aware that John Wilson owned a shotgun?'

He did notice that her eyes had narrowed. 'No, I wasn't. But if I'd thought about it, I'd have assumed he probably did – anyone with any pretension to social success round here does, and John certainly aspires, if not very successfully. So what's he done with it, then? I take it he hasn't actually fled the law.'

'He is helping us with our enquiries,' he said stiffly. 'Did you know where he kept the gun?'

She laughed. 'Hardly, since I didn't know he had one. And "kept"? Do you mean it isn't there now?' The sharp eyes were openly mocking.

That had been another stupid mistake, and somehow he couldn't brush her off as he had her boss. 'It is at the moment missing and there is a possibility it was stolen.'

'Really? Well, Sergeant, I hope you find more people who can "help you with your enquiries" but I'm afraid

I'm not one of them and we're under pressure downstairs.' She got up. 'Shall I send Ellie up to you now? She won't know anything – yesterday she couldn't remember where we kept the napkins.'

Ellie took a little longer to come upstairs and he had time to consider the elusive 'feel' when it came to Zoe Cooper. His job was to find out who had known there was an unsecured gun available – or, when it came right down to it, had actually taken it from the gun safe – but she had been so much in control of the conversation that he realised he didn't have a clue.

Ellie Donaldson, on the other hand, was plainly terrified, opening the door gradually as if she was judging how wide it needed to be before she could sidle through it. It was impossible to imagine her being significantly involved in violent crime and if he'd to go by 'feel' he'd just take pity on her and send her back downstairs – she was certainly showing all the signs of stress. But remembering that he'd mentioned to Strang the possibility that there could be a 'county lines' dimension, and that a pretty, not very bright girl could be putty in the hands of a ratbag boyfriend, he told her to come in and sit down.

'Not in school today, then?'

She reacted as if that was a threat, staring at him with big frightened eyes. 'Got exam leave.'

'It's all right, Ellie,' Kirk said. 'I just want to know if you knew Mr Wilson owned a gun?'

'A gun? No. Did he?'

Apparently that was an alarming thought in itself. 'Do you have a boyfriend?' he asked gently.

Her cheeks flared. 'Well . . . sort of.'

'So who is he?'

To his astonishment she burst into tears. 'Don't want to say.'

'Sorry, Ellie, I'm afraid you must.'

She hung her head. 'Fergus Matheson.'

Kirk would have described himself as unshockable. But Fergus Matheson, at present remanded in Glasgow on a charge of homicide, five or six years older than this wee lassie, only four years older than his own daughter . . .

'What does your mum think about that?' he heard himself saying, which didn't help with the tears. He looked desperately round for tissues; there was a box on the office desk. He pushed it towards her and said, a little more sternly, 'Now I want you to tell me whether you were speaking the truth about not knowing about Mr Wilson's gun.'

In as much as it was possible for someone in tears and only just short of sobbing to sound indignant, she did. 'I don't tell lies, sir.'

Get the 'feel', he'd been told. And police sergeants with his number of years' service weren't easily fooled when it came to sincerity, and he could recognise it when he saw it. And now he thought about it, Fergus Matheson and his pal Craig Lothian had been arrested on the M6 before the last sighting of Brodie Campbell.

Kirk stood up. 'Thanks, Ellie. That's all I need to know for the moment. Dry your eyes, and you might be better to go and splash your face in the bathroom next door before you go back. And take the advice of someone who's got a young daughter, and look for a boyfriend your own age.'

* * *

There they were at last. It occurred to Jago Innes that they could have done it deliberately to soften him up, parking outside as if they were just going to come in, then going away and leaving him to wonder what their ploy was.

And he had wondered. If they wanted to ask him about Brodie Campbell, he was, he reminded himself, pretty much fireproof – Kirk had run through all the usual stuff and hadn't found one question he hadn't been fully prepared for. But as the time passed, he'd found himself considering all his other vulnerabilities, the ones they might more successfully home in on. He'd chosen to lead his life in a world where absolutely no one had your back, where they would grass on you tomorrow, if it suited them – as he would on them.

He'd never got the jail, and if he was honest, the prospect seriously scared him. Joe and his mates – they'd first been sent down when they were barely out of their teens and now serving time was priced in as part of the job. Somehow he'd managed to fringe it for years, with just the odd fine, but it was looking as if keeping the book on the hare-coursing was going to do for him, thanks to that bastard Brodie. That *dead* bastard Brodie.

He'd spent the time trying to shore up defensive walls and surely he could handle this. But there was always Zoe – Zoe, who he knew had her own secret agenda. If necessary, he could always do his best to throw her off the troika to satisfy the wolves.

Knocking loudly on the door was, given the wind chimes bell-pull, aggressive. The man, DCI Strang according to his warrant card, was tall and lean-faced, with an expression that gave nothing away; the woman, DS Murray, was not much above middle height and sturdy with it. Noticing her Glasgow accent, Innes thought that she'd be useful on the Saturday night after the local derby between Rangers and Celtic. They went to sit down without waiting for permission.

Innes took his place on the swivelling desk chair. 'Got up your courage to enter the lion's den at last?' he said.

'We'd better fish to fry,' Murray said. 'We're busy people and I expect you are too, so let's not waste time and get straight to the point. Tell me about your courier operation.'

He had to control a gasp – that, he hadn't expected. 'I can't think what you're talking about. I'm afraid you'll have to be more specific.'

'Of course, that was stupid of me,' she said sweetly. 'The county lines ones first, maybe?'

That was OK – he'd been questioned about it before, more than once. 'I have to say I find it depressing, the degree to which the police are blatantly prejudiced against Travellers and make totally unwarranted assumptions—'

'Judging by the junk that's embedded in the grass outside here, you haven't done a lot of travelling. So you've issued the standard denial – noted. So now let's move on to the other courier operation, OK? The deluxe one?'

That really had come out of left field. That was serious stuff. How the hell could they know anything about that? Had one of his clients got in the sort of trouble that meant they needed to keep the police sweet and, ironically, *he* was the one being chucked out of the troika?

He was nothing if not quick-thinking. 'Oh, I know what you mean now. Services are very poor around here and it started because I knew a couple of people with big houses out in the countryside who have problems getting what they want delivered. I knew someone who would be willing to go to an address and take packages out to them and then word got around. That's all it was.'

'And what was in the packages, Mr Innes?' Murray said.

He spread his hands wide in the traditional gesture of helplessness. 'How would I know? I didn't undertake to arrange anything except fetching and carrying – a sort of Evri for the rurally isolated. For all I know it could be they'd run out of cartridges for the shoot or lemons for their G&Ts.'

'And where exactly did you arrange to have these mystery packages picked up from?'

Innes could feel sweat forming on the back of his neck. He couldn't think what to say.

'Oh, never mind for the moment,' Murray said. 'We'll get a detailed list of the addresses both for pick-up and delivery from you later, but we're busy people, as I said. There's something else the chief inspector wants to ask you about.'

With a desperate attempt to regain some sort of control of the situation, he said, 'Oh, if you're going to ask me about the shooting, your colleague has all the relevant information. I told him I was here all day, though I'm afraid I have no one who could speak to that, and I utterly refuted the accusation. Even with a more' – he paused – '*sophisticated* approach than his, you won't get any other reply. I may not be able to prove I'm innocent but you damn well can't prove I'm guilty either.'

He felt a little better after that, but Strang had been sitting silently watching, in an unsettling way. He said now, 'Your partner works in the Shore House Café – is that right?'

Something else he hadn't expected. 'Not exactly partner, more girlfriend,' he said, in a distancing move that was instinctive. Had they got something on her?

Strang said, 'Do you often visit her there?'

'Not often, no. Just when it's quiet and I can bum a cup of coffee.' Thrown off balance again, he eyed first one, then the other, trying to assess where the next punch might be coming from.

'When was the last time?'

He frowned. 'Couldn't tell you. Three weeks ago? Around that, I would guess.'

'Are you familiar with the layout?'

'Well yes, obviously.'

'Describe it to me.'

Innes was starting to sweat again. He'd rather deal with the attack-dog cop – this one was unnerving. 'Well, the café's on the ground floor of the house – at least, I understand it is. I've never actually been upstairs.'

'And John Wilson's studio? Do you know where that is?'

Suddenly light dawned – the bastard had shopped him! Oh God, he was in real trouble now. It wasn't easy to keep his voice steady when he said, 'Yes, I know – across the yard. I've never been in it, though.'

'But you know that there is another way into it, down the alleyway at the side?' Strang was relentless.

'Yes, I suppose I do. I've never gone down it, though, just gone straight into the café.' Then with the inspiration born of desperation, he said, 'If it's anything to do with John Wilson and his studio, you should talk to Zoe. She's artistic and she and John are pretty chummy. I'm not a possessive man – we've never had that sort of relationship – but if I was, I think I'd be unhappy about it.' Gaining confidence, he went on, 'And since you didn't ask me for the name of the courier, I assume you know it was John Wilson. He's always up for any little job going – he actually told me once that it was his "running-away money", and you might find it interesting to ask him who else contributed to that particular fund. And you could always ask Zoe what she does when she finishes work at the café and disappears for hours, allegedly to work in a couple of bars in Torridon but there isn't a bar there I've ever heard of that isn't shut by eleven.'

Innes intercepted the look that went between them. He'd scored there, then.

It was attack-dog's turn. She was smiling as she said, 'Yes, of course we know that John Wilson was your courier, and when he compiles his list of addresses for pick-up and delivery, as he is doing now, it won't take him very long since the pick-up would be the same every time – here. We'll be coming back to you about that.'

Strang said, 'Did you know that Wilson had a shotgun that he kept in his studio – a shotgun that we have discovered is now missing?'

Had that bitch Zoe known that but hadn't warned him? He came back with, 'No I didn't. Since Zoe's the one who's been in and out of the studio, shouldn't you be asking her instead of me?'

Strang didn't reply; he merely stood up and said, 'Thank you for your cooperation,' and they both left.

Innes shut the door behind them. His knees were

trembling and he sat down, his mind flicking back through the interview to assess the damage. The drugs – presumably they didn't have absolute proof of illegality or they'd have collared him at once. Wilson would have been cagey for his own protection, of course. He'd phone Joe Connelly at once and see what could be done; they owed him, after all he'd done for them, but he wasn't optimistic.

And they'd found out that John's gun was missing – he didn't know what that would mean. Nothing good, that was for sure.

But he'd set them onto Zoe. He didn't know her game but he did know that she wouldn't appreciate being questioned about it. He wouldn't mind hearing the answers to some of those questions himself.

She knew it was crazy to mix migraine medication with co-codamol, but Mairead had reached the to-hell-with-the-consequences stage, when she was prepared to suffer anything later as long as she was able to keep going. At this time of day the demand always slackened and she could leave the afternoon teas to Zoe, or even Ellie if necessary, though the girl had been upset about something recently and from the looks of her the sergeant had been treated to a burst of tears. Normally she'd have been asking her what the problem was, but right at the moment she didn't have the bandwidth to take on even one more thing.

She always felt better for a time after she'd been sick and the medication had blunted the headache enough to let her prepare for tomorrow's lunch. There'd been a run on the cakes so she had only a couple of traybakes and a fruitcake she could take out to defrost now, and Anna

Bruce was bringing in at least two of the fancier ones tomorrow. Anna Bruce – she didn't want to think about her.

She was making the pastry for the pot pies when John came back, walking straight through the café into the kitchen. He was looking pale and strained and he glanced at her uneasily as if he was scared of what she might do.

Mairead didn't have the energy to say more than, 'So they let you go.'

'Just helping with their enquiries,' he said.

'So far.' Zoe's voice came from behind him. 'What were they wanting to know, then?'

'Oh, it was just that someone's stolen my shotgun. Could have been anyone – like you, for instance,' he said to Zoe. 'Or you.'

Now he was staring at Mairead. From somewhere, she got up enough strength to come back with, 'But of course, we've only got your word for it that that's all they wanted. Now just get out of my sight for a bit, will you?'

John met her eyes for a moment, then turned without replying and walked through into the house. When she turned back to her pastry, she could see through the back window that he was striding across the yard to his studio and she could hear him swearing.

'Have we found the stink to follow, do you think, boss?' DS Murray said as they drove to Gairloch from Ardelour.

'There was certainly a rotting fish alluringly dangled in front of our noses,' DCI Strang said. 'Given that this was a desperate attempt to divert our attention from the less fragrant aspects of his own recent past, we have to put that in context, but it would certainly merit investigation.

You've mentioned this Zoe before – could you see her running this other life, apart from being a waitress and bar staff?'

'I'd believe absolutely anything about her,' Murray said. 'You'll understand when you see her – she just doesn't fit with that job description. When I went to the café with Dave and we interviewed John, I reckon she thought the whole thing was funny. Dave will have talked to her by now, of course.'

'Yes. I feel we should wait to hear what she's said to him, but after that we should definitely bring her in. What a nuisance it is to have to go to and fro to Gairloch, but it's hard to see where you could set up an incident room in Ardelour. I'll have to phone in a report to JB for the press statement tonight. She won't be happy, but fortunately I think the media will be losing interest. From what I read this morning they pretty much think that out in the wilds here where everyone has a gun the occasional fatality is hardly surprising. It was only really the dog that caught their interest, so they dusted off the "faithful friend" story they always run and they've done that now.'

Murray was a bit shocked at the cynical tone. 'Oh, poor Luath!' she said reproachfully, remembering the dignity of the creature. 'I hope he's all right. He was really pining.'

'Let's hope so, anyway.' As he spoke, the phone in his pocket pinged and he said, 'I'll just check that. It's probably Cat but she'll leave a message. Can you look?' He took it out of his pocket and handed it to her.

'No, it's not Cat,' she said. 'Alex Ritchie, it says. He's left a message.'

'Oh? Read it out, would you?'

'It says, "Kelso, I left another message earlier. Interesting development here. Get back to me."'

'Now what, I wonder, can that be? He's a DC in Glasgow – young, very bright, definitely up-and-coming. I've been dealing with him on some things with the national task force working on the freight raids, and the current live case is that recent one on the seafood van where the van driver died and two of the local youths have been charged. It's meant to be being dealt with by Inverness, so I wonder what he's got for me? I'll get back to him when we reach Gairloch.'

Murray locked the phone without saying anything. Bright, up-and-coming? How would he describe her if he was talking to someone else? Not likely in those terms, she was pretty sure, and her old enemy, insecurity, that always lurked in the thickets of her mind, slithered out to sink in its poisoned fang.

CHAPTER FOURTEEN

While DCI Strang went to the office to make his phone calls, DS Murray went to the incident room, hoping to find Sergeant Kirk there, and possibly also a cup of tea. The place was quiet; the original rush of eager witnesses had died down and now there was only a PC monitoring a computer and Kirk, who was sitting at one of the low tables with a mug in his hand and holding a biscuit taken from the cheap selection box in front of him – the kind that didn't run to chocolate ones.

'Have you eaten all the jammy ones?' Murray demanded.

'Last one,' Kirk said smugly. 'The iced rings have all gone too.'

Murray pulled a face, then took a fruit shortbread from the almost-empty box and went through to the galley kitchen to get tea before she sat down beside him.

'Well – had an interesting morning?'

Kirk groaned. 'You could say. By the time I'd had Mairead Wilson throwing up and Ellie the waitress in floods of tears, and then found out that her boyfriend is one of the pair charged with homicide in Glasgow, I was feeling it was a bit more exciting than I'd been bargaining for.'

'For goodness' sake! I'd have thought Ellie was a douce wee soul, from the looks of her, but I suppose you never can tell. And what was Mairead's problem?'

'Migraine, she said. I was definitely out my depth. I was meant to be finding if anyone was a likely suspect for having nicked the gun, but quite honestly I couldn't tell. I think I'm not cut out for this sort of thing.'

'Oh, don't worry – it's not easy for any of us. What about Zoe?'

'She breezed in, denied all knowledge and breezed out again. She could have been lying blind for all I knew.'

'Jago Innes basically told us she was up to no good, though without useful details. Admittedly, he was desperately trying to divert attention away from the courier stuff you unearthed from Wilson, but the boss reckons that's enough reason to bring her in for a little chat. We didn't get anything more than you did relating to Campbell's murder – didn't push it, in fact, since we'd nothing new to use as leverage. We've warned him we'll be proceeding on the drugs question, and given Wilson's list of names there may be some who'll be kinda keen to keep their names out of the paper – we only need one to say cocaine was involved and we've got him right there.'

'Wilson too, with luck,' Kirk was saying, when Strang put his head round the door.

'Oh, you're there, Dave. Good. Come on through to the office.'

'I'll bring tea for you,' Murray said. 'I'm afraid the biscuit selection is limited; you're offered a fruit shortbread or a Viennese finger.'

'Surprise me, why don't you. Thanks, Livvy.' He and Kirk went ahead.

When she joined them, Kirk was repeating his experiences, saying in conclusion, 'I'm sorry, boss. I don't think I'm very good at the atmosphere stuff.'

'You've been doing a great job,' Strang said. 'At least it meant that I could tell the super that we'd established that a gun had been stolen, though there wasn't much else I could say except that we are pursuing our enquiries, and I have to tell you she wasn't much impressed.

'There's another thing, though. The Glasgow DC I mentioned to you, Livvy – there was an earlier message today that I missed, but now he says he'll be here shortly. He's been involved with the case of the local males involved in the raid on the Logan Fisheries van—'

He stopped, seeing that Murray and Kirk were exchanging glances. 'I'm obviously missing something?'

Kirk said, 'The thing is, I just found out today that Ellie, the waitress at the café, is Fergus Matheson's girlfriend.'

'What a useful man you are!' Strang said. 'Alex Ritchie is being sent up here as part of the task force's investigation into the raids, working with the Inverness inquiry and interviewing the families and contacts of the two men – he's hoping for any help we can give with that. I thought, Livvy, that you could go round and speak to Anna Bruce again – she seemed to know about the youth scene and might be able to give us a steer about who else he might talk to. There seems to be another dimension to this case that he said might well open things up, so I'll stay here to wait for him. All right?'

Murray said, 'Yes, boss,' and Kirk stood up, looking uncertain.

'Will you be wanting me, boss?'

'I don't think there's a particular need for that. You've done a long shift already and it's a long drive back to Inverness too.'

She could see Kirk was torn. It was a long drive, and he'd obviously been very stressed today by the task he'd been given; on the other hand, he'd shown every sign of enjoying being at the centre of things, as he never normally was.

'We're used to it,' he said, but Murray didn't think he was all that sorry Strang was sending him on his way.

She had just got up to leave with him when there was a knock on the door and a man came in. He was fit – tall, athletic-looking, with curly brownish-fair hair and wide-set, grey-blue eyes, and he had a very nice smile he was displaying now.

Strang too was smiling as he got up to greet him. 'Alex! Well done – you must have made good time.'

'Amazingly, yes, I did, sir. For once there were no hold-ups on the A9. Must have been a reward for some act of virtue in my past.'

'Unlikely!' Strang said and they both laughed; Kirk smiled, and Murray didn't.

She knew the type – totally at ease with himself, certain of a welcome wherever he might be. This, presumably, was the young, bright, up-and-coming DC that Strang had talked about, though she didn't reckon much to the 'young' – he looked, if anything, slightly older than she was. And up-and-coming – funny he was still only a DC, then.

Strang introduced the others and The Smile was directed towards them; Murray smiled back but didn't achieve quite the same wattage.

'Livvy is just going to try to speak to Anna Bruce, Alex – you remember her? We spoke to her again today and she seemed to know a bit about the local scene. If she can suggest names, you can take that on, and Dave has unearthed Matheson's girlfriend, which could be useful.'

'Brilliant!' Ritchie said. 'But I need to put you in the picture about what's come up. It's quite significant.'

'Yes, you said. Sit down and tell me about it, and then I can brief you on where we're at. Livvy, report back when you have anything for us.'

Murray and Kirk took themselves off. 'Doesn't look as if he's going to need me tomorrow, if you've got this new guy,' Kirk said. 'Didn't take to him much, did you?'

Murray pulled a face. 'Not my type. Anyway, it sounds as if he's only here for a couple of days so no doubt you'll be needed later – unless the wonder boy has managed to solve the whole thing by then.'

Kirk looked surprised at her acidic tone, but they were outside by now and she got into her car, said goodbye and drove off.

Marjory Fleming was sitting by a window in Contini, the café below the National Gallery, conveniently accessible from the High Street – and the Law Courts – by a long flight of stairs. She had been in Edinburgh for a meeting of the Police Investigation and Review Commissioner's committee and it was a good opportunity to see her daughter – there always seemed to be wedding details to be discussed. Cat's case at the Sheriff Court today had just concluded and, she'd assured her mother, she'd be there shortly.

Cat's 'shortly' could be quite a long time and Marjory had no hesitation in ordering tea and a scone rather than waiting. After a long meeting, it was pleasantly relaxing just to sit with her thoughts, watching the streams of people walking past in Princes Street Gardens. It was so good to see Cat so happy with her career – it had taken long enough for her to find it, heaven knew – and so happy with Kelso too. She'd been worried about how Cat would cope with him going off to this new investigation after all the dramas of the last one, but mercifully it seemed to be much lower key.

And there she was now, hurtling down the steps, making Marjory wince at the thought of what a slight misstep might do to the wedding plans. Still, she made it into the café and spotted her mother waving.

However, there wasn't much sign of the happy daughter she'd been thinking about. Cat was scowling, and flung herself into the seat opposite. She didn't so much as say hello before she launched in.

'I know you're supposed to make allowances for really stupid people because they actually can't help it, but when they're senile as well someone ought to make them retire! And it wouldn't do any harm to check their hearing too. I explained my client's case perfectly clearly – indeed, better than that, if I say it myself, and the old goat gave the jury direction that was totally misleading so of course they brought in the wrong verdict.'

'So who's the guilty man?' Marjory said, smiling – not meaning the one who had just been sent down.

'Oh, Sheriff Grainger, of course – who else? He's the worst of the lot.'

'Oh, I thought Sheriff Rutherford was that,' Marjory said, all innocence.

Cat gave her a cross look. 'Well, he is pretty bad. But he's not so far past it that he's positively *drooling*.'

Marjory knew Sheriff Grainger: not, perhaps, the most brilliant jurist, but certainly not that much older than she was herself.

'I think you need tea, darling. It's a bit early for whisky but they do a very good coffee cake.' She signalled to the waitress.

'Oh, sorry about that,' Cat said. 'But I feel better having got that off my chest. How are you?'

'We're all fine. How's Kelso? I haven't seen much in the papers except about the poor dog.'

'Oh yes, I know – it was so sad. He gave me a quick call this morning to say it was pretty much plodding stuff. It was quite funny, though – apparently he and Livvy Murray are in this ghastly Airbnb that doesn't even have en suite bathrooms and they've been doing a sort of paso doble on the landing in their dressing gowns. The breakfast is terrible too – I do feel sorry for the poor lamb. Let's just hope they can get it done quickly – I think they're both hoping it's a gang from somewhere else that won't mean having to be based locally so they can come home.'

'I hope they're right,' Marjory said. 'The trouble is that

unless there's a clear link with the victim it can drag on and on – you know, there was that case twenty years ago when a blameless bank manager was shot dead on his own doorstep and they're still working on it, going back and back without ever establishing either who it was who did it or why it had happened at all.'

'Oh, don't say that!' Cat exclaimed. 'That would drive Kelso absolutely crazy.'

The waitress took the order and when she'd gone, Marjory said, 'So, with your case – are you going to go for an appeal?'

Cat looked a little awkward. 'Well, possibly not. I think from the technical point of view it might be difficult.'

'I see,' said Marjory, as noncommittally as she could. 'Anyway, Annelise was wondering if you have friends bringing babies who might need a crèche . . .'

DS Murray drove out of Gairloch in a thoroughly distempered frame of mind. To know that there was an interesting new development, and immediately be sent off without being told what it was, was completely infuriating. She would readily admit that curiosity was her besetting sin, but it was stupid anyway – there might, for instance, be something more she could usefully find out from Anna Bruce if she knew.

It was, for once, a lovely day and the views on the drive along the side of Loch Maree were spectacular, but she wasn't in any mood to appreciate them. 'See one mountain, you've seen them all,' she found herself muttering rebelliously.

And then, just to put the tin lid on it, Anna Bruce wasn't

in. Her car was there, but even on foot round here there were too many alternatives to make trying to find her feasible – she could be walking on the moors, or down at the shop or even just visiting a friend.

Murray swore. If she went back now, she'd find herself cooling her heels and contemplating the diminished biscuit box while all the interesting stuff was going on behind the closed door of the office.

There was another woman Anna had mentioned, someone local, who'd had a tragedy with her son, and had told Anna all about what went on. She couldn't quite remember the name – Shona something, wasn't it? But she had mentioned a smokehouse, out along the Applecross road – it shouldn't be too difficult to find.

She set off, along the side of Loch Shieldaig. Sea, mountains, yadda yadda yadda. Then suddenly, she gasped. There was a flotilla of what looked like small submarines, lurking in a bay. There'd been a lot in the news about shadowy Russian subs around the west coast – was this an invasion being secretly set up in this out-of-the-way place?

It was only a minute before common sense took hold. Not exactly out-of-the-way; people came from all over to drive the famous twisting Applecross road, for a start, and now she got nearer she could see right there beside the bay was a sign for Logan Fisheries – the firm whose van had been taken. Presumably, these were some sort of tanks for the fish.

Feeling foolish, she drove on and began to notice her surroundings. The hills that rose ahead were different from the usual ones everyone went on about – these were bare, dramatic, great slabs of unforgiving greyish-brown rocks. Very ancient, Kelso had said, and in some places it almost looked like those pictures they sent back from the moon.

She'd always felt before that mountains exercised an intimidating presence, contemptuously bearing down on you, despising you for your very temporary existence; these seemed too magnificently indifferent to do anything other than be what they were, entirely oblivious to the scurrying ants below. She saw the sign for the smokehouse, but, intrigued now, she drove on. She wasn't in any hurry to get back.

It was the randomness of it all that struck her: a dark, tiny lochan, sunk in the surrounding stone; double, triple waterfalls splashing down to disappear under the road; a building-sized rock, poised somehow on a logic-defying point; rubble tumbling down the side of a great hill as if it had just been spilt there by some careless giant. In clefts and valleys, there was sometimes growth but it was stunted, as if it was barely tolerated.

For the first time ever, Murray experienced the magic of place. She'd never really responded much to pretty, perhaps thanks to a tough childhood where you had to be hard to survive. This was anything but pretty – harsh, rugged, even ugly, in a way. What an amazing place! Volcanic, Kelso had said, and she could almost hear the roar of the eruption and the convulsion of the earth that had produced this.

But her mind hadn't been on the road; it had become steadily narrower and as she came up a precipitous hill she suddenly recognised one of the features that made driving in the Highlands so terrifying – she was approaching the crest unsighted, with no way of knowing what might be coming up the other side and equally blind.

A large campervan, with a similarly inexperienced driver, as it happened. By some miracle they didn't actually hit each other and stopped nose to nose, but each drove on considerably chastened.

Recalled to her sense of duty, Murray looked for a place to turn – not easy, with sightlines more and more reduced as the road became a sort of hair-rising switchback, with swoops and dips and corners that terrifyingly edged sheer drops to the sea beneath.

She was driving through what looked like a sort of pass now, with a long, narrow loch shadowed by hills on either side, and to her astonishment there was a small plane floating on the dark water – a seaplane, with pontoons beneath its wings, looking as if it had just been conveniently parked beside the road. There was no one around, no sign of habitation.

How weird – but in this wilderness where the roads were so bad that you couldn't even turn round when you wanted to, spending your millions on easy transport would probably be worth it.

She drove on, still wondering. What she needed was a turnoff into a village or even a cluster of houses, but it was miles before the first one appeared and she was shaking with tension as she switched in and out of passing places to avoid the surprising number of tourists, foreign ones among them, eager to take their lives in their hands.

With huge relief she saw a road opening at last with a generous field entrance a few yards down where she could turn round, and set off back.

It was after six now so it was no surprise that the smokehouse had a 'Closed' notice outside, but the peaty smell was still strong as she parked and went towards the house. It would be just her luck if this Shona was out as well, but if there had to be a return visit, Kelso could drive because she'd prefer to be up on a charge for disobeying an order than attempt that hellish road again.

'When it comes to impressive singing, Fergus Matheson would rival Maria Callas,' DC Ritchie said. 'He was unstoppable – he got led astray, it wasn't him, it was his pal Craig, a great lummox who more than likely has no clear memory of what happened. He was certainly completely stoned when they picked him up.'

'But what was it all about? Did he come clean about who the pal in Wester Ross Seafood was who tipped them off about the early delivery?'

'Apparently that was a red herring. There's a pub they go to in Torridon where a couple of the van drivers are regulars and apparently they're constantly moaning about times being changed for delivery on the main run – that's the ones with the frozen stuff on board, the ones that as we know are regularly targeted.

'Matheson, who probably considers himself the brains of the outfit, knew all about the raids on the big lorries and had been toying for some time with the idea of nicking the local van. He knew fresh shellfish was the most expensive and he thought it would give him a way to raid others the same and make big money.'

'And for this an honest, decent man ends up dead,' Strang said. 'It looked like amateur hour from the start, but however naive or even drug-addled you were, you couldn't think you could just pitch up at the door of some random restaurant and ask if they'd like four kilos of raw prawns. There would to be more to it than that, right? And are you going to tell me that this sort of "more" isn't just a job for the Inverness lot, but is linked in with Brodie Campbell? For heaven's sake, Alex, say it isn't so!'

'Much though I hate to be the bearer of bad news, Campbell was in this up to his neck. Apparently he got a whiff of something going on with them – Matheson didn't know how, except that Lothian probably blurted something out. But anyway, he basically took them round the back of the bike shed and told them he was about to bring in the law on them for planning a raid unless – get this – they cut him in on the profits. To be honest, I don't think Campbell is actually the brightest bulb in the chandelier either, but he told them that in exchange, he'd give them cash for things they hadn't begun to think about, like petrol and living costs, and, significantly, a list of likely outlets. Then they would go on to prey on the small seafood fisheries up and down the coast, here and in England.'

Strang shook his head in bewilderment. 'So he was at the very least in touch with someone who had a wider network? It would square with what Dave Kirk said – he was pretty sure that even though Campbell was a useful CHIS, he couldn't be trusted. But the timing of the raid – how did they know about the earlier time?'

'That was pure chance. They'd been planning to do it anyway – even at the normal time there's not a lot of traffic and you'd only have to wait for a few minutes for the road to be deserted. It so happened that just after the deal with Campbell had been put in place, one of the drivers they knew was complaining about having been detailed to meet poor Sandy Wallace at the earlier time. Then, of course, thanks to their ineptness it became a nationwide hunt for them and they hadn't even had the nous to have got false plates. Sitting ducks, they were.'

With a hollow feeling inside, Strang said, 'So where had Campbell got the information from? Do we now have a whole new set of people who as a result of this mess might be feeling exposed and have an interest in terminating him? Do you have his list of the suitable outlets?'

'Unfortunately, he wasn't that daft. He'd told them to find somewhere they could keep their heads down till the fuss was over and then he'd trickle them out to them one by one. They'd been feeling pleased with themselves and were listening to the radio in the hope their brilliant coup would be featuring and then realised it had all gone horribly, horribly wrong. They phoned Campbell in a panic and after he'd stopped swearing he told them he'd come after them if they so much as mentioned his name.'

'Asking for a bullet in the back, you'd have to think. But hang on – the timing doesn't work. They were banged up in Glasgow by late Friday afternoon, weren't they?'

'Matheson was quite blunt about it,' Ritchie said. 'It was only once they heard Campbell was dead and when he'd been killed that he agreed to make the statement.'

Strang sat back in his chair, thinking. Then he said, 'It seemed strange right from the start that there should be two unconnected violent events at the same time in a place like this.'

'That's right,' Ritchie said. 'What is it they say – once is happenstance, twice is coincidence, three times is enemy action?'

'So far we're still at the coincidence level,' Strang said. 'Let's just hope to God that we aren't entering the "enemy action" stage.'

Introducing herself was a bit awkward because Murray still hadn't remembered the surname and had to ask, while explaining at the same time that she needed to speak to her because of something her friend Anna Bruce had said.

'Macintyre,' Shona said.

Murray blinked. She looked the typical countrywoman: middle-aged with an outdoor complexion, dressed in jeans, a checked shirt and a padded navy gilet. She had a pleasant open face, though her cheeks were gaunt and there were visible signs of strain around her eyes. She certainly didn't look the kind of person who would find a visit from the police seriously unwelcome.

But unwelcome it blatantly was. She stood waiting for Murray to speak and it was with apparent reluctance that she said, 'I suppose you'd better come in.'

'We're investigating the murder of Brodie Cameron,' Murray said as they stood in the hall.

'I imagined you must be. Of course he's by way of being chummy with the police force, so no doubt you'll be pulling out all the stops. I just wonder where you all were, and come to that, still are, when it comes to the suppliers of drugs to our children, and the young men being drawn into criminality by people like – goodness me, who can I think of? Oh, I know, Brodie Campbell.'

Feeling as if she'd been punched, Murray heard herself bleating, 'I'm very sorry you feel that way, Ms Macintyre. If you can give me chapter and verse, I can—'

'Oh, of course I can't! They see to that, and another set of youngsters fall prey.'

She was, Murray realised, on the verge of breaking down. Anna Bruce hadn't described in detail what had happened to the son, but it wasn't hard to piece it together from this.

'You said Brodie Campbell was somehow involved in this kind of thing? If you were prepared to tell me anything you know, I promise I will see to it that it's followed up. It would be in our interests as well as yours.'

Shona didn't say anything for a moment while Murray held her breath. Which way would it go?

At last Shona said, with infinite weariness, 'Then you'd better come through to the kitchen. But let me tell you this at the start – I'm not going to tell you anything that might help you find out who killed that bastard and I think you'll find that I'm far from the only one who thinks like that. Whoever it was has done us all a great service and Ardelour would be a better place now he's dead – if I didn't think there was someone else just waiting to take over.'

CHAPTER FIFTEEN

'That's good!' DCI Strang said as DC Murray returned to the office. 'Alex and I are ready to pack it in for now. He's staying here in Gairloch and they've told us about a chippie with tables – it's the only place open on a Sunday night and they do good fish and chips, allegedly.'

'Sounds great,' Murray said.

As they all walked out, Strang said to her, 'There's a new complication but I'll explain in the car. How did you get on?'

'A long story,' she said. 'The polis aren't very popular around here.' Then turning to Ritchie, she said, 'What's your accommodation like?'

'Oh, standard stuff. Small bedroom, tiny bathroom, but clean enough.'

'Sounds pretty good to me. And what about breakfast?'

Ritchie looked surprised. 'Well, obviously I don't know but they've tables set up in the dining room.'

'With knives and forks and everything?'

Looking even more confused, Ritchie assured her that yes, indeed there were. Strang, who had reached their cars first, turned to say, 'Ignore it. Livvy's obsessed. We're in a dismal place and I don't envy our FCA when we get back, if your lot have done better.'

It wasn't far to the chippie and Murray listened, fascinated, as Strang rapidly filled her in on what had been happening.

'So it looks as if Campbell may have had links to some bigger organisation,' Strang said.

'Really? Now, I tell you what I saw today – this wee seaplane on a loch right beside the road – out in the middle of nowhere, no one around. What sort of person is there that might be wanting a seaplane?'

'I admit that's odd,' Strang said. 'OK, travel on these roads is desperately slow and if you're rich enough a helicopter isn't unusual, or even a light aircraft if there's space for a runway. But a seaplane – pretty restrictive, I'd have thought. File it, Livvy, and we'll keep it in mind. Oh, this looks like the place.'

There were customers queuing for chips, but the small room to one side, where there were half a dozen tables, was deserted. A woman came over to take their orders and brought alcohol-free lagers.

'So,' Strang said. 'Tell us about this woman, then.'

With the up-and-coming DC staring at her expectantly, Murray felt stupidly nervous. She needed to report what Shona Macintyre had said – and what she'd refused to say – in a very professional way.

'Shona looks on the edge of a breakdown. Those lads

who've been arrested are linked in her mind with the son who killed himself recently.'

'Drink or drugs?' Ritchie asked.

She was irritated by the interruption. 'Both, actually. She feels we haven't tackled the toxic culture infiltrating this place – haven't even tried to root it out. The kids get enrolled into county lines at school and she's going radge because there's officers on streets now that haven't seen one in years. They know Campbell was working with us so they're concerned we're just looking out for one of our own. She told me we wouldn't get anyone to give us information that would see his killer locked up.'

'So she thinks that's someone she knows?' Ritchie said.

'Or at least, someone in the community, and she meant what she said – she wouldn't answer any questions that could help us find them. She was only ready to talk about how, without support, they'd had to do their own social work as best they could – mentioned Mairead Wilson as someone who knew the young men and did her best to give them a leg up – in fact, she mentioned the chef that you said Anna Bruce knew, boss.'

Strang said, 'Interesting. And the drugs problem – was Shona willing to point a finger there?'

'Oh, no problem about that – Jago Innes, a "festering sore", according to her, but the young won't ever talk because they're scared of cutting off their supply. She admitted that the police had investigated once but couldn't pin anything on him – doesn't keep much on site, just distributes as it comes in. From Glasgow, she believes.'

'That would figure,' Strang said. 'Inverness has the names of his buddies who had a run-in with Campbell and they're already investigating them in relation to a hare-coursing event, Alex.'

'It all happens here, doesn't it!' Ritchie said. 'I'm beginning to feel Glasgow is dull by comparison. But what Shona said about them closing ranks – the protective ring would hardly extend to Jago Innes, would it?'

'Good point, Alex,' Strang said.

Murray said, 'Of course all that means is that they don't actually think it was him. It doesn't mean he didn't do it.' It came out harsher than she'd really meant it to and Strang frowned.

'No, but it means that we could start by subjecting this charmed circle to the classic assessment. So motive first: according to Shona, more or less everyone could be said to have one. Means: the missing gun could be highly significant here even if it hasn't taken us any further forward so far. Opportunity: we can examine the statements they gave of their movements and cross-reference to eliminate at least some – a nice, objective procedure that will be a refreshing change from discussing abstract theories. That might even dovetail with your brief, Alex.'

'I was just thinking that,' Ritchie said. 'My job is to suss out the general situation in Ardelour where it's relevant to the task force's brief, and someone's lined up the parents for me tomorrow, so I can work in your local questions as well.'

'Good,' Strang said. 'Though of course, what you said about the lists Campbell offered Matheson and Lothian means that's a dimension we can't possibly ignore.'

Seizing her chance, Murray said, 'So it could have been a hit arranged by someone who resented him using their lists for his own private little schemes. And there was this seaplane I saw tied up by the Applecross road, Alex – what would your standard well-off residents have one of those for? It's not going to take you to do a bit of shopping in Glasgow, is it?'

'That's really interesting,' Ritchie said. 'Whereabouts was it?'

'It wasn't really anywhere, if you see what I mean. I went on for a bit past the smokehouse just gasping at the amazing scenery and I tell you, it's the scariest road I've ever been on. I was nearly mangled by a campervan and if you want me to show you where I saw it, you'll have to do the driving.'

The food arrived just as Strang said, 'Oh yes, it's notorious. But Livvy – the scenery? Your normal reaction to landscape is something like nervous hostility mingled with determined disdain!'

She was used to being teased by Strang, but the fact that Ritchie laughed made her feel defensive. 'This was different. It's got' – she groped for the right words – 'real majesty,' which on reflection sounded embarrassingly poetical even though Strang agreed.

The fish and chips were indeed good, but there was little incentive to linger. They had to drive back to Ardelour and Ritchie was keen to get back to the guest house.

'I'm studying for my sergeant's exam,' he said. 'You'll sympathise, Livvy. You know how tough it is.'

'Oh, of course,' she said, though she didn't, much. He was the kind who'd sail through first time, barely breaking into a sweat.

As they drove back, Strang said, 'I'll arrange now to

summon Zoe Cooper to the station tomorrow. I know Innes's stinking fish was merely a distraction attempt, but from what you said about her she seems to be seriously out of context, and that's always a red light. You'd have time to try to speak to Anna Bruce before that. You never know, she might be more forthcoming.'

'Sure, boss,' Murray said, happier now Ritchie had said he had his own instructions from Glasgow, so perhaps she could stop bristling. Only perhaps, mind. She was rather holding it against him that he'd ordered scampi with his chips.

Uncharacteristically, Kelso Strang couldn't get to sleep. Army-trained to fall asleep immediately, he was finding wakefulness an unpleasant novelty.

He'd had a long chat with Cat before he turned in, mainly family and wedding stuff – Auntie Margaret and Auntie Sylvia must, apparently, be kept well apart – so they hadn't really discussed the case, mainly because he couldn't explain it in any coherent fashion.

Now he was trying to do that for his own benefit, going over the evidence again and again to make things link up, work out which cogs were driving which wheels, feeling helpless, even distressed . . .

Suddenly, he realised why: it was that diabolical toy his father had wished onto him. His relationship with Major-General Sir Roderick Strang had been difficult, with Kelso being more drawn to the arts than the sciences, subjects that Roderick despised as 'soft'.

His eighth birthday present had looked promising, but the large box contained a building set with dozens of cogs, wheels and various connectors, meant to be made into some unspecified construction. He had looked at it in dismay, then up at his father's expectant face.

'What do I do with it?' he said. He was only eight, after all.

'Oh Kelso, that's wonderful, isn't it,' his mother prompted, and hastily he said, 'Thank you, Dad.' But it was too late – the clouds had gathered on his father's brow.

'You can do anything with it, Kelso – that's the point. You can make a working model of whatever you like – make something that moves, like a tank, say.'

Kelso had looked at him blankly, with *Why would I want to make a tank*? running through his head. He wasn't yet skilled at concealment and Roderick said sharply, 'Oh, or make some sort of damn fool thing like a clock, if that's more to your taste.'

The rest of his birthday was spent trying to work out how you made this cog drive that wheel – and levers came into it somehow too – in a state of panicked helplessness until his mother said firmly that perhaps it should wait till he was older. Even so, that wretched building pack surfaced every so often in uneasy dreams.

Just like his challenge now. Two murders – seemingly unconnected, but with increasing evidence of interaction emerging. Was this rooted in the local community, where there were all too many suspects, or was it indeed an outside agency with external lines that could be investigated – Jago Innes's Glasgow connection, for instance, or the network with the sophisticated lists?

If Campbell, working for some external agency, had been using them for his own personal profit, they'd have a considerable motive for taking him out – and the sawn-off shotgun was a weapon popular with the criminal classes.

After all, these things happened all too frequently – and it would be a relief to use the firm investigative process of tracking down connections rather than the shifting sands of hearsay and deliberate obfuscation that would be involved in a local inquiry.

And then of course – Zoe Cooper. After what Innes had said about her, Kelso couldn't help wondering what, indeed, she might do late at night after the bars were shut – though there might be an obvious, and innocent, answer. He looked forward to meeting her.

They certainly needed to get hold of Anna Bruce. She would have a vested interest in helping them, unlike her friend Shona.

Kelso yawned. The longer he thought about it, cogs and wheels did seem to be starting to whirr – if that was what cogs and wheels did. He was still wondering about that as the thoughts became dreams.

Mairead had managed all her preparation before she fell into bed, and when she went down to the café next morning the headache had been replaced by the woozy, unconnected feeling that usually followed. She could cope with it; she'd been feeling that way for the last three days anyway.

She hadn't seen or spoken to John since he'd come back from Gairloch but she couldn't forget the look he had given her, before storming out to his studio. Oh, she had known for ever that their relationship was broken and had only survived because he needed money and she was determined to avoid a divorce that would mean selling up her precious home and the café, the altar on which she had sacrificed so much, but that look had shouted raw, naked hatred. She hadn't managed to hear what he said as he walked across the yard but she had little doubt the visible venom in his curses was directed at her.

It was hard to see what their future could possibly hold – but then the future was murky – no, worse than that – in any case. It wasn't a migraine making her feel sick right now – it was fear and guilt. Oh yes, certainly guilt.

The only predictable part of the future was that people would be coming in shortly looking for coffee and other people would be coming in later for lunch. She set out the standard fruitcake and sliced-up traybake under their glass domes; Anna would be in shortly with two of the fancier ones – three, if she was lucky. She went back to start grating cheese – Welsh rarebit was always popular – and then whizzed through the pastry that could be baking for the quiches while she fried the frozen onions for the filling. At least multitasking stopped you thinking about anything apart from ensuring the cheese sauce wasn't sticking.

At nine-thirty, she looked at her watch in dismay. Anna hadn't appeared; she'd nearly always made her delivery by this time, and Zoe too was late. She could only hope she'd arrive before Anna since she didn't want to be alone with her after that conversation with Shona, in case she brought up a past that Mairead had no wish ever to revisit. She might even start interrogating her about Callan, and that thought made her feel ill all over again.

Nine forty-five: still no cakes, no Zoe. Ellie was due at ten but she wasn't counting on that; she'd been completely unsettled by the police visit yesterday and had kept bursting into tears until Mairead sent her home.

At nine-fifty, Zoe phoned. She'd been summoned to Gairloch Police Station and she had no idea how long she'd be.

Mairead drew a long, shuddering breath. Anna's cakes clearly weren't coming and with no other help she'd have to shut the café. Normally she didn't do that except for a funeral, which felt like a bad omen.

While DCI Strang drove to Gairloch, DS Murray walked to interview Anna Bruce. She'd lined up a PC at the crime scene who'd take her to Gairloch afterwards; she didn't want to miss out on the Zoe Cooper interview. The woman was intriguing; she could certainly see her gunning Campbell down in cold blood, even though her own money was still on a professional hit. She reckoned even Kelso had been leaning towards that, what with the seaplane and everything.

She was feeling bloated this morning, after the fish supper and too much starch at breakfast, and the very steep slope up to Anna's house had her peching a bit. And after all that, the woman wasn't in, though the car was still outside.

Was Anna just refusing to answer the door? Cupping her hands, Murray peered into the sitting room and then went round to look in the kitchen window. There was no one there, but she could see peeled carrots lying on the table, as if they'd been prepared for something, so maybe she'd run out of an ingredient and gone down to the shop to fetch it. Muttering, Murray set off back down the hill.

Even if she found her there, it would mean coming back up here to talk to her, and the time was passing.

But Anna wasn't in the shop either, and Murray met blank looks when she asked if anyone knew where the woman was. Concluding that she must have gone to borrow a cup of sugar from a friend, Murray went back to find her cooperative constable. It was a nuisance that she'd have to try again but at least it meant she'd get back to Gairloch in good time.

DCS Borthwick was getting restive. 'Yes, Kelso, I can see that the picture is getting more and more complicated, but where do you think it's going? The Inverness investigation is clearly being bolstered by this DC they've sent up from the task force in Glasgow – I would hate to think that it will look as if they're being a lot more effective than we are. Have you something in prospect that I can use to show we're on the ball?'

Stifling a sigh, Strang said, 'I'm just about to do an interview with a female who looks like an interesting witness, so something may well come of that. I'll certainly get back to you when there's any new development.'

'Soon would be good,' was her final remark.

He ended the call with a groan. JB had been seriously rattled last year when it looked as if funding could be withdrawn from the SRCS and the result had been a sort of frantic competitiveness. The Inverness DCS being theoretically a friend had given it a personal dimension that only made things worse; the SRCS always had to rely on the local force for backup and they were supposed to be colleagues, not rivals.

He'd gone through all that had come in overnight; Campbell's phone records were still being trawled and searches around the site were ongoing but fruitless so far: it seemed to have been quick and clean. Was he really going to have to come round to Livvy's view? He still didn't quite buy it.

When Murray came in, she confessed she'd failed to get hold of Anna Bruce, but that could wait and it shouldn't be long now before Cooper arrived.

'Where are you going to start with her, boss?' she asked.

'Damned if I know. I've seen the door-to-door statement they got from her and it was bland – she was at the café, away for an afternoon meeting, very briefly at home before she went to work at a bar in Torridon, came home. I might find a crack I could work a knife in to open it up – that's our best hope. Pay close attention, anyway – she didn't agree to being recorded.'

Then Zoe Cooper was ushered in. Strang had been warned what to expect, but even so he was taken aback. Perhaps in a Mediterranean setting she would be less striking but here, where everyone seemed to have that very pale Scottish complexion with blue-grey eyes, she did indeed, as Livvy had said, look seriously out of place; olive-complexioned, with dramatic flicks emphasising dark brown eyes. As she came in she ran one hand, with its long blue nails, through her riot of dark curls. She was wearing a perfume with a strong, musky base and then there was the tattoo – well, these were commonplace enough, but this was a carefully calculated sensuous message, leading the eye to the seductive little heart at the base of her throat. The first question suggested itself:

What could have brought you to Ardelour?

But before he could say anything, she said, smiling, 'I think it's time for me to come clean with you, Chief Inspector.'

She was holding out a card, a bright blue card with a silver hologram surface, a date at the top, Security Industry Authority in the middle and a photograph of Zoe Cooper at the right-hand side – a Zoe Cooper who had a much more restrained hairstyle and very discreet eye make-up.

Murray was gaping at it but Strang had seen one before. He took the card and ran his finger over the date – yes, embossed just as it should be. 'Private detective, then?'

'On the mark,' she said.

She looked as if she was laughing at him, but it gave him the opportunity to use that opening question. 'What brought you to Ardelour?'

'The usual reason. Money. There's been a lot of problems up here in the north-west as you know with raids on the lorries carrying luxury goods – I seem to remember you were someone who gave evidence at a trial in Glasgow on that very subject.'

So she'd done her research. 'Then you'll know about the task force currently working on the problem. Have you been cooperating with them?'

It seemed to amuse her. 'I don't work for anything except money, and the police force isn't a client. My client here is a consortium of owners in the north of Scotland who find the sort of protection the police are offering is, shall we say, inadequate. It's my job to get wind of anything that may be planned so that they can take evasive action of one sort or another.'

‘The name of this consortium?’

‘I’m afraid that is not public information but I report direct to the CEO of North West Fisheries and I will give you the contact if you would like to check my bona fides.’ She sounded very professional.

‘So I come back to my original question: what brought you here to Ardelour? The Scottish raids have mainly taken place on goods coming down the main route from Inverness after they’ve reached the motorway.’

‘I have a colleague who covers the area to the north-east and of course we coordinate. But to answer your question, it became obvious some time ago that there was a lot of criminal activity centred here for some reason. It presumably comes from the place being so isolated, so unpoliced and so tightly knit as a community that any attempt at taking police action can be telegraphed to those concerned well before an officer arrives.’

‘And what forms do these criminal activities take?’ Strang asked, realising it was a naive question the moment he said it.

The mocking look returned. ‘Surely you don’t expect me to tell you? Any information I come by is the property of my clients.’

Murray had been quietly scribbling notes, but Strang had been aware for some time that she was restless. Now she burst out, ‘Whatever your professional status, it is your duty as a citizen to assist the police in a murder investigation.’

Zoe raised her eyebrows. ‘Naturally, but so far you haven’t asked me anything relating to that inquiry. Being a responsible citizen, I can tell you that working in the café I'm seeing a storm of speculation in a community that is closing ranks against the outside world. I don't believe anyone knows for a fact who did it, but there are a lot of different theories.'

She did seem to be prepared to open up a little. 'And?' Strang said hopefully.

'Mairead Wilson, who owns the café, is the one you want to ask, though you'll be lucky if you get anything out of her. She's the one they all come to with their problems – she's the keeper of a lot of secrets and she has built up a security barricade around them. A lot of the young men were kids that grew up hanging round the café and she certainly mothers them – she was beyond upset and angry about what happened to that pair you've arrested.

'As to the theories, I'm sure you have the same suspects as I would have. Jago Innes and his pals protecting their various interests that Campbell has threatened, and they're capable of anything, that lot, as you probably know. John Wilson, whose gun has mysteriously gone missing. The mates of the lads who were dropped in it by Campbell. Even one of the punters involved in the hare-coursing who got nicked thanks to him could have an outsize grudge and I can tell you they've been blowing steam – everyone's talking about them.'

She was quite an operator. Strang didn't comment on the list of suspects, saying instead, 'You mentioned Jago Innes as one of your suspects, yet you are in a relationship with him?'

Again, that seemed to amuse her. 'Ah well, we have what you might call a friendship with benefits. We don't answer for each other and we don't ask questions.'

'I see. Could I pick you up on one thing you said? How did you know that Campbell was being blamed for the Matheson-Lothian business?'

Zoe looked surprised. 'Oh, everyone knew that. They were talking about it Friday night in a bar where I work. Incidentally, that and one other bar are my principal local sources, apart from the café, and in fact on two recent occasions they've provided information that allowed us to thwart a planned raid. But no – before you ask, I'm not going to give you details.'

'Is there anything else you are able to tell us – as a responsible citizen, of course,' Strang said.

'Nothing comes to mind in that category,' she said demurely.

With a glance at Strang, Murray said, 'Just a couple of questions. What was Mrs Wilson's attitude to Brodie Campbell?'

'Oh, she hated him, absolutely hated him – even a bit scared of him, I think, for some reason. But then, who didn't dislike him? I barely knew the man myself and he seemed thoroughly objectionable.'

'Do you think there's a big outside organisation involved in what happens around here?'

Zoe looked at her with a pitying smile. 'One? There's lots of them around, big and small, all looking to find some way to make a fast buck and ready to offer payment to get in on any chance of a profit, mainly drug-related. Kids around here don't need to go looking – they'll seek them out and once they have, they never let them go.'

Strang said, 'Thank you – that's very helpful. Now, I have your statement here. May I run through it with you?'

'Of course.'

'You stated that you were at the café all morning, until you had to go for a business appointment. What was that?'

'A meeting with the CEO in Ullapool. He can confirm that. Afterwards I came back to the café in the late afternoon. Mairead had a bad migraine but had gone out to do something – I don't know what, she wouldn't say, but she was pretty much collapsing when she came back. I shooed her off to bed, closed up the café then went back home before I went out to the bar. I came home and went to bed. I knew nothing about the murder until I was stopped at the barrier when I was on my way to the café.'

'And the reason for the meeting?'

'All I am going to say is that it did not relate to this case.'

Clearly she wasn't going to budge on that – and perhaps it was even true. 'But can we rely on you to alert us to any relevant evidence that comes your way?'

Zoe considered that. 'Up to a point.'

Another dead end. After a glance at Murray, who shook her head, Strang said, 'Then I think that's all.' But he couldn't resist one final question. 'Where did you work before you came up here?'

Zoe laughed. 'Where didn't I? I'm peripatetic. I get bored easily, you see. I'm getting twitchy right now – may I go?'

Strang stood up. 'Thank you. You've been very cooperative – mainly! We may contact you again, and please give DC Murray the contact for North West Fisheries.'

She did that, then left them sitting in stunned silence. After a moment, Murray said, 'Well, what do you make of that, boss? Is she for real?'

'Certainly formidable,' he said. 'I have to say it's the

first time someone I've been interviewing has told me I'm boring them. Any organisation would pay handsomely to have that one working for them – if she wasn't on your side, she'd be bad news.'

'And which side do you think it is?' Murray persisted.

'Verify her story with the CEO, will you, but I can say that the premise is entirely plausible. The most damaging raids have all been occurring on the motorway and she's right that we haven't been able to do anything until after the event. Say a famous branded whisky distiller is in the consortium – stopping just one raid would pay for even a handsome salary for some time. Of course what she didn't say is that when they "thwarted a raid" that meant they got us in to arrest the people involved, so she owes us a favour or two.'

'I bet she doesn't see it that way,' Murray said. 'I don't think our Zoe considers anyone except her precious little self, calculating down to her cyan-blue fingertips. Even if Jago is a right wee low-life who did his level best to dump her in it, I think I'm nearly feeling sorry for him. He's like a mouse in the claws of an eagle.'

Strang burst out laughing. 'Why not tell me what you really think, Livvy? I'm pretty sure a mouse wouldn't provide so much as a worthwhile canapé for an eagle, but I see what you mean. She's a class act, certainly. Now, back to Ardelour. I want to take a look at this Mairead they're all talking about.'

He had just stood up when his desk phone rang.

CHAPTER SIXTEEN

Mairead was in the kitchen, trying to store everything that could be resurrected for tomorrow when, please God, things might get back to something closer to normal – if they ever did again! She had studiously ignored the would-be customers peering through the window and tapping on the door.

She would have to do some baking, but she'd have time to go and see Jenny Matheson, who'd been on her mind since Shona's phone call. She'd been struggling at the time, without the strength to deal with a devastated Jenny, but she felt bad about not having contacted her. They were close, and when anything went wrong with the bright, lively boy, Mairead had always been there for them.

But when she phoned, Jenny was cagey. She'd been told, apparently, that a policeman would be coming to speak to her – not about what had happened to Campbell but about what she could tell him of the situation in Ardelour itself that might explain how quite so many of their lads seemed to be going the wrong way. When Mairead suggested she could phone her once the police had gone, she didn't seem keen. She had a lot to do after that, she said.

She felt as if she'd been slapped in the face. Last time they spoke, it had been when she'd gone to comfort Jenny even when she was falling to pieces herself. What was that about? What had happened? What might it mean? She was shaking as she put down the phone, and the knocking on the café door and Zoe's voice shouting, 'Mairead, are you there?' was a most unwelcome interruption.

'You've closed the café!' Zoe said challengingly as she was let in. 'You never do that! Are you feeling ill again?'

'I'm all right. It's just that with the way everything is, and with Ellie completely unreliable and not knowing when you might get back—'

Zoe laughed. 'Thought they might keep me locked up, did you?'

Ignoring her teasing tone, Mairead went on, 'And Anna hasn't brought in the cakes she promised so we've hardly anything to offer. Perhaps I might benefit from a day off anyway.'

'That's not like Anna,' Zoe said. 'Did you phone her?'

'Yes. No reply.' Mairead turned to go back to putting things into boxes.

'Do you know anything about her?' Zoe had perched herself on the edge of a table, as if stationing herself for a chat.

'No.'

'That's what I thought. She's a bit of a lady of mystery, isn't she? Did she ever talk to you about where she came from?'

'You spoke to her more than I ever did.'

'She didn't seem to have any friends – oh, apart from maybe Shona. Anna said she was going up there one day after she'd dropped off the cakes. Did she mention her when she phoned yesterday – and what did she want, anyway? You were going to tell me when we were interrupted.'

Mairead put down the cake tin she was holding. 'Why are you interrogating me, Zoe?'

Zoe looked taken aback. 'Oh – sorry! Did it come across like that? I was just interested – I always wondered what on earth someone like Anna was doing in a place like this.' She got off the table. 'Look, you've had a rotten time with your migraine. I'll just take myself off so you can have a rest. Let me know about tomorrow.'

'Before you go, you can tell me why you were snooping in my office the other day. You left a file drawer open. What is it that you're trying to find out? I can't think what use it could be to you, so who is it that's wanting to know?' Too tired to watch her tongue, she had let that slip out; she depended on Zoe to keep the café running and now she could almost smell the bridges burning.

But Zoe just seemed puzzled. 'Snooping in your office? I wasn't! Why on earth would I do that? It must have been John.'

And now she thought about it, she didn't actually know that it wasn't. Could he have thought she'd a secret bank account or something? She wished!

'Sorry, sorry,' she muttered. 'It's all just been a bit too much for me.'

'No wonder,' Zoe said briskly. 'See you tomorrow, then?'

But the more Mairead thought about it, the less she

believed her. She began adding together the number of times Zoe had tried to find out what she was doing, where she'd been, who she'd spoken to. Her every instinct told her she was being spied on, and the implications of that were terrifying. There was something she'd been missing, and she was starting to realise just what it was.

DS Murray stood politely by as DCI Strang took the phone call. She heard him say, 'Good morning, DI Mackenzie. What can I do for you?'

After a moment, he said, 'That's excellent news.' There was another pause, then he said, 'Oh. Well, it's a bit of a facer, I have to say.' Then, 'Yes, of course. Thank you for letting me know.'

Was there anything in the world less satisfying than listening to one end of an interesting phone call? Exerting impressive self-restraint, Murray didn't say, 'Well? What was that?' the minute he put down the phone.

It seemed quite a long time before Strang said, 'Do you want the good news or the bad news first? Oh, never mind. The good news, I suppose, is that they've found what looks like John Wilson's gun. The bad news is that its barrels are still intact.'

Murray said slowly, 'So . . .'

'Yes, it means that all that time we've spent trying to work out who might have used it to kill Campbell was time wasted.' He stood up. 'I gather Sergeant Kirk has it at the crime scene in Ardelour. We were planning to go anyway, so we'd better get over there now.'

Murray followed him with quiet satisfaction. Every single little thing that had emerged so far supported her theory that someone extremely competent had come in, done the job and left at once. So she would have to be very careful about what she said; there wasn't a DCI on the planet who would welcome a sergeant being right when he wasn't.

Jago Innes was in the middle of a phone call to Joe Connelly when the wind chime by the door jangled and Zoe Cooper appeared. He ended it immediately; he hadn't expected her back until after the café had closed and he could see from her face – mouth downturned, brows drawn together – that she wasn't pleased about something.

He couldn't resist saying, 'Cheer up! It may never happen.'

She gave him the look that mixed loathing and contempt. 'I'd hoped they might have taken you away by now,' she said. 'There must be three or four things they could get you on and I doubt you have the wit to get yourself out of any of them.'

He couldn't even deny it. 'And what about you? They're going to start digging in your own personal midden-heap, and you certainly won't like that.'

Zoe smiled, holding up her crossed fingers. 'Me and the chief inspector are just like that! We're on the same side.'

'If he believes that, he's a more gullible man than I took him for,' Jago said. 'And if that's right, why are you looking like thunder?'

She reacted as if she hadn't realised that she was, and a moment later her brow was smooth. 'It looks as if it's going to rain,' she said. 'I hate this climate, that's all.'

'So they've spoken to you, then – what did they ask

you, and what did you tell them? And more importantly, what did they tell you?'

Her tone was dismissive. 'Nothing, of course. And I didn't feel inclined to share all I know with them – not yet, at any rate. I certainly shall if it becomes necessary – you would be wise to remember that.'

It was a naked threat, and Jago felt sick. He'd always known she had the capacity to be a dangerous woman – it was part of her fascination – and he had little doubt about her power to bring his world crashing down. But he'd never known enough about her doings to be able now to counter with a convincing threat of his own.

Zoe was going on, 'Mairead shut the café today – she's not very well and things are getting on top of her, I think.'

'So what are you going to do today, then?' he said.

'This and that. I've a few loose ends to tie up here. I'm wanted for a meeting later on and it may well mean an overnighter. All I'm doing now is picking up a bag.'

He'd learnt that there was never any point in questioning her – 'the cat that walks by itself', as she had always said. It had been a brutal day, and it was pretty clear that the strange, ships-that-pass-in-the-night relationship that had somehow lasted longer than he'd ever thought it would, was drifting inexorably towards the rocks.

'So – is this the sort of overnighter you come back from?' Jago said.

She gave him her sphinx-like smile. '*Que sera, sera,*' she said, and went through to the bedroom. He noticed that she did seem to be taking longer than you would need to pack a change of knickers and a nightie.

Five minutes later, she left. He watched her get into

the car and drive away before, hands shaking, he dialled Connelly again.

'What do we have to do now, Joe?' he said.

It was dry this morning, but probably not for long since the sky was low and heavy and threatening darker clouds were accumulating on the horizon – never a good sign. Sergeant Kirk, with PC Sharma, was at the park in Ardelour when DCI Strang and DS Murray arrived. The operation at the crime scene had been scaled down the previous day to a team doing a widening ground search round about, but since the gun had been found they had apparently decided they were finished and were packing up.

Kirk was holding the gun in a plastic evidence bag, ready to show them. 'One of the lads walking the cliff path leading out of Ardelour on the farther side spotted it on the shore below first thing this morning,' he told Strang. 'From the looks of it, it was probably high tide when it was thrown in but when the tide went out it was stranded between two rocks and they had to get out the coastguards to fetch it in.'

Strang took it from him. 'Definitely not what we were looking for, is it? Put someone on to checking out the tides, please, to get us some rough idea of when that might have been possible and follow that up with appeals for witnesses.'

'So someone just popped in and nicked it, Dave, then after you discovered it was gone they found it was too hot to handle?' Murray said.

'You could be right,' Strang said. 'And maybe even scared that if we caught them with it they'd be charged with murder – it's not common knowledge what kind of gun was used. We have to do an Occam's razor job on this – cut through the flannel and when there are alternative explanations, choose the simplest. Looks like a rather dispiriting dead end, I'm afraid. Can I hand it over to your team to get fingerprints from Wilson just to confirm, Dave?'

Kirk assured him that indeed he could and they went off, though Murray thought cynically that with it downgraded to simple theft, it was vanishingly unlikely that they'd do much more than they would if someone had reported a stolen mobile.

Strang said, 'We'll go down to the car park at the bottom now to wait for Alex – I've alerted him and he should be along shortly. I want to know if he's got anything out of the parents.'

That was of course perfectly reasonable but Murray had been hoping that they'd be working on this together. It had seemed the perfect opportunity to press home the point that he'd made himself about thingamabob's razor. It so clearly could be an outside hit job, by one of the formless organisations Cooper had mentioned. It was just a pity that Kelso wasn't seeing this as clearly as she did.

As they drove down and parked, she said, 'But where are we to suppose the real gun is now, boss? Did someone local who'd only had one reason for having it at all make a better job of chucking it right into the sea, or has it been stashed away by someone who knows they might want to use it again?'

She could sense Strang's irritation as he said, 'Well, I'm sure that's a good question, Livvy, but not one we're likely to solve by speculating. Oh, there's Alex coming now.'

He got out of the car to hail him, leaving her sitting in the car. The threatened rain was just starting, quite gentle at the moment, but from long experience Murray reckoned it wouldn't stay that way. Not only that, she could see that there was a 'Closed' notice on the café – bit of a downer, that. She'd fancied the look of the lunches there, even if there was a risk that Mairead Wilson might be inclined to put poison in the mac and cheese.

Strang got back in and as Ritchie climbed into the back seat, she said, 'How did the swotting go last night?'

'Oh, the usual. Went back over what I'd done last time and hardly any of it had stuck.'

It made her feel much more sympathetic. 'And it was boring enough the first time through, right?'

'Absolutely.'

Strang said, 'Livvy, while Alex briefs me, go up to Anna Bruce's again and see if she's prepared to talk to us. She's likely to be more prepared to help than Shona was.'

It was raining much more heavily now. Not only that, having been driven right down to the car park, she'd have to climb the hill up to the top level and then up the track to the house. Gritting her teeth, she said, 'Sure, boss,' and put up the hood of her jacket as she stepped out.

When she reached the bottom of the track, she could see that Anna's car wasn't there so there likely wasn't much point in pursuing her mission. But she'd better check – the car might have been taken away for an MOT or something. She went on up to the door.

There was no answer to her knock, but again, she peered in the windows. It all looked just as it had earlier, even to the carrots still lying on the kitchen surface, looking a bit dried out now.

That was definitely odd. She frowned, then with the rain starting to work itself up into a proper downpour, she hurried back to the car.

Alex, she noted, was now sitting in the passenger seat.

'What was really interesting about the interview with the parents was their ambivalence about almost everything,' DC Ritchie said.

'Ambivalence?' DCI Strang said. The word interested him; Ritchie had shown all along that he had good antennae.

'I was prepared for stark hostility. Parents whose children are charged with crime seldom want to have anything to do with the police, but the Mathesons approached us. Craig Lothian's mum was a bit more typical – has a particularly choice vocabulary.'

'I was certainly surprised when you said parents had been lined up. So it has to be a sense of injustice, right?'

'Got it in one. They're happy to cooperate to persuade us to accept that Matheson was a hapless innocent who was trapped into doing this totally uncharacteristic thing by the wicked Brodie Campbell.'

'And don't tell me – they won't point a finger at anyone who might have taken the law into their own hands.'

'You're on a roll. Very much in line with what Livvy's Shona said, they're positively anti getting any justice for Campbell – Jenny Matheson's attitude was that killing was too good for him. She was the one who did the talking – father restricted himself to muttering, "Mphm, that's right enough," whenever she stopped for breath.

'Much of it we knew already from Fergus but when he phoned his mother, he told her a bit more about Campbell's network. Apparently when what she described as "cannon fodder" was required, they'd get him to find someone around here to take on the job. The money was always good but there was a risk they'd disappear into the underworld and never reappear until something went wrong and they turned up in court – yes, you're ahead of me again, aren't you?'

'Callan McIver,' Strang said grimly. The words 'Anna Bruce' were on the tip of his tongue but he couldn't say them.

Ritchie was going on, 'You remember the girlfriend testified in the murder trial? He told her he'd done a favour for a friend, but he didn't name names. Jenny Matheson mentioned him as one of the ones who'd been thought to have escaped, with a good cooking job in Glasgow, but he'd got sucked back in. It was quite clear that she'd been terrified this would happen to Fergus, and I sensed she had some reason for that so I asked if he'd ever lived away from home.

'She gasped, and then said very hastily that he'd only been away for a wee while but he'd found he hadn't liked it. She started saying he'd never done anything wrong, and the husband said sharply, "Mind your tongue," which was interesting. She went bright red and stopped.'

'Anything come up on his record after he was arrested?'

'Not really. Brought in for questioning about a robbery but never charged, a clean sheet afterwards – gave him a scare, possibly, so he scuttled back home.

'Things were getting a bit sticky, so remembering Shona

had said Mairead Wilson was pretty much the local social worker, I thought it might lighten the atmosphere if I asked if she'd been able to help with the recurring problem. It didn't work; if anything the temperature dropped another couple of degrees. Jenny said something very non-committal and Matheson got up and said he thought they'd given us enough of their time and maybe I'd like to do something about the situation that could prove helpful to their basically innocent, if unfortunately misguided, son.'

Strang said, 'Really? Mairead is at the top of my list for interviews this morning but I might speak to Anna Bruce first to see if she can fill in any of those gaps. What's your position now? Have you other interviews to do?'

Ritchie shook his head. 'Having virtually been spat at by Craig Lothian's mother when I knocked on her door, I don't think there's much more I can do here. There's nothing new apart from the "cannon fodder" angle and it hasn't done anything to help us draw a bead on this network they're on about, which was my brief. I've got the names of the drivers that Matheson knew who drink in Torridon so I'll speak to them then head back south.'

Murray, a hooded figure in the pelting rain, appeared and opened the back door, making ineffectual brushing movements to remove the worst of the wet before she climbed in and put down her hood.

'No luck, boss. She must have been back since yesterday because her car isn't there now, but I peered in the window again and there's peeled carrots on a worktop that were lying there when I went before – looking a bit dried out now.'

Strang stiffened. 'I don't like the sound of that,' he said, and was aware that his colleagues were looking at him in surprise, but he could hardly spell it out. 'I wonder if Mairead Wilson might know where she is. Look, Alex, would you have time to come with us to this interview? It might be useful to you anyway, and if I had to go off to follow up a lead, you and Livvy could just carry on.'

'Of course,' Ritchie said, though he was still looking puzzled.

Murray was not quite as puzzled as Ritchie; at that interview with Anna, she'd realised that Strang been warning her of some sort of risk in a coded way that Murray couldn't understand. Now he seemed to her to be thinking that the situation had become dangerous, whatever that might mean. *Watch this space*, she thought, as they hurried through the rain across to the café.

It had been a good morning and now Mairead was feeling better. She'd given herself a good talking-to: *You're not stupid, you're not helpless, you run a successful business and as long as you think straight, you'll be all right.*

With a new sense of purpose, she had made a lemon drizzle and was just taking a pair of chocolate sponges out of the oven when the police knocked on the café door. Their visit was unwelcome but she hadn't been naive enough to think that excruciatingly embarrassing experience with Sergeant Kirk would be the last she'd see of them. At least he wasn't among the three officers waiting outside; three seemed a lot, though. A bit unnerving.

She recognised the woman who had come with

Sergeant Kirk then; she was identifying herself again, and introducing DCI Strang and DC Ritchie.

It was the chief inspector who stepped forward and said, 'Mrs Wilson, do you know Anna Bruce?'

That was unexpected. 'Yes of course,' she said. 'She does cakes for the café. For some reason she didn't do her usual delivery this morning.'

'Do you know where she is?'

'No, I'm afraid not.'

'Do you have her phone number?'

Mairead walked across to the till and offered him a notebook, open at a short list headed 'Staff details'. He took out his phone and dialled immediately.

After a moment, he put it back in his pocket. 'Unobtainable. Is there anyone else who might know where she is?'

'She didn't know many people. Shona Macintyre's the only one I know of.'

'That's at the smokehouse we spoke about, sir,' the woman said. 'The Applecross road, just past Logan Fisheries.'

He said, 'Right. I'll go up there. You two carry on.'

Then the chief inspector left, leaving the other two officers looking, Mairead thought, a bit taken aback.

In the moment of awkwardness after the door shut behind him, she said, 'Would you like a cup of coffee?' Politeness might bring its own reward and the woman certainly jumped at the offer.

They sat down at one of the tables and she brought over the mugs for them as well as one for herself, along with a plate of shortbread, and sat down.

‘So what did you want to ask me, then?’ she said.

As she spoke, there was a sort of jolt, short and sharp, a deep rumble that sounded like a heavy lorry passing, and everything started shaking. The crockery on the table slithered and rattled, a plate shook itself off a shelf and smashed on the floor and the woman jumped up with a scream of fright.

‘What the hell is happening?’ she said.

As the room stabilised again, Mairead said, ‘It’s all right. It was just an earthquake. They happen sometimes.’

CHAPTER SEVENTEEN

Jago Innes was on his knees sweeping up a broken bowl that had worked its way across a shelf to fall on the floor when the earthquake happened. There hadn't been one of those for ages; the last time the shock had been more noticeable and there'd been a power cut, but this time they were probably further from the epicentre or something since Mother Nature seemed to have been satisfied with just smashing the odd bowl.

He was tipping the debris into the bin when Zoe Cooper drove up, so fast that loose stones at the edge of the road sprayed up. and clearly in a furious temper. He stood back to let her storm into the house.

'You won't believe this! I'm heading out to the main road, right? Suddenly – wham! This car ahead stops dead and this enormous rock crashes onto the road. He was bloody lucky not to be pulverised. Could have been me if I'd been twenty seconds earlier. Then all these other big stones kept falling.'

'I know that rock,' Jago said. 'It looked unbalanced but with it being there for thousands of years I thought it was good for a few more. Is the road blocked?'

'Is the road blocked, he says! Oh yes, *sweetheart*, it's blocked all right. I don't know what the hell happened—'

'An earthquake.'

She stared at him. 'Don't be silly. I didn't notice anything.'

'You wouldn't, in the car. Just a wee one – might make the news on STV or a headline in the *Press and Journal* on a slow news day – though if Ardelour's cut off from the great world it might make the *BBC News at Six* as a novelty item.'

Zoe sank down on a bench. 'I must have been crazy, coming to somewhere like this. How soon will they clear it?'

Jago smiled in a way certain to infuriate her. 'As a rough guide, after the Rest and Be Thankful pass was blocked by a landslip, it took five weeks. And that was a main road.'

He was surprised at her stricken look. 'But I can't get trapped here! How can we make them clear it as a matter of urgency?'

'If you can manage, stand for the Scottish Parliament – you'd have a landslide victory!'

He was pleased with his joke. She wasn't. 'I must get out,' she said.

'Of course – the meeting.'

It was a moment before she said, 'That's right. Of course – the meeting. I'll – I'll need to call them.'

The mobile home was no place for a private phone conversation and she stood up, saying, 'I'm just going out again.'

'More odds and ends?' he said, but she only hurried to her car, ducking her head in the rain.

She was definitely scared, which made two of them. She'd obviously been planning to escape and now she couldn't. She'd had a plan that hadn't worked and any new plan would be bad news for someone else. Most likely him.

What she couldn't do now was bring in any backup – but then, neither could he. They were on their own.

Anyway, he'd better phone Joe and tell him what had happened.

Strang was on his way up the Applecross road when he felt the car give a strange sort of shudder. He frowned, then noticed a few small rocks tumbling down the side of the hill into the ditch on his left. He'd been in the north-west a while ago when there'd been a small earthquake – they weren't that uncommon in the proximity of the Great Glen, a geological fault caused by two tectonic plates that were slowly moving against each other. Fortunately, the scale of the shock was never enough to do much more damage than toppling the odd chimney pot, but it would give Livvy a fright – she'd probably take it as further evidence of the general malevolence of nature.

The smokehouse was easy to find, and open today. When he rang the bell for service, a woman hurried over from the house behind.

Remembering what Murray had said about her attitude to the police, he flashed his warrant card and went swiftly on to ask if she knew where Anna Bruce was.

She was wary, as if ready to protect her friend, but she

admitted she'd left a message that hadn't been answered and this morning when she tried again the number wasn't recognised.

'She hadn't said she was planning to be away, or anything?'

'No. Might have told Mairead, perhaps—'

'I'm afraid not. Of course, there's no reason why she should have,' Strang said, thanked her and left.

He sat in the car, thinking about it. The woman could well have gone off on holiday or something, but given the connections that seemed to be drawing Anna closer and closer to the Campbell network, he was more than nervous. He'd sensed she was casual about her personal safety; a place like this could readily lull you into a false sense of security. The NCA were mad to have let her come here, where she couldn't just vanish without occasioning comment.

And now she'd disappeared. He didn't know what to do; he wasn't supposed to know who she was and the security around witness protection was designed to be impregnable. He'd heard of a colleague trying to find out if someone he suspected of a serious crime was in the programme and he'd had to jump through so many hoops that the suspect was long gone before he could do any sort of proper investigation.

Face facts: he didn't actually *know* that Anna Bruce was Janet MacNeish. He was quite sure he had recognised her voice and he was also quite sure that she'd realised that he knew, and that she'd understood the warning he'd given her, but at no point had she admitted she was under witness protection. If he phoned the NCA and asked if they knew where Janet/Susanna was, they'd deny all knowledge.

He couldn't do nothing. There was strengthening evidence that the organisation the task force had sent Ritchie to investigate was operating here, and Anna was someone who could well have a price on her head. He would need to take it upstairs and enlist the DCS to use her influence in the appropriate circles.

JB wouldn't be at all happy, but the sooner he dealt with it, the better. He'd have to return to Ardelour to collect Murray before he went back to Gairloch and released Ritchie to do his interviews in Torridon.

Strang drove back down the road, so preoccupied that when he came round a corner just before the turn-off into Ardelour, he had to do an emergency stop. The single-lane road was blocked by a queue of three cars. His immediate thought was that there had been an accident and he jumped out to see what needed to be done.

Not a lot, he discovered. When he reached the junction, he found that there were another two cars further into the narrow passage that led onto the peninsula, and beyond them was an enormous rock and a pile of rubble, blocking the road completely.

As the senior officer, it was up to Murray to direct the interview, once she'd swallowed the last crumb of Mairead's melt-in-the-mouth shortbread, but she wasn't sure what Strang had meant when he said he wanted a look at Mairead Wilson. All she could think of was to go through the woman's movements on the day leading up to Campbell's murder – not exactly inspired, and there might even have been a formal statement taken already that she hadn't seen.

When she glanced at Ritchie, it was obvious that he was fully primed with a question and he jumped in immediately.

'Mrs Wilson, I've been speaking to your friends Mr and Mrs Matheson. I got the impression that there was some tension between you – was I right?'

Mairead's jaw dropped, and Murray felt her own sag slightly. It was a clearly a killer question; her impression of Ritchie had been that he was a bit too soft and proper, but he hadn't even been polite enough to wait for a nod from her before he asked it.

Mairead gave an uncertain laugh. 'Oh – did Jenny sound like that? Well, with the problems with her son she's been a bit on edge. She did seem a little short with me on the phone today but we've been friends a long time. I'm sure she'll get over it.'

Murray stepped in. 'We understand you've been a sort of social worker for the youngsters here?' She sensed that Ritchie wasn't entirely pleased, but too bad.

Mairead's face flushed and she said, 'I don't know who told you that. I haven't done any more than anyone else would.'

'Did you help Fergus Matheson when he got into some trouble before?' That was Ritchie again, and this time it was Murray's turn to be irritated; she'd been ready with a follow-up question herself.

Mairead was starting to look very stressed. 'Of course not. I've never done anything, except let his mother know she could always talk to me.'

'So did she tell you what sort of trouble he was in – ask

for your advice, maybe?' Ritchie said.

Mairead pulled herself together almost visibly, shoulders straightening, hands clenching in her lap. 'I don't know what you mean. No, she didn't.'

Murray seized the chance to put in a question she'd been wanting to ask ever since she'd talked to Shona. 'And did you help Callan McIver to escape to be a chef in Glasgow, to get him out of this place where so many young men seem to go wrong?'

The unexpected result was that Mairead burst into tears. She stood up, her chest heaving, and said, 'I'm sorry, if you're going to go on with this sort of aggression, I'm going to have to take a few minutes. I haven't been well, you know.' She hurried to the door leading into the house.

The two detectives looked at each other in some dismay. There was a slight edge to Murray's voice as she said, 'Oh dear. We didn't manage that very well, did we?'

'I'm sorry,' Ritchie said. 'Pity we didn't have time to work it out beforehand. I'm not used to two-handed interviews – I'm usually on my own.'

'Yes, I can see that,' Murray said tartly. 'I suppose we usually are, but I've worked for a long time on interviews with the boss and you need quite a lot of coordination to do it well. He's brilliant at that.'

'Yes, I've done a couple with him and he was really good at managing it.'

The implication being that Murray wasn't. She had a job to do, though; gritting her teeth, she said, 'Before Mairead comes back, was there anything more you picked up from the Mathesons that you want to ask about? The line I was taking came from what Shona Macintyre had said.'

'Yes,' he said. 'Look, I really am sorry. The Mathesons had mentioned the kind of thing Campbell was involved in, I wanted to put pressure on Mrs Wilson and I suppose I did jump her, to give her no time for a considered response. My bosses sent me up here to get a line on the organisation running the show and I don't want to go back empty-handed. But I'll take my direction from you—'

The door to the house opened and a man appeared – John Wilson. Murray had met him, of course, and muttered, 'Her husband,' to Ritchie.

He said, without preamble, 'You have upset my wife so that she is simply too distressed to speak to you. I suggest you make another appointment and behave in a more civilised way or we will be making a complaint.'

Murray made an embarrassed apology and they left, feeling like naughty schoolchildren. It was raining heavily again, which made it all even more depressing.

'Oh God, what will the boss say?' she said.

Her phone rang. She looked at it, and for a second contemplated pretending they were out of range.

Only for a second. 'Yes, boss?' she said hollowly. Then, 'You're kidding me, right?'

John Wilson ran upstairs to the sitting room. 'I've got rid of them,' he said to Mairead, who was sitting on the sofa, pale and tear-stained, with her head in her hands. 'You were lucky you caught me – I only came out of the studio to go to the loo. Like to tell me what that was about?'

She was looking gutted, he thought, and, well, scared, really, but the law taking an interest was enough to scare anyone. She didn't look up as she said, 'No, not really.'

'Thought you'd say that. Just remember you owe me.'

She looked up. 'My handbag's on the hall table. Take what you want.'

'It's not money I'm talking about. I want you to back up what I say next time they're questioning me – they're trying to frame me, you know. There's things you could say to get me off the hook.'

'I doubt it. Don't try to get me involved.'

'Cow!' he snarled with venom. 'Just don't ask for any more favours.'

She didn't reply. He stormed downstairs and saw her handbag on the hall table – well, she'd mentioned cash so he might as well take it. He usually did, when she was unwise enough to leave it there. He slammed the door behind him on his way to the studio.

Mairead sat on, her fingers pressed to her temples. It was all catching up with her; she'd never thought it would. Reality was ugly and not thinking had become an addiction that had left her blind to what was just plain obvious.

In her secure little world, she hadn't recognised the risks. Now for her own protection she would have to do what she should have done before.

As she heard the door shut behind him, Mairead stood up and took a deep breath. She went to her office and opened the safe to fetch the wall cupboard key.

She unlocked it and took out what it contained: a double-barrelled shotgun with its barrel sawn down, wrapped in a drape.

She laid it on the desk then went to her bedroom to fetch a heavy coat to cover it and carried it downstairs.

The rain was sheeting down as she went to the car parked in the street and backed it up the alleyway at the side, then brought out the bundle and stowed it in the boot.

As she drove off she was cursing herself that she'd put off doing this until now.

Detective Chief Superintendent Jane Borthwick was not just unhappy, she was incredulous. 'An earthquake? For heaven's sake, Kelso, whatever is going on in that place?'

And that was before he told her about Susanna Bruce. When he did, there was a silence, then she said, 'She may be in actual danger?'

'Obviously I don't know. But the group behind the freight raids that have resulted in people being killed certainly wouldn't scruple.'

'Right. Leave it with me and I'll do my best. Have you anything to report that could be described as progress?'

'I did discover there's a private detective involved.' He briefed her on the Zoe Cooper interview and she was intrigued.

'From what you say, she won't share information without payment, which we obviously can't afford. But can we assume she's straight?'

'Jury's out, quite honestly. The CEO at North West Fisheries confirmed her employment by the consortium, and I'm aiming to speak to him directly. I've been promised the techies' report on Campbell's mobile and PC from his office today so that may tell us something.'

'Well, let's hope it does. At least the two arrests took the heat off the van raid fatality inquiry, but of course that's being chalked up to Inverness. We can only hope this landslip thing won't rekindle media interest.'

You and me both, Strang thought grimly. He was feeling low as she rang off. He'd instructed Livvy to fix up a bed for Alex and he'd rung Alex's hotel to explain the situation. That had been no problem, and much as he mocked Livvy's obsession with the Airbnb's inadequacies, he had to admit the thought of a decent breakfast tomorrow was appealing. And he'd managed to source a toothbrush and a disposable razor in the local petrol station, so it really wasn't all bad.

He glanced at his watch. With luck, he'd be in time to catch the CEO guy before he clocked out.

When Murray and Ritchie arrived at the Airbnb, their hostess was nowhere to be seen.

'It's kinda weird,' Murray said. 'She never appears, but the beds get made and the breakfast, such as it is, gets put out in the morning.'

Ritchie was looking round with some interest. 'My great-granny's house looked like this until my gran inherited and changed everything to Habitat and IKEA. I'm not sure which was worse.'

Murray had never known her great-granny but she knew for sure that no house like this would ever have featured in her family's past, which confirmed all her prejudices against Alex.

'She's never seen Kelso so you could just pretend to be him, if you don't mind sleeping in his sheets.'

Ritchie grinned. 'He seemed pretty clean to me. So what now?'

'I'll show you the room and the bathrooms – no showers,

bizarrely. We'll need space to work and the breakfast room should do.'

Ritchie went to peer in. 'Ideal. If we're around we might catch a glimpse of this mysterious invisible hostess. Any chance she could rustle up supper for us later?'

'She's not the rustling-up sort. And if we're cut off for any length of time, food's going to be a problem. Everything seems to arrive in deliveries from Tesco.'

He pulled a face. 'Bloody hell! That's all we need. Anyway, I suppose we'd better confess to the boss about Mairead Wilson.'

'Mmm,' Murray said. She had previous for not sharing every little problem with Strang if she could avoid it; she hadn't always got away with it and sometimes it had been a disaster, but often enough it had worked. 'Look, it's stopped raining. Let's walk down to the shore and see what's happening, then I can give him a sitrep when I phone.'

The smile he gave her showed he wasn't fooled. 'Why not?' he said blandly. She reluctantly had to admit he had a nice smile.

The rain had stopped and as they walked, Murray said, 'What do you think will happen? If it was a hit job, getting cut off has to be a good thing – if they were thinking of coming to take someone else out there's no way they could do it now. But this place is absolutely spooking me.'

He said very seriously, 'I'm with you there – feels like a volcano's ready to blow. And that professional job – could the professional in question actually be an Ardelour native, do you think? Given what we know of them, it's entirely possible.'

She was horrified. 'You mean we could all be shut up with an assassin here? Now you say that, I could see Zoe Cooper doing it without turning a hair, and Jago Innes too, with his jailbird friends, and there's plenty of shotguns in the general population. Sawn off, though? A hot mess, isn't it?'

Reaching the shore, they could see there were more people around than usual, coming and going from the little shop.

'Let's go in and see,' Murray said. 'Maybe even grab up a couple of bridies – we might be glad of those later.'

The young woman behind the counter was looking frazzled as she dealt with the lengthy queue. The shelves were denuded already; food-hoarding had apparently swung straight into action and there wasn't a bridie, a Scotch pie or a sausage roll to be seen.

As Murray looked round in dismay, a woman tapped her on the shoulder.

'You're with the polis, aren't you? What are you doing about this? They're nearly out of everything already – my bairns are wanting their tea and my delivery never came.'

Another couple of women lined up behind with mutters of, 'Aye, that's right.'

'I'm sure everything possible will be being done.' Murray was aware of sounding defensive, but after all there wasn't a lot she could do.

Ritchie stepped forward and smiled at the woman. 'It's quite something, this, isn't it? I don't know what they're doing out there but I guess they'll be able to bring things in by boat before we all starve!'

To Murray's intense annoyance, the woman responded

with a reluctant smile of her own. 'Och, I suppose they'll be all right with beans on toast – there's some in the house. But they'll need to get supplies here tomorrow so we can do our messages, mind!'

They left the shop trying to make it look as if it wasn't a disorderly retreat.

'I'd better phone the boss now,' Murray said glumly. 'It won't be long before we'll have social disorder as well as everything else.'

Equally glumly, Ritchie agreed.

As they turned to head back to the Airbnb, Murray stopped, staring down at the harbour.

'Look! There's that seaplane I told you about!' she exclaimed. 'I wonder what it's doing there?'

And there indeed it was, sitting at a mooring a little way out, neat and elegant in its grey and blue livery. Ritchie stared at it.

'I don't suppose we have any excuse to go and check it out, but we should memorise the tail number – can you read it from here?'

It was too far away, but Murray whipped out her phone and took a snap. 'Maybe they'll be able to do something clever with that and it might give the boss something to think about apart from our failings.'

Andrew Erskine, the CEO of North West Fisheries, was very well-spoken with that trace of the Highland accent that made Strang think of peat smoke whenever he heard it, and sympathetic too. 'I don't envy you your task, Chief Inspector,' he said.

'I'm not thrilled about it myself,' Strang said. 'You've

been most helpful in confirming Zoe Cooper is employed by your group. She seems very professional but I wanted to ask your opinion of her.'

'Oh, professional, absolutely. Her charges are high, but she does deliver. She's saved us a fair bit, contriving to tip us off to switch times and routes when a raid is rumoured and even on a couple of occasions getting us information to pass to your lot that led to arrests – oh, small fry, admittedly, but you're still talking big money.'

That all sounded very positive. 'Where does she get these tips from?'

Erskine laughed. 'Puts her finger to her nose and winks, but says it's a trade secret. I know she works in a couple of bars and a café. I have to say I've sometimes wondered . . .'

For the first time Strang sensed a reservation. 'Go on.'

'We've had a couple of raids she didn't predict, but you can't win them all. It's occurred to me just once or twice that she gets credit when someone's rescheduled and the load's arrived at its destination all right, but there's no proof anything was actually being planned. That's possibly nonsense, though. I haven't heard anyone else speculating.'

'It's an interesting thought,' Strang said slowly. 'Just one more thing – you called Ms Cooper to a meeting last Friday afternoon, yes? She wouldn't say what it was about, but would you be prepared to tell me?'

'Certainly. I didn't call her – she instigated it. I didn't know why; she arrived latish but only wanted to know details about next month's schedules that we could easily have had emailed to her. It seemed odd at the time.'

As they rang off with mutual expressions of goodwill, the virtual gear system in Strang's brain started clicking and whirring. She might well have been bigging up her reputation with fake news about phoney raids, but the 'small fry' – had they been offered up as human sacrifices? Erskine had said a couple of raids succeeded; she would be in a position to provide the raiders with valuable information – say, about the place where a lorry would be likely to park up for the night, where they were vulnerable.

She was right at the centre, wasn't she? He could almost feel the hairs at the back of his neck standing up.

He needed to grill Cooper again – but of course, he couldn't. He'd have to set Murray on to it, and take Ritchie along with her.

He picked up the phone again to give the instructions.

Mairead Wilson drove through the town towards the main road with shaking hands. She needed to get well away from Ardelour; she'd seen the police searching and checking everywhere around.

West, she decided; the roads were quieter there – and thinking about it, she remembered the loch that ran alongside the road, ten, maybe twelve miles away. A moment when there was no traffic around, one splash, and afterwards she'd be safe, as long as she didn't make a fool of herself as she had this afternoon.

But there ahead was a car, blocking the road. A man in a yellow jacket got out and came over as she drew up. She could see now there were yellow lights flashing beyond the narrow neck of road that led to the rest of the world.

'It's blocked,' he said. 'Rockfall – they're trying to do something on the other side. No one can get through. All right?'

'Right,' she said, numbly.

She reversed until she reached a farm track, turned and drove home. The rain had gone off now and the shore seemed busier than usual, but she backed the car up the alley again and after a quick look round took the bundle in, up the stairs to the office, then back to the cupboard. There was no alternative.

She locked the door. But she hardly knew what she was doing; she felt so dizzy, she had to collapse onto her office chair. This whole thing was a living nightmare – a truly vicious punishment for past sins, perhaps. She had no right to complain.

And now the flashing lights were starting – the vivid, jagged lightning shooting around. She knew what that meant, and if she didn't go for the medication now and go to bed, the headache would cripple her tomorrow, just when she needed her wits about her.

CHAPTER EIGHTEEN

Having heard about the earthquake on the news as she drove back from court, Cat Fleming had phoned, just a hint of panic in her voice.

'Oh, so good to hear you! You really can't go anywhere without some drama happening, can you?' she said lightly. 'It would have been a real downer to have had a squished fiancé.'

She might be joking, but Kelso Strang could tell that the memory of that previous case was still very near the surface.

'It was the merest wobble,' he assured her. 'In the car I didn't really feel it – they're quite common all around here.'

'Oh, that's right,' she said, sounding more cheerful. 'I'd a friend who came from Comrie and she said it's known as "the shaky toun". But you're all right?'

'Well, apart from being stuck in Gairloch with the road into Ardelour blocked. I'm sleeping in Alex Ritchie's hotel and he's going to have my room in the miserable Airbnb – I've definitely got the better deal.'

'How funny! So he'll be having to do the paso doble with Livvy tomorrow – how do they get on?'

'Livvy's bristling like an irritated kitten because she suspects he's graduate entry and she's looking for evidence that he's got airs and graces. But he's a nice guy and it will do them good to get to know each other.'

'Ooh! Would he do for her, do you think? Either of them have a partner?'

'Really, Cat! I wouldn't know. That's a real bridezilla attitude – trying to fix people up.'

Cat laughed. 'Anyway, how's it all going?'

'Don't! To be honest, I haven't the slightest idea. There are so many tangled threads it might take half an hour to explain. How was court today?'

'Oh, same old, same old. Actually I'm just going out for supper with two of the girls, since I've been abandoned by my man.'

'That's good,' he said. 'I won't keep you then, darling. Love you. We'll speak tomorrow.'

Kelso was pleased to know she wouldn't be sitting alone at home, but he'd rather hoped to chat things through with her; she had a talent for highlighting things he'd overlooked that he could use at this moment.

There was no chair in the tiny hotel bedroom and he was sitting propped up on the bed, in the vest and boxer shorts that would have to do as nightwear. He'd had a drink and a fairly decent burger in the bar-restaurant, which put him one up on Livvy and Alex, who after a pint in the little pub had apparently been rationed to one microwaved sausage roll each, since supplies were short already. He consoled himself with the thought that the Ardelour situation was Inverness's problem, not his, but it was driving him crazy to be cooped up here and forced to rely on proxies.

It sounded as if their interview with Mairead Wilson had been useless, with her retreating claiming to be ill, and they'd looked for Zoe Cooper without success. And the only breakthrough he could envisage might come once they did their technical stuff on Campbell's media.

He gave a heavy sigh. He had packed a book in his holdall, the new William Boyd, which Alex was probably now enjoying, but it left him with nothing to prevent a debilitating engagement with cogs and wheels.

He wasn't short of things to think about – Zoe Cooper, in particular. Erskine clearly had his doubts about her, as any normal person would on sight, and playing both ends to the middle was becoming a familiar theme. He reckoned Erskine was being used to some extent, but because she was useful to them, he'd ignored his suspicions.

He thought back to the pattern of the interview: she'd produced her calling card, she'd done an impressively clear analysis of the most obvious suspects – and she'd definitely pointed her finger at her partner, Jago Innes, in much the same way as he had pointed his at her. For the same reason – to distract the questioners?

He wasn't sure of what her definition of 'a friendship with benefits' might mean – sex, one would assume, but there was precious little evidence of what might be called friendship. It sounded as if she might well be up to something, but he wasn't yet convinced that the 'something' had anything to do with Campbell's murder – she seemed to barely know him.

The others on her list of suspects, along with disgruntled punters, were the Wilsons, neither of whom he had interviewed as yet. What he'd been told about Mairead at least had been very favourable – little friend of all the world, it seemed – and she'd never made it to the top of the suspect list.

What Zoe had said chimed with that. 'Keeper of secrets', she'd said. She was devoted to her young friends – beyond upset and angry, after the arrests. She hated, was even a bit scared of, Brodie Campbell. She'd gone out that Friday afternoon and been ill and in a distressed state when she came home. It was most unfortunate that he hadn't had the chance to form a personal impression – and that Mairead seemed to enjoy quite a bit of useful ill health.

But he suddenly realised that there was a fascinating scenario being laid out right there in front of him. He'd seen the community uniting to protect Campbell's killer; the woman who 'mothered' the lads who'd been led astray, who, according to Zoe, had 'put up a barricade round them', might well be prepared to act to save them from the man she both hated and feared, in any way she could. And she'd left the café that Friday afternoon – where had she been?

Zoe's artless account of Mairead's behaviour had been . . . Err – artless? *Zoe Cooper*? Was it possible that he, like Andrew Erskine, was being played by a clever and amoral woman? And where was that thought going to lead him? In fact, he was almost there already. The cogs and wheels were whirring faster and faster.

Kelso had already requested that the coastguards take him round to Ardelour; they'd made no promises when his turn would come since engineers taking stock of the roadblock situation on the other side had priority, and there had already been an SOS from the shop for basic supplies.

It was all intensely frustrating. The promised technical reports still hadn't come in – typical, and until one of these things happened, there was nothing he could do.

And there was the endless niggling worry about what had happened to Anna Bruce.

Livvy Murray had scored a bottle of wine in the pub to take back to the Airbnb. It was labelled 'South African Red Wine'; as she waved it triumphantly at Alex Ritchie, she thought he looked less than wildly enthusiastic.

She was instantly defensive. 'If it's too basic for you, you don't need to have any. Oddly enough, they were flat out of vintage Burgundy.' She stalked ahead of him out of the pub.

He followed her meekly, taking the bottle from her and looking at it. 'Nothing wrong with a standard bottle of plonk. As a matter of fact, I don't even like the big heavyweight Burgundies.'

Still ploughing ahead, she said over her shoulder, 'You see, that's the difference between us. I don't even know what "big heavyweight Burgundies" taste like.'

Alex didn't reply. They walked on in silence until they reached the house. It was in darkness, apart from a couple of lit rooms towards the back, and she let them both in with the overnight key, walked into the breakfast room and went over to the sideboard, where there were glasses, bowls and plates ready to be set out for the morning.

'No wine glasses, sorry,' Livvy said. 'You'll have to make do with a tumbler – but then I expect you'll say that's all it's worth.'

Alex stopped in the act of unscrewing the top. 'Livvy, what have I done to piss you off?'

She gave a false laugh. 'Don't be daft. I'm fine.'

He opened the bottle, poured some into a tumbler for her, set it on the table then took one himself and sat down, waiting for her to join him. Feeling uncomfortable now, she hesitated, then sat down and took a swig.

'Look, I think you've got the wrong impression of me,' he said. 'I didn't come from a posh family, you know; my dad's family were quite well-off but he fell out with them when he went off to join a band that was frankly rubbish and then he didn't settle much to anything. My mum was a primary school teacher who was on my case from day one so I didn't go the same way, and yes, I went to uni, and got a job in finance, so that's how I got familiar with good wine – paid for with my own money, may I say. I was overworked, exhausted and stressed almost literally out of my mind, and with the utter pointlessness of that kind of life it seemed hardly worth living. It was my mum who sorted me out and pointed me at the police force, where as you know all too well we are daily overworked, exhausted and stressed, not to mention physically endangered too, but it's worthwhile and I love it. Right – that's my show-and-tell. How about you?'

He sat back in his chair, looking at her, and Livvy could feel her face go red. 'Sorry,' she said stiffly. 'I was right out of order.'

'No apology needed. I'd just like to know where you're coming from, if you're prepared to tell me. Tell me for a start about your name – Olivia, right?'

She never talked about it, but she'd embarrassed herself enough by being churlish already. 'Yeah, that's right. I never use it, though.'

'It's a nice name – classy, if you're into that sort of thing.'

'Which I'm not. And it isn't – not when it's because of Olivia Newton-John.'

'Your mum liked her?'

'An avid fan, for God's sake.' She saw he was trying not to laugh, but then she started to laugh herself, and they were both laughing and after that for some odd reason – the crude, rough wine that was pretty heavyweight itself, perhaps – she started to tell him things she'd never told anyone else: about her intensely critical mother, who had been a mean drunk and had instilled in Livvy a sense of her own inadequacy that made her constantly look for, and measure herself against, any competition and then fail.

When at last she ran down, she felt embarrassed all over again. 'Sorry,' she muttered.

'For a detective sergeant, you do apologise a lot,' he said. 'Seems to me you're doing pretty well. Kelso thinks so too, obviously.'

The change of subject was welcome. 'He's a great boss. Scared me silly last time out.'

'I heard it was horrific. What's the fiancé like? Do you know her?'

'Blonde, legs up to her armpits, very bright, seems quite nice. They're getting married in the summer.' She hoped she didn't sound as if it ever might have mattered to her, which it didn't by now.

'That's good. So, Sarge, what's tomorrow?'

Livvy pulled a face. 'Who knows? Try Cooper first thing, I reckon, approach Mairead Wilson again and pray that the boss gets an early boat from Gairloch.'

'A hot mess, as I think you said earlier. It's not late, but I think we're going to have a heavy day. Better get our beauty sleep.'

Livvy led the way upstairs, showed him the bedroom and the nearest bathroom. She hesitated on the landing, then said, 'Thanks. A good evening.'

Alex grinned at her. 'Not a lot wrong with basic plonk, is there?'

When she got to bed, Livvy didn't sleep immediately. The chip on her shoulder had made a fool of her yet again and he'd rescued her very generously. It would improve their working relationship, though she actually couldn't see it going any further than that – not least because he probably had a nicely brought up, blonde, leggy girlfriend just like Cat Fleming waiting for him in Glasgow.

The good thing about taking her migraine tablets was that they made Mairead sleepy. But they also gave her bad dreams, populated by ill-defined monsters and impossible tasks, that left her gasping and choking – struggling . . .

She came awake, her mouth stuffed with something so she couldn't swallow and could barely breathe. She had no idea what time it was but in the semi-darkness, she could make out a figure bending over her, could smell a familiar musky perfume.

'Don't scream,' Zoe Cooper's voice said sharply. 'There's no one here anyway – he's at the pub. But there's no saying how long it'll be before the beer runs out. Let's get on with this – all right?'

She nodded, and Zoe switched on the bedside lamp. Her dark eyes were glinting and her face itself seemed almost alight with excitement.

'Sit up,' she said.

As Mairead obediently sat up, her eye went to a knife, the Japanese steel slicing knife from her own kitchen, lying on the bed beside her, and she froze.

Zoe laughed. 'Oh Mairead, don't worry, I'm not going to use it. Unless I have to, of course – dead bodies can be an awful nuisance. I just want to talk to you. All right?'

Mairead nodded again, and Zoe's hand, with its long blue nails, reached into her mouth to pull out the wads of paper handkerchiefs. It was some relief, though her throat and mouth were so dry that that her tongue stuck to her palate.

Zoe handed her the glass of water from her bedside and as Mairead drank it thankfully, she explained.

'I'm now going to take you through to the office and you're going to write a letter confessing to the murder of Brodie Campbell. You will say that he was responsible for the death of your little protégé Callan McIver as well as others he had drawn into crime. You will say that you have no regrets, that he was a force for evil. Get up. We're going to do it now.'

Mairead followed her across the landing. Emboldened by the fact that the knife had been left on the bed, she said, 'I didn't. You did it, and I know you found the gun when you were snooping – you do like to know things, don't you? But how did you get into the cupboard?'

Zoe's eyes went to the cupboard. 'I don't know where you got it but I can't think why you were keeping it, unless to use some other time. You gave me keys to the house and to the safe so I could put in the takings when I was left shutting the café, so I could take out the cupboard key too. Very handy, when I was told there was a job that needed doing. Simple to slip up afterwards while I was getting my coat'

'Why?' Mairead croaked.

'Brodie thought he was smart. Screwing the top operators isn't smart – they don't like it. Now they're not happy because the current investigation is starting to cramp their style so when I realised you were on to me checking you out for them, I knew something had to be done. This was the obvious solution.

'Don't worry, it wouldn't suit us to demand that you detail all the things you've worked so hard to keep quiet. Oh, don't look shocked! Brodie told me most of it – mates with everyone and the great keeper of secrets, who wasn't particular about what she did to save her precious café in the hard times. And sometimes that meant getting one of the guys to do a freight raid run for him – well, for us, really – when we needed it, telling them it was easy money, which it certainly was, for you. And of course after doing it once you couldn't escape, even when you didn't need the money any more – you were caught, just like the poor benighted kids. Like Callan.'

Mairead was sitting, her head low, and now she gave a choking sob.

Zoe laughed again. 'That was the one, wasn't it? Brodie liked that; you thought you'd got him out of their clutches, but when Callan refused to get involved you were persuaded to get him to do a "just this once" favour because they were stuck – which of course it wasn't. His death wasn't Brodie's fault, you know. It was yours.'

'You don't need to tell me that,' Mairead said. 'It's haunted me every day of my life.'

Zoe looked at her wonderingly. 'I never really understand why people make such martyrs of themselves. Well, you can treat whatever sentence you get as a penance to placate your god, if you have one. Now, get on with it.' She went to the stationery cupboard and took out a sheet of A4 and handed it to her.

Mairead picked up a pen. 'What shall I say?'

Zoe smiled. 'Why not start, "Dear DCI Strang"? He might get a kick out of that. For a polis he's quite a smart guy. I put on a good show, if I may say so, but I wasn't entirely sure he bought it. He certainly gave me the feeling that sticking around was getting risky – and then your accusation made staying a no-brainer.'

Mairead had written the first line. At that she looked up. 'What are you going to do?'

'Oh, just vanish.' Her eyes were dancing with what looked like mischief. 'I was reaching terminal boredom here – you can't imagine how much I hate that. There's no point in making serious money when there's nothing to spend it on. My friends are ready to rescue me.'

Mairead said nothing, just wrote on conscientiously for a few moments, then pushed the paper across to be examined.

Zoe read it and smiled. 'That'll do. Just see he gets it tomorrow – they're in Mrs McGregor's Airbnb, for their sins. Oh, and don't even think of going back on it afterwards. As a first-time offender with a good sob story, they'll go easy on you, and if you try to go back on it I'll see to it that you won't live long enough to enjoy your freedom. Now go back to bed.'

And then she was gone.

After his row with Mairead the previous afternoon, an angry John Wilson had returned to his studio, where he had been working hard on the painting that was going to spearhead his fresh assault on the art world.

But the results were depressing; he'd always blamed his lack of inspiration on the stultifying sameness of everyday life here, so surely the cosmic energy of the drama and tension all around could be channelled into profundity on canvas? But it spoke only of ill-directed rage; looking at it again, he'd thought bitterly that it could have been daubed by a chimpanzee in a temper.

He'd got out a bottle of cheap Scotch – the Famous Grouse was long gone – and had been nursing his glass, brooding, when he'd seen Mairead's car, normally parked across the road, backing up the alleyway until it was beside the kitchen door.

Mairead had got out, opened the boot, then ducked into the kitchen. A moment later she'd reappeared, carrying what looked like her dark red winter coat wrapped around something that she'd deposited in the boot, then driven off.

What could it be, and where could she be going? He had no idea of what she got up to in her spare time; she had contacts he knew nothing about. And the other woman in his life, Zoe – if she could still be called that – was another mystery. Dear God, women! He had felt exhausted by their demands, and now the police were piling pressure on him as well.

John had just topped up his glass to aid his thinking when Mairead came back, again backing the car up the alleyway. She'd jumped out, opened the boot, lifted out the coat with whatever it was covering and hurried inside.

She'd changed her mind and returned, then. So where had she been going, why had she come back, and what had she concealed under the coat?

There had been quite a lot of people moving around on the shore – unusual at that time of night on a Monday. The pub would know what was happening and he could stay there until Mairead would be in bed – never a late bird, she'd been struggling with her migraine – so once she was asleep, he could do a search and satisfy his curiosity. Probably it'd be somewhere in the office – her very private territory.

He came home late; when the beer ran out they'd moved on to shots. He could hear her moving restlessly in bed and with his own door open, he listened until the muttering gave way to small, ladylike snores, then moved across the landing, silent in his stocking soles.

In the office, everything looked normal. What she'd been holding wouldn't have fitted into any of the filing drawers; there was a matching metal cupboard with wide, deep shelves but it only contained piles of files and stationery.

John looked around, discouraged. Apart from that there was only the old-fashioned press, built into the wall by the fireplace, and he checked it was locked. Perhaps she'd put whatever it was under her bed and he'd have to look when she was otherwise occupied.

Then a key lying on top of the filing cabinet beside the cupboard caught his eye, an old-fashioned-looking key. He snatched it up; the cupboard obligingly opened. Its contents were a shock – a severe shock.

He relocked the cupboard, replaced the key where he'd found it and then went back to bed to consider the extraordinary implications. He fell asleep with the issues unresolved.

'Now you needn't think I'll be sneering because it isn't sourdough,' DC Ritchie said, putting a slice of the distinctly basic supermarket loaf in the toaster. 'It's a work of the devil, sourdough, and, to coin a phrase, there's not a lot wrong with plastic white for toast.'

DS Murray, who had just come in, grinned. 'The acid test is how you feel about the instant?'

'Ah! Got me there,' he admitted. 'Not exactly coffee, is it – just tastes vaguely like it.'

She was still grateful for his good nature the previous night. They'd passed on the landing this morning and it hadn't had the embarrassment factor she'd felt with Strang.

'I'm having trouble deciding which is more boring, Rice Krispies or Corn Flakes,' she was saying, when looking out of the window she saw Mairead Wilson coming up the path to the house.

'Well, well, we seem to have a visitor,' she said, but as Ritchie came across to look they heard the thud of the letterbox and she walked away again.

Murray went to pick up the letter lying on the doormat, then carried it back to show Ritchie. 'It's addressed to the boss. What do we do? We can't open it but it may be long enough before he gets here.'

'Phone him, I guess, and he can take it from there.'

CHAPTER NINETEEN

DCI Strang had got up early, showered, done the best he could with the inadequate razor, and now was getting dressed. The room was above the kitchen and he could smell bacon cooking.

He was surprised by the knock on his door, and more surprised when the proprietress told him that he was wanted right now, with a coastguard patrol boat ready to take him round to Ardelour.

It was what he'd been hoping for, but with that smell in the air it was cruel to be deprived of his breakfast. 'Don't suppose they'd like to hang around for a bit, do you?' he said ruefully.

She laughed. 'No, they seem a wee bit pressed. But I've bacon ready so I can just pop it in rolls for you and the boys.'

'Heaven will bless you for that,' he said dramatically as he gathered up his belongings and went down to the hall where a big black-bearded man in a light blue uniform topped with a high-viz jacket was waiting.

'Good morning!' Strang said. 'I'm delighted to get such an early boat – I was resigned to kicking my heels.'

It was only then he noticed the man was looking very sombre, and his heart sank. 'Doubt if you'll be delighted with this, sir. I'm Garry Thomson, the cox. It's a bit of an odd one. There's been a fatality – one of our patrols was called out at first light to a body one of the prawn boats found floating way out in Loch Torridon. We had a shout to pick you up, high priority.'

The proprietress came out of the kitchen with a paper bag, saying brightly, 'Here you are, lads – there's a couple for the others as well,' then, 'Oh dear, trouble?' as she saw their faces.

'I'm afraid so. But thanks so much,' Strang said and the two men walked off down the path, Thomson explaining it was no more than ten minutes to the harbour where the patrol boat was moored.

'Any details?' Strang asked, but the cox couldn't say.

As he boarded the smart white and black patrol boat, they shared out the rolls and stood in the cuddy cabin as they set off round the headland. It was the sort of morning you see on postcards, he thought: the air clear and chilly, sky a perfect cerulean, the sea millpond calm, barely showing a ruffle, and in the Little Minch the gannets were out early, their dives white arrows piercing the dark blue. He would have liked to be able to enjoy it.

The Inverness police station had been contacted by the coastguard and it had been DI Mackenzie's decision to tell them to bring the body ashore in Ardelour and alert Strang as the nearest senior officer, explained the engineer.

A neat bit of buck-passing, Strang was thinking with some irritation, as the man went on, 'A female, apparently. Inverness has dispatched a squad to Torridon and the boat's collecting them on the way.'

Strang went cold all over. A woman was missing – Anna Bruce. There was an ugly job ahead of him anyway and if he had to identify her as the victim, her dead face would haunt him for ever. Once again, he cursed Mackenzie.

It was then his phone rang, showing Livvy's number. He'd been going to call her anyway; it would be a while before he got there and they were right on the spot.

He listened to what she had to say. 'Open it, of course,' then, 'What? Oh, for heaven's sake! What next?'

DS Murray and DC Ritchie were down at the shore in time to see the patrol boat arrive. There were four uniforms in the squad and they took charge of the body in the black bag, laying it down on the jetty as the boat backed up and sailed off.

The seaplane, Murray noticed, was gone. She was still feeling shell-shocked. One of the constables, a cheerful-looking man, gave her a reassuring smile.

'Ah, lassie, we're used to this, you know. Living around here there's aye someone getting it wrong.'

Murray smiled back. Maybe whoever it was had just drowned in a boating accident and it was only her morbid imagination that was chilling her blood.

Ritchie said to the sergeant, 'There's barriers and

sheeting up at the top of the hill, left over from the last investigation.'

'Getting themselves a bit of a reputation round here, aren't they? Thanks, I'll get a couple of the lads on to it before the place starts waking up.' He turned and started giving instructions.

'Don't know the half of it, do they?' Ritchie muttered to Murray. 'But I suppose that means we're free to go and do the needful with Mairead.'

As they walked back along the shore to the café, Murray said, 'The way she's been behaving, I shouldn't be surprised. But I simply hadn't read it that way – she didn't seem the type to deliver such a professional execution.'

'The hit job theory bites the dust, I suppose. She runs a very busy café so I suppose you have to be quite on the ball to juggle all that.'

Murray looked out to sea, shading her eyes. 'The boss said he'd probably be here in about half an hour, but I can't see any sign of another boat.' She heaved a sigh. 'I suppose it would just be cowardice to wait for him.'

'Come on,' Ritchie said. 'Over the top.'

Mairead had put the kitchen knife back in its place on the magnetic rack first thing and, after she had delivered the letter, went to the café to sit at a table by the window to wait for them. She saw them coming along the shore and her heart gave a nervous jump, but they walked on past. She leant forward to watch, but she couldn't see as far as the end of the road.

She settled down to wait again. She knew what she was

going to do and she mustn't make a fool of herself as she had yesterday; she folded her hands in her lap and took deep breaths. When she saw them returning, she went to open the door before they could knock.

'Thank you for coming,' she said politely, waving them to the table. DS Murray looked as if she thought it was an odd thing to say – and perhaps she was right; it was hard to know what would be normal, in the circumstances. She sat down again and waited for them to speak.

Murray took the letter out of her pocket. 'You put this through the letterbox this morning, Mrs Wilson,' she began.

'That's right. It was addressed to DCI Strang.'

'Yes, but since he isn't here right at this moment, he authorised me to open it. He will be here quite shortly. Are you standing by this?'

'Yes, I am. I killed Brodie Campbell.'

'And you did it because . . . ?'

She didn't hesitate. 'He was a force for evil. He was responsible for the death of Callan McIver and there were others he drew into crime.' The words were seared into her brain; she didn't think she'd ever be able to forget them.

'Yes, that's exactly what you wrote,' Murray said. 'Could you please tell us a little bit more about it? For instance—'

'No,' Mairead said. 'That is my last and only statement.'

Ritchie was leaning forward in his chair and Murray nodded to him. 'Perhaps something more general, then. Do you know how to load a shotgun?'

That flustered her. She was ready to say no, but then realised why he was asking. 'Yes – well, of course. Everyone does.' Then, back to firmer ground, 'And anyway, I've given you my statement and that is it. Whatever you ask me, I'm not going to say any more.'

She saw a glance go between the detectives; obviously neither of them knew what to do. At last Murray cleared her throat and said, 'Then I think we had better just wait until the chief inspector gets here. He shouldn't be too much longer.'

Mairead looked at her impassively, as if her pulse wasn't racing, and an awkward silence fell while they sat. And sat.

They had brought him in neatly so that he could step straight ashore, then left Strang there as they went off to their next assignment. A uniform sergeant came up and saluted him.

He noticed a little group of people gathered in the street but the Inverness officers had done a good job; they had already put barriers in place and arranged plastic screening.

'Quick work, Sergeant,' he said. 'A drowning, I believe?'

The man cleared his throat. 'Well, er – not entirely, sir, I think.'

Strang said, 'Meaning?'

'I was with them seeing her into the bag, and it'll need a post-mortem to decide. They'll be able to tell you if she was alive when she went into the water, but there's what looks like a gunshot wound in her back, poor lady.'

Feeling sick, he said, 'I'd better take a look.'

'Of course, sir.'

The sergeant held back the screening to let him go in and unzipped the bag.

There was the smell of seaweed and wet clothing. Bracing himself, Strang looked, then felt ashamed as a flood of relief swept through him. The sodden mass of tangled dark curls didn't belong to Anna Bruce and the face that looked up at him with dark eyes wide and blank was that of Zoe Cooper.

She couldn't have been in the water that long; her body wasn't bloated, but the dark make-up round her eyes was streaked into runnels down her cheeks and her lipstick was smeared. There were lacerations and bruising to the left temple and a brown strand of kelp was clinging to her hair; one leg was obviously broken and the arm with its twisting vine was at an odd angle, though the acrylic blue nails weren't even chipped. His eye went involuntarily to the pathetic little heart at the base of her throat.

The vital, confident, humorous woman who'd declared a low boredom threshold only yesterday had been snuffed out as carelessly as you would a candle. Such a pitiful waste – though he was already working out that she had probably been, to a considerable degree, the author of her own misfortune.

Strang turned back to the sergeant. 'I see what you mean. I can in fact positively identify her as Zoe Cooper, a private detective who was working for North West Fisheries. Perhaps you could put in hand informing Andrew Erskine, the CEO. As you said, the body will certainly have to be taken for a post-mortem.' He couldn't resist adding, with a certain malevolence, 'It was rather unfortunate that DI Mackenzie directed that the body be brought here, where there is currently no possibility of removing it except by boat.'

'Indeed you're right, sir,' he said, adding with the air of a man sorely tried, 'Not entirely a surprise, though. I'll get back to the patrol boat – they'll not be best pleased.'

Now for Mairead Wilson. As he walked across, Murray came out of the café to meet him.

'How is Mrs Wilson this morning? Not poorly, I trust?' he said lightly.

'Not so far, but she won't say more than what she's written in that letter to you – recites it as if she was reading off autocue. Flatly refuses to say anything else.'

'Right. Before we go in, I should let you know that the body in the bag is Zoe Cooper.' He heard Murray gasp, and said, 'I'll tell her shortly.'

He walked ahead of her into the café. 'Thank you for your letter, Mrs Wilson,' he said, joining them at the table. 'I gather from DS Murray that you have said that you are holding to the confession you wrote, but I am asking you again. Are you ready to confirm that?'

Mairead said, 'Yes, I'm quite satisfied.'

'It is still possible for you to withdraw it, you know.'

'I won't. And this is all I'm going to say.' She wasn't looking agitated and she met his eyes with such a dead stare that Strang wondered if she was heavily tranquillised.

'Let's put this to one side for the moment. I'm afraid I have some bad news for you. There has been a fatality; Ms Cooper's body was found in the sea last night.'

At last he got his reaction. Mairead came to life, the dead eyes suddenly bright.

'Did you say she was dead?'

From the look of her, it didn't seem unwelcome news, but he said formally, 'I believe Zoe Cooper was a friend of yours. I'm sorry for your loss. You must be very shaken.'

Mairead hesitated. 'Ah – yes, of course. I wouldn't say

she was exactly my friend but I relied on her greatly as an employee – I can't think how I'll be able to run the café without her. I trusted her with everything.'

Strang became aware that the house door was ajar and that John Wilson was listening; he didn't know how long he'd been there. He ignored it, and went on with the interview.

John Wilson had wakened with a start. He'd thought he wouldn't be able to sleep with all that was on his mind, but he had, and soundly. He'd wakened up only when he heard voices coming from the café but he still hadn't made up his mind what use he could make of his recently acquired information.

He dressed and started to go downstairs, then stopped. A man was speaking. The police again? He slipped down to open the door a crack. He heard Strang say, 'I believe Zoe Cooper was a friend of yours. I am very sorry for your loss . . .'

Zoe was? *Was*? It hit him like a punch in the stomach. What had Mairead done now? Brodie Campbell was no loss but the beautiful, exciting woman who had incomprehensibly let him be her lover and wakened in him emotions he'd never even imagined before was irreplaceable, unique. She'd kept him enchanted and bewildered and often resentful; he couldn't put a name to what he felt – lust certainly, even love? – but it had made him feel alive as never before. Unaccustomed tears came to his eyes.

He had no doubts now. He ran upstairs, high on the righteous wrath of an avenging angel.

* * *

Strang said, 'Did you know much about her – people she knew, the other work she did?'

'Only that she lived with Jago Innes – oh, does he know?'

'Not as yet. An officer will be going there to inform him. Do you know if she had any enemies?'

'Not that I knew of. She was often summoned away suddenly, though she never explained, and I didn't want to upset her by probing. I couldn't afford to lose her.'

Now she seemed to be opening up, it might be possible to able to persuade her to talk about her confession – it might not work, but it was worth a try.

Strang went on, 'You were very close to some of the young men in the village, weren't you? Like Fergus Matheson and Craig Lothian? And of course Callan McIver?'

Her mouth trembled. 'Yes,' was all she said.

'You said you blamed Brodie Campbell for their problems?'

Her eyes filled with tears, but her chin came up and she eyed him squarely. 'Yes. I did and I meant it. He was an evil man who drew others into evil with him, and I'm not sorry that he's dead, except for that poor little wife of his – though she's probably better off without him. But you said I could withdraw my confession – well, I'm withdrawing it now. I didn't do it.'

Out of the corner of his eye, he had noticed a few minutes ago that John Wilson had gone back inside the house. Now here he was, striding across the café to where they were sitting with something draped in a sheet in his arms. He set it down on the table and with a dramatic gesture stripped the sheet away to reveal a double-barrelled sawn-off shotgun.

'You've done it this time, you bitch,' he said to Mairead, who had shrunk back into her chair. 'Zoe didn't deserve it, whatever you might say about Campbell.' Then turning to Strang, he said, 'And you need to ask her what she was doing last Friday afternoon. She certainly wasn't here.'

Strang had been sceptical about Mairead Wilson's convenient ailments, but when she tried to stand up and pitched to the floor in a dead faint it was unmistakably genuine.

This is the sort of silence that feels as if you've hit a wall, Murray thought, *and it looks like a still from a crime series: the woman on the floor, the gun on the table, the man standing confronting the detective.*

For a stunned moment Strang sat there, then jumped up, saying to Ritchie, 'Constable, get some water from the kitchen. I think this is merely a faint. Mr Wilson, help me get your wife onto a chair.'

At least Mairead was stirring, trying to sit up. John Wilson hadn't moved; he was standing with his arms folded, his face mutinous, but he didn't have the nerve to ignore Strang's glare for long.

Between them they lifted her onto the seat and Ritchie brought through a glass. Strang said nothing as Mairead took a drink; Murray quietly picked up the sheet from the floor and wrapped it carefully round the gun, then at a nod from him got out her notebook.

He said, 'All right? Then perhaps you can explain all this, Mrs Wilson?'

Mairead coughed, then croaked, 'It's not true, what he just said – not about Brodie, not about Zoe either. It's all his lies! He's good at that, you should know!'

'Oh yes?' Wilson sneered. 'I suppose the gun that killed them wasn't in your cupboard?'

'No!' Strang said sharply. 'I am not interested in presiding over a domestic slanging match. Mr Wilson, you can make a statement later. Now I want you to return to the house. DC Ritchie will escort you if necessary.'

John said frigidly, 'No need,' and stalked off.

'Let's start again,' Strang said. 'Perhaps start by explaining how you came to have this gun, Mrs Wilson.'

That was a subject they were all feeling sensitive about, Murray thought. Mairead had been shielded from suspicion by the inherent unlikelihood of her possessing the murder weapon – an unwarranted assumption, it seemed, and they had fallen into the trap. What would she say?

Nothing again seemed to be the answer. There was another of those heavy silences, as Mairead stared at the fingers twisting in her lap.

Strang said, his voice harder now, 'I am afraid you don't understand the situation. You have withdrawn your confession, but you may well be arrested on suspicion of murder. It is very much in your interests to give me any information that might make that less likely.'

The woman was trembling now. 'It was Zoe, not me. I was stupid. She had access to the whole house, and to the safe where the cupboard key was kept.'

Murray, looking up from her notebook, suppressed a startled gasp. Ritchie was gaping, but Strang was unmoved.

'That wasn't my question. Where did you get it?'

Another silence. Then she took a deep breath. 'I will tell you where it came from. I was given it a while ago by a boy who was in with the wrong people and who feared he would go to jail if it was found in his possession. I took it from him, locked it in the cupboard and, to be quite honest, forgot about it. That's all I'm going to say – I won't name names.'

'Fergus Matheson, I assume,' Strang said blandly.

Mairead gave a cry of dismay. 'I didn't tell you! I wouldn't! Oh – you're wrong, actually. It wasn't him. It was someone else, long ago.'

She was a very bad liar, and Murray thought he actually looked as if he was feeling some sympathy. 'You needn't feel a traitor. I take it Fergus had touched the gun? Then there will be his fingerprints on it, which we have on file. And yours too, I suppose?'

'Oh, I never touched it! I hate the things – he brought it to me wrapped up and I've never even taken off the sheet. I never wanted this, but he told me the trouble he'd be in if he was found with it so I thought if I just put it away in the old press I wouldn't need to do anything – no one was going to come here looking for it, or for anything else, really.'

She looked across at Murray and Ritchie. 'It was only when you started asking me questions that I realised how stupid I'd been – and then when I was trying to get rid of it, I couldn't get out of Ardelour.'

She turned back to Strang and said, 'You won't let this tell against him, if you find his fingerprints on it, will you? After all, he was in jail when Brodie was shot and if you were to call me as a witness I'd deny that I told you that.'

Murray rather admired her spirit, but Strang said coldly, 'Given that you will be hoping to convince us of your version of events, it is unwise to reveal that you have a cavalier attitude to the truth. Perhaps we could turn to where you went on that Friday afternoon. We know that you left the café – where did you go?'

'Zoe told you that, didn't she?' Mairead said. 'If you want to know, I went to see Jenny Matheson, who needed her hand held when Fergus was arrested. But Zoe was always spying on me. I don't know why. I said that to her face, you know, yesterday. I was angry.'

'What secrets do you have that she might have wanted to find out?'

She reacted as if someone had dashed a glass of water in her face. 'I – I don't – I didn't! I don't know what she could have thought. She had all sorts of things going on and it scared me.'

He paused – reckoning he'd better not push too hard in case she collapsed conveniently again, Murray thought. After a moment, he said, 'You accused Zoe Cooper of killing Mr Campbell. Why did you say that?'

Mairead drew a deep breath. 'She had access to the safe where the key to the cupboard was kept. I didn't even think about it. And then, last night . . .'

She told them the whole story as they listened without saying a word or asking a question. Murray had cramp in her hand by the time Mairead had finished, and she couldn't think where the hell they went from there.

Strang said, 'Mrs Wilson, I am going to have you

arrested and charged with possession of an illegal weapon. DC Ritchie will take you to the officers on the jetty. DS Murray, would you take the gun and have them get it fingerprinted as a matter of urgency. I'm going to have a word now with Mr Wilson.'

Murray and Ritchie looked at each other and she could see they shared the same thought: *God, he's good.*

There was one more thing to do first. Strang went to the door leading to the Wilsons' flat and called, 'Mr Wilson!'

John appeared down the stairs like a rabbit out of a hat. 'That poisonous bitch will have told you all sorts of lies. I'm glad I'm going to be able to give my side of the story at last,' he said, sounding thoroughly aggrieved.

'Not at the moment, I'm afraid. Just a couple of questions. When did you know about the gun?'

'Yesterday. I saw her driving off with something wrapped in an old coat, and then not long afterwards she returned and brought it back inside. I wanted to know what she was up to, so when she was asleep I went to have a look.'

'How did you get into the cupboard?'

'Left the key lying on the filing cabinet, didn't she? Complete shock when I saw the gun – and then she claims—'

'I don't have time for that. I have to tell you that there is no likelihood that your wife was involved in Zoe Cooper's death. Thank you, Mr Wilson. That is all for the time being, though of course we will be in touch about . . . other matters.'

Strang left, leaving John Wilson standing in the little

hall looking stunned. As he walked back to the Airbnb he reflected that it was probably only luck that they weren't investigating the murder of one by the other, to add to everything else.

CHAPTER TWENTY

DS Murray said, 'I don't know about you, but I feel it ought to be bedtime by now.'

'It's only midday,' DC Ritchie said. 'In fact, it's pretty impressive what they've pulled together.'

The next coastguard patrol boat had come in and Mairead Wilson had been taken away in the custody of the Inverness police, along with Cooper's body on its way to the mortuary in Inverness. The shore was very busy, with boats of various descriptions queueing up to bring in workers to tackle the rockfall, and boxes of supplies now too.

They were back in the breakfast room in the Airbnb, where DCI Strang had arrived earlier to negotiate with Mrs McGregor; she had accepted its commandeering with a bad grace and grudgingly brought back the breakfast supplies, though only after being assured this could be charged to the police.

'So what happens now, boss?' Murray said, lavishly spreading three packets of butter on a slice of toast.

Strang was preoccupied; she noticed that he almost jumped when she spoke to him, and that his mug of, admittedly unappealing, coffee hadn't been touched. 'Sorry? Well, I managed to get through to the DCS earlier and she wants me back in circulation ASAP. They're going to find a boat that can take me to Gairloch and they'll phone when they've found one.

'Livvy, Jago Innes will have to be told. Can you take that on, please? Alex, I'd like you to go round to the Mathesons' again and see if you can pin down exactly when Mairead was with them that afternoon. Tell them we now know about Fergus's gun and they'd better come up with every detail they know about the little "arrangements" with Campbell.'

Murray said, 'Are we accepting what Mairead said as gospel? If it isn't, she should definitely be writing fiction.'

'I don't think we can quite do that. Fingerprint evidence from the gun might be revealing, though of course there's no way of telling whether a particular shotgun was the one that was used. There's no direct evidence as yet that Zoe had any contact with Campbell – she certainly said she hardly knew him, for what that's worth. But there are . . . well . . . connections, I suppose, that have been making a kind of pattern that fits with something I was considering before.'

Just as well someone was making something of this complete sotter, Murray thought. 'But Zoe,' she said. 'What was it that actually happened to her?'

Strang said, 'That'll have to wait for the post-mortem. I wasn't able to have more than a cursory look but the sergeant who was involved in transferring her into the body bag said that she'd been shot in the back. There was no visible bleeding but there was considerable other trauma that would suggest to me that she must have been dropped into Loch Torridon. If it was from some height, it would have been like hitting a concrete floor.'

It was Ritchie who said, 'As it might be, from Livvy's seaplane.'

Saying 'I told you so' isn't pretty and given the ghastly circumstances Murray wasn't even tempted, but it was a good feeling to know that there might be a way of bringing Zoe's spine-chilling assassin to justice, if the tech wizards could do something with her snapshot.

'Do you think she was dead before she knew what was happening?' she asked.

With a grimace, Strang said, 'It would be good to think that. Let's just hope the autopsy doesn't show water in the lungs.'

His phone rang, and he seized it. The conversation was brief, and then he was on his feet. 'They're waiting for me. Livvy, well done. Even if the enhancement doesn't come up to scratch, it still gives us a basis we can proceed on.' Then he left.

Murray, pouting, said, 'All right for some. We're stuck here. I'm certainly starting to go stir-crazy, and now I have to go and give my condolences to Jago Innes when I don't believe he possesses one genuine human emotion or could even feel pain anywhere except in his wallet.'

'Oh dear. Now, me, I'm quite looking forward to turning the screws on the Mathesons. They made it quite clear they didn't think much of the way we seemed to be more concerned about poor Sandy Wallace than about their precious son.'

'Put the boot in, then, why don't you, and wish me luck!' Murray said as they went out.

The previous day had been difficult. The mobile home simply wasn't geared for the two of them being home at the same time except when they were in bed, and with Zoe in a bad temper and restless as a cat on hot bricks, Jago hadn't been able to get on with the things he needed to do – like cancelling deliveries and explaining why to suppliers.

He'd had to seize his chance when Zoe had a phone call herself; there were several and each time she'd gone outside to take them, marching to and fro even at the height of a rain shower. He could see that she was making calls too and this evidence of planning made him even more nervous than he was already.

She'd issued a definite threat, but he had no idea what she was specifically referring to, or which of his vulnerable areas she even knew about. When she'd gone out to take another call and then started walking off down towards the shore, he'd taken the opportunity to call Joe Connelly again.

'I know she's concocting something,' he'd said. 'I've no idea what she might be aiming at, none at all. The trouble is we have so many irons in the fire. What are we going to do, Joe?'

'For God's sake, Jago, I'm no' yer mammy! You're waiting for the next shoe to fall – think we're not? You're cut off from the outside world, so what could anyone do, even if you knew what would help? Face it – you're on your own, sunshine.'

But he'd known that already and what he certainly didn't need at that moment was another visit from the attack-dog detective and a sidekick, but there they'd been on the doorstep. Mercifully it was Zoe they'd wanted to speak to; he took some pleasure in saying she was out, and no, he didn't have any idea when she'd be back.

On her return she'd treated this news with complete indifference. After that he'd played a lot of computer games while Zoe sat absorbed in her phone, and at six o'clock when he'd announced he was going to the pub, she'd only raised her eyebrows and shrugged.

When he had come back around ten she was still looking at her phone, but she seemed to be very edgy. He'd tried making conversation about how the pub had been absolutely hoaching and how at that rate they'd be out of beer by tomorrow, but though she'd looked up and made a suitably anodyne reply, she'd returned to her phone, phubbing him without hesitation. He'd swivelled his desk chair, tuned in to Sky Sports and found a football match.

She'd never liked football. After half an hour she had stood up and said, 'It's beyond me why you want to watch that stuff. I'm going for a walk.'

It wasn't the sort of night you'd choose for a walk – damp and dark too by then – but he wasn't the one who was going. She hadn't come back by the time the game finished so presumably she was enjoying it.

It had been nearly midnight and he'd given a huge yawn. There were few things more exhausting than doing absolutely nothing all day and he certainly wasn't going to wait up for her.

He slept late and in the morning she wasn't around. Gone out already, he assumed, but then noticed her side of the king-size looked as if it hadn't been slept in. So where had she spent the night? She'd put her overnight bag in the car the previous day – was there perhaps another lover around that he didn't know about?

Well, she'd turn up when it suited her, no doubt – and if she didn't, he'd be OK with that. She'd always been the cat who walked by itself and as they said, all good things must come to an end – and by now he wasn't sure how good they'd ever been, anyway.

He was washing up his breakfast dishes when the wind chimes jangled and he went to open the door. The attack-dog sergeant was standing there, alone this time; he could only hope she'd come to look for Zoe, rather than because they'd found her and she'd carried out her threat.

He was just about to say she still wasn't there when she said very quietly, 'Mr Innes, I'm afraid I have some bad news for you. You may want to sit down.'

He did as he was told, but with his mind on looming danger, Jago took a moment to take in that his partner had been found dead in Loch Torridon, and longer than that to take in what it meant.

'Do you mean she was drowned?' he said, thinking, *Suicide? Surely not.* Self-love was one of Zoe's main characteristics.

'I'm afraid we have reason to suspect foul play,' the sergeant was saying.

From the way she was looking at him, he realised there

was an expected reaction and unless he demonstrated it, he'd probably find himself under arrest.

'How – how dreadful.' he stammered, inserting an artistic little gap to indicate emotion. Perhaps he went on too quickly to say, 'Of course this was nothing to do with me.'

The sergeant's voice hardened. 'No one is suggesting that, at least at this stage. Perhaps you could tell us when you last saw Ms Cooper?'

'Last night, when I came back from the pub. She was in a bit of a weird mood, to be honest. She spent the whole day going to and fro getting phone calls and making them herself.'

'Do you know who was making the calls?'

'No. She had a lot of interests I knew nothing about.'

'Or who she made calls to?'

'I have absolutely no idea. It may be hard for you to understand but our relationship was built on never asking questions, so she didn't know any more about what I did than I did about her activities.'

He hoped that might open up a chance to explain that anything Zoe might have said about him was based on spite and ignorance, but she wasn't diverted.

'Is her phone still here?'

'I haven't looked.' He got up. 'Had it on her, I would guess. Never went anywhere without it being in reach.'

At the sergeant's suggestion, he checked in the bedroom and rooted through her tote bag without success.

She said, 'Thank you, Mr Innes. Do you know if your partner had any enemies?'

He almost said, *Apart from me* – but that wasn't entirely

true, was it? The news was beginning to hit him now, and he took a moment to think about crafting a reply.

He said, 'Not specifically, but she was someone who could well antagonise people. She was very self-assured and not much interested in what anyone else wanted. I would also say that in my opinion she was involved with some very unsavoury people.'

The question came back like a bullet. 'Who are they?'

'Oh God, I wish I knew. I might sleep better at nights if I did.'

He hadn't meant to say that; it had just popped out. But its effect was all that he could have hoped for – the sergeant got up to go.

'Thank you, Mr Innes. I'm sorry for your loss – you are bearing it very bravely.'

'Sarky bitch,' he snarled as the door closed behind her. It was only then that the shock really struck him and he was, after all, glad to sit down.

Zoe had pretty much spelt it out the day before that she would be leaving. It was what he'd always expected she would do, but he'd been finding it hard to sort out what he felt about it. The heady early days of the relationship were long past and latterly they'd been circling each other like cage fighters, looking to seek out a weakness. Even so, there were still occasions when they struck sparks off each other and when they did it gave him a buzz that compared to what he got from cocaine, and was similarly addictive.

Jago had been considering how best to cope with having to go cold turkey when she had thrown his calculations out by returning. Being closeted with a frustrated, irritable and unreasonable Zoe had got his rehabilitation off to a good start and this morning in her absence he'd been thinking the sooner she left the better.

But Zoe dead? He just couldn't assimilate that – she wasn't that sort of person. *Category error*, they called it. He had never known where she came from; he'd accepted that in due time she'd go and he wouldn't know where she was going either. This idea – her being actually, physically dead – simply wasn't convincing.

But it had started conjuring up images he had to put out of his mind if he wasn't to be physically sick. He didn't even have any of his usual medication for a low mood to hand; he'd cleaned the place out completely in anticipation of a police raid, and the smell of her perfume that lingered on the air wasn't helping.

He noticed now that there seemed to be a lot of traffic – cars, even vans, going to and fro. There must be quite a lot happening down at the shore and perhaps if he went down he might find people who knew more than the police had been prepared to tell him. Around here they usually did.

DS Murray got back to the Airbnb well before DC Ritchie did. She was at a bit of a loose end; DCI Strang was presumably still on the high seas on his way back to Gairloch and hadn't communicated with any further instructions. She could hear Mrs McGregor hoovering somewhere but she hoped to avoid a discussion about how many more nights they might need the rooms for since she was devoutly hoping that the answer was none.

From the front window she could see promising signs

that goods were being brought ashore from a variety of boats so the breakfast-cereal-for-lunch threat must be receding. Even so, it would be a considerable challenge to provision the whole Ardelour peninsula and she'd find herself caught up in that unless rescue came.

When Ritchie did come in, he was looking pleased with himself. 'Well, that was quite a useful little excursion. How was yours?'

Murray shrugged. 'He didn't appear exactly inconsolable. Nasty bit of work, him. The Inverness lot will have quite a gratifying charge sheet when they follow up on the leads they've got already and add the ones we've trailed to them, and with any luck he'll go down for quite a stretch.'

She was putting on the kettle. 'Want a hot drink? Now tell me about the Mathesons.'

'The interesting thing was that there was a girl with them, Ellie Donaldson – not long out of school, I'd say.'

Murray nodded. 'That's right – the little waitress. Still at school, in fact. Dave Kirk said Fergus was her boyfriend. Silly girl.'

'She'd certainly got his parents' approval. Jenny Matheson was beaming as she listened to Ellie standing up for him when it came out about the gun – *just the result of people taking advantage of him*, of course.'

'There's one born every minute – an unending supply of young women who think they can reform bad men,' Murray said with feeling, having been one herself.

Ritchie pulled a face. 'He's not so much bad as weak and opportunistic and the best thing for him could be to get married young and have a wife find him better friends. But that wasn't the main thing. When I asked about

Mairead's visit, Jenny confirmed that she had been with them for almost an hour that day and not only that, Ellie said that she'd seen Mairead leaving and she came back shortly before closing time. There wouldn't have been enough time for her to do anything else.'

Murray was gratified. 'I did think there was the ring of truth in what she was saying – Mairead didn't strike me as the imaginative sort.'

'No indeed. But when we got on to the reason for the sudden chill I'd noticed before, they clammed up again. I had to wave the gun around a bit, saying it might well be possible to ignore its history if they told me what that was all about.

'It really wasn't very savoury. The secret was kept by those involved right up until the pressure got to Fergus. He cracked and burst into tears on the phone to his mother and told her what Mairead had been doing. During Covid, the café was all set to close and Campbell made her the offer she couldn't refuse: recruiting youths for him who'd welcome a lucrative handout for occasional work when needed for planned freight raids, while raking off a commission for herself – young men like Fergus, though they denied he'd been one, for obvious reasons. Once the café was back on its feet she seems to have tried to bail out but certainly in the case of Callan McIver she'd persuaded him to do it.'

'Campbell tweaked her tail?'

'Blackmail would look almost irresistible to him, wouldn't it? She more than likely hadn't realised at the start that it would be a disastrous pathway into crime for the lads she seems to have been genuinely fond of.'

'So in a word, she demonstrably didn't kill Campbell but she's going to get the jail anyway?'

'Always supposing we can find witnesses who'll testify, which with the Ardelour attitude to *omertà* isn't a given.'

Murray took the mugs of coffee over to the table and they sat down. 'So,' she said, 'what does that tell us about the network – or networks, according to Zoe Cooper – that are behind this?'

'I wish I knew. Getting even one of the big boys as opposed to the steady trickle of sacrificial lambs is the objective of the task force Kelso and I have both been involved in. I suppose this is one small piece to add to the jigsaw but I'm distinctly relieved that working out where you go from here isn't up to me.'

'Hmm,' Murray said. 'To be honest, I'm at the point where there's only one thing I'm interested in, and that's when we get off the desert island.'

With a sigh of relief, DCI Strang sat down at his desk in the Gairloch police station and logged on to the computer. There was a list of reports waiting that he'd been unable to access and with a practised eye he scanned them.

Reports were the bane of policing; for obvious reasons everything had to be recorded but it did mean that there were slag heaps of dross cluttering up the feed that would have to be scanned and sorted – the sort of thing you had subordinates for, but since his sergeant and his constable were playing Robinson Crusoe and Man Friday at the moment, he was on his own. Probably it was good for him and would make him more sympathetic about irritating delays. Possibly, anyway.

It had come in at last – the printouts from technology on what they had gleaned from Brodie Campbell's phone and computer. It took him a few minutes to work out their presentation but once he did, it was revealing.

Campbell had only three names registered in his phone book as contacts so that the name would come up before he answered a call: Kirk, Home and XXXX. The first two were self-explanatory, but who was XXXX? Someone whose name he wouldn't want to have appear if he was in company, at a guess.

They were going to go on digging to find whose name was on the contract for that account. He made a note to point them in the direction of Cooper's private investigator's licence, which might save time – if her details were genuine, though he wouldn't put money on that.

Going through the other numbers would be a painstaking job. Impatient now, Strang went on to the email list from Campbell's office computer and ran his eye down it.

The vast majority concerned purely estate business. He ran his eye over these; they could eliminate the businesses and follow up names that were clients for the shoot or members of the syndicate that ran the place.

What he didn't see was a repeated name that would suggest 'XXXX'. Not really surprising – Zoe Cooper as a sophisticated operator would know to ensure all communication was done by phone, where what had been said vanished into the ether, leaving ne'er a rack behind. A class act, you could say.

Mairead, on the other hand, was there, pinned to the board like a collector's butterfly. 'mairead@shorehousecafe' made no attempt at disguise; contacts were occasional but given that dates were imprinted they might even match up with known raids. And once they got round to printing out the messages, he would even be able to see what Campbell had asked her to do.

The cogs and wheels were starting to mesh now. All they needed now was something to impel them into motion.

When Strang's phone rang and DC Ritchie spoke, his first reaction was guilt. He should, of course, have thought about their situation but he had been so keen to get stuck into the files that he simply hadn't.

He listened to the account of his interview with the Mathesons and then said, 'Excellent, Alex. It's one whole investigative area we don't need to pursue, which is good because the phone and email records have opened up a few more. What I certainly don't think is necessary is for you and Livvy to stay on in Ardelour. I'll get them to find you a lift back here. Perhaps you can break the sad news to Mrs McGregor.'

Livvy had clearly been listening in. He could hear a faint cheer in the background as Alex pointed out that he still had a car stuck in the car park.

'I'd forgotten that,' Strang said. 'That's a bit tricky. Come here anyway and we'll take it from there. But now I think about it, there might be a use for it. Put me on to Livvy.'

An idea had been hovering while he was looking through Campbell's phone book: the entry 'Home' suggested that Iona Campbell must have her own mobile.

When Murray came on the line, he said, 'While you're waiting for a lift, perhaps you could speak nicely to Alex and see if he'll let you borrow his car to go across the moor to see Iona Campbell.'

He explained what he wanted and she said with alacrity, 'I'd really like to do that. I want to see how that poor dog is. Just so long as you tell the boat not to leave till I get back.'

The moor looked more benign today with the sun shining and only puffy little clouds in the sky, but it still wasn't the sort of place where you'd want to live if you were a young wife and mother. Murray's arrival hadn't been noticed; when she went to knock on the door she could hear a baby gurgling with laughter and a woman's voice singing 'The Wheels on the Bus' until she too started to laugh.

Murray was smiling in sympathy as she knocked on the door and Iona was still smiling when she opened it, though her face changed as she recognised her visitor.

'Oh,' she said. 'You'd better come in.'

She'd had warmer welcomes, and Murray hastened to say that it was only a minor thing she wanted to check. The baby, still jiggling about in her little bouncy chair, stopped and gave her a solemn stare.

'Mrs Campbell, am I right in thinking you have a mobile phone?'

Iona frowned. 'Well, of course.'

'I wonder if there's someone down in your phone book as XXXX?'

'No, but I remember seeing that on Brodie's phone when it rang once or twice.'

That was promising. 'Did he tell you who his caller was?'

'Certainly not – kept his business to himself, did Brodie. But it's funny you should ask – that Zoe Cooper from the café came yesterday and she asked if I had Brodie's phone, which I don't, of course, because you took it away, and when I said that, she was a bit put out for some reason. Then she said, just like you did, did I know who XXXX was, so I said I didn't and she just went away again then.'

Murray hesitated – should she tell her what had happened? Iona wasn't on any need-to-know list, and she'd hear soon enough as the story spread. It would take up time and Murray's mind was already on the boat that hopefully would be waiting for her at the jetty.

'Thanks, Mrs Campbell, that's all I needed to ask you – except I've been wondering how Luath is? He was so sad about his master.'

'Oh, he really was. Just lay there, wouldn't eat a thing, and a day later he didn't wake up in the morning. Broken heart, if you ask me. I always said he was a real gentleman to Rosie and me but nobody mattered except Brodie.'

A great dog wasted on a worthless man, Murray was thinking as she said goodbye. His wife, on the other hand, had better things to do than mourn him. The horn on the bus was, apparently, going *beep! beep! beep!* by the time she got into the car.

When she got back to Ardelour, she drove down to the shore car park, partly in hopeful expectation and partly because she didn't think Mrs McGregor would welcome an abandoned vehicle being left on her premises.

And Ritchie was waiting for her there, talking to the crew of a coastguard patrol boat. It was nice to be greeted with cheers, even though it had more to do with their being able to leave than her arriving.

As the boat pulled away from the jetty, Murray stood in the stern looking back. It looked such an idyllic little place on a day like this, with sun sparkling on the water and the majesty of the hills behind demonstrating a whole range of shades of blue, from indigo through to mauve and shading into grey. It was hard to reconcile its innocuous aspect with the seismic events that had toppled boulders and changed human lives for ever.

CHAPTER TWENTY-ONE

DI Mackenzie came into the office where Strang was working, looking awkward, rather like a schoolboy aware that misdemeanours might have consequences.

'Ah, Chief Inspector!' he said. 'I'm glad they have managed to get you back. This has been a most unfortunate business – barely credible, really.'

Strang got up to greet him. 'Quite extraordinary, indeed. I take it they've told you that Mairead Wilson has been taken to be charged in Inverness? There's also a gun that I'd be grateful to have fingerprinted as soon as possible.'

'Certainly, certainly – I'll get that moving for you. I trust you didn't mind being landed with dealing with the body from Loch Torridon. It was just that we have this enormous territory to cover – the size of Belgium, you know – and knowing that you were right on the spot, it seemed the obvious thing to do.'

If he mentioned Belgium again, Strang wasn't sure he could be responsible for his actions. 'It was certainly fortunate that given the current situation the coastguard have been able to find another boat to transport the body of the deceased to where it's possible for it to be removed to the mortuary. Now, I'm just preparing a dossier for you that should allow you to move on the drug problem in this area – it seems to have become pretty much endemic.'

Mackenzie tried to look as if this was good news, dutifully murmuring thanks as Strang said, 'I don't feel there is any need to spend more time here and I will be leaving today with DS Murray and DC Ritchie, once they are ferried back from Ardelour. Just one or two loose ends – I'm told Zoe Cooper's car is standing in the Shore Street car park, so I'm sure I can leave you to deal with arranging for it to be examined, and DC Ritchie's car is still in Ardelour too, so perhaps at the same time you can liaise with Glasgow for it to be returned when that's possible?'

Mackenzie was looking depressed as he left but Strang wasn't feeling as sympathetic as he might have been. He'd dealt with too many senior officers whose one idea was to spare themselves trouble, no matter how it might affect anyone else. The 'dossier' he was planning should keep the inspector fully engaged with the Ardelour problems that had been ignored for far too long.

The A9, of course, was plagued with the roadworks that might at last bring the long-promised improvements. Strang dropped Ritchie off at Perth station, where a train could take him to Glasgow in an hour, then Murray in the centre of Edinburgh before he was able at last to head for Newhaven.

He'd told Cat he was coming but that it would be very

late; of course he'd told her not to wait up, but he was still hoping she would. When he parked his car there were welcoming candles in the window above, and the front door opened before he had reached the top of the steps and she came to throw her arms round him.

There were tears in her eyes when at last she let him go. 'It's just so good to see you. I know it's neurotic, I knew you were all right really but what with the earthquake I kept wondering what would be next. Anyway, come on in – I got picky bits so you could have whatever you want.'

'Genius idea,' he said, looking at the tray of appetising little plates and bowls laid out on the table between their favourite chairs. He went to get drinks for them both, then sat down with a sigh of relief. 'Long day.'

As Cat nibbled delicately and Kelso got stuck into chicken liver pâté, she said, 'You have to tell me what's been happening. There's been hardly any news reports apart from about that dog staying with his dead master and the two arrests that didn't seem to have anything to do with that.'

'Well, they did and they didn't. There was an elaborate network linking them all that only became apparent in the last couple of days. But you'll get plenty on the news tomorrow. A body was found by fishermen out in Loch Torridon and brought into Ardelour – Zoe Cooper, a woman who worked in the local café, among other places, and it's looking as if she was shot in the back and then pushed out of a plane.'

Cat stared at him. 'But that's really heavy stuff! I'm glad I didn't know about that before you got home. Who would have done that?'

'You won't be surprised to hear that we don't know – one of the big crime syndicates, quite possibly. Livvy spotted a seaplane around the place and we'll be following up on that.'

'And what about the gamekeeper's murder? Oh, and the faithful dog?'

'Sadly, he died of what looked remarkably like a broken heart. As for the murder, we're hoping to prove Zoe Cooper killed him, if the technology wizards do their stuff. The gamekeeper had been ripping the bosses off and it looks likely she was told to take him out, then realised she was under suspicion and asked to be lifted out, not realising she'd become the sort of liability to them that warranted a bullet in the back. It was just their bad luck that the prawn boat happened along before the body had sunk.'

Kelso noticed her stifling a yawn. 'Darling, it's very late. The rest is far too complicated to go into tonight and I'm going to have to prepare a package to present to JB first thing tomorrow morning. Off you go to bed.'

Cat got up reluctantly. 'I suppose if I don't it would mean you'd get there later yourself. Just tell me before I go – how did Livvy and Alex get on? It sounded as if you might have an uncivil war on your hands.'

'No, it was all right. They were stuck in that wretched Airbnb and perhaps it was the paso dobles that brought them together, but they seem to be getting on fine now. I'd give the credit to Alex – he's quite a tactful sort of chap.'

'That sounds promising,' Cat said. 'I tell you what – we can ask them both to the wedding.'

Kelso shook his head at her. 'Why not, but I can't at all see it working out.'

'You never know.' She stooped to kiss him. 'Good luck – I hope your package comes together easily.'

'A pious wish,' he said with a groan as he went to fetch his papers.

DCI Strang wasn't looking forward to briefing DCS Borthwick as he drove through the rush hour next morning to the Fettes Avenue police station. Somehow or other, Borthwick, who'd famously been summed up by four Fs – firm, fair and effing formidable – had lost her nerve after the problems last year and had starting finding fault in a way that Strang thought actually wasn't effing fair.

He had a good story to tell now, though – at least, it would be good provided that a few crucial cogs could be meshed with the appropriate wheels. It wasn't a given that it would work out like that but there was a good chance – a very good chance. Positive thinking – that was the key.

It didn't help that the DCS greeted him with, 'Well, Kelso, good to see you back in one piece. Another catastrophe would have been very unfortunate.'

He managed a smile. 'Indeed. However, things are shaping up well. There's going to have to be a lot of technical wizardry matching dates and phone conversations, but every piece of evidence that has come in so far points to the conclusion I'd come to already.

'There was a lot of coincidental stuff that made it harder to see how it all fitted together, but there were two key figures – Brodie Campbell and Zoe Cooper. They both seem to have been on the books of a syndicate masterminding the freight raids – and more than likely other criminal enterprises as well – but each had their own little side-hustles, like Campbell being a CHIS and Cooper having her work for the fisheries consortium, where they could both run with the hares while hunting with the hounds. There's evidence that neither was above a bit of private enterprise as well and in Campbell's case that meant running the sideshow with Matheson and Lothian.'

Borthwick was, for once, looking impressed. 'And you say that the woman who had the shotgun has been cleared?'

'Only of Campbell's murder. We've released her on bail and by the time we finish there will be quite a bit more on her charge sheet, and we've been able to pass on details to the Inverness police that should let them deal with the local drug dealer as well.'

She beamed. 'Excellent! I'll have a word with DCS Anderson and see how it's going.'

Have a bit of a gloat over your pal, you mean, Strang thought. 'Inverness is running a fingerprint check on the gun, though we'll only have Zoe Cooper's prints for comparison once we get the post-mortem report. She's quite savvy enough to have worn gloves, but I'm going to send them in to dust the cupboard where the gun was secured, and the key to it as well.

'I think she was commissioned to do the hit job when her bosses realised that Campbell's incompetent private enterprise was endangering theirs. But it hadn't been quite as clean as they had expected it to be; too much was starting to emerge and when Cooper realised she was in the frame she devised the panicky plot I told you about – that Mairead would confess – and then got on board the plane they sent to whisk her away, believing she was a treasured asset when in fact she was entirely expendable.

'As regards Campbell's murder, I believe his phone records will show that Cooper made a phone call to him that morning, after which he told his wife he had to go to a meeting "to sort things out". I don't think we have anything more to do there.'

'At least that's one less drain on the budget,' she acknowledged. 'Though of course we still have her murder on our hands, and I don't know how we follow that up, without another hugely expensive investigation.'

'There is a chance that we have a lead on that. Assuming the autopsy confirms that the injuries are consistent with a fall from a considerable height, we will be linking it to a sighting of a seaplane in the area. Livvy Murray had noticed it previously, moored on an isolated loch in the hills up behind Ardelour, and when she saw it actually in the bay the night before last she took a snapshot of its registration. It wasn't visible to the naked eye so we're keeping our fingers crossed that technology can enhance it enough to be readable.'

'I always said she was a very promising young woman, though I know you had your doubts,' Borthwick said with marked satisfaction.

God! She never missed an opportunity to point that out, but Strang had a previously prepared smile stashed away for these occasions and took it out now.

'Anyway, thanks to having access to Campbell's phone, we should be able to home in on other calls made by Zoe Cooper. It seems safe to assume that there would be multiple calls made to whoever was directing her, and we could risk a leap of faith and assume that the loch where Livvy saw the seaplane moored would be relatively near the pilot's destination. There are a few big houses in the area and though burner phones are always possible, they may still find one registered to a local address. In any case, we can commission enquiries all round the area – a seaplane is highly visible.'

Borthwick had clearly been impressed by the logic, but as he explained the procedures to be followed, her brow furrowed. 'But, Kelso, that would be a phenomenally expensive operation. We just don't have these resources at the moment with everything pared to the bone.'

He was well ahead of her. 'The beauty of it all is that this relates directly to what the task force I've been working on with Glasgow is investigating. DC Ritchie, who was a most welcome addition to our team, had been sent from them up to Ardelour specifically to see if there was some way to get at the big guys, instead of being fobbed off with the occasional little one. So this will be their pigeon. We were tasked to find the killer of Brodie Campbell, and I am reasonably confident that we will be in a position to say that we will not be looking for anyone else in connection with the crime.'

It was a long time since JB had looked at him with such warm approval. 'We're not out of the woods yet, of course, but it's been a very complicated business and this is certainly a most impressive result. I know you'll have a lot to finish up but I hope you may have some time to spare to prepare for the wedding.'

Strang groaned. 'I'm actually hoping *not* to have time for wedding preparations!'

'Tut!' Borthwick said briskly. 'I'll clype on you to the bride. Six weeks, is it? It's in my diary.'

'We'll look forward to seeing you then. There's just one thing: the Anna Bruce who was, I reckoned, in witness protection – did you have any luck with the NCA?'

'To some extent. But you know what they're like – not prepared to confirm or deny, not obliged to give us information, but the request will be making its way slowly around the chains of command. No doubt we'll get an answer sometime.'

Strang thanked her, but his upbeat mood had gone. After the relief when he had seen that Anna Bruce wasn't the female fatality, he had barely spared her a thought as he laboured on tying up the ends and producing a coherent summary, but he was thinking of her now.

Yes, the witness protection programme was strictly regulated, with security walls even inside the organisation itself. Given the red tape, it might well take some time for any answer to come back – which didn't matter if the answer was yes, they were in touch with her.

But if they weren't, if something had happened to her, and no one even knew . . .

The trial where she had given the crucial evidence had direct links to events in Ardelour. Brodie Campbell and Zoe Cooper had been ruthlessly dealt with: he had been shot; her body had been found in the sea. But who was to say that there wasn't another body that had fallen from the sky being tumbled about as it drifted on the currents until it was washed up somewhere as an unidentified female?

There was nothing he could do now – or even could have done then. He'd done all he could to warn her but his hands had been tied. The worry was a niggle at the back of his mind even as he did as JB had told him and got involved in wedding preparations.

It was a fortnight later that the phone rang in his office and the desk asked if he would be prepared to accept a call from someone called Anna Bruce.

His heart gave a sudden leap. 'Ms Bruce, you're all right?'

'Oh yes,' she said. 'I'm fine, but feeling guilty. They've only just told me that a request had been put in to check that I was all right. They told me there was no need for me to speak to you, but I should have told you I'd left and thanked you for warning me as you did.

'It was immediately after your interview that I was contacted by the NCA. They do keep a very watchful eye and they'd felt all along that my being there was risky, even before all this happened. I'd been feeling I was getting into deep water anyway and after what you'd said as well, I seized the chance of an immediate escape. I should have realised just vanishing would be alarming – it was thoughtless and I'm sorry.'

'Ms Bruce, the only thing that matters is that you are safe and well. And now you can leave Ardelour behind you and start on a new life – an interesting prospect.'

'Yes,' she said, with a deep, deep sigh. 'Ardelour was an ill-conceived idea in the first place and I made serious mistakes, so yes, I'm glad to have been offered a clean slate. But it's hard never to be able to tell the truth and by moving on I'll only be creating another fiction and then living a new lie for the rest of my life.'

Strang said, 'We have recently had a considerable breakthrough in our investigations that has given us the hope that possibly the threat to you can be neutralised. It's not guaranteed, but if you hear that a major arrest has been made in Torridon, make contact again.'

'They say it's the hope that kills you, don't they?' she said. 'I won't count on it.'

But he could hear the lift in her voice and as they said goodbye he too was feeling optimistic. And after all, the 'deep water' she had felt herself to be in had not been of the sort that had engulfed poor, deluded Zoe Cooper.

It was, Livvy Murray decided, the loveliest wedding she'd ever been to. The weather had been kind, the little church had been filled with friendly people and she'd been welcomed by Kelso's sister as if she was family too. The bride's dress, a cream midi with an elegant lace top, was perfect for the occasion – certainly in Kelso's eyes, to judge from the way he was looking at Cat. The little flower girl, his niece Betsy, in a simple, pretty pink print dress, had, according to her mother, needed lavish bribery not to sulk about its lack of frills but basking in the attention she now looked positively angelic – and smug with it, especially when her little brother yelled in the wrong place.

The setting for the marquee, looking out across the farm to the low Galloway hills, was entirely charming. Cat's brother, Cammie, whom Livvy recognised as having been one of Scotland's rugby heroes, officiated as sommelier while the Australian sister-in-law managed the waiting staff, holding a baby on her hip. Cat's father, oozing with pride, made a typical father's speech, while her mother looked as if the typical mum's tears weren't far away. Kelso's father, the general, was distinguished-looking and a bit forbidding, but his mother, a sweet-faced woman, seemed to be sharing Marjory Fleming's emotions. Even the DCS, also seated at the top table, looked as if she was moved by the prevailing mood.

Once the meal was over, the band arrived and they adjourned to the barn, where haybales as seating were stacked all around. As the older guests withdrew it developed into the best hoolie Livvy had ever attended. Strip the Willow, as perpetrated by the Young Farmers, only just stopped short of GBH.

The best part was that Livvy found that she could wholeheartedly rejoice in the couple's happiness. Lucky, lucky Cat, certainly, but she was envying her for her big warm family, not her spouse. Looked at now, the crush on her senior officer that she'd cherished for years bore some embarrassing similarities to the one she'd had for a time on Johnny Depp some years before.

And it had been good to meet up again with Alex Ritchie. His partner was with him – not the blonde, leggy woman she'd imagined, but Jenna, a dark, attractive journalist with *The Herald*, who was really interesting to talk to. Alex had told her about the enhanced photo that had given them the registration number of the seaplane and, strictly off the record, about the Romanian who'd been living on an estate near that loch who was now helping the police with their enquiries.

Jenna had been very impressed and, much like little Betsy, Livvy had enjoyed basking in the admiration. She and Alex were great company and they ended the evening planning to meet up next time Livvy was in Glasgow.

It was liberating that she'd been mature enough not to be drawn into another hopeless fantasy and had recognised that what she and Alex had become was good mates – and having got all this out of her system, she might even be more ready to think about her friend's brother who was actually quite a nice guy.

'Was it all right – the wedding, I mean?' Cat said to Kelso as they sat over a positively last glass of champagne in their bedroom, having been taxied to stay in Knockinaam Lodge. 'I've just been so afraid that it might feel sort of weird for you the second time round – too many memories.'

'I'd be lying if I said there were none, but they were all the kind that reminded me how lucky I've been to have a second chance at that sort of happiness. It was perfect, just as you are, my love.'

She blew him a kiss. 'You know, when I was a little girl and thought about what my wedding would be like, it actually was just like that, right down to the hoolie afterwards. Did you see JD giving it laldy in the Eightsome?'

'She was in good form, wasn't she – and purring like a kitten about the results in Torridon. But Livvy and Alex didn't take, did they? I told you that.'

'Remember the rules – whenever you're wrong, admit it, and whenever you're right, shut up. And now I'm absolutely shattered. Let's go to bed.'

In truth he was reluctant to let this moment of perfect happiness finish – one of the rare golden moments that shine in the memory for ever after. But 'I thought you'd never ask,' he said flippantly, draining his glass and getting up.

ACKNOWLEDGEMENTS

My thanks go to my agent, Jane Conway-Gordon, and to Susie Dunlop and all the team at Allison & Busby, especially Becca Allen and Emma Hawes.

Aline Templeton grew up in the fishing village of Anstruther, in the East Neuk of Fife. She has worked in education and broadcasting and was a Justice of the Peace for ten years. She has been a Chair of the Society of Authors in Scotland and a director of the Crime Writers' Association. Married, with a son and a daughter and four grandchildren, she lived in Edinburgh for many years but now lives in Kent.

alinetempleton.co.uk
@AlineTempleton